CONUNDRUM'S BOOK

BY THE SAME AUTHOR

Yemen Rediscovered (*Longman*)
Bahrain: Gulf Heritage in Transition (*Longman*)
Syria in View (*Longman*)
Scotland through the Ages (*Michael Joseph*)
London Heritage (*Michael Joseph*)
Traveller's Companion to the West Country (*Michael Joseph*)
Journeys into Medieval England (*Michael Joseph*)
Ireland through the Ages (*Michael Joseph*)
Architectural Heritage of Britain & Ireland (*Michael Joseph*)
Victorian Britain (*Weidenfeld & Nicolson*)
New British Architecture in Germany (*Prestel*)
FlipDesigns (*Prestel*)
FlipSigns (*Prestel*)
Mrs Mulroony's Fly-Away French Bloomers (*Lulu*)
Off Course (*Lulu*)
Dream of a Summer Night (*Lulu*)
Farthing Abbey (*Lulu*)

CONUNDRUM'S BOOK

Michael Jenner

ISBN 978-0-9558480-2-5

With love to Hilary who passed this book
fit for human consumption.

ABOUT A BOOK

One day, when I thought I knew him fairly well, I made so bold as to suggest to Conundrum he should write a book. I had in mind some sort of personal memoir to encapsulate all his mercurial wit and devious wisdom.

"A book, Henri?"

"Yes, a book. Why not?"

"What for? There's no market for what I have to say."

"But surely ideas are more important than money?"

Conundrum shook his head.

"As dear old Sam Johnson so rightly observed, no man but a blockhead wrote for any reason except money. And you are not suggesting that I am a blockhead are you, Henri?"

"No, of course not, but…"

"Writing books is the summit of human vanity. Penning deathless prose for posterity. What an absurd notion."

Foolishly I persisted.

"But you have so much to say about everything."

"Everything, Henri?"

"Yes, everything. As in life, the universe, everything."

I immediately regretted my paltry attempt at levity. He treated me to a withering silence before responding.

"A book about everything would be an encyclopaedia."

I blushed at the naivety of my suggestion.

"Well, maybe not everything in one book. But there must be something or other you would like to write about?"

"Anyone can write about something or other. Every book ever published has been about something or other."

My embarrassment deepened. I wished I hadn't started on this cursed writing a book nonsense. But Conundrum now had a gleam in his eye. He was mulling something over.

"Now, a book about nothing. About absolutely nothing, mind you. That would indeed be something."

"Yes, why not a book about nothing? It would be such a shame if all your thoughts disappeared into thin air."

Conundrum groaned.

"Don't be such a bore. Thin air is a perfectly good place for things to disappear into. Especially thoughts."

"Yes, but they don't have to disappear, do they?"

Conundrum gave me his dreaded gimlet look.

"Don't lock horns with me, Henri."

Lock horns? A sinister turn of phrase. There was a clue here. A big one. I should have suspected something. Conundrum quickly steered the conversation in another direction.

"Don't you think it's enough if one pair of ears registers my ramblings? Or would you like the whole world to be listening in on our little conversations?"

It was unexpectedly generous of him to dignify with the word 'conversations' my humble role as attentive listener.

"You must not underestimate your own contribution, Henri. I might not speak at all if it weren't for you."

I basked in the unaccustomed warmth of his words.

"Indeed, I have come to depend on you."

Music to my ears.

"Furthermore, you are essential to my purpose."

Recognition at last.

"You are indeed quite indispensable."

I held my breath.

"As an anvil to a blacksmith. Inert in yourself, yet the perfect foil for my sparks to fly."

Ouch! Another cruel jest at my expense. But I deserved no mercy and got none too. In that respect, if only in that, Conundrum never let me down.

I shall leave this conversation unfinished. It has given you a flavour of the man. You will hear enough from the old scoundrel in the pages that follow. Let me just say for now that there was a cold quality to his laughter. He lacked a real sense of humour. He could be extremely funny in an ironic, acerbic, cynical, sarcastic sort of way. But the bubbly stuff of humour for humour's sake, the vintage champagne that cannot help popping its own cork, that particular quality was alien to his nature. Though it was something he could mimic passably well, like an intelligent performing monkey.

At this point, permit me a few words from my personal perspective. For I often wonder what perverse stroke of fate brought me under his sway. Could I have escaped Conundrum's clutches? Suppose I had slipped away just before his physical presence registered itself as an optical image on my retina? Sorry, I can only excuse that awful formulation by coming clean. I am not a writer by trade. Most definitely not. I'm a photographer. I don't really 'do' words. They are not my natural element.

What I mean to say is I can't recall the exact moment I first laid eyes on Conundrum. Suddenly, there he was standing before me, right in my face, and no escape. Yet somehow he was already familiar, as if he had been hovering on the fringe of my consciousness long before our actual encounter. Perhaps stalking me, sizing me up as his chosen victim. But why me?

I can only think Conundrum must have seen me coming from a long way off. There I was, sailing along head in the clouds, brain full of air, all at sea, an unmanned vessel waiting to be boarded. If only I had been at the helm steering my own ship to its proper destination then he could not have grabbed the tiller and diverted me onto his chosen course. Everything would have turned out very differently. For a start, my life would not have been hijacked. And I would still know who I am.

I must now own up. Henri isn't my real name. And I really don't know what is. But I can tell you who I am not. I am definitely not Henri. And it is most important to know who you are not, is it not? At least, that's what Conundrum once said. He went on to say that particular ignorance was his most precious piece of knowledge. He also told me my personal redemption could only commence when I had stopped thinking I knew who I was and started knowing who I wasn't.

On the other hand, he also said that when I had found my true self then I could be anyone I damn well pleased. But I fear it is too late for reclaiming my own person. Far too late. And anyway, deep down, I really don't want my old self back. I have invested too much pain and suffering to settle for that.

In retrospect, it's obvious where I went wrong. From the outset I made the basic error of seeing Conundrum as part of my story. Whereas, in his eyes, my role was nothing more than to play a part in his plot. Not a small or insignificant part, but a part nonetheless. By way of an excuse I can only say that we all tend to regard other people as supporting characters in our own grand drama, with ourselves occupying centre stage. That's what makes being an individual such a perplexing business.

Enough of these tortured reflections. Let's get on with the story. I don't want to give the game away except to say there is plenty of action in exotic locations with the Holy Grail of *Conundrum's Book* hovering over us like a ghost at the banquet through every twist and turn. The dramatic grand finale is not one I could have envisaged as I set out on this quest for nothing more precise than whatever I might find.

Although I had no idea what Conundrum would write in his book, I was sure it would be very special indeed. For he gave me to understand that everything previously written by others fell short of the mark in relation to what needed to be said.

"Our finest minds have poked with their sticks just about everywhere but in the turd itself."

That comment alone – however unsavoury – left me in no doubt that Conundrum was the man to take things to the next level, that he had something amazing tucked up his sleeve. And so my burning desire to possess what was in Conundrum's head and hence in *Conundrum's Book* was to keep me shackled to his baleful presence right to the bitter end.

WELSH WALES

My first conversation with Conundrum was as surreal as any of the many that followed.

"Eat up your John Julius."

"My what?"

"Your John Julius."

I was still none the wiser.

"It's getting cold."

Conundrum's impish eye flitting across the table dropped a clue so heavy even I should have picked it up.

"I thought you were a Londoner."

"What's that got to do with it?"

"Rhyming slang, dear boy. John Julius Norwich ...."

At last the penny dropped.

"Porridge!"

"Better late than never. I suppose."

"Must say I haven't heard that one before."

"You won't have. I just made it up."

But hold it right there. I've jumped into the middle of things without even setting the scene. So permit me to add that we are seated at a breakfast table half concealed behind a dusty aspidistra in the dingy dining room of a rather faded country house hotel somewhere in south Wales.

I don't know what possessed me to accept the invitation to join a press group on this weekend trip. The aim was for us to witness the cultural and economic rebirth of the mining valleys, then to carry the glad tidings back to the outside world. As a freelance photographer, there was nothing much in it for me except to add a few more images to my portfolio. But I was at a loose end. So off I went.

Rendez-vous was, as I said, at this country house hotel in south Wales near, well actually not near anywhere. That turned out to be the start of my troubles. There were about a dozen hacks, mostly provincial press, not a distinguished gathering. Some had brought along their wives as a special treat. I shared a table for dinner with a Birmingham couple whose intimate conversation took no account of my presence. Throughout the meal, I felt worse than a stranger at the feast, more like an intruder in the marital bed.

Then there was a taciturn fellow from I don't know where. He didn't say. He only opened his mouth to shovel away another consignment of food with the practised rhythm of a stoker. He went at it diligently; as if afraid his congealing gravy dinner would be snatched from him.

With such company and a gloomy, wet Welsh weekend closing in over the hills, I was already regretting the whole enterprise. So I congratulated myself that at least I had come in my own car. I could take off the following day whenever the spirit moved and be safely back in London for a lazy Sunday at home. That was a great consolation.

Where Conundrum was on that first evening I'm not at all certain. It's hard to be sure. But I can't recall anything like a formal or even a casual introduction. However, when our paths crossed at breakfast the following morning, he treated me with all the breezy familiarity of a regular travelling companion.

"I've bagged us a table by the window. Just over there, behind the aspidistra."

I vaguely resented being collared by this stranger. But my annoyance didn't amount to much. So I joined him at the aspidistra table without protest. And it was he who made most of the sparse conversation over breakfast.

"Ghastly bunch, don't you reckon?"

"Who?"

"All those Yorkshire folk, of course."

"Yorkshire?"

"Exactly so. For, as Tacitus once remarked, England is divided into two parts. First, there is Londinium. Then there is the rest. I reckon Yorkshire is as good a name as any for all those other places outside London. It's as simple as that."

So Conundrum's Yorkshire began where London ended. On his mental map, Yorkshire stood for everything that was not of the capital city. It was a provincial no-man's-land, a kind of black hole into which he seldom ventured.

"Yes, all a complete load of Yorkshire apart from us."

How he identified me as a fellow Londoner, I really don't know. He must have been sitting within earshot at dinner and heard me introduce myself to the Birmingham couple. But there was no time to reflect, for he now fixed me with eyes of such luminous penetration they shone in their own right independent of their owner. Then he smiled. Some people should never smile. Conundrum was one such. His lop-sided grin, revealed a set of yellow, stained, gapped, crooked and decaying teeth.

And that's when Conundrum glanced at my untouched bowl of porridge.

"Eat up your John Julius."

"My what?"

"Your John Julius."

Oh dear, I've gone and repeated word for word exactly what I told you just a moment ago. Please bear with me. I hope I'll soon get the hang of this narrating business. Anyway, so there I was contemplating my bowl of John Julius at a complete loss what to say next. To excuse myself from further comment I took a spoonful to my mouth and slipped it between my lips.

"Pig snot. Looks just like a plate of pig snot."

I almost gagged as I pulled the spoon from my mouth, wiped the porridge from my lips and pushed the bowl away.

"Well, if you're not going to eat it."

I looked on in dazed silence while Conundrum hoovered up my porridge as if he hadn't eaten for days. Quite amazing. I'm sure there was a message in this, some key to his personality I should have noted and analysed for future reference. But I just sat there with my brain switched off unable to comprehend such eccentric manners. And no sooner had Conundrum polished off my porridge or John Julius or pig snot or whatever you want to call it than he resumed the conversation as casually as you like.

"Not much chance of getting a Melvyn on this trip, eh?"

This seemed a bizarre observation to make.

"A Melvyn?"

"Looks like I'll have to make do with a Barclays."

A Melvyn? A Barclays? I had no idea what he was talking about. And that must have been written all over me.

"The basic rules of rhyming slang aren't too difficult, you know. I'm sure you can quickly figure it out."

"More rhyming slang? OK, let me see. A Melvyn ... Melvyn ..."

Suddenly, I twigged.

"Melvyn Bragg?"

"At last."

"Melvyn Bragg. OK, fine. Melvyn Bragg....."

Then I twigged again. I was too embarrassed to say it.

"Well?"

"Shag?"

"Well that wasn't too painful, was it?"

I shrugged modestly.

"And now Barclays."

"Barclays? Barclays Bank?"

"Yes? Come on, don't be shy. Out with it!"

"Wank?"

"Well done. Problem is you often have to make do with a Barclays when you're dying for a Melvyn. Aye, there's the rub. And at others you would have been better off with a quick Barclays and shouldn't have gone for the full Melvyn. Ah, the mysteries of love. Why can't we always get a good old-fashioned Aylesbury when we need one?"

"An Aylesbury?"

"I thought you were getting the hang of things."

"You mean as in Aylesbury Duck?"

16

"No need to spell it out."

Then without warning Conundrum changed subject.

"So you're a photographer are you? Can't imagine what you think you're going to shoot here. Going to be a hellish bore. On a par with the fish house at Meare. I feel it in my bones."

"The fish house at Meare? More rhyming slang?"

He threw me a disdainful look, as if to say surely everyone knew all about the fish house at Meare.

"But if you want a rhyme, then I shall give you one."

In response to my continuing blank look, Conundrum recited the following in a curious form of verse:

"The fish house at Meare, the fish house at Meare,
T'was the absolute pits of my writing career.
For what could be more drear, my dear,
Than doing a piece on the fish house at Meare?"

I got the message. As a photographer I had had to render 'interesting' many a boring old pile of stones. I imagined the fish house at Meare was the writer's equivalent.

Conundrum's premonition about the weekend in store turned out to be well founded. Immediately after breakfast our PR minder – a pert, prim young lady – informed us we were all to travel together as a merry group in a minibus. This would be our communal transport until Sunday afternoon when we would be brought back here to the hotel to collect our own cars and drive home. Saturday night would be spent at another charming little hotel in a charming little town in a charming little valley. So my escape route was cut right from the start.

Better if I gloss over the details of a long, tiresome day. All morning we were carted from one industrial heritage site to another. Lunch came as a blessed relief. With several glasses of wine to keep out the weather and generally blur the mind, things didn't look so bad. The afternoon saw us squinting at more supposedly rejuvenated valleys through the steamy windows of the minibus. The drizzle, so it turned out, was but the advance guard of a serious storm still in transit over the Irish Sea.

Conundrum spoke little as we were shuttled about. With no scenery to look at, I studied him instead. There was something detached and otherworldly to his whole way of being. His thoughts were adrift somewhere out there in the falling rain. There was an odd quality to his eyes. Even while wide open they glazed over at times as if he had a second set of lids like net curtains behind which he retreated into a kind of private inner space from which he could peer out indifferently.

His grin was suffused with a faint amusement I can only describe as post-modern irony. And something else struck me. He seemed strangely out of focus. Can a human being be out of focus? Well, Conundrum was. There's no other way to describe it. Bits of him were sharp, don't get me wrong, he wasn't completely blurred. But other bits were fuzzy and it was constantly shifting. The point is it was virtually impossible to catch all of him totally in focus at the same time.

As for his age, my estimates varied. At breakfast, when he was fresh, I might have put him in his late fifties, a good twenty-five years older than myself. But as the fatigue and hassle of the day took their toll, the years settled on his face like so much wax coagulating on a candlestick. Come teatime he looked almost seventy. And I feared he might expire of old age by nightfall.

Just as it was getting dark, our patrol leader informed us she wouldn't be staying on for the theatrical entertainment that evening. Sadly, she had to drive home that very instant. Home. It was a lovely thought. She was gone before we knew it. Just before she left, she let slip there wouldn't be a dinner 'as such', but a sort of buffet laid on at the theatre courtesy of the local council who would be out in force to welcome us.

Sure enough, there was a great rattling of mayoral chains, moist handshakes, warm beer and sweet wine. Through a smog of cigarette smoke we heard wheezing voices extol the virtues of the lovely fresh air now available in the post-industrial paradise of the valleys. Some of the 'Yorkshire folk' dutifully took down quotes from spokespersons in their reporters' notebooks.

Conundrum looked suspiciously at the buffet, which consisted entirely of serried ranks of greasy chicken *vol au vent* laid out on flat metal trays.

"That could do a lot of damage, I fear."

This hunch proved well founded. Not five minutes passed before a councillor manoeuvred Conundrum into a tight corner and engaged him eyeball to eyeball, chicken *vol au vent* in one hand, beer glass in the other. When I caught sight of him after his ordeal, he was almost unrecognisable. His head and shoulders were flecked with flaky pastry and gobbets of pale gooey stuff that might have been fired through a spray gun.

Conundrum wiped his spectacles and sighed.

"Seems I put up a pretty poor show in the *vol au vent* spitting contest."

He sighed stoically, almost apologetic about it.

"Lack of practice, I suppose."

That was the extent to which he gave vent to his feelings. Conundrum was evidently not the type to whinge.

"I must have done something extremely bad in a past life to deserve this."

I could tell from his thoughtful expression he was earnest about this notion. He was searching his memory for some minor misdemeanour to explain his present punishment.

"Everything catches up with you in the end. But quite what I have done to merit that vicious assault by *vol au vent* is for the moment entirely beyond me."

The metallic ring of a stainless steel knife on a beer glass signalled speeches about to begin. The Chairman of the Tourism and Leisure Committee drew breath.

"Ladies and gentlemen of the press from across the border. Before I bid you welcome to our vibrant valleys, permit me to make an observation on the deep roots of our Welsh culture. You of the Anglo-Saxon persuasion may be clever enough in the brains department. But we of the Celtic race are more passionate in the theatre of the emotions. Our souls are resonant with music and poetry. Mere water flows in your English veins compared to the …"

The Chairman paused for dramatic effect. Conundrum took advantage of the silence to address the barman.

"Whisky! Neat whisky!"

The Chairman attempted to rekindle his oratorical fire.

"Our Welsh veins flow with a rich stream of …"

Again, Conundrum spoke loudly to the barman.

"Whisky! Whisky! And make it a large one!"

Guffaws of mirth gathered in volume. The remainder of the welcome speech was a hesitant mumbling affair that failed to live up to its early promise.

After that, our hosts gave Conundrum a wide berth. I joined him by an open window. Together we inhaled deep gulps of cold night air. We knew our fate was not in our hands. We would have to wait for the minibus. At last, proceedings drew to a close and we were driven away.

Relief at deliverance was short-lived. Our new hotel was a gloomy establishment on the main street of a deserted town with lights out and curtains drawn. The 'hotel' turned out to be a row of five terrace houses knocked together. A grumpy individual, more security guard than night porter, admitted us. Or was his real job to keep us in? He called out the names and room numbers of our party from a crumpled piece of dirty paper. We raised our hands like schoolchildren to receive our keys.

We struggled up a narrow staircase. Conundrum's room was next to mine, the two doors unnaturally close. One modest room had evidently been divided by some unspeakable act of DIY into two tiny singles. With the resigned stoop of condemned men, we entered our adjoining cells. I've never seen Conundrum look quite so old, lost and baffled by things.

My room had a suicidal air. A naked bulb cast a pool of light on the white candlewick bedspread. A funeral shroud waiting to receive someone. Me? I pulled it back. The sheets were crumpled. A solitary pubic hair – thick and curly – coiled like a scorpion in the nether regions. Unwilling to undress or even to open my suitcase in such sordid surroundings, I sat for a moment in the clammy grip of the armchair and counted the cigarette burns in the upholstery. The air stank like an ashtray in a toilet. I stood up and looked for the bathroom. Finding none, I took a piss in the hand basin, as doubtless many others had done before me. Then I perched on the edge of the bed and began to reflect on my fate. Once, I had had such high hopes and expectations. How had it come to this?

A series of sharp taps on the wall brought me to my senses. It was Conundrum sending an SOS. I tapped back to acknowledge the message. Then he spoke and I practically jumped out of my skin. For it sounded as if he were in the same room, so thin was the plasterboard partition between our places of confinement.

"Listen. Things are pretty grim in here. And I don't suppose your room is the Ritz either. So it's a question of *sauve qui peut*. I invite you to join the escape committee. Here's the plan. Hitch back to last night's hotel, jump in your car and be back in dear old London by daybreak. In short, let's do a runner, get the hell out of here."

Dear old London by daybreak. A promise of paradise regained. The matter was settled. A minute later, we slipped out into the street. Now the full force of the storm was directly overhead. We sheltered under the awning of a shop. Water cascaded before our eyes in a bead curtain just like studio rain in a movie. My first instinct was to look for the tap and turn it off. My second was to abandon our bid for freedom.

It was only 11 pm but it felt like the dead of night. Things really were bible black. We scanned the rain-lashed street. Suddenly, the awning split and burst, releasing a load of water all over me. Conundrum had avoided a similar fate by stepping out into the road a moment earlier to flag down a passing car. I heard snippets of an animated conversation. Conundrum seemed to be talking Welsh. Then he grabbed my arm and bundled me into the back seat of a battered old Land Rover. He took up his position next to the driver, to whom he began talking once more.

"Don't mind if I speak English for the sake of our young friend? He's had a terrible shock. Just heard that his poor old mother is at death's door. I simply must get him back to London. Awful, god-forsaken place to die, London, don't you think?"

That cemented the understanding with the driver, who to judge from the friendly collie salivating on my shoulder was a sheep farmer. I only saw the silhouette of the man's head as he drove through the torrential downpour along narrow lanes between high stone walls, but my heart went out to this stranger. He was our saviour. I have special sympathy for all Welsh sheep farmers ever since. And I have an abiding fondness for the heady whiff of warm, wet dog. A perfume so elemental and basic in all its doggy virtues of trust and affection. With this companion at my side I felt nothing could touch me.

I had no idea how far we travelled. Time was suspended. At last we came to a halt in front of the now darkened hotel where we had spent the previous night. Through the falling rain I saw my own car standing there on the gravel. We took our leave from the sheep farmer, thanking him profusely, Conundrum speaking Welsh, me English.

"I do hope your poor old mother lasts the night."

"My mother?"

I had already forgotten the little fiction Conundrum had cooked up to win the sympathy of the driver. Fortunately, the rain driving right into my face gave me a convincing expression of tearful grief, so at least I looked the part. I thought it wiser to say nothing further. For good measure Conundrum stopped me giving the game away with any careless talk by landing a sharp kick on my left shin, much harder than was necessary. It drew blood. So I limped over to my car, adding a poignant touch of physical injury. But as I turned the ignition I felt a rush of adrenaline that dulled the pain. The engine started first time. I slammed it into gear. And off we went.

One curious spin-off from this hastily curtailed wet weekend in Wales was that Conundrum would occasionally pretend to forget I was a fellow Londoner and make teasing references to my supposedly Welsh ancestry. When I confronted him after yet another tiresome jibe about my cultural attitude being just typical, coming as I did from 'the land of our fathers', he came straight out with it.

"Wales is where I found you. And that makes you Welsh in my book. End of story."

Me in his book? But I'm the one doing the writing here. You do start to see the extent of my problem, don't you?

ON THE M4

The drive through the night that followed was undoubtedly the defining moment of my life. Afterwards, nothing would ever be the same. How I wish I had been able to study the expression on Conundrum's face as he spoke. But my chauffeur duties obliged me to look straight ahead. All I could see were the wipers endlessly removing the same spots of rain, an epic exercise in futility. That was hypnotic enough, but it was the ceaseless torrent of words from Conundrum's lips that held me spellbound. He started the moment we were underway.

"Now we've escaped like thieves in the night, let's savour the open road that lies before us. A well constructed journey belongs to you just like a book on your shelf, to be revisited in the memory whenever the mood dictates."

Another book reference. I didn't pick up on this one at the time. Was Conundrum already manipulating my mind for his great project? But I was too intent on getting home.

"London by daybreak. A sweet prospect, is it not? Back to the big city. Far too much empty scenery around here. I might retire to the country one day. Actually got my eye on a nice little garden flat in Bayswater as it happens."

I smiled.

"So let's hit the trail, Henri! Can't you feel the pull of the mother metropolis drawing us back to her maternal breast?"

It was the first time he called me by that name. Why I didn't challenge him then and there before it took root, God only knows. But I let it pass.

"Yes, Henri. Point the bonnet towards dear old London and give it some wellie. For they like us none too well in Cymru. Mind you, I don't blame them. Let's face it, we English are annoying bastards. Get on everyone's tits. Ask any Scotchman. I'm not sure we even like ourselves, if truth be told. Yorkshire loathes London for its so-called dominance of national affairs.

Dominance, my arse! London hasn't enjoyed a scrap of dominance since the Conqueror built his flaming White Tower to subjugate the unruly populace. But don't start me on the Normans, Henri. Suffice it to say London is my true country. I am a citizen of that fair city. I think we should set up our own People's Republic. England has had its day."

I feared I was going to be treated to a history lecture or some political rant. But quickly, Conundrum changed tack.

"Now, when I was out East, Henri."

I distinctly heard Conundrum pronounce East with a capital E. For myself, who had never been further east than Athens, 'out East' betokened an exotic realm of rich experience entirely beyond my ken. I was instantly hooked.

"Go East, Henri. Get yourself well outside Europe, then look back and see what a self-important, small-minded place it has become. Such a bore having to live here. But then living anywhere is a bore in the long run. And travel can be a frightful bore too. Never know who you will have to pass the time of day with. On the other hand, travelling is most definitely preferable to staying at home. Home. God, what a frightful word. Pains me just to say it. Sometimes the memory of a particularly dull day 'at home' comes wafting back across the years to oppress me with the deadly smell of boiled greens trapped in an airless corridor of cracked linoleum."

That was another elusive clue to the circumstances of Conundrum's early life.

"Home is a terrible place, Henri. Wherever it may be."

It occurred to me this contradicted what Conundrum had just said about the joys of getting back to dear old London. But somehow Conundrum had this trick of contradicting himself without contradicting himself. Or rather it didn't seem to matter. Anyway I let it pass.

"Things always catch up with you at home, Henri. Not just the brown envelopes, smarmy letters from Tom Champagne, financial advisers projecting your benefits. Bad habits adhere to you at home. Ridiculous routines. Meddlesome neighbours. Friends and … even one's nearest and dearest."

The last sentence was spoken under his breath.

"A true traveller should never settle or marry. For he is already married, married to his journey. So may the Good Lord preserve us from the horrors of Home Sweet Home. Better to hit the highway. The departure lounge, the roadside café, the 2-star hotel: these anonymous places of transit are my real home. And a pox on the pretty view from my own little window."

"But what if everyone were to hit the road?"

"Excellent question, Henri. And the answer is, it would be quite intolerable. Other people should have their roots, be of the place where they are. That gives interest to my journeys. Just imagine if everyone was travelling. For a start, the transport system would never cope. And when you did get to a place there would be no one there. Except of course for all those people from somewhere else."

A brief pause for breath, no more than that.

"As for family, I'd rather have surly waiters, thieving cab drivers, misinformed tourist guides, sundry pickpockets and muggers. Scoundrels one and all, God bless them. These are my people. Take it from me. Anything is better – even the Black Hole of Calcutta – than the bondage of home."

This didn't really surprise me. From the little I knew of him I couldn't imagine Conundrum settled in a domestic situation of any sort. But clearly he wasn't going to say more on that subject for he now fell silent and began fumbling in his pockets. From the corner of my eye I saw him pull out an old tobacco tin and roll a cigarette. As he lit up the car suddenly filled with pungent smoke.

"Homesickness should be outlawed. They should make a huge bonfire of all the carpet slippers in the world."

"Burn carpet slippers?"

"Yes, why not? If they can burn books, then why not carpet slippers?"

26

"But they're not supposed to burn books."

"You seem very keen on books, Henri. Commendable. Most commendable. I shall have to make a note of that."

Books again. This time a direct hint at his secret purpose. Why didn't I nail it then and there?

He now introduced a note of sadness in his voice.

"You only get to realise how attached you are when on the point of leaving. An early farewell on a cold morning. The loved one rises from bed and comes to the door. For a fleeting moment you hold her in your arms. Soft and warm as a freshly baked croissant. But already the frosty breeze tugs at your sleeve, whispers in your ear. Time to go. A sweet pain like the loss of a milk tooth. The child's tongue sucks at the empty socket out of which a fresh molar will grow. Oh to be an oriental sheikh who divorces one of his wives on the eve of a journey to make room for a woman he might meet along the way."

I had the feeling Conundrum was recalling a particular farewell from a long time ago that pained him to this day.

"But if parting is such sweet sorrow, then staying put is the bitter pill of contentment. So you might as well go quickly and be gone. Make no fuss about it. And when you are travelling, then discard all memories: where you come from, friends and family. Forget even your name, who you are. Discount the very possibility you will ever go home again. Just go! Go!! Go!!!"

He struck the dashboard three times with clenched fist.

"That, Henri, is what travel is all about. Renewal of the soul. Disguise, masquerade, subterfuge. Being someone new somewhere else. If you take your tired old self with you to the uttermost corner of the world, then you have completely missed the point. You might just as well have stayed at home."

His voice tailed off like a great wave that having pounded the beach draws back bruised through the shingle.

"But what about discovering the various different ethnic cultures of other peoples?"

27

Even as I spoke I could hear how lame and pathetic my words sounded. But for once Conundrum spared me the sharp edge of his tongue.

"Real travel is hardly possible now. Thank heavens I did the serious stuff when it was there to be done. I have whirled with dervishes in Damascus, boiled beef with bandits in Bolivia, chewed cheroots with Cheyenne chiefs in Chattanooga, made love under Arabian moonlight in the Pool of the Virgins. I have entered the blue doors of Sidi Bou Saïd, had my most intimate places massaged with jasmine-scented almond oil. Penetrated the purple pussies of Pnom Penh. But it's not been all wine and roses. I have sniffed the pong of premium pigeon shit from the High Atlas in the tanneries of Marrakech. Seen heads chopped off in Riyadh. Watched bloated bodies float down the Mekong to the China Sea. Whiled away hot afternoons counting floaters in the port of Smyrna."

I must have smiled.

"I am serious, Henri. In Bangkok I slept on teak temple floors and saw a Buddhist monk pin a portrait of Adolf Hitler on the wall of his cell next to a poster of Manchester United. That taught me to take everything at face value."

I gave him a quick sideways look. Against my better judgement, I interjected.

"Everything? Surely you mean to say, take 'nothing' at face value?"

"Don't presume to tell me what I mean to say."

I bit my tongue in self-chastisement.

"Cultivate superficiality, Henri. And take it to the greatest possible depth. There is nothing more enlightening than to be profoundly superficial."

I was about to take issue with this. It sounded like one of Oscar Wilde's throwaway lines. But I didn't want to risk another rebuff. In any case the unspoken comment was plucked from my mind as if Conundrum could read my thoughts.

"Ah yes, dear old Oscar. Now there was a man on the right track. But he had no idea where it was leading. Too drunk on his own genius to figure it out."

"Figure what out?"

"The bigger picture."

"The bigger picture?"

"Of course. There's always a bigger picture. Surface impressions, however shallow, contradictory and nonsensical they may appear, actually have more substance than so called underlying truths. At least the superficial exists. We can see it. Whereas with truth or truths, who knows whether they exist at all? Or if we discern them, we may be entirely mistaken about what they are. And when all is said and done, how can all the conflicting truths be true? So I make it my mission to respect superficiality. And to piss on profundity."

He drew a sharp puff on his smouldering cigarette. It responded with a brief red incandescence.

"We live in a surprising world. Estate agents and chartered accountants in cornflower blue shirts, sporting yellow ties like exotic birds of the Amazonian rainforest."

He continued virtually in the same breath.

"Meanwhile, I take my pleasures where I may. Tread the permissive path here. Ride the inclined railway there. Dally in the dingle dell. I should have liked to be a long-distance truck driver. Ensconced in my cabin after a hearty lunch at some roadside watering hole with fantasies of big-bosomed waitresses while my mind roams free over the map of Europe as I dictate an epic pornographic novel into a tape recorder while cracking horrendous farts for my private delectation."

To prove the point, Conundrum now cracked what can only be described as a most horrendous fart. A real dog's egg. I immediately opened the window.

"Don't be such a sissy, Henri. Just pretend it's one of yours. Besides, it's the silent ones you must beware of."

I allowed a decent time to elapse before shutting the window. I was grateful for the pungent cigarette smoke.

"There's nothing like the pure mountain air of the high Himalayas. Or the scentless perfume of Saharan silence, a silence, so intense you can almost hear it. But it requires the buzzing of a solitary fly to reveal its awesome extent. Like dropping a stone down a well to gauge its depth. That's one of the things I learned out East, Henri. In the land of the one hand clap."

Conundrum's voice lowered into a conspiratorial tone.

"Actually, I penned my first literary *oeuvre* 'out East'."

What had Conundrum been up to 'out East'. Foreign correspondent? Diplomat? Missionary? Academic? Spy? He proceeded to tell me about his great *oeuvre*.

"Called it *'Major Henry Spiffin's Handy Hints for Lewd Acts of Sexual Gratification with the Indigenous Fauna in Remote Corners of the British Empire'*. Jolly fine title, don't you think? Zoological *Karma Sutra*. I brought some creative flights of fancy to the subject. Want to know how to goose a moose, stuff a puffin, bugger a baboon, get eager with a beaver? Well, for all that and so much more, Spiffin's your man."

I must have betrayed my scepticism.

"Many a true jest is spoken in earnest. When I got back to London, I tried to get the *magnum opus* published. No takers. Then I hawked it all over as a series of risqué articles in tune with the brutal spirit of the age: *'Things to Shag in Foreign Parts'*. Still no takers. Is the world losing its passion for a good old-fashioned Melvyn? Yet another sign we are approaching the end?"

He sighed.

"Men once fought to plant their seed in the fertile folds of the fat ladies of prehistoric Malta. Now thinness is *à la mode* and no thought for procreation. Women more desirable if they look like boys. *Fellatio* is all the rage. Everyone wants it, from the President of the USA down to the Secretary of State for Wales. Did the two ever meet, I wonder? Not that I'm immune to such temptations. Once won a fiver on the nags, had a great night out and still had enough to treat myself to a blow job from the Duchess of Denbighshire. Ah, those were the days. You didn't have much money but it went a long way. What was I talking about? Ah yes, *fellatio*. Then there's our old friend *cunnilingus*. Have-a-look Ellis[1] reckons it is always popular at periods of high civilisation. So perhaps there is some hope for the human race after all. By the way, I note that Peregrine Worsthorne has come out marginally against Barclays in *The Telegraph*."

Conundrum paused to relight his cigarette.

"But I don't give an Aylesbury. Not any more."

I may have chuckled. Conundrum paid no heed.

"I should have suggested they put a cat on the jacket."

"A cat on the jacket?"

"Yes, a cat on the jacket of my, I mean of Spiffin's book. That would have done the trick. Want the advice of an old pro, Henri? A cat on the jacket will sell any book."

"Even a book on dogs?"

"Oh, very good, Henri. Excellent. Yes, even a book on dogs. Why not indeed? That is precisely my point."

I felt rather pleased for once I'd managed to amuse him. Then I opted for silence, anxious not to interrupt him as he set off in another direction.

"Walking down Drury Lane the other day, I thought Dreary Lane would be more apt. Later on in Frith Street I had this notion. Why not Froth Street? Or even Frath, Freth or Fruth Street? That got me thinking. Why are some words invested with meaning, while others are complete nonsense? Then the great idea dawned on me. I should collect all the words that don't yet have a meaning. If I snapped up the copyright on all those that haven't found a use, I could make a fortune. Sell them off over the counter as and when required to describe something or other no one had ever thought of before. Conundrum's Word Bank. That has a certain ring to it, don't you reckon?"

---

[1] Havelock Ellis, Stud. Psychol. Sex IV, 21

Another cigarette sprang from Conundrum's metal tin and materialised in his hand already lit as if by a conjuror.

"If you can have a hot totty or a cool chick, then why not a tepid tart? Man, she was seriously tepid. I mean like mega temperate. That's one helluva lukewarm lady. Did a bit of script writing in my time, don't you know?"

There was no stopping him.

"How can you trust words? Slippery little devils. The more you look at them the less they mean. A missing apostrophe can turn man's laughter into manslaughter. And who put the 'turd' in Saturday? Once spotted impossible to ignore. Weekends always begin with a feeling I've just stepped in something unpleasant. Saw an ad the other day offering free, no obligation quotations. Quotations? Sounded just up my street. Wondered what they'd give me. If music be the food of love…? Once more into the breach …? My kingdom for a …? And do you know what it was? Some crap about bloody motor insurance!"

I smiled.

"Actually, I detest cars. Work of the devil. Present vehicle excepted of course, since it is the instrument of our deliverance. Anything with an internal combustion engine should come with a health warning. When we write the epitaph of the human race automotive insanity will be engraved on the tombstone. Have you noticed how they always give cars lovely names like Zephyr, Espace, Explorer and Mustang? Would be more honest to call them Cockroach, Cesspit and Stinkpot."

Conundrum the environmentalist?

"But since we live in a global age, everyone has the right to fuck the dear old globe for all she's worth."

He barely paused for breath before charging off in another direction.

"Dandruff, Henri! That's it. Dandruff!"

"Dandruff?"

"Yes, the end of the world as we know it will come about not through carbon emissions and greenhouse gases but by common or garden dandruff. The atmosphere clogged up with trillions of minute particles of dry skin blocking the sun, removing the earth's source of energy."

Conundrum looked and sounded completely mad.

"How subtle and devious is mother nature. We are doomed to be the instruments of our own destruction. The balance will be restored by the scattering of human dust. Isn't that a wonderful prospect?"

"But that's a horrible prospect."

"Not so. The inevitable must by definition be sublime. We're privileged to witness our own demise. Seeing the final curtain of a long running show as it folds. I wonder if it's worth taking off my coat and hat, getting comfortably ensconced for something that close to the end."

I shook my head.

"Just a thought, Henri. An idle thought. A trifle wayward, I must confess. But a thought nonetheless. I must make note."

Then followed yet another broad hint that Conundrum was indeed working on a book or something.

"Always write things down, Henri. One night I dreamed up a script and screenplay for a full-length feature film. Ran it twice through the mental cinema to make sure I had the subplots sorted out. God, it was cracking stuff. A real blockbuster. The casting couch was ready and waiting. Come morning, I leapt from bed, sharpened pencil, grabbed piece of paper. But it had all gone. Not even a vestige of the story to jog the memory. All I had left was the fuzzy afterglow of how sodding brilliant it had been. Absolutely sodding brilliant. Like having the right lottery numbers in your brain and then forgetting them."

Conundrum stared for a while into the driving rain.

"On another occasion, and this was no dream, worse luck. I had just written a sensational travel book, a hair-raising account of my perilous trek through the Amazonian rainforest on a pogo stick or some such nonsense. But this absent-minded author drops his priceless MS in the paper bank and delivers an armful of old magazines to the publisher instead. By the time I realised my mistake it was too late. The great work has since been recycled as toilet paper. A good wipe rather than a good read. But what difference does it make?"

He sighed as if reliving the loss.

"Something similar happened to Lawrence of Arabia. Left the manuscript for *Seven Pillars of Wisdom* at Reading Station. Just imagine. Reading of all places, I ask you. But T.E. wasn't the sort of chap to let little things like that put him off. Only went and wrote the whole damn thing all over again. Spelling mistakes and all. Well, I couldn't be bothered to rewrite my great opus. My heart wasn't in it."

So Conundrum had already written a book. I wondered what the content might be.

"Eventually I understood this was life's way of telling me something. I decided not to become a best-selling author. After all, a real artist has no need to publish. The true believer works in secret, an undercover agent not courting the attention of the common herd or plaudits from snooty critics. And besides, being a celebrity would be such a pain. Difficult to know if folk were being friendly just because I was famous. How could I be sure? So I had to think of other ways to make my fortune. Next venture was a chain of antique shops called DPF."

"DPF?"

"Dead People's Furniture. That's what antiques are all about. Can't think why it didn't catch on."

He reflected further on this quandary.

"Am I in bad taste, Henri?"

"No. Not at all."

"Oh dear, I rather hoped I was."

Another pause.

"Or how about Socks Reunited? For what can match the joy of finding a lost sock? Bound to be a winner."

Then he was off again.

"Let me tell you a story. One fine day in Baghdad all the moustaches of the male population detached themselves from their hosts and flew off. The men stayed indoors for a whole week to grow new ones. Meanwhile, their liberated mustachios were flying about merrily somewhere over the desert wastes between Tigris and Euphrates. Like a vast flock of crows. But when they tired of this and returned home to roost, there was nowhere for them to land. All the upper lips of the men had grown brand new mustachios that were the pride and joy of their owners. A flock of disembodied mustachios has been fluttering over Babylon and Nineveh ever since."

Conundrum looked out of the window.

"We are all one step away from being utterly ridiculous. Greek philosopher Harry Stottle. Russian Czar, Knickerless the Second. Austrian psychiatrist Dr Fraud. French painter Henri Sewer Rat, singer Jacques Pervert. And don't forget the Elector of Hangover. Had Baroque tendencies, you know. And what was so civil about the Civil War?"

I didn't answer.

"Have you ever entertained a myth, Henri? I once had Helen of Troy, Achilles, Hector, the whole flaming Greek chorus round for tea and cakes. Most entertaining it was too."

A brief pause to pull on his cigarette.

"I promised her I'd spank her..."

He exhaled slowly for dramatic effect.

"When we got to Salamanca."

Conundrum was coming completely off the rails.

"But when we reached Plaza Mayor,
It suddenly seemed such a bore."

This doggerel, terrible and eminently forgettable as it was, somehow would not be forgotten. It lodged obstinately in the mind. The more I tried to forget it the more I seemed to remember it. And now I have committed it to paper.

"Oh, for the wisdom to accept the decline of one's advancing years. To be contentedly collapsed in the crotch, gently sagging in the scrotum. To savour the joys of lingering without intent. What relief to be no longer on active service and permanent standby, never knowing when the call to arms will come. First got the summons when I was hardly out of shorts. In the Round Reading Room of the British Museum of all places. Regular den of iniquity and no mistake. This red-blooded blue stocking gave me the eye, graciously initiated me in the arcane ways of the *General Retrospective Catalogue*. Afterwards a spot of lunch at her lodgings in Coptic Street. Coptic Street! How could I resist? By God she buttered my parsnips and salted my radishes. I was a quick learner and progressed swiftly from sniffing melons to sucking mangoes. Since then I've had my fair share of rumpty-tumpty in the *Great Bed of Ware*."

I lapped up all Conundrum's outrageous remarks and tall stories. The way he talked you'd think he'd been everywhere, met everyone, done everything. He was larger than life. Being on the road with Conundrum, even for this short trip along the boring old M4, was as good if not better than going coast to coast with Dean Moriarty.

If he'd told me he'd shagged the Queen of Sheba, I would have believed that too. He made everything sound so plausible. I swallowed it all. Hook, line and sinker. I thought how wonderful to look back on a life lived fearlessly to the full, so unlike my own, barely lived at all. Conundrum had plunged into the deep ocean of existence, while I stood timidly on the shore. I had done nothing, been nowhere. I was hugely envious.

Unquestioning, I hung on his every word.

"The world is spinning like a demented yo-yo through imploding galaxies in an exploding universe. Yet you can go away for a month, or a year, and the three-penny bit left standing on the mantelpiece remains upright until you return. Then you can knock it over with the slightest touch of your little finger."

Like so many of his observations this sounded so full of meaning and yet I struggled to get my head round it. I put this down entirely to my own lack of imagination.

"You do know what a three-penny bit is, Henri?"

I could only nod, struck dumb by the slippery, erratic flow of Conundrum's ideas dancing, darting and swirling without rhyme or reason like shoals of fish. It was not just individual utterances but their general effect, framed by the deep darkness of the night, that held me mesmerised. His thoughts flowed through him like an untamed river. Or rather they nested briefly in his head like bats in the belfry of an ancient Gothic folly. The attic windows of Conundrum's mind were open to all comers. Every mental winged creature, from wise owls and sinister ravens to playful house martins and bright butterflies, came and went as it pleased them. All seemed dear to him in their own fashion. Conundrum made no attempt to direct them for any apparent purpose. Indeed, he gave the impression he considered the thoughts not really his own, but friendly aliens paying him a fleeting visit. Here one moment, gone the next.

"We can create nothing new, Henri. We are only playing about with stuff that is already here. Could the human being invent a tomato, a cucumber or a lemon if these didn't already exist? Yet we believe there's an answer to everything if we can only go back to first causes. But the further back we go, the more we find answers to questions we haven't put. But we can't recognise them as answers because we haven't yet thought up the questions. You do follow, don't you, Henri?"

Frankly, I didn't follow. And I'm not sure Conundrum did either. There was a speculative quality to so much of what he said. It seemed he was not really 'behind' his thoughts with any conviction. They came 'from' him but they were not 'of' him.

Suddenly, he barked an order as if to a chauffeur.

"Turn off here."

"Why?"

"Just do as I say."

"But where are we going?"

"To our destination."

"Where's that?"

"Just follow the road."

There was an imperative of steely authority behind the quiet voice. So I turned off as instructed and continued along the A4 towards Avebury.

"We'll take in a bit of megalithic sightseeing on the way."

"But it's pitch dark. We won't see a thing."

"There are certain things you don't need eyes to see."

Obedient to his wishes, I drove through a darkly invisible countryside while he spoke of earth magic, prehistoric burial grounds and the ritual landscape. I could see nothing but the beams of my headlights drawing me ever onward through an endless tunnel of rain.

"This place really gets my bones jumping. My skeleton wants to shed its flesh and race on ahead without me."

Conundrum's face lit up momentarily in the headlamps of an oncoming vehicle. He had the crazed eyes of a man possessed. I began to feel scared.

"Stop here, Henri. Right now. Just do it."

I pulled over onto a grass verge. Without another word, he opened the door and stepped out into the pouring rain. Before I could ask him what he was up to he had disappeared into the black wetness of the Wiltshire night. After a minute or so I switched off engine and headlights then sat there staring into the gloom through a windscreen streaming like the underside of a waterfall. As I waited for Conundrum to return, it dawned on me he might not return at all. What had he meant about his skeleton going on ahead? What on earth was he up to?

I opened the door and got out of the car. Still I couldn't see a thing. Impossible to tell in which direction he had gone. The storm lashed down. In a couple of seconds I was soaked to the skin. I slipped back into the shelter of the car. I don't know how long I sat there staring out into the empty night before I nodded off. But I was awake long enough shivering in the wet cold to regret even that sordid hotel room from which we had made our escape. I had sunk into an uncomfortable, fitful kind of sleep when a sharp tapping on the window awoke me.

"Wake up, Henri. Damn your eyes. Open up."

I leaned over to release the catch. Conundrum wrenched open the door and slumped onto the seat. Although drenched right through, he wore a blissful expression.

"Avebury to Stonehenge as Greece to Rome. The mother culture. The fountainhead. But so many of the ancient stones have been destroyed. Once a holy hotspot where great circles harnessed massive forces of global energy. Alas, all ruins now. No wonder the world is in such a mess."

Conundrum fell silent for a moment.

"Pay and display in all around I see. Our forefathers tossed iron swords and shields of bronze into sweet flowing rivers to placate the gods of the sacred wellspring. Now we tip supermarket trolleys into stagnant canals and litter motorway verges with plastic hubcaps. Oh, give me a hard shoulder to cry on! But I suppose we must learn to love all this, along with mobile phone masts, electricity pylons and cooling towers. For these are the monuments we need to believe in."

Conundrum paused just long enough for me to ask something that was puzzling me.

"And what do you believe in?"

After a powerful sneeze, he replied.

"Oh, everything. Just about everything."

Then he paused.

"And nothing. Mostly nothing, I believe passionately in nothing. Too many thoughts have been thought. Too many words spoken. What the world needs now is a hundred thousand years of sweet silence. At least, after I've had my say, of course."

I was relieved to detect a hint of laughter in his voice. I feared I'd been cornered by a fanatic. Then he was off again.

"Great mistake to get involved in the so-called big issues of the day. Same sex marriage, proportional representation, single European currency, carbon trading, genetically modified crops, war on terror, multiculturalism, that sort of thing. To be a man of your times is to be ensnared by trivia, tied down like Gulliver by the Lilliputians. To let the spirit soar, you must unshackle the imagination from the paltry concerns of the here and now. You must have no truck with actuality in any shape or form."

Conundrum stopped to draw breath.

"And while we are on the subject, if you can trade carbon emissions, then why not other things? Self esteem, for example. Someone with too much of that commodity, could give a boost to someone lacking in the same. Aaaatisho!"

Another violent sneeze shook the car.

"You should take something for that cold."

"Not likely. A cold is not a sickness in need of treatment, Henri. Just nature rebooting the system."

When Avebury was several miles behind us he ordered me to rejoin the M4 motorway. He now resumed his rambling discourse. I was born aloft once again on the wings of his words. The subject was now transience and mortality.

"So why do we footle away our lives? We spend the first half scared of living. The second half scared of dying. If we are lucky there is a brief intermission, a kind of fool's paradise in between. They've discovered that babies smile in the womb. Well, let them. There's precious little to smile about once they get out. We are born knowing everything we need to know but from then on it's downhill all the way. If you want to know the answer to life, the universe and everything, just ask a new borne babe. They know it all. If only they had the words to tell us. But the more we learn to think and to speak the less we actually know. Everything we learn is an illusion. Our lifespan transports us willy-nilly from total knowledge ever closer to total ignorance. And on it goes ad infinitum. World without end, amen."

He puffed hard on an extinguished cigarette.

"World without end? I don't think so. Even the solid earth beneath our feet is but shifting sand on unstable tectonic plates. Our eternal white cliffs are made of billions of corpses of tiny sea creatures that once had aspirations of their own. And so it'll go with us. We'll end up as a bit of geology."

He struck a match. In its brief glow Conundrum's face was as ancient as a rock.

"Curious thing getting old, Henri. You become virtually invisible to the young. They look through you as if you aren't really there. As if you're already dead. Young folk don't want to see a reflection of their future selves. Prefer to dismiss you as a trick of the light. But that has its advantages, mind you."

A dry chuckle followed this last remark.

"And why are we so obsessed with the future? Do we really need it? Is it not enough to be enjoying a particular mood at a particular moment with no thought for the morrow? The greatest obscenity is growing old without growing up. Senile faces with adolescence still writ large on their vacuous chops. Where is the dignity in that? Anyone with an ounce of tragic insight into the human condition should have had the stuffing knocked out of them somewhere along the line."

A short pause. Another sneeze.

"Used to worry I wasn't growing old physically. Doomed to stay young while everyone else was maturing and ageing. Then one day I noticed in the mirror the first signs of decay. A tiny crease around the eye I hadn't spotted before. An extra fold of flesh under the chin. What a relief! I too would go the way of all flesh. Now it's full speed ahead. A runaway train. I feel the hoary hairs of senility sprout from ears and nostrils. Toe nails thicken by the minute. Soon my chief hobby will be pruning my nasal garden. Actually did some jottings on the subject of *The Well Cultivated Nose*. Think I might be on to something there. I'm told you can sell anything to do with gardens."

A strange urgency entered his voice.

"The point is, life isn't a life sentence. Well of course it is if you want to be literal. What I mean is there's an end to it. If you get my gist. It's finite. So what's all the fuss about?"

He paused for another sneeze that refused to come.

41

"One day in Yemen, I came across a pair of shoes in the street, abandoned in mid-stride as if their erstwhile occupant had on a sudden whim launched himself into space. That was when I first saw the light. I didn't fully grasp it at the time. Only later did I realise that once someone sees the cosmic joke, then that soul simply dematerialises, ceases 'to be', or rather begins 'not to be'. Hence the absence of the 'former man in shoes'. And that is precisely how I shall hope to end, Henri. Vertical lift-off, in mid-stride, leaving my shoes behind me."

The cosmic joke, a curious expression. I reflected that the removal of the letter 's' transformed cosmic into comic. I smiled at the thought but said nothing.

"And what's so funny? That nothing makes sense, never can make sense? Millennia of philosophising all in vain. Was that the Age of Enlightenment flashing by? Ephemeral as ice cream on a hot afternoon. Same with Existentialism, Romanticism, Post-Modernism, Deconstructivism and all the other isms. Just blink and they're gone. Just blink and I'm gone too."

I didn't cotton on that Conundrum was giving an order.

"Just blink, Henri. For God's sake, just blink."

I blinked. Suddenly Conundrum was gone. I was on my own. I blinked again and just as suddenly he was back.

"How the hell did you do that?"

"Do what? I did nothing. You are the one who did the seeing and the non-seeing."

What was more worrying? That Conundrum could disappear and re-appear just like that? Or that he could get inside my mind and make me believe it? Or was there another possibility? Maybe I was too tired and starting to hallucinate? At any rate, it all happened so fast it soon seemed totally unreal.

"I fear our telescopes have been pointing in the wrong direction in this cursed quest for Truth. In fact, the telescope is entirely the wrong instrument. A microscope shows more neurons in a human brain than all the galaxies of the universe. That makes us all gods, I suppose, with the divine inside us not out there, everywhere and nowhere. But the microscope runs smack into a brick wall of meaningless detail just as the telescope fails to focus on infinity. Something else is required. Perhaps a macroscope? An instrument of that name needs to be invented. A macroscope would allow us to see through the opaque skin of reality, not magnifying, but getting so close to the heart of the matter that whatever is right there in front of our noses, staring us in the face, moves from the invisible to the visible. Simple as that. Unattainable as that."

His mood became increasingly melancholic.

"Meanwhile, I still dabble in the daily grind of living. I'm mostly there much of the time. Occasionally I'm possibly all there just for a bit. Don't think you'd want to see me in my entirety, at least not for very long. Believe me, Henri."

I did believe him, most earnestly.

"Occasionally I go in search of myself. Like a child playing hide-and-seek. But the moment I step towards the mirror, so my reflected self steps towards me. We collide, yet the two of us are destined never to meet, never to be united in the same sphere. And so it is with the world and its essence. Our reality is the shadow image of something far greater. You do see what I'm getting at, Henri?"

To tell the truth, I had no clue what he was getting at with this talk of macroscopes, mirrors, shadows, the cosmic joke and shoes abandoned in mid-stride. I later realised these were all perfect metaphors for Conundrum's...

But I mustn't race ahead. All I can say for now is the potent spell his words cast on me. I started to come pleasurably adrift from the narrow confines of my own thoughts. I became detached and remote from myself. Hard to describe it. Not so much an out-of-body as an out-of-mind experience. But in a way that was completely sane. Yes, that was it. For the first time in my life, I had taken a few timid steps outside the tedium of my own mental prison. I felt the joy of floating free in the great universal void outside myself. No longer trapped, I was a loose projectile hurtling down a great tunnel of darkness.

During that period of suspension, the world became wondrously transformed into something quite out of this world. Even the service stations along the M4 with their ridiculous Little Chefs and fatuous Happy Eaters were no longer banal everyday objects, but infinitely fascinating phenomena offering an excitingly new reality. I don't know what trick Conundrum had played that I should start to perceive things in this way. Perhaps it was my fatigue and the thrill of driving through the night to escape the clutches of that hotel from hell.

Somewhere between Swindon and Reading, Conundrum fell silent. He took forty winks while red streaks of dawn stained the sky. On waking, his mood changed.

"Well, that's quite enough of questions and answers."

This was perplexing. I hadn't been asking that many questions, one or two at most. Had I known this was a unique opportunity to interrogate him, I would have quizzed him thoroughly. But the moment had passed. The free flowing mode was replaced by an uncomfortably inquisitorial tone.

"You have to understand your own destiny, Henri. Are you merely passing the baton? Or are you running your own race? You must know. And if you don't know, you bloody well should. So get a grip. Find out what part you are playing. Where precisely are you at? Time to spill the beans."

I was now the object of his scrutiny. I had no option but to explain myself as best I could. How I found the way most people lead their lives messy and pointless. Me still searching for substance, meaning, purpose but finding none. Between Reading and Heathrow I revealed to this curious stranger the frustrated ambitions of a freelance photographer who still yearned for the Holy Grail of Art, Truth, Beauty, but at the same time feeling an enormous urge to dump that silly stuff, put the lid on all those hopelessly idealistic schemes and dreams.

"Sounds like you have given up, Henri?"

I said nothing. But my lack of denial spoke volumes.

"You're far too young for that. Giving up is the prerogative of the old. You'll have to wait your turn. Meanwhile, you must put up the pretence of believing in something. Doesn't matter what. Anything will do."

Was he sending me up? I ignored the edge of mockery and gave vent to my personal frustrations, all the hassle I had suffered with my various projects. I concluded lamely with some banal remark about it being good to unburden my feelings.

Conundrum chuckled.

"A trouble shared is a trouble doubled. Bring me your problems and I will multiply them."

There was a deeply cynical, world-weary, all-knowing tone to his laughter. I felt I had been outplayed before I had grasped the rules of his game.

"But let's assume everything is for the best in this best of all possible worlds. Consider the shabby compromises, failures, deceptions, all the gratuitous insults endured from shysters, shits and charlatans. Just think on them for a moment, Henri."

What a ghastly parade passed before my eyes. All the bastards who had trampled on my noble feelings, bright ideas, or thwarted my ambitions one way or another.

"Take your leave of them, Henri. But first, embrace them, press them to your bosom and thank them from the bottom of your heart. Then kiss them goodbye."

"Thank them? Thank them for what?"

"Suffice it to say all those petty villains are no more than grains of sand, a kind of abrasive to mould your contours and transform you from a rough lump of rock into a fine work of sculpture with smooth polished surface."

So there might be some sense in my suffering after all. I felt relieved. But something disturbed me. It was as if Conundrum already knew my tangled emotional labyrinth far better than I knew it myself. Somehow, he was intimately acquainted with the workings of my innermost being.

"Unless you accept how you got to where you are now, there can be no moving on."

"Moving on?"

"But of course. What else?"

"But where to?"

"Nowhere in particular."

"So how will I know when I arrive?"

"Arrive? Maybe nowhere. Who said anything about arriving? But at least you will be no longer trapped where you are. And if you persist in asking such ridiculous questions you won't even achieve that."

I bit my tongue. One moment I had been released into an exciting new dimension. The next, I was back in jail.

"You really should experience things out East, Henri. As a photographer I mean. In some places people smile and thank you if you take their picture, thinking they will travel with you in your image of them. But elsewhere, they suspect you are trying to steal their soul. And so they throw stones at you. Both are valid reactions. You must know in your heart what you deserve. So what is it to be? A smile or the stones?"

He made everything sound simple. So amazingly simple.

"When the wind takes your hat, you reckon there is still time to reach out and grab it. Invariably it is too late. The hat is gone even as you raise your hand. Like the spontaneity of those pictures of yours that vanishes even before you have taken them. The trick is to act on the wing of the thought. Anticipate the wind and grab the hat just before it even thinks of flying away. Action before thought, Henri. Not thought before action. There is a whole new world of possibilities out there."

Action before thought? I gasped at the very idea. I had already knocked back the cocktail in one fateful gulp.

"There is so much you can yet achieve at your tender age, Henri. You have everything before you. You haven't even reached your starting point. As for an old fart like myself, I haven't stopped living as such, but most of my time is now spent making mental notes of what I will do next time round. But you have it all before you. The whole script can be rewritten for your personal benefit and entertainment."

Just contemplating the myriad possibilities and complexities of life made me panic. I'd gladly have swapped places with Conundrum who had it all behind him. He now rolled another cigarette and with it another thought.

"Never think or do the obvious, Henri. Anything but that. Just when you think you have arrived, that is the moment to press on. Above all, be bold. Weak people are like quicksand. Fear is the enemy of life. To the faint-hearted even the scratching of a dry leaf on the garden path sounds like the paws of a hellhound closing in for the kill. Do not be mean with your thoughts and feelings. Don't measure yourself out in tiny portions. When you open the bottle throw away the cork."

Conundrum's eyes narrowed.

"Think bold. Bend the spectrum."

Bend the spectrum? That had a certain ring to it. Conundrum saw my reaction and became evasive, as if he hadn't intended to be that specific.

"Live dangerously, Henri. A life without risk is no life at all. No point in worrying about things until they happen. Live in the now, the blessed here and now. Most people are machines for turning future into past with no sense of the present. Break free from the shuffling rank-and-file of those zombies whose only claim to life is that they are not yet physically dead."

Conundrum was frightened of nothing. I was scared of everything. But in his company I felt strong. All things were possible. Or at least, they would be if I could make Conundrum's knowledge my own. Deep inside I was on fire.

"Well, Henri? What's it to be?"

"I don't know what to say. You surprise me."

"Surprise you, do I? That must be exciting for you. But what's the point in surprising you unless I can surprise myself too? If I know in advance what I'm about to say, what is the

47

purpose of my saying it? One day I should like to say or do something that will leave even myself gasping in disbelief."

For someone who claimed that nothing really mattered, Conundrum gave the clear impression with every ounce of his being that everything did matter to him and to an intense degree. Yet for all his passion, he spoke in a cool, deliberate manner. Like someone who had done the calculations, figured the odds, knew he could make it happen.

"So think daringly, Henri. Forget about peace and enlightenment in this life. Wisdom is most destructive to a thinking man. Forget about progress too. Our universe is powered by the dynamism of chaos, the titanic struggle of opposing forces. That which tears us apart actually holds us together. Sufficient unto the day is the evil thereof. Just keep faith with your madness."

Now he sounded like a demented biblical prophet.

"The trick is to start where others leave off. Go over the edge. Meditate on the dark side of the moon. Walk on the water. Dance on the ceiling. Fly without wings. Be the fist not the jaw, the boot not the arse, the sword not the neck. Unless you are constantly thinking ideas unthinkable, doing the undoable, you are going nowhere. Not moving on."

Moving on? Those words again. 'Moving on' as if in quotation marks, like a pair of birds fluttering around his head. Then it occurred to me that everything Conundrum said came with inverted commas. Like reported speech, his thoughts were fragments from a lost scroll, pages from an unknown book by an unknown philosopher-poet. His whole person had stepped out of a forgotten manuscript.

"Don't be alarmed, Henri. I am not asking you to sell your soul."

Sell my soul. Was that the deal? Conundrum eyed me in an appraising manner before continuing.

"Even if I were to buy that commodity, I would only be acquiring something you are clearly all too eager to part with."

Was I that transparent? Without any conscious assent on my part, had I picked up the gauntlet?

By the time we arrived back in dear old London, Conundrum had had his way with me. My pack of cards had been reshuffled, my hand dealt. Henceforth, ensconced deep in my subconscious was the germ of an idea, the small seed of his great project. It would take a long while to flower and even then I would deny it existed. But there it indubitably was. Yet ultimately, like with the cuckoo's egg, I would be duped into accepting it as my own. Having hooked me, Conundrum now tugged sharply on the line to make sure his catch was secure.

"Beware the old leading the young down the primrose path, Henri. Handing on dreams they abandoned long ago. On the other hand far too much fuss is made of the young who are merely tomorrow's old farts waiting in the wings."

"Surely you haven't abandoned your dreams?"

"Take careful note, Henri. Everything I say comes with a health warning. But it is one you would do well not to observe."

With the end of our journey approaching, I felt the need to set the record straight about my name.

"I wanted to say… My name isn't Henri. Actually, it's…"

Conundrum cut me off with some urgency.

"No for God's sake, I don't want to hear it. Since you have aspirations to be a real Henri, I shall call you thus."

"A real Henri?"

"Don't be dense. Surely you've heard of that famous French photographer chappie?"

"You don't mean Henri Cartier-Bresson?"

Conundrum appeared to nod.

"Since you aspire to be a real Henri, I have anointed you one straight away. Saves a lot of confusion. It's a new spin on Cartesian logic. I call myself such and such and therefore ….?"

"I am such and such!"

"Excellent, Henri. Bravo! You do appear to be grasping the essentials."

Only then did it dawn on me I didn't know his name.

"And what is your name?"

He hesitated before replying.

"It's a conundrum."

"A conundrum?"

"Precisely so. But don't ever call me that."

"But what shall I call you?"

"Call me? You don't have to call me. I'm not a dog. So you don't have to call me anything."

He fended off any further enquiries.

"Well, that's quite enough of the personal stuff."

A conundrum? Was that supposed to be his real name or just a comment on it? Whatever, from that moment on I knew him simply as Conundrum and never by any other. That is, not until well after ... But I mustn't talk about that awful business yet. As for my new name Henri, Conundrum continued tagging it to almost every utterance, so that it was soon an embedded object in my consciousness. I must admit I was highly flattered by the reference, however spurious, to Henri Cartier-Bresson, legendary French photojournalist.

We were now driving along Piccadilly. The morning sun reflecting off the wet streets almost blinded me with its radiance.

"Drop me at Cambridge Circus. I shall walk from there."

As we parted company by the Palace Theatre, I suggested he might care to meet up for a drink one evening.

"What a ghastly idea, Henri. Couldn't possibly. There's no need to socialise. I never do. Except with strangers."

I mumbled an incoherent apology.

"No offence taken, Henri. I assure you. In fact, I owe you my deliverance. I shall see to it we do better next time."

"Next time?"

"Indeed so. For with this little outing we have scraped the bottom of the barrel. I'll see what is to be done about it."

"Let me give you my card."

"Good lord no, Henri. No need for silly stuff like that."

I delivered a violent triple sneeze. Conundrum grinned. He seemed pleased he had passed on his cold so quickly.

"I wouldn't take anything for that. Embrace the virus. Let the system renew itself. That's my advice, Henri. And on this occasion I do advise you to take it."

Conundrum wandered off down Old Compton Street in a vague meandering fashion. His trousers were spattered right up to the knees with mud from his nocturnal walk at Avebury. But that wasn't what struck me as peculiar. Something about the nonchalant way he swung his battered old suitcase told me there was nothing in it. I also had a suspicion he was not heading directly for home. He looked like a man going nowhere in particular. It was as if – for some unfathomable reason – he wanted quite deliberately to put me off the scent.

Now, the strain of the journey was beginning to tell. I drove the short distance to my flat in a crumbling mansion block on the shabby fringes of Bloomsbury and Kings Cross. As I opened my front door and kicked aside the brown envelopes of Saturday's post, I was wondering whether I hadn't dreamed up the whole bizarre encounter. The sane part of me hoped I had. The mad part of me hoped I hadn't.

Within minutes, I'd fallen into a dreamless sleep.

SURREAL IN SPAIN

Conundrum's cold laid me low for several days. I heartily cursed him for those infectious sneezes, surely released with malicious intent, on the drive back to London. But I followed his advice and took no medicine. I sat tight and embraced the cold. It quickly developed into a nasty bout of flu. Soon I was seriously ill. But just when I felt at my lowest, I began to emerge from the fever. My whole body tingled with a curious sensation of newness. My system felt decidedly rebooted.

Several weeks passed. I heard nothing further from Conundrum. This came as a relief. Deep down I sensed in him a sinister threat as well as a heady promise. I was glad we hadn't done the ritual exchange of visiting cards. I couldn't contact him, and I was pretty confident or at least hopeful he wouldn't bother getting in touch with the likes of me. In all probability he was too busy winding up some other impressionable young person with his dark thoughts and dangerous dreams.

Besides, I had other things to keep myself busy, a project of an artistic nature. The sort of thing Conundrum would have scoffed at. Soon after I moved in to my present flat in Bloomsbury, someone had dropped a tin of red paint on the pavement right outside my block. The contents spread over the stone slabs like a thick pool of blood after a brutal murder. No one bothered to clear up the mess. The paint congealed into a monstrous red blob that looked like a permanent feature.

Then as the days and weeks passed I noticed how the sun and rain went to work eroding its edges, modifying its contours. I was fascinated by this mutating apparition on my doorstep. I got into the habit of taking pictures. I soon became obsessed with making a daily photographic record of the reductive process. It seemed like a powerful metaphor of something very personal, as if my fate was bound up with this blob of red paint.

The idea grew that when it finally disappeared a chunk of my life would also be at an end. Once this notion got a grip on me it became scary to monitor progress each time I went out or returned home, like watching the sands of time dribbling through my own existential hourglass. Somehow, my own life was shrinking before my eyes in the shape of this crimson stain on the pavement. Taking pictures could not halt the process but allowed me to face up to the reality of my transience.

You may correctly deduce from this I wasn't too busy in a professional sense. In fact, my photographic commissions had almost dried up. Only when I badgered a picture editor did some small job come my way. And if I didn't bother, the phone would hardly ring. Then one day, the phone did ring with an offer of work. But it was more an order, not an invitation.

"Pack your bags for sunny Spain, Henri."

Conundrum's voice at the end of the line had a self-mocking tone, which suggested that everything it said was too ridiculous for words.

"Sunny Spain?"

"You don't have to repeat everything I say, Henri. And before you ask what this is all about, we're going there to look up my old friend Salvador."

"Salvador?"

Conundrum didn't comment on my mindless repetition.

"Yes. That's Salvador, as in Salvador Dalí. Greatest genius of all time."

"Oh him. But I thought Dali was dead."

"Very droll, Henri. Now, Dalí – and do stress the accent on the final i – may have expired, but that does not prevent us from paying him a visit. We're to do a travel piece on the Catalonian landscapes that inspired him. You're in charge of the snaps. Leave the rest to me. We leave tomorrow. Rendez-vous, 10 am, Iberia ticket desk, Heathrow Terminal Two. Don't pack your bucket and spade. This is work."

The line went dead. I dialled 1471 to call back Conundrum and ask for more details, like what was the deal, who was it for, how long would we be away. But the number was withheld. Ex-directory or even a pay phone perhaps?

It now occurred to me that Conundrum – damn his presumption – hadn't even deigned to ask if I was available. But I soon overcame my petty annoyance. A surge of anticipation even excitement welled up inside me. Yes, in spite of all my misgivings I was up for the challenge Conundrum had placed before me. It was time to grab life by the balls. I spent the rest of the day packing, stocking up on film and paying a few urgent bills. In truth, I was ready for a trip. Sunny Spain didn't sound too bad. Catalonia had a pleasant ring to it.

The following morning, as I left the building, I almost forgot my daily ritual. Hurriedly I paused to take yet another picture of the blob of red paint on the pavement. I realised I was no longer engaged in the act, just going through the motions. I would reapply myself when I got back, whenever that was.

At Heathrow, I hovered around the Iberia ticket desk for almost half an hour, eventually feeling rather like someone about to be stood up. Just as the flight was about to close, Conundrum finally put in an appearance.

"I've got the tickets, Henri. Follow me."

Once on board Conundrum made sure we took full advantage of the free champagne on offer in business class. I browsed through the glossy mags, studying all the artful tricks and dodges of trendy travel photographers to make their pictures sexy and appealing. His conversation was unpredictable as ever.

"A country with an upside-down question mark at the beginning of a sentence and two verbs meaning 'to be' is clearly a force to be reckoned with."

He waved a book right under my nose. I could just about read the title as *A SPANISH COURSE* by B.J.W. Hill.

"How about this for a useful phrase? *'Conchita is a naughty girl and needs to be punished'*. Might come in handy. You never know your luck."

Conundrum grabbed more champagne from a passing trolley and proposed a toast to the moustachioed genius of Catalonia who was the pretext for our trip. After that he did not utter another word during the rest of the flight. He stared out of the window or sat there eyes half closed, hardly breathing. It was neither sleep nor meditation, but a state of suspended animation. Nothing was said until we had cleared customs in Barcelona.

"I trust you brought your driving licence, Henri?"

"You didn't mention it."

Did he note the petulance in my voice?

"But you did bring it?"

"Well, yes. As it happens."

"So no need to quibble. Just toddle over to Hertz and do the necessary. They'll know all about you."

While waiting to be served, I read a warning about motorway bandits holding up tourists and making off with their luggage. Well, they were welcome to mine. I always pack too much and inevitably all the wrong things. So do help yourselves, gentlemen. But please no violence. I can't stand the sight of blood. Especially my own. Suddenly I found this rather funny. Couldn't suppress a giggle. I was not used to whimsical dialogues in my head. I now realised I had drunk too much champagne and was not best pleased at being the chauffeur.

"*Señor?*"

The Hertz lady smiled at me. All I had to do was sign and take the keys. She scribbled on a piece of paper how to get out of the airport. It looked amazingly complex. So I thought I'd leave the navigating to Conundrum.

"Let's hit the road, Henri."

"Which way?"

"Just follow the signs for Girona."

No sooner had we left the airport car park than I spotted a sign for Girona and followed it confidently.

"Should be a doddle now. Don't think we will need this any more."

Conundrum casually tossed out of the window the directions carefully written by the Hertz lady. We were on an overpass at the time and I watched the scrap of paper waft down like an autumn leaf onto the cars racing along below.

"We shall not pass this way again, methinks."

But we did precisely that. Half an hour later we were back where we started. For after the first sign, there was no more mention of Girona. Nothing at all. As if the town had been wiped off the map. And with no idea where to head for and absolutely no help from Conundrum, who gave an excellent impression of not being remotely concerned where we were going, I resorted to guesswork. I eventually came full circle and ground to a halt in the jaws of total gridlock. I reversed up a slip road into a petrol station to seek help.

Conundrum still seemed completely unperturbed and left me to make enquiries of the pump attendant. In my non-existent Spanish, the conversation went approximately as follows.

"Girona?"

"Tarragona!"

"Girona??"

"Tarragona!!"

"Girona???"

"Tarragona!!!"

I think that was about it before I concluded this might go on forever. So I thanked him and returned to the car.

"Don't understand why, but he's telling us to go to Tarragona."

"Well, get on with it, Henri. Go to Tarragona."

"But that's 100km in the wrong direction."

"Don't be such a bore, Henri. Always looking for logical flaws. Just do what the man said."

So I followed the signs to Tarragona. They led us slowly but surely away from the airport and towards a huge motorway intersection. Right at the last moment, Girona appeared as one of several hitherto unmentioned destinations. Phew.

I relaxed at the wheel and took a fleeting sideways look at Conundrum. He was daydreaming just as he had been in the plane. The only sign of conscious life was an occasional movement of thumb and index finger, as if rolling a cigarette in the vicinity of his upper lip. This little tick, often repeated over the coming days, I came to recognise as the grooming of a phantom Dalinian moustache.

"Salvador never drove a car. Always got someone else to do it for him. That's another thing we have in common."

"Did you really know Dali?"

"Who's that, Henri?"

I now placed the accent on the final i.

"Dalí?"

My effort seemed to satisfy him.

"Know Dalí? Intimately of course. Blood brothers. Kindred spirits. Virtually inseparable. A dying breed of wayward geniuses. Now sadly in Salavador's case, dead as a doornail."

"How did you meet him?"

"Meet him? Who said anything about meeting him? We didn't need to meet in order to communicate."

"So you didn't actually know him?"

"Don't be tiresome, Henri. As Salvador would say, there is much more to reality than the surface dross of facts."

I recalled Conundrum saying completely the opposite during the drive back to London, namely that the meaningless facts of superficial reality were all that counted. But I decided not to risk another rebuff and opted for silence. Then without any warning Conundrum suddenly barked an order.

"That's our turning, Henri. Quick. Look lively."

There was just time to change lanes and make the exit.

"But that's not the way to Girona. It says Lloret de Mar."

"Your point being?"

"You said we were going to Girona?"

"And now I am saying go to Lloret de Mar."

"OK, Lloret it is. That's one of those tourist resorts on the Costa Brava, isn't it?"

"Just get on with it."

The sun was close to setting as we drove into downtown Lloret. Conundrum tapped on the dashboard to indicate I should stop in front of a nondescript seafront hotel. It didn't feel like the sort of place where Dalí would have dipped his brush.

I sat waiting in the car while Conundrum engaged in animated conversation firstly with the lady receptionist and then with a man in a suit. Through the large plate glass window and between the leaves of a potted plant I could see him gesticulating in a convincingly Spanish manner as he pointed melodramatically to a crumpled letter. At last, matters appeared to be resolved. Hands were shaken, smiles exchanged.

Conundrum returned to the car.

"Bit of a hiccup, Henri. But it's settled now. We'll put up here for four nights. It's not the Ritz. But a freebie is a freebie."

It certainly wasn't the Ritz. Several listless British tourists lingered in the lobby. They eyed us suspiciously, sensing we were not holidaymakers of the packaged variety like everyone else. Glazed eyes sussed us out. We took the lift to the fifth floor. Our rooms were located near each other with one room in between. Just as we inserted the keys, the door of this room in the middle opened. A silver-haired man in an amazingly colourful shirt and unnaturally white slacks stepped out.

"Allo, allo, allo. You must be the two that missed the plane. There's always someone, isn't there?"

He waited in vain for a reply before continuing.

"I'm Arthur. And this is Gladys."

A lady now peered timidly out of his shadow but she said nothing.

"Have you two heard the latest bullfight results?"

58

Arthur was clearly dying to tell us.

"Bulls 0."

We must have looked mystified.

"Matadors 8!"

We stared uncomprehendingly at Arthur, now doubled up with laughter.

"Another bad day for the poor old *toros*. Get it?"

Conundrum winced visibly. This was a rare occasion when I saw him at a complete loss what to say. Perhaps it was the shock of hearing broad Yorkshire in Spain that deprived him of the power of speech.

Arthur now waved the *Daily Express* at him.

"Here, have a read of my paper, if you like. News isn't as fresh as I like. All happened day before yesterday."

Arthur chortled again. His parting remark was delivered as he steered Gladys towards the lift.

"We'll have a nice long chat later. But it's dinnertime now, and we must be first in the queue. You've got to be ahead of the game. Even on holiday. The early bird catches the worm. That's what I always say, isn't it Gladys?"

"Yes, Arthur. It's what you always say."

When they had gone, Conundrum took a deep breath.

"An advanced case of SRS, if you ask me."

"SRS?"

"Silly Remark Syndrome. Uncontrollable urge to crack poor jokes. The English disease. Very tedious. Take it from me Henri, there is nothing quite so unfunny as cracking jokes. Thank heavens we're only on B&B. So we won't be having to share a table for dinner with the likes of Arthur and Gladys. I'll see you downstairs in half an hour and we'll find a local restaurant ."

When we met in the lobby, Conundrum looked about anxiously over his shoulder and ushered me out of the hotel. We found a pleasant enough restaurant nearby with a pavement terrace and ordered wine and paella. The food had only just arrived when Arthur and Gladys passed by on their after-dinner stroll. Arthur stopped to inspect our plates.

"Wouldn't touch that foreign muck if I were you. Won't look much different when you have to throw it up, mind you. So hardly worth eating it in the first place."

Gladys pulled on his arm and filled the awkward silence.

"Arthur's just dumped his stock, you know. And I advise you to do the same. Arthur always knows what's best."

"Indeed I do, Gladys. World economy going down the pan. Get out while you can. Take my word for it. I bailed out yesterday. Sold the whole bloody lot. Not top prices, mind you. But at least I can relax on my well-earned holiday safe in the knowledge I'm well off out of it. Footsie can bloody well go through the floor and I'll be dancing on the tables."

Arthur and Gladys continued their evening walk along the seafront. I looked at the paella. Arthur had put a damper on my appetite. Conundrum appeared totally unaffected. He rapidly cleared his plate and promptly helped himself to what was left on mine. It was as if he hadn't eaten for a week. I wondered where he put all the food in his bony frame. When he had finished he ordered more wine and rolled a cigarette from his metal tin.

"So who or what is Footsie? And what on earth does 'dumping stock' mean, Henri? Sounds painful, I must say."

"I think it means Arthur has sold all his shares."

"Shares? Shares of what, Henri? Don't talk in riddles."

I tried to explain matters in terms of the ups and downs of equities, index tracking, long-term growth versus short-term risk, market volatility and so on. I knew all the jargon from my pension adviser. But I should have saved my breath.

"The ugly sisters of fear and greed, Henri. That's what drives markets. I hate money. Detest the stuff. Had some once. Quite a bit actually. Damned nuisance it was too. Caused me no end of bother figuring out what to do with it. In the end I got rid of it with some spectacularly bad investments. Seemed I had this gift for buying dear and selling cheap. Undid the work of many a financial consultant. Pretty soon I was cleaned out. I'd reduced my cash pile to a pocket of loose change."

Conundrum puffed a cloud of acrid smoke at me.

"Then it dawned on me that if I'd done the opposite of what I actually did, I'd have made a fortune. So I thought I could earn a few bob selling my valuable expertise as Conundrum's reverse investment strategy. All I had to do was advise people to do one thing and they should go off and do the opposite. But I turned my back on that too. Decided to make a virtue out of impecuniosity. And in this respect I've been hugely successful."

He downed a glass of wine in a single gulp.

"At least I didn't amass a sordid little nest egg to worry about like our Arthur. I may have done many shameful things in my time, Henri, but I have never saved a penny. I have spent my all. Nor have I ever accepted the bondage of regular employment and final salary pension schemes. What greater servitude can there be than shackling oneself to a paid job?"

I kept silent. I would have given anything right now to be in receipt of a monthly brown envelope. Being a freelance, far from making you free, only made you beholden in a different way. As if reading my thoughts Conundrum continued.

"You deserve full credit, Henri. Standing on your own two feet. Chancing your arm. Taking things on the chin. Not one of those cowardly time-servers. Being a freelance has a certain dignity. Even when we apply the tongue – as occasionally needs must – to orifices unspeakable, there is still a certain nobility in our abasement. Not so with the salaried man who has sold his very soul."

I dared not say how much I had come recently to hate selling myself as a freelance photographer. There was a degree of subservience in that act infinitely worse than any life sentence of paid employment.

"And that's precisely why travel writing has such appeal. I can live like a king without the tiresome business of making my own stash of filthy lucre to pay for it. No sleepless nights over the ups and downs of Footsie, like poor old Arthur."

So that was it. Conundrum was a professional freeloader.

"I see what you're thinking, Henri. But being a freeloader isn't demeaning. Quite the opposite. It's an elegant response to a painful reality. Almost an art form if you like. I retain my personal integrity while being a recipient of hospitality and largesse. It's a pure existence, living off the land like our ancestors the hunter-gatherers of prehistory. Now this hotel is ghastly enough, but at least we haven't been so foolish as to pay for it. Thus we are free to enjoy it for what it is. We are not tainted by it. So it's an honourable profession. More's the pity. I should so like to have done something dishonourable."

Conundrum blew a smoke ring in the air and watched it drift away over the Mediterranean.

"Luxury hotels are much more fun of course. But the principle remains the same. Ultimately there's nothing grand about the Grand, majestic about the Majestic, or splendid about the Splendid. Such places are mere excuses for the well-heeled to spend too much money. But we freeloaders are a cut above the paying clients since we don't need to settle our bills. And we help to propagate the myth that luxury is paradise on earth. We are flies grazing freely on an expensive cowpat that without us would resemble any other pile of farmyard manure."

I was rapidly learning that Conundrum had no idea about money. He didn't possess a credit card and only dipped a hand in his pocket – and most reluctantly at that – to fish out a bit of small change for some minor item of expenditure. He seemed to have no attachment to material things. And yet his instinct for physical survival was as keen as that of any predator. As I was about to discover, he could smell a free lunch a mile away. And the unalloyed joy he took in such treats denied the received wisdom that there is no such thing as a free lunch. With Conundrum, it was one free lunch after another, not to mention all the free dinners, free hotels, free cars and free flights.

"Yes, I'm glad I don't have money, Henri."

This last statement coincided with the waiter presenting the bill. Conundrum deftly steered it towards me.

"Do the honours will you? You can charge it, of course. I'm no good at paperwork."

Me doing the honours became a ritual often repeated over the next few days. Our meal over, we returned to the hotel. I was ready for bed. But as I lay down to sleep I heard the voices of Arthur and Gladys through the wall.

"Tight-lipped pair, don't you reckon, Gladys?"

Silence from Gladys.

"Typical bloody southerners. Admit it, woman."

"I suppose so, Arthur."

"Takes all sorts though, Gladys. That's what I say."

"Yes, Arthur. It's what you say."

"So glad I dumped my stock, Gladys. To hell with the Footsie. Just another bit of London trickery, if you ask me. Reckon yourself lucky you can count on me to get things right. You'll never want for anything with good old Arthur, my girl."

Next morning, I awoke to the sound of a flushing toilet followed by a resumption of the Arthur and Gladys dialogue. As usual, Arthur was speaking.

"Good result this morning, Gladys. Nice solid primary movement. Just what I need to set me up for the day."

Arthur grunted.

"Don't think much of the plumbing though."

I went down to breakfast. Conundrum was already there. A couple of minutes later Arthur and Gladys came and sat at the adjoining table. Arthur seemed very pleased with himself after his nice solid primary movement.

"Very neighbourly, I must say, isn't it? Next door rooms. Next door tables. I don't think I caught your names last night."

Conundrum introduced me as Henri. Then he swallowed a large mouthful of cornflakes. Arthur extended a hand.

"So that's Henry and er ... ?"

Conundrum mumbled inaudibly through his cornflakes. Arthur didn't press the point. He started on his own breakfast.

"There's only one thing I like less than lukewarm milk on my cornflakes, you know what that is?"

Foolishly, I responded.

"And what's that?"

"Cornflakes! Can't stand them!"

Arthur roared with laughter. Conundrum groaned.

"Can't think how they can call this stuff a cup of tea. No one out here makes tea just how you like it, do they Gladys?"

"No, Arthur. They don't."

"Never tastes right. And yet every morning you hear our fellow tourists rabbiting on about the 'nice cup of tea' they've just had or are so looking forward to."

Conundrum pulled a face at being included as a fellow tourist. Arthur didn't notice. He was back with his obsession.

"If you two want to do yourselves a big favour, bear in mind what I said about a market crash. Sea might look calm right now but there's a big storm brewing. Real monster. Take my word for it. I'm never wrong in these matters."

Gladys chipped in obligingly.

"Arthur's never wrong, you know."

"And when the market crashes, folk will feel the pinch. Property prices will go down the drain. Then there's bound to be a few nice villas up for sale at bargain basement prices. And then we'll snap up our dream home in the sun, won't we Gladys? I think you get more for your money in Lloret than Marbella. Now what do you say to that as a nice little business plan?"

Conundrum didn't express an opinion. He stood up and headed for the breakfast buffet. I watched him pull from his pocket a polythene shower cap, presumably taken from his bathroom, and rapidly fill it with an assortment of meat, fish, eggs, bread, jam, butter and fruit. Within seconds he hoovered up enough for a substantial family picnic. Impressive proof of his skill at living off the land.

"Come along now, Henri. Salvador awaits."

We left Arthur and Gladys pondering their golden future in the sun. Conundrum muttered.

"A pox on dream homes in the sun. They've built their goddam Guildfords and Godalmings from the Pyrenees down to Granada and the Guadalquivir. It's bad enough with Surrey folk living in Surrey. But now they're everywhere and Yorkshire wants to get in on the act. Is nothing sacred? Spain is finished."

With that Conundrum lapsed into a sullen silence as we drove in a north-easterly direction. His hawkish eyes surveyed the scenery. He nodded from time to time, as if ticking off familiar sights in his mind. He made no use of a map, but gave directions as and when he saw landmarks he recalled from long ago. Eventually, we left the coast and climbed a narrow track twisting its way in a series of tight loops over a sinuous and stony mountain terrain.

"We are now entering Dalí country."

We meandered through a fantasy landscape of contorted rocks that might have been designed by Dalí. At last we reached the jagged promontory of Cap de Creus. The only building in sight was a forbidding hostelry perched on a bluff.

"Stop here, Henri. We shall begin by paying our respects to the Great Masturbator."

I recalled Dalí's famous surrealist painting of a grotesque piece of rock like a man's head bursting with erotic fantasies.

"Since you are clearly not adequately conversant in the local lingo, I will make the necessary enquiries."

Conundrum climbed a steep path towards the hostelry. I followed behind. He was met by a barking dog and an unshaven man in a grubby chef's outfit. From his dramatic body language I could tell he was speaking Spanish. But clearly he was not getting his message across. He resorted to sign language. I looked on in disbelief as he attempted to mime the Great Masturbator with deft wrist movements. The chef seemed to hover on the brink of two possible courses of action: to run away from this sex-crazed foreigner or to set the dog on him.

In the nick of time, a young waitress arrived. She soon picked up the gist of Conundrum's meaning.

"*El grande masturbador? Sí! Sí! Sí!*"

She entered into the spirit of the charade, making rapid jerks with one hand in the region of Conundrum's crotch while pointing with the other towards a small inlet in the rocky shore.

"*Muchas gracias, señorita.*"

And so we located the rock that had inspired Dalí's Great Masturbator painting. While I took pictures, Conundrum twirled his phantom moustache. For a moment I thought he had actually become Salvador Dalí. The resemblance was uncanny. I strained to get a better view. But the sun was in my eyes and I had to look away. When I looked again, Conundrum was himself once more.

We drove on to Port Lligat to visit the house that had been Dalí's home throughout his adult life. Conundrum moved through the rooms in a manner both hesitant and self-assured, like a former owner come to see what has happened to his old place. He groaned at the sight of the two separate beds with a yawning chasm between them.

"See that mirror on the wall, Henri. Dalí put it there so he could watch dawn break while lying in bed. This is the most easterly point of Spain and Dalí boasted he was the first Spaniard on whom the sun shone each morning. But I reckon the lighthouse keeper at Cap de Creus might have been just ahead."

Conundrum entered an oval chamber at the heart of the house. He gave another twirl of the phantom moustache.

"Gala's inner sanctum. A real womb of a room."

I left him there and went outside to take some pictures of the phallus-shaped pool, then of a pink plastic sofa in the form of female lips. When he joined me some time later, Conundrum had a sly grin on his face, as if enjoying a private joke.

"Dalí would have loved all that souvenir kitsch, those ugly Great Masturbator T-shirts. Delicious. Quite delicious."

Next we headed for the port of Cadaqués. The sky was overcast as we walked along the waterfront. Conundrum pulled out his picnic lunch. The contents of the breakfast buffet had coalesced into a revolting mess in the polythene shower cap. He proffered it towards me.

"Fancy a spot of lunch, Henri?"

I recoiled. It really did look as if someone had thrown up.

"No thanks. I'm not hungry."

Conundrum perched on the harbour wall and scoffed the lot. Between mouthfuls, he continued to speak, spraying crumbs and gunge all over the place. I reckoned he could have put up a better show, had he wanted, with the *vol au vent* in Wales.

"They say that Gala, the sex-crazed Mrs Dalí used to proposition local fishermen whenever the flesh moved her."

I looked at the men fixing their nets. What stories they could tell. But their bronzed leathery faces were inscrutable.

Suddenly, the sun burst obliquely through the clouds. A dazzling shaft of light beamed onto a small beach. In a flash, this nondescript bit of strand was miraculously transformed into a vast landscape. Here in microcosm were all the familiar elements of those searing Dalinian deserts stretching into infinity. Through a trick of the light tiny pebbles had become huge boulders. A short stretch of shore stood for an entire coastline. Even a dry stick looked like the trunk of an enormous tree. In a flash, I understood how Dalí had worked his magic. He could conjure up an entire surrealist universe from a tiny patch of sand.

I jumped down onto the beach and started shooting. Framed in the viewfinder, I could see one Dalinian tableau after another. Yes, yes, yes! I shot off the best part of a roll. After several minutes frenzied activity, I looked up to find Conundrum eyeing me with a quizzical expression.

"Why bother to record the outer surface when the real stuff lies within? Dalí used his artistic imagination. Not like that old buffer Monet who only painted what he saw. Endless lily ponds like aquatic wallpaper. Even frogs get bored with that.

Dalí painted what you couldn't see, revealed what you didn't want to see, because it was too dangerous. So why not let Dalí inspire you, Henri? Take pictures of the 'real' things the eye can't see. What interest can there be in visual facts? There is nothing so boring as facts, Henri. I'm jolly glad I'm not in your trade."

Conundrum had punctured my moment of artistic truth. I promptly hit back.

"And what about your writing? Why don't you do proper journalism, cover big news stories, world events and suchlike?"

"News, Henri? World events? What an absurd idea. That is the stuff you wash off your fingers when you have read the paper. It goes straight down the drain. Believe me, there is nothing so futile as actuality. Here today, gone tomorrow. So I don't even bother to inform myself of the news, let alone chase it, notebook poised like a cub reporter."

Conundrum brushed a piece of fluff from his jacket, as if it were a nasty piece of news adhering to his sleeve.

"So where do you get your information?"

"Information, Henri?"

"Yes, information. Surely that's the key to everything."

"The last thing the world needs right now is more information. All the cards were dealt long ago. No point in looking for new ones. We already have more than enough to go on. More facts, more data only create more confusion. The more we know the less we understand. I go in fear and dread of more information. Intellectual progress may be on fast forward, but spiritual understanding goes backward with equal velocity. More information equals less knowledge. As I may have mentioned already, we come into this world knowing everything and leave it understanding nothing at all. Our entire lives are a long process of forgetting and unlearning."

We were sitting at an outdoor café by a bronze statue of Dalí. A stray dog was repeatedly laying a stick at the feet of a couple of French tourists, waiting patiently for them finally to give in and throw it for him to chase. I knew how the animal felt. I was equally determined to get something out of Conundrum.

"Then how can you find the meaning in anything?"

"Meaning, Henri? Meaning what precisely?"

He spat out the word 'meaning' like a bad taste lingering in his mouth.

"Meaning whatever you want, I suppose. I mean, there has to be some kind of meaning. Otherwise, …."

Suddenly, Conundrum snapped.

"To hell with your 'meaning', Henri. All your supposedly meaningful thoughts are base lies cleverly concealed in pretty language. The human face is the beginning of falsehood. There are more bacteria in a man's mouth than a dog's arse."

"But surely…."

"Oh, spare me. This conversation is becoming tiresome. A pox on all meaning, Henri. Stuff it. Just give me magic."

I sensed a door opening. I rushed straight in.

"Magic? What do you mean by that?"

"Alas, poor Henri. Your question is meaningless. Magic doesn't 'mean' anything. It can't. That's why it's magic. Get it?"

I didn't get it.

"Time to grow up, Henri. Only children expect meaning. There is no meaning. Just learn to live with the random, arbitrary nature of things. The eternal plan, if you want one, reveals itself in the very lack of a plan. It's all a chaotic chain of stray events. The search for meaning – religious, philosophical or artistic – is something humans have invented in their ignorance to make things intelligible for themselves. But meaning is an impossibility. We are in a murder mystery without a body. The scene of the crime is littered with signs of foul play and ambiguous clues. Amateur detectives sleuth about in the undergrowth for a weapon, witnesses clamour to tell their incompatible stories. But the corpse of meaning, where is it? Conspicuous by its absence. End of story. Accept the basic truth that everything is essentially meaningless and you need never be confused again. Then one day you too can laugh at the cosmic joke. Nothing makes sense. Just remember that."

Conundrum's cosmic joke again. Surely there had to be more to it than that? For I was convinced, in spite of all his protestations to the contrary, that there was a meaning, some kind of secret knowledge or awareness to which Conundrum had gained access. But I sensed this wasn't the moment to press him any further. So I gave up my interrogation. And then, as if that had been the precise moment he had been waiting for, he continued in what was a loud whisper.

"So I don't believe in thinking too much. At least, not in the conventional sense. Would advise strongly against it. Deep thinking is bad for the mind. For me thought is a natural process, allowing things to crystallise. I let the thoughts think themselves. Indeed, only thoughts that come of themselves are worth having. The rest are artificial. Thus I am happy for the frontal lobes to graze at will. Let them chew on whatever takes their fancy. The real fun comes when the deep brain digests and turns things over like the second stomach of a cow. Occasionally, something of note is relayed back to the conscious surface. For those rare moments I like to be ready. So I stare vacantly into space and wait for magic to materialise on the blank screen of my mental cinema in which I am the only interested spectator. That, Henri, is the limit of my intellectual enquiry."

I noticed the stray dog had at last succeeded in prevailing on the French tourists to throw him a stick. Seconds later, the dog returned and dropped it back at their feet. Again they obliged. Once more the dog returned. The game looked set to continue for ages. For my part, I contented myself with the one stick Conundrum had deigned to throw for me to pick up. It was more than enough to go on, at least for now. Conundrum pulled a silver watch from a waistcoat pocket.

"We'd better be getting back to lovely Lloret."

"And another little chat with Arthur and Gladys?"

"God help us."

We stopped off for dinner on the way and arrived at the hotel so late that Arthur and Gladys had already retired to their room. But they were not yet asleep, as I quickly discovered from the conversation being broadcast through the wall.

"I'll have the window shut, thank you very much, Gladys. Don't want those Spanish breezes and disco music disturbing my kip. I'm quite happy with the roar of the air-conditioning. At least we've paid for that. So it's ours."

Gladys now spoke, but in a much quieter voice I had to strain to hear.

"Arthur, why don't you come and visit me? I'm sure we didn't ask for twin beds. I feel ever so lonely on my own."

"Not right now, if you don't mind, Gladys. Must say it'll be a relief to see that the Footsie really did take a nosedive. So let's hope for the worst. Might even play a round of golf just to celebrate. They say the local course isn't bad."

"But what happened to good old intercourse, Arthur?"

I couldn't believe what I'd heard. So there was more to Gladys than the timid, long-suffering spouse. As for Arthur, he pretended he hadn't heard her right.

"The local golf course is very nice, Gladys. You'll like it."

"If you say so, Arthur."

"Indeed I do. Good night, Gladys."

"Good night, Arthur."

Like a machine, Arthur switched in an instant from speech mode to sleep. His snoring blended with the hum of the air-conditioning.

The following morning, I caught Arthur glued to the Daily Express. When he saw me, he hastily turned to the back page and began reading the sports results. The front-page banner headline stared me in the face: FOOTSIE FLYING HIGH. The predicted falls hadn't happened. In fact, the complete opposite was happening. Now the markets were soaring to dizzy new heights. Arthur had dumped his stock at bargain basement prices. In a word, he had got it wrong. Badly wrong.

Mysteriously, Conundrum appeared from nowhere.

"I see our friend Footsie lives to fight another day. You didn't suppose it would crash just for you, did you Arthur?"

Arthur muttered grimly through clenched teeth.

"All right, have your little laugh. It's early days yet. The interesting bit with markets is what they call dead cat bounce."

"Dead cat bounce? That's the interesting bit, is it? Well, I can't wait to hear the boring bit."

"Just mark my words, you southern smarty pants. I'm never wrong on these matters. You'll see."

I admired Arthur for that brave riposte. How I wished I had the nerve to talk to Conundrum like that.

Gladys tried to pour oil on troubled waters.

"I suppose the papers could have got it wrong, Arthur."

"Don't be so daft, woman. This so called recovery is only a blip. Some bit of City trickery to hide the true facts long enough for the smart money to jump ship. I'll be proved right in the end. Just you wait."

Arthur stood up. A pale layer of apprehension could now be detected showing through his newly acquired suntan.

"Come along now, Gladys. I feel an urgent secondary movement coming on."

Meekly, she followed her husband out of the restaurant.

Conundrum sighed.

"Our Arthur does seem to have made a dog's dinner of things, doesn't he? Meanwhile his breakfast remains untouched."

Conundrum plucked a sugary bun from the pastry basket on the table vacated by Arthur and Gladys.

"Mmm, excellent. Now, Dalí didn't bother with stocks and shares. Not that he didn't appreciate money. But his notion was just to coin it and then squander it as fast as possible."

As he passed the buffet Conundrum again scooped up some edibles into a shower cap and stuffed it in a jacket pocket.

Our first stop that morning was the famous Dalí Theatre-Museum in the town of Figueres.

"See the tourists trampling on the tombstone of the Marqués de Dalí et de Púbol. That must be Salvador's ultimate surrealist joke. The *hoi polloi* dancing on his grave."

I sat in on Conundrum's interview with the PR man from the Gala-Dalí Foundation. And so I witnessed for the first time a novel journalistic technique. I did not understand much of what was being said since it was entirely in Spanish. But I couldn't fail to notice that Conundrum's questions were invariably much longer than the answers. He was not conducting an interview so much as holding a conversation, in which he played the leading part. Afterwards, he commented.

"So they're trying posthumously to sanitise poor old Salvador. The man spent his whole life being as shocking, perverted and deviant as only he could. He really put masturbation on the map, you know. And now, they – the guardians of the Dalí flame – want to get rid of all that and leave the world with just 'the great artist'."

Conundrum seemed genuinely upset.

"What a load of crap. Dalí once said painting was the least interesting thing he did. Well, that's all they want to credit him with now."

On the way back to Lloret, we stopped at the ancient Graeco-Roman city of Empúries where Conundrum devoured his ghastly picnic among the crumbling ruins. I dined on the solitary apple I had purloined from the hotel buffet. We had the place to ourselves until a coach party of British pensioners turned up. The lecturer, a red-faced fossil, droned on about classical urbanism and various layers of dead civilisations. Names and dates spouted from his mouth and fell like dust at his feet.

Conundrum cracked an ugly smile.

"I bet he won't show them the most interesting bit."

When the tourist guide announced he was giving his group ten minutes free time, Conundrum quickly intervened.

"Your kind attention please, ladies and gentlemen. As one familiar with the intimate secrets of Empúries, may I invite you to follow me? Your attention will be well rewarded."

They followed Conundrum like children. He led them out through a gate of the city and pointed to a stone carving set in the outer wall. It was an erect phallus of great stature.

"Impressive isn't it? Well, gentlemen, how does your own equipment measure up to this proud specimen here?"

The OAPs admired the rampant stone erection.

"Folk once came from far and wide to pay homage to the stone phallus of Empúries. A single touch restored even the most jaded geriatric to the full Priapic vigour of youth. And it still works. Oh yes, gentlemen, you can throw away your Viagara."

Conundrum spoke like a quack doctor flogging some elixir of eternal youth. A couple of tourists shuffled forward. Now he raised a hand like a traffic policeman.

"Let us stop and reflect. We're all a bit over the hill, aren't we? Pretty soon we'll all be dead. So should we not accept our mortal fate and go quietly into the dark night purged of all earthly lusts? For was it not Sophocles who described impotence as being unchained from a wild beast? Perhaps real happiness begins with a withering in the loins department. As for myself, having long sojourned in the sweet regions of Much-Bulging-in-the-Bollocks I now know that true contentment only comes to the residents of Much-Shrivelled-in-the-Gonads."

His audience on the point of drifting away, Conundrum now stirred them up once again into a frenzy.

"But, if you still fancy a final flourish, if you want to play one last tune on Pan's pipes, the answer to your prayers is nigh. One touch of the magic stone phallus of Empúries and you'll go like the clappers. So step up to the plate gentlemen please."

Several pensioners, prodded into action by their wives, staggered forward, hands outstretched. Conundrum, like an old satyr, was about to help the first of them reach up and touch the stone phallus, when the official guide re-entered the scene.

"Ah there you are, ladies and gentlemen. But time presses and I would draw your attention to the toilet facilities by the main entrance before we return to the bus."

The tourists dutifully heeded the familiar voice. With a wistful look at the stone phallus they straggled off. I overheard an old lady saying she thought she had seen Conundrum or someone very like him on TV.

"Yes, wasn't he that mad professor of archaeology?"

I looked for Conundrum, but there was no sign of him. He had spirited himself away among the broken stones and wild flowers. I smiled to myself. I figured his flowery words in praise of impotence, though delivered in jest, probably concealed a painful personal truth. This must be his way of dealing with declining sexual powers. As it turned out, I couldn't have been more wide of the mark. I was the real dupe, buying the foolish notion that Conundrum suffered from what he so disarmingly called a withering in the loins department.

That evening in Lloret we ate once again at a seafront restaurant. It wasn't long before our Yorkshire friends put in an appearance. Arthur was clearly upset. Gladys was trying to calm him. As they walked by, completely oblivious to our presence, we overheard part of a curious conversation.

"I'm bloody well going to get my money's worth, Gladys. I'll damn well walk up and down this perishing promenade until I've worn the bugger out!"

"Don't take it so hard, Arthur. You did what you thought was best at the time. I'm not blaming you."

"But I do blame myself, Gladys. Don't you see? It's my job to get things right. How can I ever trust myself again?"

Evidently, Footsie had gone from strength to strength. Arthur walked like a broken man. Gladys supporting him.

"But I'm sure it will crash, Arthur. If you said so, then it certainly must."

"We'll see. We'll see."

Conundrum did not speak until Arthur and Gladys were distant specks on the promenade of Lloret de Mar.

"There is something quite magnificent about our Arthur. No surrender, no compromise, a brain like a battering ram. A will as unyielding as the Rock of Gibraltar. His personal happiness can only be realised by the world economy falling on his head. I think he would like to see the entire universe collapse, just in order to maintain his self-belief."

That night Arthur reached his lowest ebb. I heard him voice all the doubts now plaguing him. Suddenly he was worried about everything under the sun. Had he remembered to cancel the milk? Had they bought their lottery ticket? Had he mislaid the keys to the potting shed he had taken on holiday along with his Northern Rock account book? Gladys reassured him on every count. But there was no stopping him.

"I do wish the waiters wouldn't smile at me. Don't want their cheesy grins. I know their little game. Just a ploy to get a tip out of me. Well, I'm damned if I'm going to smile back. I won't be fooled as easily as that."

"I don't think they mean any harm, Arthur."

"Hell they don't."

Finally, he fell asleep snoring fitfully. Next morning Arthur and Gladys did not appear at breakfast. I found Conundrum tucking in to his usual hearty meal.

"I expect you heard the latest in the Arthur and Gladys saga. A horrible reminder of the cringing fears lurking in the human soul. Now Salvador's answer was to splash his angst all over a surrealist canvas, shock the world and make a fortune. Not a bad solution, eh?"

That day we drove to Gala's castle at Púbol. Statues of fat elephants on thin locusts' legs stalked through the garden. The interior had many Dalinian touches. Like a chess set where the pawns were tips of index fingers painted gold and silver. Gala's *haute couture* seduction wardrobe filled a whole room.

"Púbol was Gala's knocking shop, Henri. The scraggy old bird was a frisky 78 when she finally got her own love nest. But even at that age she was so sexed up just a glimpse of her empty dresses can still stir the blood."

Around mid-afternoon we drove into Tossa de Mar. I shot a few pretty postcard views without enthusiasm. Then through a long lens I spotted two familiar figures. Arthur and Gladys were walking along the cliff path. As they drew closer, I could hear Arthur, still upset by the obstinacy of Footsie defying his gloomy predictions that it would crash.

"Suppose we must get on with our holiday. Haven't videoed much yet. I'll do a shot of the cliffs, pan across to that bush. You stand over there and admire the flowers, Gladys."

"Do you have to video everything, Arthur? Why can't we just look at things? I'm really not in the mood."

"I'm doing this for you, Gladys. So you can look at things later and enjoy your holiday when we get back home."

"But why can't we enjoy it now, Arthur?"

"That's just my point, Gladys. There's too much on my mind to enjoy the holiday right now. So we'll bloody well have to enjoy it when we get home. Stands to reason, doesn't it? Now get ready for a take. Action!"

Arthur executed a slow sweep of the camcorder far out over the sea, then down to the shore to show just how steep and high were the cliffs at this point. But he didn't get to zoom in on Gladys waiting obediently by the flowers. A small step in the wrong direction and suddenly he lost his footing. For a few seconds Arthur swayed to and fro like a clown wobbling on the high wire to scare the audience. But this was for real. After several desperate turns Arthur performed one last pirouette, staring poignantly at Gladys one moment and down into the abyss the next. His face was a study of dread. Finally, he tossed his beloved camcorder up into the air.

"Grab it! For heavens sake! There's good footage in there. Make sure you enjoy it when you get home, Gladys."

Arthur caught my eye as he said this. But there was nothing I could do to catch the machine without falling over the cliff. And so fixed were we all on the camcorder thrown up in the air, we completely took our eyes off Arthur. Thus we failed to register the moment of his disappearance. Unremarked, he toppled over the edge. I only realised what had happened when Gladys rushed forward, yelling hysterically.

"Arthur! Arthur! Come back! Come back!"

Conundrum removed his sun hat with the ceremonial flourish of an undertaker out of respect for the departed Arthur. For a while no-one spoke. I imagined Gladys already planning how to spend the insurance money. Then a low moan reached our ears, mingling with the cries of the seagulls. Now it sounded more human. I peered over the cliff. There was Arthur spread-eagled on a grassy ledge not ten feet below. His forehead was bleeding profusely, presumably from a knock inflicted by the camcorder that lay by his side.

I scrambled down and helped him up. Apart from a cut to the head, Arthur was basically unharmed, though much shaken and chastened by the experience. He even shook my hand, said not to worry about the broken camcorder. It was only a material object after all. What did money matter as long as you had your health and the love of a good woman? Arthur embraced Gladys contritely. The reconciled couple came slowly together. Their moist lips touched like two snails pressing cold mucous on cold mucous. Conundrum looked away.

We gave them a lift back to the hotel. They insisted we had a drink with them at the bar, and on their account too. Conundrum accepted like a shot. Arthur took a brief look at the day's newspaper. The Footsie had continued its meteoric rise to ever-new highs, making yet more mockery of his panic dumping of stocks and shares. But he now showed strength in adversity. He was a changed man.

"It's good news for the wider economy, I suppose."

In the conversation that followed, Arthur even admitted he had once met a half-decent southerner in a London pub.

"Chap from Birmingham, as it happened."

Arthur's new life didn't stop there. At bedtime he made it up with Gladys. I heard it all through the wall.

"Sorry I've made such a mess of things Gladys. Thought when I retired it would be one long, happy walk into the sunset. I've made a right pig's ear of it and no mistake. But I will get you that villa in the sun. I promise. Then we can enjoy our holidays in the peace and comfort of our own home."

After a pregnant pause, Gladys spoke.

"No, Arthur. I don't want that. Anything but that."

Gladys seemed to have a new sense of purpose.

"And what's wrong with enjoying holidays in the peace and comfort of our own home, Gladys?"

I wondered if Conundrum in his own room was listening as intently as I was to the dramatic scene that followed.

"There's nothing comfortable about our home, Arthur. It's been the most uncomfortable place on earth these past twenty years. So why should a villa in Spain be any different? As for peace, can't you see we've been at war all our married life?"

"At war? Speak for yourself, Gladys."

"I am, Arthur. That's precisely what I'm doing. And about time too. You know I've often wanted to kill you for your cursed, know-it-all, pig-headed stupidity."

"Why didn't you mention this before, Gladys?"

"Don't be such an oaf, Arthur. Just imagine me coming up to you and saying 'you bore the tits off me and I want to kill you'. That's not the sort of thing you can tell your husband."

"Don't see why not. I always said you can tell me anything, Gladys. Anything you bloody well like."

"Oh yes, that's right. Just so long as what I happen to say happens to be what you want to hear or what you've just told me to think, Arthur. You don't want to know what I really think or who I really am, do you?"

"Know who you are, Gladys? Don't be daft. Of course I do. You're my wife. That's who you are. Besides, we promised we'd never discuss anything we didn't agree on. That's why we've been so happy all these years."

"Happy? Will you stop telling me I'm happy?"

"But I know you're happy, Gladys. Admit it."

"That's just it. There you go again. You're a bully, Arthur. And you've always been scared to find out what I really feel."

"So what's brought this on all of a sudden? I've apologised about the Footsie. Anyone can make a mistake."

"Do you really want to know, Arthur? Well, I'll tell you. It was that silly look in your eyes when you were about to go over the cliff. You were about to die and all you cared about was that perishing camcorder. Made me realise what a pathetic creature you are, Arthur. And how little I'd miss you."

"Oh, Gladys. Tell me this isn't true. This can't be real. This isn't you speaking, is it?"

There was a long pause before Gladys spoke again. It was as if she had been looking for the right words.

"The twin beds, Arthur? That's was all your doing, wasn't it? Admit it. You didn't ask for a double, did you?"

Another long silence ensued. I fell asleep. Later that night I was woken by a series of grunts and squeals to indicate that the couple were as one. This was confirmed by the happy expression of Gladys at breakfast the following morning. Her suffering was behind her. The accident at Tossa de Mar had returned to her the man she had married all those years ago.

Conundrum and I were out all day still following the Dalí trail. When we got back to the hotel that evening, we immediately knew something had happened. Arthur waved a tabloid newspaper in our faces. We read the banner headline: FOOT FOOT FOOTSIE, GOODBYE! The Stock Market had crashed after all. Big time. Gone right through the floor. The great meltdown predicted by Arthur had really happened. He looked as pleased with himself as an Old Testament prophet on hearing

Sodom and Gomorrah were utterly destroyed. His face shone with a bright glow of I-told-you-so smugness.

"So what do you say to that?"

Turning triumphantly to Gladys, he continued.

"You can always rely on good old Arthur. That's right now isn't it, Gladys?"

Arthur rampant once more. Gladys back under his heel.

"Yes, Arthur. That's right."

Then Arthur fixed me in a deadly stare.

"As for you, butterfingers, I've half a mind to charge you the replacement cost for dropping my camcorder over the cliff."

And with that Arthur hurried from the lobby as if an urgent tertiary movement was on the cards.

That night all was quiet but for Arthur's contented snore that had the wall vibrating. Next morning Conundrum and I overheard the final act of the drama from our respective rooms.

"I'm going to the bathroom for one last try, Gladys. Meanwhile, make yourself useful. Check we've got everything. That you haven't gone and lost your ticket or passport."

"Yes, Arthur."

"And make sure the suitcases are locked and labelled."

"Yes, Arthur."

"And don't forget to put the cat out, Gladys."

After a delay, Gladys replied.

"But we haven't got a cat, Arthur."

"Well, use your initiative, you daft woman. Find a flaming cat and then put it out. There are plenty of strays about."

"Yes, Arthur."

Arthur was back in the groove. Silly Remark Syndrome in full flow. Gladys's spirited rebellion had been snuffed out. Arthur had been right after all. A loud bang of the bathroom door indicated he was turning his mind to more serious matters. Several minutes later I heard the flushing of the toilet.

"No result, I'm afraid. Bomb doors wide open. But no payload. Can't manage a bloody thing. *Yorkshire Water* will have to deal with last night's dinner. Serves them bloody right too. All those fat cats and their big bonuses for doing nowt. Hope they've lifted that hosepipe ban. The flower beds will need a good sprinkling when we get home."

Well, at least Gladys had seen a temporary lifting of Arthur's hosepipe ban. Her flowerbed had had a brief watering.

"I'll be glad to be home, Gladys. And no mistake."

We too were setting off that morning. I met Conundrum down in the lobby. He had hung on every word just as I had.

"At least Arthur appears to have learned one thing."

"And that is?"

"The only point to a holiday is to make you want to go home. If, on your last day, you would like to do it all over again, then the whole thing has been utterly wasted."

Conundrum brightened.

"You know what, Henri? I liked that bit about putting the cat out. Inspired. Quite inspired. Perhaps an excess of sanity is a form of madness. There is more to Arthur than meets the eye. And Gladys too. Now that she's had a taste of power."

"Do you think we should say goodbye to them?"

"What for? Don't be sentimental, Henri. You might end up exchanging Christmas cards for the rest of your life."

Suddenly Arthur loomed up behind Conundrum.

"And what would be so wrong with that? I only ask for a civil exchange of common courtesies. That's not too much to expect of one's fellow man, now is it?"

I held my breath, waiting for Conundrum to respond. He was completely unrepentant.

"No, it's not too much to ask. It's not enough. Not nearly enough."

And with that Conundrum turned on his heel. Sheepishly I avoided Arthur's eye as I made tracks to the car.

We stopped in Barcelona en route to the airport. We had only half a day to 'do' the city and Conundrum went into overdrive. He appointed himself art director making me jump through the hoops as if I were a complete novice. First off, he had me take some corny photos in the covered market off Las Ramblas. Did he know how much I hated this kind of photography? Some market traders grinned ridiculously waving salted cod, smelly cheese or red peppers in my face. While others turned their backs, telling me in no uncertain fashion that photographers were a pain in the arse.

Conundrum made my ordeal much worse hovering behind me, attempting to orchestrate my efforts. He seemed to take intense pleasure at my discomfort. For some reason he had it in for me. Finally, I couldn't hide my annoyance.

"I've done this sort of thing before, you know. And I have my own way of working."

"Only trying to help, Henri. I do happen to know what the magazine wants."

At last I decided to throw in the towel.

"I think I've done enough."

"Do you really, Henri? Well, I say you do some more pictures in the fish market. I will be writing about the seafood."

What choice did I have? Half an hour later I returned with several gobbets of fresh tuna blood on my shirt.

"Wounded in action? I shall see that you are mentioned in dispatches."

At last we called it a day and retired to a café. But before we were served, the barman – at Conundrum's instigation – held up our two glasses of *café con leche* and beamed at me like a halfwit. Conundrum elbowed me in the ribs.

"Photo opportunity, Henri."

Cursing under my breath, I did the shots. Meanwhile, Conundrum helped himself to a donut, ate it, then another.

"Do the honours, Henri. I'm right out of washers."

Patience exhausted, I paid up. Afterwards, we took a ride in the old cable car high over Barcelona's harbour. Suspended between grim towers of rusting girders like abandoned border posts on the Iron Curtain, the flimsy cabin swung alarmingly as it made its painfully slow way across the water. I suffer from vertigo and felt immediately unwell. But Conundrum was in high spirits, almost thriving on my unease.

"We'll need some pretty views. Brave new Barcelona. You know the sort of scenic stuff. Huge panoramas."

I framed a shot as Conundrum tugged at my sleeve.

"Look lively, Henri. See over there. The other cable car is coming. You'll get a double page spread. Stunning *señorita* staring out of window. Bloody perfect. Money for old rope."

I foolishly allowed several vital moments to pass while the other cable car drew level. My camera remained dangling around my neck as a superbly attractive Spanish girl stared me right in the eye. Her look challenged me to take her picture. But I was too late. A second later, she was gone. Numb with regret, I watched her disappear from sight. Conundrum had been right. With the sultry *señorita* in the foreground and the sun-dappled vista of Barcelona harbour spread out far below, it would have made a superb double page spread in any magazine. I rued my petulant refusal to be ordered into action.

"No good pulling a face, Henri. You've gone and missed your 'decisive moment'. And what a picture you make! You have the tormented look of a man dying for a piss who on the brink of release discovers he has his underpants on back to front."

Anger and frustration bubbled up inside me. But I couldn't speak. I'd been found wanting. I had never been much good at those 'decisive moments' that made the reputation of the real Henri. My photojournalistic efforts tended to be rather of the indecisive kind: shots of people staring vacantly into space or lost in a mood of self-absorption, doubt or daydreaming. Suspended animation I suppose you could call it.

"I've been observing you, Henri. You don't have the killer instinct of a natural photographer. You want the images badly enough. Indeed, I see you panting for them like a thirsty dog. But when they are there staring you in the face you hesitate, as if you have to overcome some inner barrier. You draw back at the 'decisive moment' and then struggle to push yourself forward by an effort of will. I wonder why. Perhaps you don't believe sufficiently in what you are doing?"

This was too close to the bone. What business did he have to question my professional motivation? Suddenly, I wanted to open the door of the cable car and push Conundrum out. Guessing my thoughts, he eyed me with amusement.

"Won't solve anything, Henri. I am not the problem."

Judging from his superior tone of voice, I guess he found my reaction as petty as the tantrum of a small child.

"Don't go hunting for pictures, Henri. Wait for them to come to you. All you have to do is be ready to shoot when they present themselves so obligingly."

I was still so angry with myself, it didn't occur to me to ask how come Conundrum pretended to know so much about photography. Glum and speechless, I stared down at the sparkling Barcelona waterfront.

"Travel pics are mere child's play. You can do them in your sleep. Why not aspire to the real stuff? What wonders can a well-tuned mind not perceive? Just imagine you could see something the world has never seen before. An undiscovered primary colour perhaps. Who knows? I am deadly serious, Henri. Out there beyond the spectrum there may be a world of colours beyond your wildest dreams."

Now my frustration bubbled over.

"Beyond the spectrum? There's nothing beyond the spectrum. I'll have you know we studied colour theory in art school. Science has mapped every shade of the spectrum and defined the limits of the human retina."

"Damn your silly art school education. And a pox on the limits of the human retina. How do you know there isn't a dormant colour sensor in your brain just waiting to be woken up? A third eye that one day will open and allow you to go beyond the spectrum, over the rainbow and see what has never been seen before? How do you know you are not the owner of such an amazing eye? Think about it, dream about it, Henri."

I'd never seen Conundrum so passionate. By God, he was serious about this crazy notion. A new primary colour indeed! What nonsense! But at some deep level I began to thirst for something beyond the rainbow. An entire parallel spectrum perhaps? And in time I came to cherish the insane hope that I Henri would be the one to perceive it.

I Henri? What on earth was I talking about? Had the bogus name he'd given me already supplanted my own knowledge of who I was supposed to be? But at the time I was still hopelessly unaware of this significant shift in my self-perception. Nor had I spotted the magic trick by which Conundrum so easily had me thinking his thoughts, dreaming his dreams. In all I was as unsuspecting as a stray kitten lapping milk from a saucer left outside the door of a stranger.

There was one final incident in Barcelona. Walking through the old town off *Las Ramblas* we heard a man singing *When I Fall in Love* by Nat King Cole. A beautiful voice. The singer wore a shabby raincoat and in one hand held a heart-shaped red balloon. Conundrum commanded me to take a picture. I did so. But having spent what remained of my Spanish currency I had nothing to give the man. I shrugged apologetically as I departed. Unbothered, he continued to sing with a look of utter peace on his face. As if all he ever asked for was the air to carry the sound of his beautiful voice. I felt I deserved a stone but came away with a smile instead.

On the flight home we again drank champagne. I tried to make conversation but without success. Only once did Conundrum's thoughts break through into speech.

"Our Arthur which art from Yorkshire is entirely devoid of the gift of tragic insight. He has not one iota of awareness how ridiculous he is. The man is barking mad but regards himself as the summit of sanity. How petrifying it must be to have such unshakeable belief in one's own rightness? My heart goes out to poor old Gladys. How can she put up with such a man?"

This passing concern for someone else's feelings took me by surprise. Conundrum downed the last drops of champagne with a flourish. Then he turned away and stared out of the window. Not another word was spoken. I could feel him draw a curtain of silence over the Arthur and Gladys episode. But their memory lived on. Henceforth, Conundrum would occasionally say *"As our Arthur which art in Yorkshire would have put it..."*

For some reason he had come away with a grudging respect for this obstinate piece of northern grit. As for Gladys, I eventually learned something to suggest she at last got to deal her Arthur his come-uppance. But that comes later, much later.

At Heathrow, I had to wait ages in the baggage hall for my luggage. Conundrum, having retrieved his battered old leather case, headed for the exit. I don't think he would have said anything if I hadn't spoken first.

"I shall look forward to reading your article."

"Oh, I wouldn't if I were you, Henri. Oh and I'll tell you where to send the snaps."

Lobbing this final grenade over his shoulder, Conundrum turned and strode off through the red channel, pausing merely to address a cheery greeting to a tired customs officer. Probably wanting to declare his genius, I shouldn't wonder. I could just imagine him coming out with a stupid wisecrack like that. He went through unchallenged and I was glad to see him go. It took an eternity for my case to appear. But I was grateful for the delay. That put more space between him and me. And as I waited, I grew calmer in the knowledge that Conundrum was fading away out of my mind with every second and every minute that passed.

I had the pictures processed the next day: a mixed bag, I had to admit, little better than snaps to be honest. But just about good enough for the magazine. Again I regretted the missed opportunity of the sultry *señorita* in Barcelona. As I studied the results on the light box, I noticed Conundrum had strayed into several shots. There he was poking about among the rocks at Cap de Creus. And there he was again in the garden of Púbol Castle, framed by the elongated locust legs of the Dalinian elephants. I inspected every shot and found two more with him intruding. Somehow, he had even managed to wander into the edge of the panoramic shot at Tossa de Mar I'd taken just a second before Arthur fell over the cliff.

I ran a magnifying glass over the images. Something peculiar caught my eye. I had distinct memories of Conundrum wearing three different waistcoats: red, yellow and green. That much I could recall with certainty. But from what I could now see on celluloid, his waistcoat appeared in all four pictures as a dull muddy brown, the sort of effect you get when all the colours in the paint box are mixed together. I had no memory of a fourth waistcoat. So I wondered if I had not remembered this shade because it was so neutral and nondescript?

Anyway, that meant Conundrum must own at least four separate waistcoats: muddy brown plus red, yellow and green. Four waistcoats? Wasn't that just a little bit extraordinary? What mystery lay behind this sartorial extravagance? But while my rational mind accepted the 'man of many waistcoats' theory as the most logical explanation, I remained perplexed and even a trifle uneasy about it. It struck me as odd, to say the least. And why hadn't the three colours showed up on the film?

ETERNAL CITY

More than a week passed before Conundrum rang and told me where to send 'the snaps'. This time, I wasn't offended. Snaps is what they were, no more no less. And that was that. He made no mention, dropped no hint of another trip. I knew I had blown it in Catalonia. Lack of killer instinct. End of story. My immediate reaction was relief. His merciless critique of my photography and digs at my person had done more than wound my pride. It went deeper. I found it disturbing that a stranger could get inside my head, read my innermost thoughts and strike home where it hurt the most. No, enough is enough. Let him go and find someone else to torment.

I was happy to tell myself a painful episode was over. The mystery of *Conundrum's Book* need concern me no longer. Why should I care about that? As for his various coloured waistcoats and an undiscovered spectrum beyond the rainbow, well I could dismiss all that as pure Wizard of Oz talk. And so I put the weird stuff out of my mind. Or at least, I tried to. But can one consign anything to oblivion? Is it possible to forget something to the extent of actually un-knowing it? Especially when it's so out of the ordinary the mind cannot help but file it away in some hidden recess for future reference.

Deep down I was intrigued by what I might learn from this singular if uncomfortable personage. Here was someone who clearly knew all about something definitely worth knowing. I had this idea of Conundrum communing with forces beyond the reach of most mortals. That phrase of his 'meditating on the dark side of the moon' had etched itself in my mind, fired my imagination. There was a touch of the supernatural, a dash of wizardry in his being. But was his magic real or phoney, benign or evil? Did such distinctions matter? The point was, the master puppeteer had only to pull the strings, and I Henri, being his creation, would dance. I really I had no choice.

On a human level, if one can use that term with regard to Conundrum, I had no doubt whatsoever that he was a nasty piece of work. Thoroughly nasty. So for that reason I was glad several weeks passed without any further contact. Left to my own devices, I was able to fool myself I was still my own man with freedom of choice. Whereas in reality I was primed and ready for a new assignment, to hell with the consequences. And of course I wasn't really being left alone, at least no more than a sleeping undercover operative waiting on a mission that would only be divulged at the last moment.

I sat back and watched the days peal off the calendar and float away as in an old movie. I allowed myself to be reclaimed by the routine side of life. The big red blob of paint on my doorstep received my daily scrutiny and its strange contortions were duly recorded for my great photographic project. Gradually, Conundrum faded into forgetfulness. Then one day without warning, just when his memory was so faint as to be almost invisible, he came back suddenly into sharp focus.

I received from the editor, not from Conundrum himself, I hasten to add, a copy of the magazine with the Catalonian story. My pictures looked fairly ok, though I again regretted missing the shot of the *señorita* in the cable car in Barcelona. That double page spread would have doubled my fee. I noted the title of Conundrum's article. An inspired sub had called it *DALLYING WITH DALÍ*. I shuddered to think what the great man would make of that.

I read the piece. It was polished and informative but conveyed none of the personality of the writer. Frankly, I found it a bit flat. Anyone could have written it. As for Conundrum himself, still no news. Another week or so went by. And I'd just about concluded I was off the hook when the phone rang.

"Get ready for a spot of *la dolce vita*, Henri."

He told me he'd landed a nice soft commission for a travel feature on Rome. For my part, the job would involve nothing more strenuous than the usual 'snaps'.

We met up on the plane. Conundrum sat across the aisle wedged next to a large Italian gentleman. His enormous bulk made Conundrum's scrawny frame appear less substantial than ever. His several chins coalesced into a single majestic fold of pale flesh flowing soft and smooth like wax from an invisible jawbone directly into his chest. Three cooked breakfasts disappeared down his gullet in quick succession. I caught a fleeting glimpse of small tough eyes which made me think of a tough Mafioso godfather or a sinister Renaissance cardinal. They bored through me like hard nuggets of coal.

Conundrum and the godfather/cardinal spoke, switching from English to Italian as the mood dictated, of many things: ancient history, medieval art, Italian rugby, beautiful women, Albanian crime syndicates, the burgeoning bureaucracy of the new Europe. On the last subject, Conundrum, for someone who professed utter contempt for the news, seemed remarkably *au fait* with the latest developments.

I was glad to be excluded from the discussion. That left me free to recall my previous stay in Rome about ten years ago, although it seemed much longer, when I had headed straight from art college to the Eternal City and idealistically thrown myself into some serious creative photography.

I had experimented with abstract colour compositions and black and white reportage style photojournalism. The results, though modesty forbids me to praise them, were good enough to persuade me at the time that creative art photography was my mission in life. But enough of past dreams. They hadn't exactly been realised as I had hoped. So their memory was bitter-sweet.

Wanting to keep such personal stuff to myself, I decided not to breathe a word to Conundrum of my youthful Roman days as an aspiring artistic spirit for fear of opening up yet more of my private ambitions to his cynical scrutiny. I resolved to put up a more professional front on this trip. I would make a greater effort with my travel photography. Hopefully, that would put

Conundrum off the scent of my earlier arty endeavours in Rome and spare me more mockery in the process.

The strategy I'd devised was simple. I would not drop the slightest hint this city meant anything special to me. Instead of trying to sneak off and relive precious times in Rome while Conundrum was around, I would do all the corniest, cheesiest snaps without batting an eyelid. Then, on the last day I would casually announce I was going to stay on for a while to do some private sightseeing. That would be my chance to go down memory lane, revisit old haunts and recapture the thrill of the life I had intended to devote to Art. I recalled how deeply I had been moved in those days. I was a true believer. And God how dearly I wanted to be moved again, and to believe.

Such was the plan. But so wrapped up was I in my own agenda, it hadn't occurred to me Conundrum might have a Roman agenda of his own in. This now dawned on me as he interrupted his *conversazione* with the corpulent godfather/cardinal and raised a glass of champagne to me across the aisle.

"Rome always induces in me a dose of acute melancholia, Henri. A poignant nostalgia for past glories. Pathetic ruins on all sides with *tempus fugit* and the sheer vanity of human ambition writ large on each and every shattered stone. The monuments may be majestic, the statues sublime, the vistas picturesque, but the essence of Rome is undeniably futile, irredeemably sad. "

Conundrum leaned back and shook an entire sachet of roasted peanuts into his wide open throat. He washed it down with a swig of champagne just as the captain announced we were about to land in Pisa.

"Pisa? I thought we were going to Rome?"

"So we are, Henri. But first a brief sojourn among the Etruscans. And then we shall descend on the Eternal City."

I did the formalities for the rental car. No sooner were we out of Pisa airport than Conundrum ordered me onto the fast road, the *autostrada* to Florence.

"But what about Pisa? And the Leaning Tower?"

"What about it indeed? It can lean over backwards as much as it likes. For me its sole fascination lies in the possibility of actually being there when it finally comes crashing to the ground. Until then it's just a news item waiting in the wings. But I fear it will not happen today. So we shall ignore it."

We checked in at the classy *Villa San Michele* in Fiesole. The hotel façade was designed, according to the brochure, by Michelangelo. Late afternoon, we sipped *Bellini* cocktails on the *terrazza panoramica*. A golden light suffused the scene, as if the finest olive oil from Lucca had been poured all over the city. Centuries of time-hallowed culture wafted up on the evening breeze. Conundrum's face had a 'thus far and no further' expression. He seemed to breathe in the hallowed atmosphere through the pores of his skin. When he broke the gentle silence I reckoned I was about to witness another side to his character. Perhaps the aesthete, the man of culture?

"Fiesole, where we now sit, was once an Etruscan hill town slowly starved into submission by the Romans. Farewell fair phallic fantasy. I trust you have read your D.H. Lawrence, Henri? He claims the Roman world was built on the brutal destruction of Etruscan civilisation. Let us be mindful of that."

He rolled a cigarette from his battered old tin.

"So the Etruscans can join the Picts and the Canaanites to form an international league of lost peoples, wiped off the map by the Romans, Scots and Hebrews respectively."

Conundrum lit his cigarette and inhaled deeply.

"But peoples who don't survive in flesh and blood live on in other ways. They take up residence in our memory as archaeological relics to be displayed in a glass case."

We downed another *Bellini* before dinner. Conundrum was in reflective mood throughout the meal. I observed the diners at the neighbouring table. An American couple ordered Diet Coke with the gastronomic menu. The waiter met their request with a polished equanimity born of long experience.

"*Si. Perfetto.*"

The tone of his voice allowed them to believe they had made an excellent choice. The waiter even presented the little red can for their inspection as if it were a noble Barolo.

"Va bene? Perfetto."

Then he poured an elegant half glass and left the can standing on the table.

Conundrum remained in a world of his own, as if he were not really present, but still communing with the spirits of those unfortunate Etruscans two thousand years ago. The only remark he made was one muttered to himself as we sipped an *espresso* and he had the bill charged to my room.

"One day all this history will be history, perhaps even prehistory, I suppose. And after that, nothing at all."

Next morning we plunged down into Florence through narrow streets between posturing *palazzi* whose rusticated façades and iron-barred windows were designed to intimidate. Engaging a French tourist in conversation, Conundrum managed to position himself at the head of the queue for the *Uffizi*. I was not included in this cultural excursion.

"Snap the *Ponte Vecchio* and all that touristy stuff, Henri. And don't forget David. The magazine expressly said they didn't want him. Too much of a cliché, would you believe? But they are bound to ask for him. They always do."

I made quick work of the trinket shops and milling crowds on *Ponte Vecchio* then headed for my tryst with David in *Galleria dell'Accademia*. Afterwards I came across Conundrum drinking a *cappuccino* at an expensive-looking café in *Piazza dei Signori*. He hailed me with uncommon enthusiasm.

"*Buon giorno*, Henri. So what did you make of David?"

I mumbled some rubbish about feeling uplifted by the fresh energy of an awesome piece of Renaissance sculpture.

"Oh dear. What a predictable response. But just wait until you are as old as I am and you may see it differently. On the surface David and Goliath is an inspiring tale of a small guy outwitting a big bully. But there is a more sinister side. The not insignificant matter of a young boy killing a grown man. As an adolescent I admired David. But now he seems not such a lovely lad, more an agent of retribution, youth slaying maturity."

I couldn't imagine Conundrum as a boy. It seemed to me he might have been dropped into the world ready made at his present age. Meanwhile, he was warming to his subject.

"Shouldn't David's countenance be flushed with the joy of victory? Savouring the triumph of good over evil? But a shadow of doubt flickers across his furrowed brow. Has he just had a glimpse of his own mortality? The monster he has slain is actually himself in twenty years time. The cocky adolescent knows his days are numbered. All too soon it will be his turn. In his moment of glory David suddenly sees the fatal flaw in the perfect picture. Youth is but a brief prelude to old fartdom and death. That is the tragic insight, the inescapable message at the heart of Michelangelo's work. Only a fool could find it simply uplifting as a sculptural ode to the body beautiful."

I was saved further discomfort by the arrival of the waiter. Conundrum managed with a mere flick of the eyes to have him leave the bill on my side of the table.

"*Mille grazie*, Henri. Make sure you charge it."

But Conundrum wasn't finished with David.

"On the other hand, Michelangelo deserves the eternal thanks of all averagely endowed men who may take comfort from the modest proportions of David's tackle."

And that was it for my Renaissance art history lesson in Florence. Next day we left the city after breakfast and drove south. But we didn't get far.

"Stop right here, Henri. Do you see what I see?"

We were in the middle of nowhere. I stopped the car outside a terracotta works. Behind a wire fence an entire regiment of diminutive Davids stood in serried ranks, replicated *en masse* like garden gnomes.

"Get some snaps of that little lot, Henri. The mag shall have more Davids than they bargained for."

It was really amazing. Dotted among the dozens of Davids were other items, all equally incongruous. A statuette of the Virgin Mary seemed to be looking with concern at the private parts of one particular David.

Suddenly, a crude falsetto voice exploded in my ear.

"Don't worry, lad. I'm sure it will grow. Our Jesus had a tiny one at your age. And he ended up with a real whopper."

Conundrum cackled wickedly as he skipped like a demented ballet dancer among the terracotta figures. Had he lost the plot? But he soon fell back into his previous melancholy as we continued our winding route through the Tuscan hills towards Siena. His mood brightened at the discovery of a cassette in the car stereo. As he hit the play button, so we bathed unexpectedly in the wonderful sound of Maria Callas. Her sensational voice came to us with an emotive hiss and crackle performing before a live audience many years ago.

Conundrum was beside himself.

"That's how I love my music, Henri. Stealing up on me unsummoned, unscripted, unpremeditated. A stray snatch of violin wafting forth from an open window in the old town of Prague on a summer night is infinitely more precious, however badly played, than an entire symphony immaculately interpreted by the world's best orchestra in an acoustically perfect concert hall kicking off at 8 pm precisely."

"And the cassette will make a lovely souvenir."

Conundrum looked at me aghast.

"What a shocking suggestion. I am deeply disappointed in you, Henri."

"So you aren't going to keep it?"

"Certainly not. There is nothing worse than amassing a collection of one's own music. Playing personal favourites over and over again to accompany one's moods. Where is the magic in orchestrating a pleasure that should be spontaneous? "

"But there can be no harm in playing it again?"

Conundrum smiled as I hit the play button. Again, we bathed in the divine sound of Callas singing. Conundrum sighed when it was done, taking final leave of a sweet moment.

"I hope your enjoyment wasn't ruined by the persistent cougher who punctuated all 5 minutes 35 seconds of Vicenzo Bellini's *La Sonnambula* recorded at *La Scala* on the fifth of March 1955 with his bronchial tubes variations? Who was this nuisance of a man whose raking cough is superimposed over the immortal Callas? Civil servant, accountant, gangster? Is he still alive? Why did he go to the opera on that particular night? Would he rather have been watching AC Milan? Alas, we shall never know."

He lit a cigarette.

"And the spooky sound of that so called live applause from long ago. All those dead hands clapping. So many autumn leaves rustling on the forest floor of yesteryear. That's what I'd call real phantoms at the opera."

Suddenly Conundrum snapped out of his reverie, ejected the cassette and tossed it out of the window.

"That's enough sentimentality for one day. Foot to the floor, Henri. Time we were in Rome."

We entered the city late afternoon. Our hotel was an exclusive little establishment set in an ancient *palazzo* every bit as classy as our lodgings in Florence. This trip was turning out to be seriously upmarket. A huge antique mirror with a gilt Baroque frame covered one entire wall of the lobby. Conundrum walked up to it, inspecting not so much his own reflection as interrogating the space beyond the dark glass.

"To pass through a mirror of memories and mingle with all who have been reflected in this ancient piece of glass. What would you say to that?"

A mirror of memories? What was he talking about? Can a mirror contain everyone who has been reflected in it? I was beginning to think the impossible. And then I noticed something. Conundrum's waistcoat shone with the glow of burnished gold. What was going on? Anxious for any logical explanation, I put it down to a trick of the light caused by the fact that I was seeing him in the gilt-framed mirror. That seemed to be the case, for when Conundrum turned to face the hotel receptionist his waistcoat was revealed fully restored to its previous shade of bright mustard yellow.

Immediately after we'd checked in, Conundrum insisted we go straight to St Peter's. It struck me as strange for a fearless freethinker to visit that great citadel of religious dogma. But he wouldn't take no for an answer. And since I'd decided to keep my own Roman agenda to myself, I trailed dutifully along.

First we inspected the recently refurbished exterior of St Peter's. Then Conundrum lit a cigarette and inhaled deeply.

"Gothic seeks to point the soul up towards heaven while Baroque serves us paradise on a plate. Fluffy clouds. Cherubs all aflutter. Humanity awestruck by the heavenly host. Celestial visions made real in paint on plaster. But the dazzling display is by definition unreal. Understand that simple fact and you will be able to distinguish between illusion and reality. For if there is one thing Rome can teach you, it is that. It is that."

Conundrum's words touched a raw nerve. It was precisely on the tricky business of illusion versus reality I'd come unstuck during my previous stay in Rome. The harder I'd tried to penetrate the mystery the less I understood it. Art and life forever swapping places. I could see real live human beings when photographing marble statues of two thousand years ago. As for living people of flesh and blood, they generally had less substance than cardboard cut-outs in a make-believe theatre. But occasionally they could be transformed into something special I could only describe as statuesque.

Conundrum now headed with great purpose towards the entrance of St Peter's. I hurried after him across the great oval piazza. Once again I thought how incongruous for such a man to display a religious side to his character. So I wasn't entirely surprised when he stopped halfway up the stairs, scratched his head and performed an abrupt about turn, as if he had thought better of it. But why had he insisted on coming here? And the strangest thing about this strangest of incidents was that I'm fairly sure I saw him make the sign of the cross in a hasty, surreptitious gesture as he turned away.

There was one other minor happening before we left St Peter's. A group of nuns alighted from a bus and fanned out over the piazza, ducking in and out between the pillars of the curved colonnade. I was spellbound by the elaborate choreography of their black and white habits in powerful graphic patterns. I had shot about a dozen pictures and could have finished the roll when Conundrum tapped me on the shoulder.

"Don't get the brides of Christ excited, Henri?"

I said nothing. I didn't want to explain myself. My arty vision of abstract figures on a canvas would have caused more derision. But from his theatrically arched eyebrow I had an uncanny sense Conundrum knew exactly what I was up to.

That evening, after a simple dinner in a small *trattoria*, we strolled up to a terrace overlooking the *Foro Romano*. It was a popular place to hang out and see dusk fall like a shroud over the Eternal City. Conundrum watched the lights of countless flats and houses come on and twinkle in the dark.

"We are all gazing at the stars, Henri. But at least I have my feet firmly in the gutter."

"Shouldn't that be 'we are all in the gutter but some of us are looking at the stars'?"

No response, so I thought I'd further impress him with my literary knowledge.

"Oscar Wilde, if I'm not mistaken."

"Stuff your Oscar Wilde, Henri. Always stating the bloody obvious. And to hell with your mealy-mouthed 'if I'm not mistaken'. You are indeed very much mistaken. For down here is where the true stars of the universe are to be found. Down here in the squalid gutter of human life. Not up there in the germ-free galaxies of outer space. Oscar was far too busy being clever coining witticisms to think things through. So forget the stars in the sky, Henri. Take a look instead at our stars on earth. Just imagine each tiny flash of light in those flats and houses as a surge of love, an orgasm of ecstasy, a moment of beauty or perhaps just the passing whim of some wonderful idea."

I let myself drift away on this unexpectedly lovely thought. So there was a sentimental, poetic side to Conundrum after all? But if so, it was quickly spent.

"On the other hand, imagine those twinkling lights to be outbursts of anger, stabs of torment, flashes of pain. Would they look any the less pretty for that? I think not. For the universe is supremely indifferent to our petty ideas of beauty and ugliness. Bluebottles basking on a cowpat are in essence just as lovely as butterfly wings, peacock tails and spring flowers. So in the final analysis the ceiling of the Sistine Chapel is no better than anarchists' graffiti scrawled on a toilet wall. It all looks the same from a distance: good and evil, happiness and misery just colourful dots and daubs on a canvas with no ethical meaning at all. Is this what the creator sees? The whole universe as one sweeping celestial panorama of abstract cosmic design devoid of all moral content stretching into infinity?"

Conundrum lit another cigarette.

"So let there be life. Let there be suffering. And He saw that it was good. For you can't have one without the other."

Eternal truths in the Eternal City. I would have expected nothing less from Conundrum. There were more to come.

"But what is the point of all this idle speculation, Henri? It's high time we put away our childish illusions. I may think my precious thoughts and develop some tentative ideas on this and that. But I'm only pissing in the dark. And as I listen for the reassuring splash in toilet bowl to know my aim is true, what do I hear? Only the soft splatter of piddle on the bathmat. Once again I am off target. But so what? Everything one can possibly say is bound to be so wide of the mark it's hardly worth saying."

Conundrum dropped his cigarette and trod it underfoot.

"Oh dear, I feel a touch of my old Roman melancholia coming on. A bit more than melancholia actually. I've had a dark thought, Henri. Not just any old dark thought, but the darkest thought it is possible for a man to have. It's been with me a long time. Try as I might I cannot unthink it or force it back in the bottle. It hangs over me like a black cloud, a veil of soot."

I held my breath. Was this what Conundrum had meant by meditating on the dark side of the moon? Was I about to be initiated into his innermost thoughts?

"I would dearly like to spit it out like the acrid taste of a great blasphemy on the lips of a true believer. But I dare not speak its name, Henri. For once spoken it will spread like contagion extinguishing all you and your precious humanity hold dear with your ridiculously romantic ideals. So I must keep silent, hold my peace. My peace? That's a joke. I can have no peace with this ghastly piece of knowledge lodged in my soul. I may not utter it but it pollutes my every thought."

Conundrum a true believer protecting humanity from an unpalatable and unspeakable truth? From what I knew of him to date that seemed unlikely. But what other interpretation was possible? That would explain why he had turned back on the steps of St Peter's. The reluctant heretic unfit to enter the holy of holies? If so, that would make Conundrum something like a defrocked priest, perhaps even a fallen angel?

Not having any knowledge of theology, I am soon out of my depth in matters metaphysical. But here I was compelled by the seriousness of his discourse and the way he pronounced the words 'great blasphemy' as if some foul taste really did sit on his tongue. I held my breath to listen carefully, anxious not to miss a single word or a tiny nuance. Even while doubting my ability to understand, I felt poised on the brink of a great revelation. I was about to be shown the first few pages of *Conundrum's Book*. Or at least be permitted a rapid glance at the table of contents.

In the event, however, he went no further. He fell silent while continuing to gaze at the heavens. His lips moved as if interrogating the night sky. Then he clammed up completely. It seemed he had thought better of it. Perhaps he didn't consider me ready to hear what he had to say. Or his immediate purpose was simply to lay down a marker for future reference?

At any rate, I was not to discover the specific nature of his dark thoughts on this occasion. Though when Conundrum eventually revealed all, under very different circumstances in Paris, I had to agree that the great blasphemy was indeed best kept to himself, and for the very reasons he hinted at here in Rome. For it offered a bleak vision that squeezed every last drop of hope and joy from any idea of life as a precious gift.

As if his dark mood were a spot of cramp Conundrum shook his limbs and proceeded to walk it off as we performed the ritual of the evening *passegiatta* on a delightful moonlit terrace above the *Foro Romano*. His low spirits lifted with every step. Suddenly, he stopped and pricked up his ears as he registered snatches of a lively conversation in English. A handful of young Americans, between bites of hamburger, were trying to respond to a verbal onslaught delivered by an elderly Roman gentleman with the impish face of an ancient satyr.

"Why have you bothered to come to Rome? To wander about gorging yourselves on McDonalds and Coca Cola? The Eternal City isn't a theme park. Not Disneyland. You bring your kindergarten culture with you wherever you go. You may grow old, my dear children, but I fear you will never grow up."

That rang a bell. Hadn't Conundrum said something similar? Now the old satyr waved aside the brave attempt of a young American girl to have her say.

"Be silent, my dear. Listen to old Arturo and you might learn something. A country having the pursuit of personal happiness enshrined in its constitution has taken leave of its senses. Happiness is not a consumer package to be plucked from the shelf of a supermarket."

A mocking edge to Arturo's voice suggested he was taking his young audience for a ride. But a hard glint in his eye suggested the charade had a more serious purpose. Before I knew it Conundrum had joined in.

"*Complimenti*, Arturo. *Complimenti*. But we old Europeans must also take our share of the blame. American culture is essentially what resulted when the countries of Europe dropped their surplus fanatics into a virgin continent and left them to stew for several centuries. Children they may be, but the Americans are our children. Family is family. Mickey Mouse is a descendant of Montaigne and Michelangelo."

Arturo enfolded Conundrum in a respectful embrace, kissing him on both cheeks.

"*Maestro! Maestro!*"

The young Americans were forgotten as Conundrum and Arturo now engaged one another in philosophical matters. Silhouetted against the ink blue night sky, dramatically framed between fallen columns and cypress trees, the two men were soon hard at it, stroking one another's vanities like a pair of old goats grooming mutual beards as they droned on and on about the Old World and the New.

I sidled off unnoticed, leaving Conundrum with his new friend. I didn't return directly to the hotel but traced a circuitous route via the Trevi Fountain to *Piazza Navona*. Here I planned to pay respects to the muscular Bernini figures in the Fountain of the Four Rivers. I'd photographed these statues many times during my previous stay. But *Piazza Navona* now resembled a building site, shrouded in scaffolding. The magic was gone. I had better luck at the Spanish Steps. Immediately I recognised the smooth sweep of polished stone I'd once shot under the flat gleam of a full Roman moon. But something prevented me from taking any pictures. A spark was missing.

I found Conundrum in extremely high spirits at breakfast next morning.

"Pity you didn't hang around, Henri. Most illuminating. Tourists might think the world is their oyster. But the likes of Arturo are there to remind them of the inalienable right of the natives not to wish them 'a nice day' and to be as awkward as they bloody well like."

Our first visit that morning turned out to be *Piazza Navona* of all places. Coincidence? I couldn't be sure. I opted not to tell Conundrum of my nocturnal stroll. By day, the effect of the Baroque sculptures was much worse. The marble statues had been cleaned so blindingly white I had to avert my eyes. They looked fresh from the factory like items of garden statuary for the ornamental fountain of a rich man's *palazzo*. I wondered if someone had switched the originals.

Conundrum droned on about how *Piazza Navona* had once served as a stadium for athletic contests, whose outline was preserved in the form of the Renaissance square.

"Well, so much for ancient Rome, Henri. Now we shall enter the hugger-mugger of the medieval city."

Conundrum darted down a shadowy, crooked alleyway.

"Fasten your seatbelt."

He soon had me taking snaps of colourful washing festooned in garlands across the street. Suddenly a man in string vest appeared at a window and hurled abuse at me. I turned to Conundrum for a translation.

"He is asking what kind of pervert you are taking pictures of his mother-in-law's knickers."

In the event, Conundrum placated the man with some soothing words in Italian and we took our leave. We didn't get far before we ran into real trouble. A wild-eyed ruffian stepped out of the shadows and flashed a glinting knife blade right under Conundrum's nose. His other hand gestured in a way that needed no translation. We were being invited in time-honoured fashion to hand over our valuables.

The knife was held in his face as Conundrum began to go through his pockets. Knowing how long it usually took him to find a spare coin, I reckoned the mugger might quickly lose patience. But Conundrum seemed remarkably unperturbed. He spoke calmly, as if dealing with an overbearing waiter.

"How much do you want?"

"*Inglese, no! Italiano!*"

Conundrum obliged in Italian.

"*Quanto volete?*"

"*Tuttto!*"

"*Tutto?*"

"*Tutto!!*"

"*Momento, signore.*"

Fumbling once more through his pockets, all he could produce were some crumpled traveller's cheques. So he did have some money! The mugger reached out to grab them. But Conundrum snatched them back, miming with a rapid flick of the hand that he had to sign the cheques. Then he resumed his feverish frisking of his own person in search of a writing implement. The mugger, clearly taken aback by this unexpectedly generous co-operation, contented himself with a few more stabbing gestures with the pointed end of the knife. Finally, Conundrum gave up the search for a pen.

"*Mi dispiace, signore. Avete una penna, per favore?*"

The mugger now went through his own pockets for a pen. It didn't take him long to find something which he promptly handed over. Conundrum held it up in the thin shaft of golden Roman sunshine that managed to penetrate the dark labyrinth. It was an exquisitely fashioned *Mont Blanc* fountain pen. Doubtless, our thief had stolen it from someone else.

"*Bellissima!*"

The mugger seemed to take this as personal compliment, the way some people do if you praise their choice of motor car. But suddenly, he remembered the business in hand. With *staccato* movements of the sharp knife, he repeated his demand.

"*Tutto! Tutto!*"

It was just like a fencing match as Conundrum stabbed back with a flourish of the *Mont Blanc* fountain pen.

"*Momento! Momento!*"

I peered over Conundrum's shoulder. Instead of signing the cheques, he was totting up columns of figures.

"How much do we need for extras, Henri? Then there's the taxi to the airport. Oh dear, that won't leave much for our friend, will it? But I suppose if we took the bus, then I could afford to be a bit more generous. I'll explain as best I can."

Conundrum now presented his tiny scrap of paper scrawled with rows of figures ending in plenty of zeroes. The mugger looked distinctly unimpressed and hissed in an alarming manner. The knife was less than an inch from Conundrum's scraggy throat. Seeking to avoid disaster, I held up a 50,000 lire note. A desperate hand reached out to grab it. In a flash my money was gone. So too was our mugger. With a theatrical snarl, a flash of hungry eyes and a glint of *stiletto* he was off.

I was shocked and shaken. Conundrum was all smiles. And no wonder. He was now the owner of the beautiful *Mont Blanc*. He screwed the pen in its holder with the respect of a jeweller fastening a priceless bracelet. Then he twirled it lovingly between his fingers before placing it carefully in a pocket.

"Quite a bargain, Henri. These beautiful pens are outrageously expensive. Well worth however much you gave him. Not that you had to give him anything, of course. So that's entirely your own affair."

He patted his chest to feel the object in his jacket pocket.

"A genuine *Mont Blanc*, if you please. I'm not remotely covetous of costly trinkets, but if the Gods are offering, who am I to refuse? At any rate, this calls for a celebration. I'll treat you to dinner this evening. That should make good your loss."

Conundrum inviting me to dinner? I couldn't wait to experience such a novelty. But an eventful afternoon still lay ahead. First we visited the Protestant Cemetery near *Porta Ostiensis*. As we made our way through the shady grove of cypresses, Conundrum kept touching the *Mont Blanc* fountain pen, caressing it with his thin fingers. Suddenly, he stopped.

"Here lies one whose name was writ in water. Young Keats dictated his own epitaph, Henri. What shall be mine, I wonder? One who took a walk on the dark side?"

A posse of stray cats rubbed their furry flanks against our ankles as Conundrum succumbed to the sad spirit of the place.

"The dead have come to be more real to me than the living. I derive a great sense of peace from the knowledge that I'm now on the last lap and will soon be moving on to join them. But this handsome pen reminds me that my work is not yet done. I have not yet written that which is in me to write."

Another reference to *Conundrum's Book*, and with it a clear hint that he was struggling. Writer's block most probably, I told myself. But had he even made a start? I held my breath while he twiddled the pen between his fingers with a preoccupied air.

"And I'm beginning to wonder if I ever will..."

So it was as I feared. I resolved to make it my mission to encourage him, to coax the words from him if need be. How exciting to be that close to a genius, privy to his thoughts. At this point the cats concluded we would not feed them and slunk off towards an old lady carrying two large plastic bags.

"...and if it is really worth the candle."

That last confession saddened me. For I had imagined Conundrum must be above all the usual human doubts. So I was mightily relieved when his spirits rallied.

"But seriously, Henri. The game is not over by a long chalk. Plenty of running in me yet. Come along now, time is pressing. We must just say a quick hallo to Percy."

Percy? Our visit to Shelley was indeed a quick affair.

"Chap called Trelawny plucked the poet's heart from the funeral pyre on the beach at Viareggio and buried it here. I wonder if it was nicely grilled?"

Soon after we left the cemetery we arrived at a squat circular hill. It might have been an enormous burial mound.

"This obscure corner of Rome has an important message on our subject of the day."

Our subject of the day? I had the impression Conundrum was addressing an audience much larger than myself.

"Human mortality."

Oh no, not that again. Conundrum now climbed the hill nimble and eager as a mountain goat. What was the old fool up to? I scrambled up behind him as best I could, weighed down as I was by all my camera gear. He did not stop until he had reached the summit, where he began picking up pieces of pottery and throwing them up in the air with wild abandon.

"Welcome to *Monte Testaccio*, Henri. This great heap, 100 feet high and half a mile in circumference, is composed of shards of *amphorae*. It is the belly of ancient Rome, all that remains of the great flood of oil and wine imported into the city through the port of Emporium. Some of these jugs might have contained wine drunk by Horace, Mr *Carpe Diem* himself. So with that happy thought in mind let us imbibe a well-earned *aperitivo* as we ruminate on the transience of all things physical."

The venue for our drink was a dingy dive, one of several cave-like cells gouged out around the perimeter of *Monte Testaccio*. Nothing indicated this was a bar except for a scattering of rickety wooden chairs and metal tables evidently 'acquired' from various other establishments or refuse tips. As calmly as if entering his local pub, Conundrum strode boldly through a grubby bead curtain that hadn't deterred a thick fuzz of flies from making the place their own. I followed hesitantly.

"Don't be shy, Henri. You are far safer here than in St Peter's Square with the Supreme Pontiff giving his Easter blessing in 57 languages. Believe me, once you have tasted the hospitality of this thieves' kitchen, not one of the neighbourhood villains will touch you. Your person will be sacrosanct."

The landlord was hardly reassuring. A sour grin of crooked teeth set in a sallow, unshaven face heralded the landing on the tabletop of a carafe of red wine and two smeary glasses. Conundrum poured ample portions of the dubious liquid as he proposed a toast to our good fortune, and in particular to his own, in having come by the *Mont Blanc* pen. This he now held aloft as a prize trophy.

"I don't know what mysterious force has led our steps to this insalubrious neck of the woods, but I sense that there is something fateful about our presence here."

He turned the fountain pen between his fingers like a fat cigar. Then he ignored me completely for several minutes while he scribbled away busily in his notebook. I tried to see what he was writing but was unable to read his scrawl upside down.

Glancing around the gloomy bar, I now became aware of a pair of flashing eyes. A young girl was sitting in the corner. She was a real Roman beauty. All the fire and pride of the ancient race shone defiantly out of her noble features. The tawdry setting and her shabby clothes only enhanced her loveliness. But who was she? From the way she perched on a chair at the back of the bar, I assumed she must be the landlord's daughter.

My throat tightened as our eyes met. My tongue felt dry. I reached for my wineglass. It was empty. So too was the carafe. The young girl now stood up and walked toward me with the predatory grace of a panther. Before taking away the carafe to refill it, she hovered for a moment while casting a haughty glance of appraisal over the pair of us.

Conundrum continued to scribble in his notebook in rapt concentration. At last, he replaced the pen in his jacket pocket. Then he picked up the grubby hand-written menu on the table.

"Fancy the *strigoli al pesto*, Henri? Fresh home made pasta hand-rolled on the silky inside thigh of that winsome wench, I wouldn't be surprised."

Suddenly, the young girl stood before us once more. She poured my glass confidently enough. But when it came to serving Conundrum she came over all clumsy. Her hand shook, slopping wine on the table. Several drops fell on his yellow waistcoat. Mumbling apologies, she whisked out a cloth, mopped the table in a great flurry of movement and gave Conundrum's waistcoat a comprehensive wipe. Then, without another word, she stuffed the wet towel under her arm and scuttled away.

She didn't return to her former place in the corner of the room but strode straight through the bead curtain and vanished into the street. I looked at Conundrum staring after her, his eyes full of wonderment. I thought the old cynic had been well and truly smitten at last. And so he had in a manner of speaking.

For several long seconds neither of us spoke. When Conundrum finally broke the silence, he held open his jacket, looked me in the eye and asked me to ascertain whether his *Mont Blanc* was still *in situ*. But there was no trace of the fountain pen. It was gone. On receiving this news, Conundrum's eyes sparkled and a broad smile spread across his thin lips.

"*Dio mio!* How very satisfying to have been relieved of something so beautiful by someone so beautiful."

He was positively purring with contentment.

"Who cares about the loss of a pen? It was never really mine anyway. I have scribbled a few words with it and now it has moved on. And rightly so. I shall never cease to wonder at the power of inanimate objects to have their way with us."

He downed the last drops of red wine in his glass.

"Nor let us forget the power of inanimate objects to outlive us. Here we are, two lowly mortals sitting inside *Monte Testaccio*. All around us shards of pottery which have seen off the likes of Nero, Augustus, Caligula, Julius Caesar *et al*. Perhaps that exquisite fountain pen will still be beautiful in fifty years time when *la bella ragàzza* who took it is all shrivelled up and possibly no more. Pottery is the worst. Virtually indesctructable. Even this humble dish can make fools of us."

Conundrum picked up a white saucer and looked at it as if he were about to deliver an address to Yorrick's skull.

"Do you realise that this banal piece of cheap china could outlast the span of our two lives multiplied many times over?"

His eyes gleamed.

"Unless, of course, it meets with a small accident."

110

He raised his arm and dropped the dish. A hundred tiny fragments of broken china exploded on the concrete floor.

"That's one bit of pottery that isn't going to make a mockery of human mortality, don't you think?"

The crash brought *il padrone* scuttling out of the back room where he had been watching football on TV. He treated Conundrum to a string of foul curses ending with the pithy observation *"Non siamo in Grecia qui!"* – we're not in Greece here.

When presented with an exorbitant bill for the broken saucer as well as for the sour wine, Conundrum conveniently discovered he had also lost his wallet to the nimble fingers of the sultry maiden. So I had to fork out yet again.

As we walked away from *Monte Testaccio*, I didn't have the heart to remind Conundrum of his blithe assertion we would be safer here than in St Peter's Square.

"The wind has changed, Henri. Although the *Mont Blanc* is gone, I would still invite you for dinner to celebrate my acquiring it. But alas now that my wallet is gone too, it will have to be on you this time. Don't forget to charge it."

His mood brightened once we were back in central Rome. As we entered the lobby of our *palazzo* hotel he even extracted a consolatory lesson from the day's mishaps.

"Amazing how that knave of a landlord reminded us we are not in Greece. How very true. For Athens may show us the world as we would like it to be, a place where once gods and goddesses walked the earth. But Rome shows us the world such as it is. Here, all is cynicism and posture. Calculation and artifice are rampant. This is where idealism was transformed into fascism and beauty prostituted for profit. *Mille grazie, bella Roma.* I salute your artful deceits and wicked wisdom."

The hotel concierge handed us each an elegant embossed envelope containing an invitation to a reception the manager was holding that evening for his distinguished guests. The party was already in full swing when I arrived. I spotted Conundrum in a far corner of the courtyard deep in conversation with the most stunning Roman beauty. She was the luxury version of the poor young girl who had stolen his fabulous fountain pen. I made my way slowly through the throng. The lady was clearly impressed enough with Conundrum to confide in him her intention to give up fashion modelling and take up photography.

"So how would you advise me to learn photography?"

At this critical moment, Conundrum, who had his back to me, turned and drew me in to the conversation.

"Ah, Henri. Excellent timing."

Turning back to the girl, he continued.

"Here is a seasoned exponent of the photographic art, my dear. Henri is just the person to give *la bella signorina* the benefit of his vast experience."

What a generous build-up. Such a rare dose of flattery. I looked deep into the burnt almond eyes of the young lady. A *bella signorina* indeed. A fiery flicker met my gaze.

"But first, you must get us all a drink, Henri."

He capped my humiliation with his next remark.

"There's a good boy."

I went about my master's bidding. I returned clutching three glasses of something bubbly. Conundrum was in full flow.

"The secret, my dear, is let the pictures take themselves. Don't go running after them. They will come to you."

"But what sort of camera should I start with?"

"Doesn't really matter. Just get used to seeing pictures. Look at life and frame things in an imaginary viewfinder."

Conundrum formed a crude rectangle with thumbs and index fingers and peered through it with a lascivious leer.

"Then if you still think it's interesting enough, do get yourself a camera and take a peep through that. And once you see a shot that really needs taking, pop in a roll of film. That's basically all there is to photography."

"But what sort of film should I use?"

"Film? You haven't been listening, my dear girl. Don't waste celluloid before you've learned to see properly."

"Learned to see properly? How long will that take?"

"Depends. Couple of minutes. A lifetime."

The lovely features of *la bella signorina* fell from bright expectancy into a dark frown. Thinking I might endear myself to her with a few comforting remarks, I chose this moment to step forward with the three glasses of *spumante*.

"Ah, Henri. Something to drink. At last."

Her dark eyes fell hopefully on me.

"No point asking Henri, my dear. He wastes far too much film. I can't imagine what he's snapping half the time."

This seemed to annoy the young lady as much as it did me. She turned brusquely to go off in search of more congenial company. Brushing me aside, her elbow knocked my arm. The bubbling wine slopped over my fingers. As if in slow motion I saw my hands desperately trying to hold on to the slippery glasses. It was like juggling three bars of wet soap. For a moment I thought I could hang on, but then the inevitable happened. One by one the glasses crashed to the marble floor.

"What a clumsy fellow you are, Henri."

A deep silence fell. All eyes were on me. It seemed like an eternity before a waiter came along to clear up. Meanwhile, Conundrum slipped away. But in his haste to latch on to other company, he got cornered by an elderly British academic. At a distance I could hear a serious art-historical lecture on the threatened churches of Venice. I ignored his signals to create a diversion to get him out of it. Let him suffer. I'd had enough.

Eventually Conundrum freed himself.

"I have changed my mind, Henri. Venice should not be saved. And certainly not by the likes of that old bore."

The following morning was our final day in Rome. Conundrum elected to wander off on his own so I grabbed my chance to revisit old haunts. I soon wished I hadn't. *Campidoglio*, Michelangelo's exquisite little square had been tarted up like a stage set. The statue of Marcus Aurelius had a phoney feel about it. Surely a replica? I had fond memories of *Campo de' Fiori* and its seedy market that left the cobbled square littered with trampled vegetables and squashed fruit scattered all over the place like bloody entrails on a battlefield. Now it was another building site, doubtless to be transformed into a sanitised heritage attraction.

Wherever I went, I took note of the walls. But the *graffiti* were not as powerful as I remembered them. The great splashes of vibrant colour I'd photographed as works of art, were now mere daubs of no artistic interest. Were these changes real or simply a result of my changed perception? Surely it wasn't just me that had changed. The rough edges and raw passion were gone. Rome used to be a city with its wounded soul plastered all over the walls. Now it was just like anywhere else. Arturo was wrong. The young Americans were right. Rome had turned into a theme park, so why shouldn't they treat it as such?

Rome had died for me. I decided not to stay on. What swung the decision was the realisation that Conundrum, even after he had gone, would cast a shadow over everything. His malignant spirit would dog my steps, tap me on the shoulder, tug at my sleeve, mock my thoughts before I'd thought them and whisper his own devious truths into my ear. That was an awful prospect. But the reality was about to get worse.

My last visit on our final morning in Rome was *Castel S. Angelo*, the mausoleum-fortress housing the remains of Emperor Hadrian. It was a popular picture postcard view to add to my archive. Just as I was framing the standard shot of statue-lined bridge leading up to castle, my attention fell on a priest coming slowly towards me. His eyes were cast downwards. He wore the traditional black cassock and flat clerical hat like a soup dish.

I tracked him through the viewfinder. When he drew level on the other side of the road, I shot a single frame. I caught his stooped posture, an aged back arched like a human question mark, artistically framed by the carved balustrade of the bridge. A great shot, I hoped.

Something must have alerted the old priest for he looked up and gave me an enigmatic smile. It was all over in a flash, as he turned the corner. I could hardly believe my eyes. It took me a couple of seconds to fully register what I'd seen. The old priest was the spitting image of Conundrum. No, it was more than that. He was Conundrum. I knew those jesting eyes and that rotten lop-sided smile anywhere. I almost called after him. I blinked to make sure I wasn't dreaming. But when I took a second look, the priest had vanished into thin air.

When I got back to the hotel, Conundrum was alone in the foyer and apparently in a world of his own. I waited outside and observed him through the glass door. For a while he just stood there contemplating his reflection in the huge blackened mirror that occupied the entire wall between two columns.

Then he approached the mirror, not looking at himself so much as looking through himself. No, it wasn't that either. His eyes were focused on the tip of his nose as it almost touched the mirror. Somehow he was searching for the space where his face ended and his reflection began.

Next he began to pace up and down, keeping a beady eye on his moving reflection. The two Conundrums put me in mind of rival stags performing a parallel walk to size up their respective strength. During this routine Conundrum made various changes in pace and gait, carefully noting his reflected image follow the same routine. Then, on reaching the end of the mirror, instead of turning back as he had been doing with the regularity of a caged tiger, he took a sudden spring forward and sprang back even faster, eyes still riveted to the mirror. I had the impression he was seeking to outwit his reflected self, trying to detach himself from his own reflection, or something like that.

But that wasn't anything compared to what happened next. I found myself looking straight into Conundrum's eyes staring at me out of the mirror. I thought he'd seen me and I was about to wave to him when I noticed that the 'real' Conundrum was not where he should be in relation to his reflection. He was still by the mirror though momentarily looking the other way. And while the attention of the 'real' Conundrum was otherwise distracted, his reflected image struck up an independent posture of its own. Stranger still, the Conundrum in the mirror was wearing a toga like a senator of ancient Rome.

This was scary. Then it got scarier. The Conundrum reflection winked at me in a conspiratorial fashion and made a lewd, mocking gesture towards the 'real' Conundrum as if to say what a stupid old goat he was. At this moment the 'real' Conundrum sprang back in front of the mirror to resume his game of cat-and-mouse. At precisely the same moment his reflection started to behave just as a conventional reflection is supposed to, dressed no longer in toga but in the very same clothes as its master and mirroring his every move. Conundrum regarded himself even more closely in the looking glass with a raised eyebrow before continuing the stalking game.

The whole episode lasted just a few seconds, but it sent me reeling. Conundrum's reflection had recognised me, even acknowledged me. A communication had passed between us behind the back of the 'real' Conundrum. What was going on? To steady my nerves, I took a stroll round the block. When I returned to the hotel Conundrum was shaking hands with the manager, thanking him for his hospitality. I tried to think no more of it, nor of the old priest on the *Ponte Sant' Angelo*.

My thoughts were turning to home and a Conundrum-free existence. We hardly spoke in the taxi on the way to the airport. When it came to paying the driver, Conundrum darted off with amazing speed on the pretext of finding a trolley. As the plane headed north from Leonardo da Vinci airport Conundrum tilted back his head and threw a handful of peanuts into his open mouth. He washed them down with a swig of champagne.

With a rhetorical flourish Conundrum shook the powdery remains of the peanuts into his open mouth. Some of the contents cascaded down his waistcoat like volcanic ash on a mountainside. I looked at this garment with suspicion. During our time in Rome I'd kept an eye on the alternating colours of Conundrum's waistcoats. I now knew for sure some trickery was afoot, for I had noted changes of colour when he'd had no opportunity to change. Perhaps it was a reversible waistcoat? But that could give two different colours at most. Then, eureka! I thought I had cracked it. It must be a reversible waistcoat with different shades back and front, inside and out. This could account for the three colours of red, green and yellow plus the muddy brown. It would have to be a sophisticated piece of tailoring. But why would he go to such lengths?

Then, in a flash I knew it could only be the one waistcoat. For the dark stain the red wine had made on the left side of the yellow waistcoat when the waitress at *Monte Testaccio* had spilled the carafe now stared at me from the identical spot of the green waistcoat. The implications were mind-boggling. Conundrum wasn't changing waistcoats. Instead, his one waistcoat was changing colour like a chameleon.

My bafflement must have been stamped across my face.

"Anything the matter, Henri?"

"Er, no. Nothing. Nothing at all."

I pretended to look away. But Conundrum wasn't fooled.

"So you've noticed at last, haven't you? Well, you are making progress, Henri. Very good. Very good indeed."

I decided to challenge him head-on.

"So how many coloured waistcoats do you have?"

"Its colours are of such infinite variety."

"So just the one then?"

Conundrum gave a slight nod. It was as I had feared. My throat felt dry. This was indeed magic. But of what kind?

"You may be wondering if other people see it too?"

The thought hadn't yet occurred to me that I might be the only one to perceive this weird phenomenon. But even as I contemplated the question I dreaded the answer.

"Well, they can't."

"And *I* can?"

I recalled the shots I'd taken in Catalonia in which the waistcoat had been the same muddy brown in every one of the four pictures. Not even the camera had been able to record the colours I had seen with my own eyes.

"But how? And why me?"

"It's what you are seeing, Henri. That's the secret."

I was too scared to press the point. The man was clearly a wizard of sorts. And I was caught in his web. I'd become an initiate without knowing it. Did I really have a particular kind of vision? Could I see things others couldn't? I recalled Conundrum's heady promise in Barcelona of the undetected primary colour, the dream of a parallel spectrum waiting to be perceived by someone with the third eye. Was that person really me? Was this what this circus was all about? The implications were too alarming. I didn't want to hear any more. And as for that moment when I had been face to face with Conundrum's detached image, I didn't even dare to ask.

Mercifully, he now changed the subject.

"Why the devil didn't you show me all those places you photographed last time you were in Rome?"

Embarrassment must have been stamped all over me.

"No need to be ashamed of youthful artistic leanings, Henri. Rome has that effect. I saw your show. Bad venue. Some pretentious little place in Notting Hill. More furniture shop than art gallery. But not all of your work was beyond redemption, I seem to recall. I wonder why you didn't pursue that line."

I refilled my glass and downed the champagne in a single gulp. I was dumbfounded. What was there Conundrum didn't know about me? At the same time I was totally disarmed by his positive comments on my Roman show. Not all of my work beyond redemption. Praise indeed coming from him.

"So you think photography can be art?"

Conundrum practically choked on his champagne.

"Photography? Art? What silliness am I hearing?"

"Seriously, though. I mean, can it?"

"You want me to be serious? Well, I suppose I could give it a try. So what would you like me to say? That if painting can be art, then why not photography? And besides, what is this sacred Art of yours with a capital A, Henri? Just a four-letter word spelled with three letters. Nothing more than that."

"I do so wish I'd done art instead of photography."

Conundrum gave me a pitying look.

"Art schools should be banned, Henri. You've had a narrow escape. Why encourage young artists? They should be positively discouraged. They've hardly been anywhere or understood anything. Yet we hail their juvenile efforts with uncritical rapture, as if the contents of their potties had some universal significance. No wonder they nail their soiled underpants and knickers to the wall and call the *oeuvre* 'browned off'. Well, sod the young. We should cherish the old geezers, who have clocked up the mileage, taken the hard knocks, drunk the sour wine, eaten the stale cheese, had youthful ideals crushed out of them, seen their dreams sullied in the cesspit of life."

More champagne fuelled him further.

"The only thing we can usefully teach the young about art, Henri, is the inevitability of failure. So much more important than success, which is a total illusion. Take it from me, there is no such thing as success, just varying degrees of failure. Failure is the real lifeblood of the human saga. So, what have we to learn from the young but the impossibility of their dreams? Alas, something we know too well already."

"So you would do well not to believe in things like Art and Truth, Henri. In Rome, all truth begins with a lie and all art manifests itself through artifice. And *vice versa*, of course. For every lie contains some grain of truth. That's the real message of Rome. Rest assured everything here comes complete with an authenticated certificate of genuine duplicity. Learn that and you will take away something of lasting value."

He sighed wistfully, as if he was a trifle saddened by the harsh facts of life he'd just spelled out for my benefit.

"I'm not sure I will ever return to the Eternal City. Did I mention Rome always induces in me a touch of melancholia? I did? Well, now I need cheering up. Spot more bubbly, Henri?"

What a relief to get home and shut the door of my flat behind me. Rome could reach me no longer. Neither could Conundrum. Or so I thought. But that night I had a dream in which Conundrum's toga-clad image leered out at me from an antique looking glass. Then it was the turn of his *doppelgänger* on the *Ponte Sant'Angelo* dressed as a Roman Catholic priest. Even the carved stone faces on the tombs along the *Via Appia Antica* looked like more versions of Conundrum.

Waking in a cold sweat, I tried to dismiss these apparitions as the stuff of dreams. But they were real enough. Conundrum could travel like a wizard back and forth in time, disguising his appearance at will, merging and morphing his being as it suited him. Wherever I looked were undeniable signs of his presence. I could even imagine graffiti on the walls of ancient Rome declaring: *CONUNDRUM WOZ HERE.*

Then there was the magic waistcoat. So what was all that about? Had I developed a sensitivity to Conundrum's varying moods? And it was these shifting states I could detect as colour impressions. Or had I acquired the skill to project chromatic images onto the neutral screen of his waistcoat? But even this 'logical' explanation flew in the face of logic.

Whichever way I argued the matter, I overlooked the bigger picture, namely that my free will and my very being were no longer my own. I had ceased to exist as an independent individual. But, as tends to happen in cases of hijacked identity, the afflicted person is the very last to realise the sad truth.

I didn't know what to make of the latest offerings from Conundrum's box of tricks. But if he was indeed a magician, then he was my magician. Of that much I was certain. For I had convinced myself of one thing. All that I was going through had to do with me, not with him. It was my destiny at stake, not his.

After Catalonia I'd been minded to go my own way. Now after Rome, I'd passed the point of no return. I was fully enrolled as Conundrum's acolyte at the Academy of... the Academy of what? Most probably the exact term didn't exist and therefore didn't matter. By the same token nor did it matter that I didn't know what I was meant to be studying. I suspected the essential part of the course would be to find out what the course was actually about. Then, and only then, would all the pieces fall into place. But whichever way I looked at it, I was signed up for the duration and with no escape clause.

I resolved not to think too much about where things were going. What was it he said about thought getting in the way? Perhaps all I had to do was absorb his knowledge passively like a sponge? So I let Conundrum retreat steadily to the back of my mind. Though I sensed he was still there always lurking in the shadows waiting to resurface at any moment.

In fact, only a few days passed before I was suddenly plucked from my mental retreat. I clearly remember the day he called. The main item on the news that evening when the phone rang was the Queen Mother's second hip replacement.

"Listen carefully, Henri. I have a most excellent wheeze."

"Oh, really?"

I even contrived a stifled yawn, my idea being to feign indifference to whatever he proposed.

"Drop whatever you're doing, and jump in a cab. I'll meet you at the back door of the King Edward."

"The King Edward? Is that a pub?"

"Not a pub, Henri. A place of healing. As in King Edward Hospital. Do I have to spell it out?"

"Well, it would help to know what's going on."

"And bring a pair of scissors."

"Scissors?"

"Yes, scissors, Henri. Implements for cutting."

"Cutting what?"

"Or a sharp kitchen knife. Anything to slit open a few black plastic bags."

"Black plastic bags? What exactly do you have in mind?"

"If we're lucky we might get hold of the original."

"The original what?"

"Don't be so dense, Henri. If only I had thought of it last time round we could now be on a pair. Even so, one Queen Mum hip will make a valuable royal relic."

"Royal relic?"

"Yes. Should be worth a fortune."

The line went dead. An evening foraging through hospital waste for the Queen Mother's hip? Was there no end to Conundrum's madness? Well, to hell with that. I wouldn't do it. In that instant, I realised I had revolted. For once I was actually going to say no to Conundrum. So there was a limit to my dumb obedience after all. I sat down, determined not to budge from the spot. Several minutes later the phone rang again.

"Put away the scissors, Henri. Queen Mum hip is on hold. Something else has come up. Call back soon."

So much for my bold act of rebellion. Conundrum would never even know about it. Nor did he call back soon. A couple of weeks passed and I began to believe I might be in the clear. Perhaps he had sensed my changed mood and decided to drop me? But I knew I could make no such assumption. There was only one thing I could expect from Conundrum, namely the unexpected. He was the one who called the shots.

I fell to speculating what became of him between trips, how he passed his time. Where did he live? But even this basic fact remained a mystery. On a couple of occasions, when he hadn't scuttled off without a word, we had taken the tube from Heathrow into town. On these journeys Conundrum had got off the train at Leicester Square. That and Cambridge Circus, where I had dropped him on our return from Wales, were the only clues I had to Conundrum's home. Somewhere in Soho then?

If he concealed his private address like a spy, then he was equally secretive about his phone number. Perhaps he didn't have one? Several times I dialled 1471 right after he called. But the result was always the same. Either the number was withheld or a payphone that went unanswered. After these futile efforts at detection I gave up trying to track him down. In fact, I came to prefer the mystery. It was somehow more satisfying to believe Conundrum had no material existence between our trips. Like a genie, he simply popped out of the ether.

So imagine my surprise actually to come across the man himself in the flesh one fine day right out of the blue and in broad daylight. I was walking along Piccadilly towards Green Park when I spotted him lurking just inside the Burlington Arcade. He was scrutinising something in a shop window with such intensity that his thin frame was bowed over like a question mark. It made a great picture, and I was able to snap him while his attention was distracted.

I was about to hail him like any normal acquaintance one sees by chance. But some devious instinct stopped me. Here was a unique opportunity to observe Conundrum in his natural habitat. I resolved to find out what he was up to. For a few moments, he stood there, eyes riveted on the shop window. Then he took a few paces up and down, always returning to the same spot for further scrutiny as if there were a puzzle to crack. A memory from Rome came back into focus. This was how he had behaved in front of the antique mirror in the hotel.

Since I had a copy of a newspaper I hid behind it like they do in films. Thus amateurishly concealed I felt even more conspicuous and uncomfortable with what I was doing. But it was too late for second thoughts. I had committed myself. I waited patiently for something to happen.

Now Conundrum looked about furtively, like an animal sniffing the wind, as if he sensed he was being observed. Then, apparently reassured, he wandered off. I followed at a discreet distance, curious to know where he was heading. Perhaps home? Would I at last track the beast to its lair? Never mind. Any scrap of new information would be a revelation.

Wherever he was going, he was in no hurry. He sauntered casually through the Burlington Arcade like a gentleman of leisure with an hour or so to kill before drinks and lunch at his club. On reaching the northern exit he turned sharp right along Burlington Gardens and into Vigo Street. He hesitated at the junction with Regent Street, uncertain which way to go.

Then, all of a sudden, he was off. Now there was a real sense of purpose to his progress. It didn't take me long to figure out what had galvanised him into action. Walking just in front of Conundrum was a girl. Her long legs disappeared alluringly into the most minimal of miniskirts. My attention wandered between her languorous movements and the predatory prowl of Conundrum on her tail. I tried not to be too distracted by the girl. If I let the wily old fox out of my sight for a single second he might vanish into thin air like a leprechaun. But it was no trouble to keep both targets in my view since Conundrum maintained a constant proximity to the sexy girl. He bobbed and weaved through the crowds in a fresh and sprightly manner, like a ballroom dancer gliding along on the balls of his feet.

When the girl disappeared inside a boutique, Conundrum hung about for a bit before giving up and walking away. Now the spring had gone out of his step. He continued listlessly towards Oxford Circus, dragging his heels. Then in a flash he found his sense of purpose again. On the spur of the moment, he wheeled right and crossed Regent Street. It didn't take me long to spot the reason for his fresh burst of energy. Not far ahead of him, two beautiful girls walked arm in arm. So that was it. Conundrum was a dirty old man trailing behind sexy, young females. A kind of opportunistic stalker, no less.

Then something miraculous happened. A burst of morning sun split the clouds and turned the girls' flowing tresses into golden crowns, lighting up the scanty white silk dresses that clung to their lithe bodies. An aura of luminescence centred around them while everyone else remained in the shade. For a moment they looked like a pair of angels. Another great photo opportunity. This celestial spotlight seemed to track the two girls like supermodels on the catwalk. By now, I was almost walking on air, deliciously uplifted. My legs bore me effortlessly down Great Marlborough Street as if driven by a force of their own.

A thick cloud blotted out the sun just as the two girls scuttled into the back entrance of Marks & Spencer. Conundrum stumbled, as if he had stepped off a moving pavement onto solid ground. Then the sky darkened and rain came teeming down as people rushed for cover. It was like a monsoon. But Conundrum wandered along bareheaded, coatless, oblivious to the storm.

On an impulse, I opened my umbrella and, pretending I had just happened to spot him by chance, rushed up and held it over him. He spoke to me without bothering to turn round.

"Ah, Henri. Thank goodness you have nabbed me at last. Must admit I am rather tired of following you."

"You following me? Surely I was the one following ...?"

I bit my tongue. Too late. I had stupidly revealed my childish game. Conundrum revelled in his triumph, dismissing any further protestations with a scornful laugh.

"Of course you thought you were following me, Henri. But it was the other way round. What may have fooled you was my cunning technique yet to be discovered by the surveillance plods as portrayed in B movies, where you seem to have learned the trade. Do you really think you make yourself inconspicuous hiding behind newspapers, diving into doorways, looking at your watch every two seconds?"

I was too embarrassed for words.

"Still don't get it, do you? Where is the one place you never suspect to find someone following you?"

"Well, er….."

"Why, in front, of course. And that is exactly what I was doing. Following you from in front. Simple as that."

"And let me tell you something else. By the same token, if you ever want to lead someone, do it from behind."

I was still too embarrassed to say anything.

"And do remove that brolly, Henri. The rain has stopped, the dust has settled and there's a whiff of something exciting in the air. Must be the rites of spring. Phallic forces rumble in the nether regions. Time to pay a little visit to Raymond."

"Raymond?"

"Yes, Henri. Raymond. An old acquaintance. Follow me and all will be revealed. Quite literally."

Was I about to learn something of the real Conundrum? But we didn't get far before disaster struck. As we waited on the kerb to cross the road a van came roaring along with three young lads in string vests on the front seat. The driver took aim at the large puddle right in front of us. Before we could take evasive action we were covered head to foot in dirty water. The echo of raucous laughter only added insult to injury. Conundrum shook an angry fist at the departing white van.

We brushed the dirty water off our clothes. Then, as we walked around the corner into Poland Street we saw just ahead of us, the offending vehicle, a white Ford Transit stuck in traffic. As we drew level, Conundrum snatched the umbrella from me and smashed it with an almighty bang against the side of the van.

"Sounds like thunder inside. That'll teach them."

The van door opened. Two lads in string vests jumped out. Conundrum scuttled off like a hermit crab. I tried to placate them with a feeble gesture of conciliation. They brushed me aside. As I turned to follow them, I could hear them shouting.

"Fuck you, grandad! Up yours, grandpa!"

Just as the attackers were about to pounce, Conundrum stopped in his tracks, dropped his trousers and underpants to reveal an ugly pair of wizened buttocks. Each cheek was decorated with a tattoo. One with a couple of grotesque beasts engaged in an obscene act. The other some kind of ancient runic inscription. To add to the alarming effect, Conundrum's leering face appeared upside down between his legs.

"Come on and help yourselves, lads. What are you waiting for?"

The two ruffians froze, seemingly mesmerised by the shocking spectacle of Conundrum's backside.

"Bleeding pervert! They should lock you up!"

The string-vests raced back to their van. Watching them depart, Conundrum stood there instantly trousered up once more and calmly composed as if nothing untoward had happened.

"Good to know the ancient charm still works."

His voice was without the merest tremor of alarm.

"Once, the troubadours sang of knights in white satin. Now it's all yobs in Ford Transits."

For want of anything better to say, I quipped.

"Well, *sic transit*, I suppose."

At this, Conundrum's mood brightened.

"*Sic transit*, Henri? A witticism? Oh very good. It may be only a humble pun, but quite excellent all the same. You could be at risk of acquiring a sense of humour."

I shrugged nonchalantly, secretly delighted to have delivered a *bon mot* of my very own, however unintended.

"Well, I suggest you buy me a drink to celebrate. *Sic transit* indeed. Good stuff, Henri. But don't start telling jokes. A jest is fine. But a joke is no laughing matter."

Conundrum steered me into the door of the *Admiral Duncan* in Old Compton Street.

"Strictly backs to the wall in here, Henri."

Rather than say anything that might ruin the warm glow of my *sic transit* quip, I wrapped myself in silence, waiting for Conundrum's next comment.

"Oh, dear. Perhaps I shouldn't have brought you here?"

I had no clue what he was talking about.

"I mean, how can I put it?"

It was so unlike Conundrum to be lost for words.

"You're not happy, are you Henri?"

I could hardly believe my ears. Was he taking an interest in my wellbeing? Today was full of surprises. But having been so often the butt of Conundrum's jibes, I was not about to be taken in too easily. I opted for a cautious response.

"I'm not really sure. Being happy is rather relative, don't you reckon?"

Now it was Conundrum's turn to look perplexed.

"I really don't see how being happy can be relative, Henri. Relative to what?"

"Well, perhaps not entirely relative. What I mean to say is that it's not always easy to know if you are truly happy."

"Good lord, Henri! I think you would be the first to know something like that."

Conundrum seemed genuinely amazed at what I thought was fairly obvious. Ignoring the danger signs, I plunged on.

"You see, when I now look back at the past, I think I might well have been happy without knowing it."

"Happy without knowing it?"

"What I mean to say is I may not have been really aware of being happy at the time."

"Were you not indeed?"

Conundrum was now beside himself with astonishment.

"I don't think we are talking of the same thing, Henri."

He lowered his voice to a conspiratorial whisper.

"How can I put it, Henri? What I mean is, you're not one of those cheerful chappies, are you?"

My silence only encouraged him further down this track.

128

"What is the word I'm looking for? Glad? Don't be so obtuse, Henri. Do help me with this. What I mean is, you don't bat for the other side, do you?"

Finally, the penny dropped.

"So you're asking, if I am gay?"

"Gay? Gay! Yes, that's the one. You're not gay are you, Henri? Often wondered why you live near Russell Square."

"No, I'm not gay as it happens. What's it to you?"

Seeing his mistake, Conundrum quickly changed subject.

"Anyway, I expect you're dying to know how I came by the tattoos that put the fear of God into those yobs. Well, just fetch some more drinks and you'll get the full story."

I dutifully fetched the drinks. What followed was one of his tallest yarns.

"It was like this. Got myself into a small spot of bother in the former USSR. Had to get out of Leningrad in a hurry. Didn't fancy an extended holiday in Hotel Gulag. Rode a tourist hydrofoil out to Peterhof on the Gulf of Finland. Then a local bus further west into Kyrelia. Got off a few miles short of the Finnish border and took to the forest. Got lost and wandered about for a day or so. Luckily, it was late summer, plenty of berries to eat. First touch of autumn though and a bit cold at night. But what bothered me was the uncomfortable feeling that someone or something was following me. Always out of sight but forever on the fringe of my consciousness."

Conundrum swallowed a mouthful of whisky.

"So I climbed a tree and kept lookout. Eventually, I discovered the identity of my pursuer."

Another gulp of whisky.

"Can you imagine who it was?"

I shook my head.

"Or rather what it was?"

I shook my head again.

"A bear, Henri. I was being followed by a big brown Russian bear. What was I to do? No way could I shake it off. So I had to continue with this shaggy beast always on my tail. Only now the bear knew that I knew he was following me and made no more attempt to conceal itself. Maintained a respectful distance, mind you, but noticeably closer than before. The bond between us was getting tighter all the time. We were fellow travellers. We dined off the same berries and mushrooms. We saw the same scenery of birch and aspen tinged with the golden rust of autumn. But I'll spare you the poetic details."

Conundrum downed the rest of his drink.

"Gradually, I felt the bear was less of a threat. Almost the opposite. Like a bodyguard watching my back. I wish it could have been my guide too since I hadn't a clue where I was heading except in the general direction of west."

Conundrum lifted his empty glass and wiggled it.

"Be a sport, Henri. You'll have to drop a large one in there if I'm to get through the rest."

A couple of minutes later, I placed yet another double whisky in front of him.

"Now, where was I? Oh yes, the bear. Well, one morning I had the fright of my life. I awoke to find the bear cuddling up right next to me, breathing down my neck as if we had been sleeping together. Like marital spoons. That intimate. I almost jumped out of my skin. The bear gave me a guilty look before scuttling off into the forest. As if out of shame for inappropriate behaviour. And it was inappropriate."

"Inappropriate?"

"The bear had taken a shine to me, Henri."

"Taken a shine to you?"

"Do I have to spell it out? It was gay, don't you see? Imagine being stalked by a gay Russian bear. Made the KGB seem much less of a threat. Anyway, after that it kept its distance but was still tagging along out of sight. But I knew it was only a matter of time before it made its next move."

Conundrum eyed me through his whisky glass to make sure I was paying attention.

"So I made greater haste to reach safety. Couldn't face another night in the forest. Around sunset, I came across a log cabin on the edge of a lake with a tattered Finnish flag flying from a mast. Somehow I had slipped into Finland. An old man took me in. I told him the story of the bear. He said he knew what to do. We had a sauna and flogged ourselves with birch branches. Then he had me lie down on a wooden table. I think I must have fallen asleep. When I awoke a couple of hours later he had tattooed my buttocks exactly as you saw them earlier. Any hint of danger to my person, he said, all I had to do was expose my backside to my assailant."

I thought the unlikely tale was over. But it wasn't.

"That night the woodcutter's daughter came to my bed. Simply offered herself to me without a word. Next morning I studied her as she lay beside me, flaxen-haired, eyes a tender blue of Arctic berries, docile doe-like innocence. We made love again. I recall every detail of that simple room: ceiling soft pastel green, door pale dove grey, walls warm apricot, floor of scrubbed pine. And the whole time we didn't utter a single word. That, Henri, was the Faustian moment when I would have stopped the clock and declared myself at the summit of human happiness."

Conundrum sighed.

"Alas, it was not to last. That day I had to set off with her father in a rowboat. As we pulled away I watched the girl on the shore by the log cabin, a small figure in a bright blue dress slowly shrinking until she was no bigger than a cornflower in a distant meadow. Then I saw her no more.

We rowed for hours through a maze of islands until we reached another log cabin. It was a smoke sauna. A dozen or so people sat in the dark. Everyone invisible in the gloom, just the sound of voices. Between times we took a dip in the cold lake. Faces like ripe pumpkins glowing with contentment. Slowly people disbanded. I ached to return to the young girl. I looked about for my friendly woodcutter. But he was nowhere to be seen. Even his boat was gone. Then I spotted him far away rowing back over the lake. I stood frozen to the spot, tracking his progress until he vanished behind the nearest island. There was no way back. I had tasted paradise. I had devoured it whole. Now I was consigned to outer darkness. Nothing would ever attain the perfection of that fleeting embrace in the soft arms of the woodcutter's daughter. And nothing ever has."

Conundrum sighed as he came out of his reverie.

"Happily, the tattoo has lost none of its potency. Good to know the old Norse magic still works and…"

He paused in mid-sentence. A huge muscled man loomed over us, a terrifying sight in black leather and bristling with steel studs, shaven head, and a six-inch nail piercing his nose.

"Well, let's have a look at those tattooed buttocks."

Conundrum downed his drink in a single gulp, slid off his seat and moved toward the door, all in one fluid movement.

"Another time perhaps. Must be going."

We made it outside without further incident.

"Well, Henri, the night is young. We can catch the early show at Raymond's. I just happen to have a couple of freebies."

A short walk brought us to the *Raymond Revue Bar*. We took our seats in the front row. Conundrum settled back as if in a favourite armchair. The lights dimmed.

WELCOME TO EROTICA 2000! A smooth voice promised a feast for the senses. The curtain opened.

What followed was no traditional striptease. After a brief appetiser of swirling veils and sparkling g-strings the girls treated us to a highly explicit private view. Their every movement was carefully crafted to expose tantalising glimpses of what I can only describe as a gynaecological close-up.

The male interest was provided by two hulks, evidently chosen for their ability to fill their massive black leather jock straps. But there was something eerily detached about their demeanour. They displayed as much libido as a pair of eunuchs. In fact, they looked more interested in one another than in the lovely ladies they were supposed to be lusting after.

132

Conundrum confirmed my suspicions.

"Gay as geckos the pair of them."

It was raining as we exited Raymond's. Gaudy Soho neon gleamed on wet pavements. Only early evening and Conundrum was still up for more mischief. We drifted into the *Coach and Horses* and squeezed ourselves into two seats at the bar.

"Did you note how Raymond's temptresses attract the eye with their sequined triangles and tiny jewels? Like X marks the spot. Men must be such mindless spermbrains that without something bright to identify the target they might end up trying to shag bottle banks instead."

Conundrum downed another large scotch and soda.

"Women are the real guardians of the sexual wellspring. When Venus commands, Priapus must obey. We were not designed to say no. Hardly rates as consensual sex if we can't refuse, does it? Anyway, that's our humble role in the order of things. We are quite literally nature's dickheads. Men are the ones doomed to be led astray through the weakness of their flesh."

"Yes, but surely not all women are like that?"

I felt ridiculous even as I made this pious statement.

"Have you tried bananas, Henri?"

"Bananas?"

"Yes, bananas. It's obvious when you think about it."

"It is?"

"Why yes. Bananas ripen other fruit. Put a couple of Fyfe's finest next to a hard mango and it will be ready to eat in no time. I once tried it on a frosty young lady. Just to soften her up, if you follow my gist. Slipped into her room in the middle of the night and laid a ring of bananas around her bed as she slept."

"And did it work?"

"Did it work, Henri? I thought it would take a while to bring her on. But when I went back to monitor progress an hour later, she reached out and grabbed me. She was amazingly warm and soft. Like a ripe fruit. Only problem was afterwards, when she commented on the curious smell. You know bananas make a bit of a pong? Well, she thought it was me. Sent me packing."

Conundrum hesitated.

"Now where was I, Henri? Ah yes, Raymond. That's it. So, where does that leave your poetic notions of the 'Eternal Feminine' now that you have had the essentials of femininity waved in your face in such graphic detail?"

I started to protest. Conundrum would have none of it.

"The exposé of what women keep in their panties always sends me away curiously at peace. I am ready to be released back into the community. And thanks to good old Raymond, the streets of London are a safer place."

Conundrum now stood up and addressed the crowd at the bar of the *Coach and Horses*.

"I would like to propose a toast. To good old Raymond!"

No one took notice as he raised his glass in military style as if saluting the memory of an old comrade in arms. Clearly, such eccentricities were par for the course in here.

"Lest we forget."

He downed his drink in a single gulp and banged the glass on the bar. A woman next to us caught his eye. Conundrum returned her look far longer than is polite.

"What are you leering at me like that for? I'm not one of those tarts in Raymond's, you old pervert."

If what Conundrum said next wasn't exactly action before thought, it was certainly an act of the utmost audacity.

"Not even in my dreams, dear lady, I can assure you, would I consider leering at you."

"You rude old tosser! Take that!"

Quick as a flash, he brushed aside the lady's hand as she aimed a half pint of Guinness at him. The black stuff splashed all over me. Conundrum was unmarked.

"Thank you so much, dear lady, for sharing your drink with us. Now come along, Henri. Time we were going."

Mopping my clothes for the second time that day, I followed Conundrum out of the *Coach and Horses* into the crowded Soho streets. I had never seen him so drunk, so abusive, so wantonly offensive. Normally, the more he drank the less he said. *In Vino Brevitas* was a matter of principle, or so he had once confided in me. I was hugely disappointed. As ever, Conundrum was able to read my mind.

"I really can't see the point of going to a pub and not getting drunk, seriously drunk."

Without a word, I took my leave.

"Hang on a moment, Henri."

I was halfway across Cambridge Circus when he called me back. I reluctantly retraced my steps.

"I haven't told you about tomorrow's assignment."

"Tomorrow? Not sure I can make it. Sorry."

"Travel piece for an American mag. Quick rummage through the old jumble in the heritage attic. Stately homes, thatched cottages, dreaming spires, vicars drinking warm beer on village greens. All the sights and sounds of Merrie England. And a seaside resort too, if you please. God, what a bore! But if we get our skates on we can wrap up the whole thing in one day and be back in dear old London before closing time."

It was pointless to argue.

"So pick me up tomorrow. 8am sharp. Right here."

Conundrum stamped his foot to indicate a precise spot on the pavement of Cambridge Circus.

I trudged home in a bloody mood. How could I have put faith in this man? My master magician was just another dirty old man, a drunk with intellectual pretensions, one of a dying breed of pub philosophers still hanging on in Soho hostelries like the *Coach and Horses*. Was this to be my fate as well?

MERRY ENGLAND

I drove to Cambridge Circus next morning as instructed and was there at 8 on the dot. Conundrum didn't show until gone 8.30. The moment he spoke with a dull groan, I could tell he was nursing a monumental hangover.

"I'm afraid the day has started without me and will have to continue without my active participation."

Was this his pompous way of acknowledging he was late? My anger of the previous evening was rekindled.

"So much for your theory of *In Vino Brevitas.*"

"Nothing wrong with the theory, Henri. Trouble is, I devised it when I was stone cold sober. Even as I lifted the first glass I had that awful sense of *déjà bu.*"

I ignored his attempt at a witticism.

"So where to now?"

"Didn't I say?"

"No, you didn't."

"Southend."

"Southend?"

"Yes, afraid so. Wake me up when we get there."

Conundrum promptly fell asleep. Already the morning sun shone bright and hot on the tarmac. A scorcher was in prospect. Pretty soon we got stuck in the Easter Sunday traffic. Everyone heading for the coast. Rivers of hot metal flowed out of London like lava from a great stinking volcano. It took ages to grind our way through the East End via a girdle of urban expressway out into the realm of golf courses, gravel pits and caravan parks that is suburban Essex.

At last we reached Southend. Conundrum awoke to the sight of bodies of every shape and size laid out in rows on the beach, some tightly muscled, others wobbly as waterbeds, quivering like blancmange. Tattooed limbs and bellies with mermaids, dragons, tigers, death heads grimacing. A whole menagerie cavorting on winter white skin exposed to the first rays of summer. A young girl with tampons and inflated condoms hanging from her hat wandered up and down the promenade, a lone Saturday night reveller shell-shocked as a war zone survivor. A baby's nappie oozing shit lay discarded on the ground next to folk eating ice cream.

I took in these details at a glance, expecting Conundrum to deliver a withering judgement about the general ghastliness of England at play. But he didn't say a word. He had other things on his mind. I followed his meandering progress through the vaguely drifting Sunday crowds towards the pier.

He strode the boards of the great jetty sticking out across the mud flats of the Thames estuary. Soon we left far behind the tawdry promenade and entered a purer space suspended midway between sky and sea. We were just tiny blobs of organic life in an infinite universe. Conundrum didn't look back over his shoulder to make sure I was there. Maybe he didn't care? Or he just knew I would be following him, powerless as ever to do otherwise.

A cluster of ramshackle wooden buildings stood right at the end of the pier, their blistered white paint stained by rusty iron bolts. A recent fire had apparently removed the rest. What were we doing here? Conundrum sat down on a bench next to a small shack. A creaking sign swayed in the breeze: *Madame Renée Clairvoyante*. I peered through the window. I could make out a crystal ball on a table next to an overflowing ashtray. My view was suddenly cut off by a hand drawing the curtain.

Next thing I knew, the door inched open. Conundrum was admitted by a theatrical old crone in a gipsy costume. She ushered him inside in a respectful manner that suggested he was a cut above the ordinary punter to be sent away with vague hopes of good fortune in love and business. As she closed the door, *Madame Renée* gazed into my eyes. We looked at one another for no more than a couple of seconds, but I had the sensation it was long enough for her to read me completely in that single glance. Was I being sized up as a prospective customer?

I made several circuits around the end of the pier while the door remained closed on the secret doings of *Madame Renée* and Conundrum. What was going on? It wasn't in character for Conundrum to have his fortune told. To pass the time I snapped a few pictures of nothing in particular and then stared vacantly into space. The horizon seemed both infinitely distant and extremely close. Gradually, my spirits took wing across the wide expanse of air and water. I still had solid ground beneath my feet, but it felt like I was hovering, almost flying. Hard to tell how long this delicious state of suspension lasted. All of sudden, the spell was broken and Conundrum stood before me.

"Come along, Henri. Time we were pressing on."

He offered no word of explanation about his rendez-vous. I looked to *Madame Renée* for a clue. She was just shutting the door of her salon. Again our eyes met. She spoke in a whisper so soft she might not have been speaking at all.

"No. Not now. Not yet."

In spite of the heat, a shiver ran down my spine. I turned away and followed Conundrum. He had unbuttoned his jacket. It flapped about in the breeze that was scudding in over the mud flats. I noticed his waistcoat had acquired a new tone, or at least one I hadn't seen before: a dark, reflective colour, like burnished gunmetal. So the tricks with the magic waistcoat were starting again. Evidently, something of significance had happened behind the drawn curtains of *Madame Renée Clairvoyante*.

Walking back along the pier, we observed a golden Labrador neck high in the water barking angrily out to sea. His contented owner roared him on approvingly.

"That's it, George. Keep the Germans away. Good dog."

Conundrum surveyed the ooze and slime of the shore.

"How I love the foetid, swampy pong of low tide: the seaweedy, protozoon realm where we humanoids began the long journey into the curious shape we assume today. Our true roots are right here, Henri, among these unprepossessing pools."

Conundrum fished a watch from his waistcoat pocket.

"And now, Lord Ponsonby awaits."

"Lord Ponsonby?"

"The article needs a dose of British nobility. So we must proceed forthwith to Ponsonby Towers. To join a group of American lady travel writers being lunched by his lordship. Must be desperate if he's asking in stray hacks for a bit of scoff. I know it sounds ghastly, but *noblesse oblige* and all that."

Ponsonby Towers announced itself with a dilapidated gatehouse, of which the gate was half shut. I pulled over onto the verge and got out of the car to open it. The rusty iron grill – a humble five bar farmyard affair – promptly fell off its hinges and collapsed into the long grass with a sigh. Meanwhile, Conundrum took the opportunity to urinate on the crumbling masonry of the gatehouse. As he did so, a minibus drove past. Conundrum was too occupied to notice the half dozen or so ladies, their faces pressed to the windows. Finally, as he adjusted his clothing, he permitted himself a brief observation.

"Second-rate Gothic Revival. Hardly worth pissing on. Doesn't augur well for the house."

Meanwhile, the minibus sped off up the drive towards Ponsonby Towers bearing the American lady travel writers. What on earth would they make of Conundrum after he had relieved himself so shamelessly on his lordship's gatehouse? There was no time for further conjecture. A yapping dog now came tearing towards us. It was a small Jack Russell. It looked like it had very sharp teeth. Conundrum made haste to regain the safety of the car. I did likewise. We shut the doors just in time.

"Drive on Henri. Lunch *chez* Ponsonby awaits."

I drove down the long potholed drive. The barking dog raced alongside, yapping excitedly as it tried to take bites out of the tyres. Once or twice it bounced high in the air, leaving smeary tongue and nose marks on the window. Conundrum attempted ineffectually to shoo it away.

"Must be jealous I put my own marker on its territory. If it's one of Ponsonby's brutes, we can expect no quarter."

"It's not very big. Perhaps it just wants to make friends?"

"I doubt it. Have you seen those teeth?"

As we turned a bend in the drive the main façade of Ponsonby Towers came into view. Conundrum groaned.

"God, even worse than the gatehouse. A bungled attempt by some local builder to ape the Strawberry Hill look."

The Jack Russell now spotted Lord Ponsonby's peacocks parading proudly on the croquet lawn. The tiny hound took off like a rocket. Soon feathers were flying as the squawking birds sought to run for cover. Conundrum, seeing his chance to make it to the front door of the house without being attacked by the dog, quickly got out of the car. But he was thwarted in this by the sudden appearance of Lord Ponsonby, alerted by the raucous cries of his terrified peacocks.

The aristocrat was a tall figure in cavalry twill trousers. The leather buttons on his Harris Tweed shooting jacket were shiny as fresh conkers. A slight stoop of the shoulders, the product of his advanced age, softened an otherwise rigid military bearing. The aquiline face was flushed red with anger as it confronted Conundrum.

"Is that your Jack Russell, sir?"

"And what if he is?"

Why Conundrum elected to assume custody of the dog was beyond me. Lord Ponsonby was livid.

"Well, he's a mess, sir. A first rate bloody mess. I'm within my rights to shoot him. And I'd shoot the owner too for that matter. Do you realise how long it takes to get peacocks settled? Call him off immediately!"

Conundrum looked evasive.

"Call him off, I say. Or I'll set my own dogs on him. And on you too while they're at it."

Conundrum remained obstinately silent.

"Well, get on with it man!"

Still, nothing happened. I feared Lord Ponsonby would self-ignite from sheer incandescence. At last, Conundrum spoke.

"Actually, I'm not sure I can oblige."

"What's that? You just said he's your dog, dammit! So call him off my peacocks before they have a heart attack."

"Actually, if you care to recall, I didn't exactly say he was mine. I only asked, what if he is."

Lord Ponsonby focused a twin-bore gaze of pure hatred on Conundrum, as if about to exterminate an item of vermin.

"Don't split hairs with me. Call him off! Your miserable cur is disturbing Lady Ponsonby."

"Disturbing Lady Ponsonby? I am so sorry. How very inconvenient. Is she resting?"

"I'll have you know my dearest wife is buried under the croquet lawn. Laid her to rest myself. You wouldn't want to incur her wrath even now, I can assure you."

Conundrum adopted a softer stance.

"And let me assure your lordship that the wee pup has nothing to do with us. Followed us up the drive. We thought he must be one of yours."

"One of mine? How can you even think any dog of mine would dare behave so disgracefully?"

Lord Ponsonby shouted angrily at the Jack Russell.

"Stop tormenting my peacocks, you miserable cur!!"

Lord Ponsonby now squared up to Conundrum. I thought fisticuffs were about to fly.

"Well he came with you. And I'm holding you personally responsible. Do something!"

Conundrum shrugged as if accepting his fate.

"Oh, very well. I'll see what I can do. But I have no training in canine discipline."

Cool as a cucumber, Conundrum inserted two fingers in the corners of his mouth and emitted a high-pitched whistle, barely audible. Immediately, the dog froze. A second whistle brought it bounding towards us. It crouched obediently at Conundrum's feet, waiting for further orders.

"Good boy. Now go home. Go!"

Conundrum pointed towards the gatehouse. The dog obeyed instantly. Stupefied, Lord Ponsonby watched the Jack Russell race back up the drive in a cloud of dust.

"And you still expect me to believe he's not your dog? How did you get him to obey you then? Answer me that!"

At this point, a round of applause erupted. Conundrum was enthusiastically engulfed by the Lady Travel Writers of America who had witnessed the entire spectacle through the drawing room window. They too were anxious to know how he had performed his trick.

"My dear ladies. It's just a question of natural authority … and respect for animals."

Lord Ponsonby eyed Conundrum with suspicion.

"Well, now you're here, you'd better come in."

Sherry was served by a butler in a shabby, ill-fitting uniform that might have been borrowed from a theatrical costumier. Lord Ponsonby sought to revert to his regular role of *grand seigneur* graciously condescending to impress his visitors.

"Welcome to Ponsonby Towers. In the family since the Norman Conquest. Lineage doesn't come more ancient than that. Over 900 years and still going strong. Not bad, what?"

At the mention of the Normans, Conundrum snorted. It was the dangerous sound of an animal whose hackles are up.

"Anything wrong?"

Lord Ponsonby's remark was intended as a shot across the bow to tell Conundrum not to dare spoil his show.

"Wrong? Why should anything be wrong?"

Lord Ponsonby wasn't quick enough to stop Conundrum answering his own question.

"Unless of course you think it right for the Norman invaders to have robbed the native Saxons of their lawful inheritance: their land, their property, their human rights, their culture, even their wives and children."

Lord Ponsonby looked apoplectic. Bereft of speech he was powerless to get a word in.

"But I've got to hand it to you Normans. You are still in possession of the spoils nearly a thousand years later."

The American lady journalists turned on Lord Ponsonby with mute accusation. He bravely stood his ground, feet planted firmly on a tiger skin rug. One of the ladies broke the silence.

"I don't want to pass comment on your ancient British history, Lord Ponsonby. But I can tell you that's an endangered species you're standing on. I trust you didn't shoot it."

Another lady chimed in.

"Like you did those poor, defenceless Saxons."

Lord Ponsonby looked flustered.

"And what if I did shoot the bally tiger? What's the harm in that? We hunters actually protect the wildlife."

Murmurs of disapproval spread among the American ladies closing ranks around Conundrum.

"You probably think I'm some unfeeling old aristocrat, all blood and feathers, and no concern for the lower orders."

"I wouldn't put it that mildly."

It took Lord Ponsonby a second or two to grasp how Conundrum had regained the initiative. He now decided frontal attack would be the best form of defence.

"And where do you stand on this hunting issue?"

Conundrum pretended he hadn't heard the question.

"Well? Where do you stand?"

Conundrum waited until he had everyone's full attention.

"Oh, here. There. Everywhere."

"Everywhere?"

"Yes, everywhere. And nowhere too."

"Nowhere?"

"Yes, but on balance, more like everywhere."

"But you must have an opinion on the subject. Stand up and be counted. Either you are for or against."

"An opinion, Lord Ponsonby? Only a half-wit has just one opinion. Anyone with more than half a brain is perfectly capable having two, three or more opinions on any given subject you care to mention. As for myself, I try not to have opinions, especially cherished ones, certainly not those of the deeply held variety. Yes, I think I can agree with myself on that."

You could have heard the proverbial pin drop. Lord Ponsonby's eyes bulged in their sockets. But behind them all was doubt and confusion.

"I expect decent manners in my house. It's my right to insist on that. I don't care who you are."

"Well, that makes two of us."

"How so?"

"I don't care who I am either. Never have done. Hope I never will. Don't see the point."

Lord Ponsonby, shaking with impotent rage, now opted for a tactical withdrawal to consider how best to deal with this unexpected and totally unpredictable nuisance.

"We shall resume this conversation anon. But first, if you will excuse me, there are some urgent things I must attend to."

His lordship barked an order to the butler who followed him out. Conundrum now had the stage to himself. He turned to the Lady Travel Writers of America with an ingratiating grin.

"England is full of old buffers like Ponsonby who boast they came over with the Normans. Bunch of carpetbaggers. They forget to mention they stole the country from the Saxons and exploited it for their own imperialistic purposes. And now they pretend to be the true sons of England's green and pleasant land. Don't call themselves Normans any more, but they are still running the show. Actually used to hunt Saxons you know, until they discovered foxes were more fun."

The Lady Travel Writers of America hung on his every word, scribbling in notebooks. They had discovered instead of the tired old story of a genuine British lord, a red-hot social issue. Conundrum expounded further on his theme and even spoke of his work in progress for *A Real History of England*.

"First chapter is entitled *Rape of the Saxons*. In which I indict the Normans for all their crimes from the brutal invasions of England, Wales, Scotland and Ireland to the bloodshed of the Hundred Years War, the worst excesses of the British Empire, the barbarous practices of public schools and the ridiculous accents of the British upper class. And to cap it all, the Normans now claim to be English. While the native English have had their very identity stolen and their national destiny hijacked."

The American ladies were outraged. Condemnation of Lord Ponsonby and his Norman henchmen was unanimous.

"Did you see how meanly he treats that butler of his?"

"As if he were less than a man."

A mischievous glint sparkled in Conundrum's eye.

"Thereby hangs a tale, good ladies. And a sad one too."

Conundrum's voice assumed a conspiratorial tone.

"Have you wondered why Ponsonby's butler does not speak? Well, if you will permit, then I shall tell you."

There was a silent nodding of heads.

"The following events happened in a charming stately home not dissimilar to this. The host, like our gracious Lord Ponsonby, was most attentive to the needs and desires of his guests. One of them praises the delicious goat's testicles served for lunch. Says he would love some more. Bollocks the Butler is summoned by his lordship. Goes off to consult Cook. Returns with solemn tread. Presents apologies. No more goat's testicles, my lord. Guest is disappointed."

Conundrum paused.

"His lordship reckons it's not a good show. In fact, a damn poor show. Will Bollocks make positively sure Cook isn't hiding any goat's testicles in her private larder? Butler departs. Absent a long time. His lordship says what a sterling fellow Bollocks is. *Would do absolutely anything for me. Decades of loyal servitude. Won't come back empty-handed. Matter of breeding, don't you know?*' At last, Bollocks returns. White-faced, tight-lipped, limping slightly. Lifts the silver salver. *'I managed to find just the one, sir.'* Serves the guest who wolfs it down greedily. *'Damn delicious. Even better than the others. I'd give anything for just one more.'* His lordship exhorts his butler. *Do go and have another look, Bollocks, there's a good chap.'* Pained expression masked behind a long suffering professional smile, Bollocks hobbles off. This time, he is gone for a very long time."

Conundrum drew breath.

"Eventually, Bollocks returns, dragging himself along with the greatest difficulty. *I found just one more, sir. It's definitely the last.'* His voice has assumed a strange falsetto. He serves the guest who now looks suspiciously at the small piece of meat, then goes pale and pushes the plate away. The butler faints on the floor. His lordship offers the meaty morsel to his gundog. The slavering Irish wolfhound makes short work of it. Was self-sacrifice ever so cruelly rewarded?"

At this critical moment, a gong sounded and the butler drew open the double doors connecting to the dining room.

"Lunch is served, ladies and gentlemen."

Suddenly the room fell silent. Everyone noted that the butler's voice was a bit on the high side for a man. Conundrum gave a knowing wink, then pulled his watch from a waistcoat pocket and consulted it carefully.

"Gosh, is that the time? Alas, we'll have to skip lunch, I'm afraid. Prior engagement, don't you know?"

"Skip lunch? Prior engagement? What the deuce?"

Lord Ponsonby looked as if he was about to explode.

"Sadly time's winged chariot and all that. Perhaps we might just trouble you to pose for a snap in front of the ancestral pile. Henri will take care of that. Then we really must press on."

Lord Ponsonby's anger abated instantly. As if he had suddenly spotted the delicious prospect of being instantly shot of this troublesome guest.

"Why, yes. Of course. Be my guest. Or rather, don't be my guest. Capital. Absolutely capital. Don't let me detain you."

Conundrum waved a fond farewell to the Lady Travel Writers of America. But they weren't ready to let him depart.

"Do you really have to go? What else should we visit? Do you have any savvy tips? They say Cambridge is a must-see."

"Cambridge? You don't want to go there."

"We don't?"

"Good lord, no. Go to Ely. Imposing Norman cathedral built by Ponsonby's ancestors. The Bishop of Ely is a big cheese. He gets to kick ass in Cambridge."

Lord Ponsonby looked as if he were capable of one last eruption. But when I pointed to my camera he followed me outside and stationed himself next to a lichen-encrusted statue of a griffin. He looked like a warrior straight out of the Bayeux Tapestry, presenting the rugged profile of a Norman battle-axe.

I could click only once before he turned on his heels and, without a word, went back into the house to work the old aristocratic charm on the Lady Travel Writers of America.

Conundrum was in the car, prising small chunks of Lord Ponsonby's gravel drive from the soles of his shoes.

"If only it were as easy to rid oneself of this cursed Norman legacy, Henri. That old fool with his thousand years heritage of robber baron. I wonder why the sun bothers to rise on a place like this. Why the flowers don't just wilt and die."

We stopped for lunch at a thatched pub in a picture postcard village. The bill of fayre (sic) informed us in quaint old lettering that good food takes time. I went out to take some snaps. When I got back, Conundrum took one look at the meal.

"And here is proof that bad food takes time too."

Conundrum was in a foul mood.

"Oh ye inglenooks of Olde England! Ye copper kettles and horse brasses. Ye hunting prints and jolly yeomen of days of yore. Ye drying up cloths with the laws of cricket. Ye oak beams on which to bash one's bonce. Ye surly landlords with your soapy lager and inedible pub grub! From all these works of the devil, may the Good Lord deliver us. Amen!"

After lunch we drove on through country lanes full of horses being driven about in their boxes as if their human owners were no more than hired chauffeurs. I parked the car by the church in Grantchester.

"Oh, to be in England now that April's there."

Conundrum stood solemnly with bowed head by the War Memorial. It was dedicated to the memory of *MEN WITH SPLENDID HEARTS*.

"Splendid hearts are the stuff of ancient history. Where Rupert Brooke once lodged, Jeffrey Archer now resides."

We strolled into Cambridge along the river through grassy meadows. Soon the sinuous footpath took us away from the banks of the Granta onto an asphalt strip that ran straight as an arrow. All romance and mystery were banished. A gang of young folk on mountain bikes forced us off the track. Conundrum lost his balance and came a cropper. Surprisingly, he had an almost beatific look as he dusted himself off.

"Young life pushing aside the old. An autumn leaf blown away by a fresh spring breeze. A good stiff broom to clear the path. We must not get upset. That is nature's way, Henri."

Paradise Nature Reserve, full of dog shit and beer cans, was but a prelude for the scene awaiting us on the patch of green by Silver Street Bridge. There was more garbage strewn about here than in the whole of Southend. And a great throng of people sat contentedly in the midst of it all.

I went off in search of more shots of Merrie England for the magazine. I thought my luck was in when I spotted a band of Morris Men waiting on a street corner for the lights to change. I grabbed a couple of snaps. A couple of the men with bells on their knees and ribbons on their boaters gave me a filthy look. Had it not been for the presence of children, I suspected they would have dragged me down a side alley and, with a hey ho sweet nonny-nonny, given me a damn good thrashing.

I beat an apologetic retreat. We now proceeded to the famous Backs, those lush meadows by the Cam spanned by comely bridges. With a broad sweep of his hand, Conundrum encompassed the noble prospect.

"Oh, ye city of deluded dons. Earth hath not a spectacle to show more fair and more farcical than this."

Young lads and lasses in amorous embrace were dotted all over the grass among the spring flowers. Some couples came as close to penetrative sex as was possible when fully clothed. I felt we were intruding on an orgy of epic proportions. Conundrum stepped gingerly between the bodies, taking note of this and that, not like a *voyeur* but more the good shepherd admiring the lustful antics of his rams and ewes.

"Let professors pontificate on Kierkegaard, Socrates, and the Critique of Pure Reason. While more enlightened souls tune in to the harmonious hum of happy hormones. Life straining to reproduce life. For this is the real truth of the universe."

As if he had been seeking her out, Conundrum carefully threaded his way through the bodies in the meadow towards a solitary young girl. She was studiously reading a book, oblivious to all the love making around her.

Conundrum sat down on the grass a few yards away and propped himself against a tree. He shut his eyes and appeared to doze off. I squatted on the grass and watched the young girl as she read her book. Her eyes scanned the pages with a singular intensity. Her lips trembled as if mouthing the words out loud.

Then the most amazing thing happened. Conundrum began speaking softly as if in a trance. He seemed to be talking in his sleep, reciting something that was neither poetry nor prose, but somewhere in between. I hung on his every word.

"Let me be the wind in your willows. The mill on your floss. The little house on your prairie. The midnight in your children. The great in your expectations. The riddle of your sands. The lord of your rings."

At first, the young girl did not react. Then her eyes stopped moving across the page. She let the book lie unheeded on her lap. Next, she removed her glasses and looked up as Conundrum's voice droned on like a magician casting a spell.

"Let me be the catcher in your rye. The remains of your day. The seven pillars of your wisdom. The sense in your sensibility. Your passage to India. Your flight from the enchanter. Your lost illusions. The dream in your midsummer's night. The labour of your lost loves. Your comedy of errors. Your much ado about nothing."

With Conundrum partially concealed behind the tree, the girl looked around to see who might be talking to her. But her eyes, myopic and unfocused, couldn't figure it out. She now lowered her eyelids and allowed herself to drift away on the magic carpet of Conundrum's mysterious words.

"The name of your rose. The perfume in your garden. The tender in your night."

The girl was enmeshed in this wondrous web of literary love. She looked truly beautiful. I was amazed that Conundrum was capable of such delicacy of feeling even if for him it was nothing more than a babble of words. But whatever his purpose, he now brought the girl down to earth with a cruel bump.

"Let me be the turn of your screw. The pride in your prejudice. The grapes of your wrath. Your year of the plague. The decline in your fall. The war in your peace. The end of your affair. The death in your soul. The elegy in your graveyard."

The young girl winced as if she had been struck in the face. Conundrum had broken her like a twig. Her look of horror remains etched in my memory to this day.

He stood up and grinned.

"Come along now, Henri. The party is over."

I stole a last, anguished look of shame at the young girl. Her face was ashen white as if she had seen a ghost. How dare Conundrum mock her with his devilish mischief? I wanted to talk to her, soothe her with words of my own. But how could I step into a place Conundrum had just desecrated?

"What was all that about? What business is it of yours to hurt someone's feelings like that?"

"All for your benefit, Henri. As is everything I do."

"For my benefit? How do you figure that?"

"What a hopeless romantic you are, Henri? What are feelings but a *bouillabaisse* of electro-chemical reactions. Nothing more. The lass couldn't even see me and yet she felt love for a complete stranger. I think I proved my point."

"But didn't you see that look on her face?"

"Don't get on your moral high horse. Only more painful when you fall off."

There was sinister menace in Conundrum's voice. We walked back in silence to Grantchester. I was disturbed by this latest manifestation of Conundrum's gratuitous nastiness. He really seemed to have it in for the human race. But there was something that troubled me even more. His comment that it was all for my benefit. What on earth had I got myself into?

"And is there honey still for tea?"

Conundrum's keen eyes surveyed the scene.

"Yes, I do believe there is."

In Grantchester Village Hall we ate home-made cakes baked by the good ladies of Grantchester Women's Institute in aid of the Grantchester Boy Scouts, one or two of whom stood awkwardly in attendance. After tea we took a walk along the river to Byron's Pool. The place where once the poet bathed naked by moonlight was an inert expanse of stagnant water beneath a concrete weir. On a mouldy tree stump some wit had scrawled in a crude hand: "What ho, Jeeves! Has anyone seen Byron?"

After that we headed home. Not a word passed between us. As we entered London Conundrum ordered me to make an unexpected detour. A drive through Docklands brought us to the Woolwich Free Ferry. The weather was now overcast. A dull leaden sky merged imperceptibly into the slate grey of the Thames. Low tide exposed glistening banks of cement-coloured sludge. Enough greyness to swallow the entire rainbow.

Dreaming of one day being able to see a brand new spectrum seemed utterly foolish. I finally gave up the thankless task of trying to take an interesting photograph. I stared silently out over the slimy waters. I wished I was somewhere else, far away from Conundrum. But not only was he standing beside me, annoyingly close, he was also inside my head.

"To the disbelieving eye, the Ganges is not a pretty sight. But that doesn't prevent it being a holy river to many millions."

"But the Thames isn't a holy river."

A gleam infused Conundrum's expression.

"How do you know it isn't, Henri? Monet thought so. Until he came to London and painted the effects of sunlight filtered through the polluted smog over the Thames, no one thought there was an ounce of beauty here. Even now, long after his pictures have been hailed as masterpieces of world art, people still don't believe it. They see the beauty of the canvases while failing to see any beauty in the scene that inspired them."

I now spotted a bright blue plastic container floating downstream on the slime-grey waters of the river.

"Well, Henri, there's a splash of colour for you. And if it comes courtesy of a discarded drum of toxic chemical, so what?"

Suddenly the sun shone through a gap in the clouds. The bright blue container was bathed in a halo of golden light. Next I noticed another object materialise in the distance. A boat had detached itself from the far bank and was heading towards us.

"So perhaps the Woolwich Free Ferry is awaiting its artistic liberator, Henri?"

The camera leapt into my hands. The burst of sunshine lasted a couple of seconds, long enough to shoot some stunning pictures of the approaching vessel through the red-golden haze. It was exquisite. Yes, Turner would have loved it.

For me this sublime end to the day helped put to the back of my mind the various unpleasant things that had gone before. It was late evening when we finally got back to central London. I dropped Conundrum at Cambridge Circus precisely where I had collected him and went straight home.

Next day I went for a swim at the local pool. The slimy, ill-ventilated corner that accommodated the showers looked more evil than ever. In this tiny space four naked bodies were wedged in close together. I tried to pretend it had the makings of a noble scene like Cézanne's bathers. If I only I could see things with the eye of an artist. But I couldn't. One chap was engaged in what looked like the annual spring clean of his foreskin. Another executed a deep anal probe with a sponge. It was too horrible. I dressed hurriedly and took my shower at home.

Only later did it occur to me that the originals for Cézanne's bathers might have presented an equally sordid scene. But the artist had painted not what he saw but what he wanted to see. Perhaps Conundrum had got it wrong. Not that beauty is everywhere but that someone with an eye thirsting for beauty can create it anywhere. Was that why I was unable to see beyond the surface ugliness? Did I lack a nobility of vision? Perhaps beauty can only be perceived by those who have beauty inside them already. And if this was so, how could I acquire it?

Surely not from Conundrum?

CHARADES

Conundrum phoned a couple of days later.

"Editor wants us to attend some charity do at the Savoy. Says it'll be high society, the glittering London social scene for heaven's sake. But a free meal is a free meal."

The thought of Conundrum socialising with high society seemed incongruous. I was shocked.

"It's a black tie bash. Hire yourself a monkey suit, Henri. Tomorrow evening, 7.30 for 8. No need to bring a camera. See it as a night out, a small reward for services rendered."

Something so completely out of character should have put me on my guard. However, the following evening I turned up at the Savoy in an ill-fitting dinner jacket hastily hired from Moss Bros. I had cut it a bit fine. The drinking was already well underway. So I joined an animated throng quaffing champagne and gobbling canapés in the River Restaurant. I hadn't eaten all day so I availed myself of whatever the waiters and waitresses presented on elegant silver trays: quail's egg and caviar, lobster, melon balls, prawns and other delicacies. Snatched conversations were equally of the finger food variety.

It was not an enormous gathering. I quickly established that Conundrum was not present. No matter. Plenty to eat and drink. Sociable crowd of people. Many snatched conversations soon terminated by cries of 'must circulate'. Women outshining men, not only in their striking dresses. Their presence stronger in all departments. A pair of real stunners with more balls than a snooker table guffawed like beery blokes at a bar. Their male escorts not taking part, more in attendance, deferential even. The buzz of competing conversations merged into an abstract noise where individual words had no meaning.

Then I saw a beautiful picture. Lurid colours of pink and green décor and through an illuminated arch the timeless tableau of a waiter poised with a yellow-labelled bottle frozen in the eternal pose of his profession. The recipient of the champagne was a stylish young lady, blonde hair set off magnificently by the electric blue of her off the shoulder cocktail dress. A perfect expression of a single moment to encapsulate an entire era of refined pleasure. Worthy of an oil painting and certainly the vintage stuff of the very best photo reportage.

But, faithful to Conundrum's instructions, I had left my camera at home. Damn! What an idiot! This was a picture to die for. A defining image. A masterpiece. A slice of social history. All I would be able to do is talk about it like an angler describing the one that got away. To make matters worse, I caught sight of myself in a mirror and saw what a sorry figure I cut.

Oh, Henri, you really don't have what it takes, do you? It was then the awful realisation hit me. I was talking to myself in exactly the way Conundrum would talk to me. He didn't even have to be present to mess with my mind, tinker with my thoughts. I recalled his comment about everything he did being for my benefit. Surely not this too? But hadn't he told me I needn't bring my camera? So perhaps the lesson was not always to do as he said. God, this was getting confusing.

Then something else struck me. The crowd was thinning. People were saying their farewells. I noted with alarm I was the only man in a dinner jacket. The others were all wearing lounge suits. Dinner? A black tie dinner? Conundrum had said that, hadn't he? Yes, of course he had. Oh Christ! I had just spent half an hour filling my boots at the wrong party. Trying to appear casual I slipped past the hosts shaking hands with their departing guests and made my ignominious exit.

I caught up with the correct function well after everyone else had sat down to eat. With the help of a table plan I soon located my seat next to an empty space with a name card that was marked: A CONUNDRUM. The absence of a dot after the letter A suggested this could be the indefinite article rather than the initial of his first name. At least that's how I saw it. Besides, the very idea of Conundrum having a first name like ordinary mortals struck me as improbable. He was simply Conundrum, even though I dared not address him as such.

But whatever truth lay behind the name card, his place at the table remained mysteriously unoccupied throughout dinner so that his absence – or what he would have called his 'lack of presence' – remained, quite literally, a conundrum. Indeed, it was just as the card so clearly stated. I thought I was quite clever to have twigged the point of this little joke, albeit one at my own expense. But that was probably the champagne talking.

A five course dinner came and went. Still no sign of Conundrum. During the interval before the speeches I joined the rush for the Savoy gents. I undid the flies of my rented Moss Bros trousers, wondering how many other chaps had stood in similar pose in this very suit fumbling with an unfamiliar zip.

On the way out I noticed an old drunk propping up a urinal by the door. There was something so settled about his slouched posture, he might have been there for ever. To my surprise, he started talking to me as I passed.

"Should remember to wash my hands before taking a piss. After all the unsavoury mitts I've had to shake, I might risk infecting the dishonourable member."

God knows why I didn't just respond with a polite smile and continue on my way.

"Been here since Armistice Day. Problem is I can't seem to stop pissing, would you believe it? Don't suppose you could get these cloakroom Johnnies to stop brushing dandruff off my shoulders? Can't they see I haven't got any hair?"

He now lifted his wig to reveal a shining dome of a pate. Then he gave me a hideous grin. His dentures dropped down from his upper palate and snapped back up like a sprung trap.

"I've pissed on far fancier porcelain than this. Everything from Villeroy & Boch to Royal Copenhagen. In the end you can't beat good old Armitage Shanks. Want a word of advice from someone who knows? Avoid the stall by the plughole. Everyone else's piss comes flooding past right under your nose. Talk about the river of life. I've had my boots splashed by everyone from Lloyd George to Boy George. I say, that's pretty damn good. Lloyd George to Boy George. Didn't realise I was that funny."

At this point the door of the gents opened. I heard the master of ceremonies introduce the first after dinner speaker. I grabbed the opportunity to beat a retreat. After the speeches, which made hardly any sense at all, I did a tour of the tawdry social scene as it slowly ran out of steam under the influence. Still no sign of Conundrum, so I headed for home.

On the way to the exit I almost tripped over another old drunk dressed in an old-fashioned dinner jacket who might have been the brother of the one who had spoken to me in the gents. This one was sprawled out in a leather armchair, legs akimbo. Looked like he had been sick all over his DJ. His eyes flickered as he seemed to recognise me.

"Good lord, is that you Muffy?"

I said nothing.

"It's me, Buffy. Do remember your dear old Buffy, don't you? Of course you do. Long time no see, Muffy old fellow. What a topping time we had celebrating whatever it was. Coronation of George VI, I think. God what a night! You were so blotto you buttoned up your flies with a cigar smouldering away inside your pants. Must have mistaken it for something else. Surely you remember? Took you ages to realise your pubes were on fire. Smoke pouring out of your crotch before you noticed. By God, you were smashed. Unforgettable. I can still see you racing through the ballroom like a human firework. We had to put you out with a soda syphon in the end."

Buffy scratched his head and looked at me again.

"No, it wasn't you, Muffy. It was Fluffy. Dear old Fluffy. It was Fluffy's stag night. Yes, that was it. Caused severe damage in the conjugal region. Fluffy wasn't the same chap after that. Nuptials cancelled. On account of grilled gonads. Bloody original excuse, mind you. Fun went right out of him. Became a recluse. Gave up smoking altogether. Poor old Fluffy. But a damn good laugh we had all the same. I can see it now. God, how fast he moved. As if his balls were on fire. Which of course they were, as a matter of fact. Trousers were a complete write-off. Expensive night out for poor old Fluffy all told, I'm afraid. But by God, Muffy, what a laugh we had. Couldn't lend me a tenner for a cab, could you? Buy you lunch at the club next week."

Buffy started up again with another long yarn about dear old Fluffy. I must have missed the point of the story because the *dénouement* made no sense at all.

"And do you know what Fluffy said next? Keep the tiara on, darling. How else can I know I'm shagging a duchess? Absolutely bloody brilliant it was. Vintage fucking Fluffy. Don't know how he thinks them all up. Never says the same thing twice. That was it about Fluffy, wasn't it? Always so unlike himself. Invariably so. Typical of the man. So, where was I? Oh, yes. After that, he said something unforgettable. Bloody unforgettable. Now, what was it exactly? I'll be buggered. That's the trouble with Fluffy's unforgettables. I can never bloody well remember them. God, that's funny too, isn't it?"

Buffy now looked me over again as if still struggling to recognise me.

"So who did you say you were? No, don't tell me. Doesn't bloody matter."

Why didn't I walk off? The man was clearly barking mad. But I was held riveted to the spot by some higher force. I simply couldn't move a muscle. And then things got even more strange and uncomfortable. Buffy started to recite a poem.

'I drank Rosé d'Anjou
Out of her shoe
Which was really a treat
On account of her feet
Simply massive in size
Took me quite by surprise.'

Then to my horror, Buffy broke into song. It was one of those lewd ballads they love to sing in rugby clubs.

"The Mayor of Bayswater,
He has a lovely daughter,
And the hairs on her dicky-di-doe,
Hang down to her knees."

I'll spare you the complete chapter and verse but the real embarrassment came when Buffy tried to get me singing along with the refrain, waving his arms like a deranged conductor.

"One black one, one white one,
And one with a bit of shite on,
And the hairs on her dicky-di-doe,
Hang down to her knees."

Thankfully, Buffy didn't seem to mind continuing solo as he romped through several more verses with extreme gusto.

"The aroma it lingers,
It smells like fish fingers".
"I've licked it and kissed it,
It tastes like a chocolate biscuit."
"You can drive a Morris Minor,
Right up her vagina."

But then Buffy suddenly became even more insistent that I should join in the chorus.

"Come along, Muffy. There's a sport. Sing lustily withal."

I don't know what possessed me – perhaps I felt inclined to humour him by acting my part as his old chum Muffy – or maybe I was simply too drunk and incapacitated to offer further resistance. At any rate my actions were taken out of my hands. Oh what the hell, singing along made no less sense than the rest of this highly surreal evening at the Savoy. Slowly my lips started to move of their own accord.

"One black one, one white one,
And one with a bit of shite on,
And the hairs on her dicky-di-doe,
Hang down to her knees."

At first my words sounded disembodied, as if coming from a long way off. But by the end I was giving it full voice. In the brief silence that followed the chorus, I heard sniggering and a slow hand clap. I turned to find I was the object of amusement for a half dozen revellers. I turned back to see how Buffy would deal with the hecklers. But the chair was empty. There was no Buffy. No one there at all. Had I been singing to myself?

My audience was now hooting and guffawing out loud. I beat an ignominious retreat. Staggering out of the Savoy, only now did I realise how drunk I was. The night air hit me like a sandbag. I weaved my way along Aldwych and practically crawled up Kingsway. Boozed as Burlington Bertie. God knows how I made it home in one piece.

Early next morning a call from Conundrum pierced my splitting headache. I was summoned to the Travellers Club in Pall Mall that afternoon to take some pictures. I arrived ready to confront Conundrum about his non-appearance at the Savoy and those strange encounters. But he brushed my questions aside

"Something cropped up. But I trust you had an amusing evening. You must tell me all about it, Henri. Later."

And that was that. Conundrum paused by the entrance like a tourist guide to deliver a short speech.

"Before we enter the sacred portals of the Travellers Club, permit me a few observations. Admire the threshold polished by countless leather soles of weary explorers dragging themselves back to regale fellow clubmen over a decanter or two of port with unlikely tales of desert heat, of jungle smells, and of natives true and shifty."

Conundrum was as ever in a world of his own.

"Membership of the Travellers was once restricted to gentlemen who travelled out of the British Isles at least 500 miles from London as measured in a direct line. What a delightful idea! All those rectilinear gents pushing forth like laser beams, walking through houses, crossing fields, fording rivers until they had accomplished their 500 miles on the straight and narrow."

I followed Conundrum inside The Travellers.

"Since most members nowadays can hardly manage 50 yards in a direct line, the criteria have been altered. The sort of journey they are looking for now? Crossing the Gobi Desert in a dugout canoe, riding a penny-farthing up K2. Something intrepid with a sense of adventure and a taste for the utterly pointless."

Conundrum charted an erratic course through the vintage leather armchairs.

"Extra points for getting underpaid porters to carry your thunder box to some remote spot offering gratuitous danger, genuine discomfort and a high likelihood of catching some life-threatening disease. Top marks for real eccentricity and resourcefulness. Like leaving a trail of diarrhoea through the rainforest – so the rescue party can eventually find you – as you dodge the poison darts of treacherous tribesmen while leeches suck the life blood from every square inch of exposed flesh. That's the sort of caper to get you a modicum of grudging respect in the Library or possibly even the Smoking Room."

We were now entering the Smoking Room, the club's inner sanctum.

"But the real purpose of The Travellers is to provide explorers a virtual home to dream of when they are far away, a place to hanker after when marooned in some frightful pit, somewhere for one's spiritual slippers to be always waiting by the fireside, a notional nursery where you can return to suckle on the maternal breast. Indeed, you may only appreciate the real value of club membership when you are many miles away."

Conundrum left me to get on with the snaps. I worked first in the Smoking Room where the afternoon light glinted off the bookcases, soft and golden. I thought the place was empty, until I spotted what I took to be an aged 'Traveller' emerging from a deep snooze in one of the leather armchairs. Slowly his watery eyes took me in. A few more seconds careful scrutiny and I obviously looked real enough for him to address me.

"I say. Is that you, Squirters, old thing? Remember that time I danced with Carruthers under the desert moon?"

I couldn't think of a suitable reply. There was no need.

"Damn fine dancer, Carruthers. Have you ever had the pleasure?"

The old explorer looked through me rather than at me. My image might have shimmered hazily on his retina like the mirage of a desert oasis. He seemed uncertain, as if he didn't trust his eyes. Finally he accepted I really must be Squirters.

"Good God, how long has it been, Squirters? Remember that torrid summer in Rangoon? Hot as a whore's crotch before the rains. So much time on our hands we taught the cockroaches to play cricket. Winter in Siberia was a different story. Cold enough to chill the blood in your veins. Piss froze straight from my pecker. Had to snap it off like barley sugar. The piss, that is."

The piss? Surely the old explorer was taking it well and truly. I made to leave.

"Hang around, Squirters old thing. I'll give you some handy tips for your next expedition. A half price pith helmet from Henry Heath's Hat Factory. How to get a discount on your tropical underpants from Turnbull & Asser. Or how about a few tips from my masturbation master class? A devilish two-handed technique I learned in Mongolia? All you need is a half-pound of rancid camel butter and a strong pair of wrists. Guaranteed to blow the roof off a grass hut. Boom! Shall I give you a demo?"

"No, please don't."

"It's really no trouble."

He was now fiddling with his flies.

"No really, I think I can imagine it."

"Not like you to be squeamish, Squirters."

He stopped undoing his flies but left them half open as if he might return to the task.

"Fancy your chances with a giraffe? Need a trampoline for that. An hour of strenuous work for a hard-won climax. Or for the fleet of foot, how about an ostrich on the run? Or do you fancy bigger game? A rhino perhaps? First prime the honourable member in a termite hill. The resulting swelling brings it up to the required size. One of the trickiest manoeuvres is giving it to a goose on the wing. But don't confuse your goose with your gannet or you'll be in for a damn good ducking."

I sensed he was only just warming to his subject.

"Even tried a hippo once. Shagged it all the way up the Nile to Khartoum. Then it shagged me all the way back to Cairo again. A rum do that was. Not really my cup of tea."

The old traveller drew breath.

"I owe it all to Spiffin. The second edition of his *Handy Hints for Lewd Acts of Sexual Gratification with the Indigenous Fauna in Remote Corners of the British Empire* also describes various ingenious methods for shafting inanimate objects, everything from orifices in trees and cacti to letterboxes and even holes on golf courses. Lost my membership at Rawalpindi caught *in flagrante* with the 18th green. After that I stuck strictly to fauna."

Spiffin? I shut my eyes to retrieve a memory. Only now did the penny finally drop. Henry Spiffin was Conundrum's *nom de plume*. He had mentioned his outrageous book during our drive along the M4. But when I opened my eyes the old explorer was nowhere to be seen. The armchair was empty.

"Everything all right, Henri?"

I spun round. Conundrum was right behind me. Giving me a quizzical look that told me I had been wrong-footed yet again. There was no need to ask about the old explorer. Now the truth of those two weird encounters at the Savoy dawned on me with blinding clarity. Conundrum playing his Buffy to my Muffy. As well as the old drunk propping up the urinal.

How did he do it? Pointless to speculate. Why did he do it? No idea. But one thing was clear. Conundrum could pop up in my life in any guise and at any time. So how could I ever be sure if I was dealing with a 'real' person and not an outlandish projection of his deranged imagination? I was up to my neck in something I couldn't even begin to understand.

LOVE VERSUS LECHERY

After those surreal encounters in London I needed a break from Conundrum, but just a couple of days passed before he rang with instructions for another assignment. Somewhere abroad this time, I can't recall where. Things get pretty scrambled from this point. The pace of our travels became unrelenting. No sooner did we get back from wherever it was and delivered our story than we went off again on another trip.

Before I knew it, travels with Conundrum took over my entire life, supplanting whatever had made up the daily routine of my previous existence. Such was the intensity of our journeying I had no time to gather my thoughts. Was Conundrum quite deliberately spinning the merry-go-round faster and faster in order to keep me permanently off balance and prevent me from seeing things too clearly? If blurring my senses was his purpose, then he succeeded admirably.

One week I'd be snapping Greek ruins under a hot Mediterranean sun, the next shivering under torrential rain at Auschwitz contemplating a tangle of metal spectacles the Nazis had removed from their victims. In Brussels I drank beer in surrealist cafés. Prague was truly Kafka-esque, the monolithic castle on the hill tracking my every move, its hundreds of windows eternally vigilant like so many eyes. I reckoned Franz Kafka had every reason to feel acutely paranoid.

In a strange way the hectic pace of travel disembodied me from what I experienced. I did my snaps as if I were an inanimate recording device storing nothing but visual memories, with no reference to personal emotions. Click, click. Job done. On to the next place. Click, click. Strangely, the quality of my work did not suffer. I was certainly more efficient.

On and on it went. My home life vanished. I was never in London long enough to do more than achieve a quick turn round between trips. My photographic record of the red blob of paint on the pavement outside my front door became a haphazard affair. I could only grab a hasty picture as I rushed past. In short, I lost track of everything, swept up in the slipstream of my travels with Conundrum. Past and future dissolved in the constantly moving present. Was I at last learning to live in the now, the blessed here and now?

On our travels my attention was increasingly absorbed by the spectacle of Conundrum the master sorcerer. I don't mean things like seeing his face in statues, reflections in mirrors or his waistcoat changing colours. In fact, he seemed to dispense with party tricks of that kind. I wondered why. Perhaps he had achieved his primary aim. He had me believing in the power of his magic. So there was no need to impress me with yet more tricks. For once the onlooker has been hypnotised by the conjurer he is primed to see magic in his every action.

But Conundrum continued to weave his spell in other ways. There was a powerful aura about him. He could hold me spellbound through his very being. I was to witness first hand the amazing effect he had on others. He seemed to have an uncanny ability to connect with women at a deep unspoken level and get behind their defences. He could get away with anything and took full advantage in an increasingly outrageous manner.

Up to this point, I'd taken Conundrum's frequent sexual innuendo to be the embroidered reminiscences of an elderly man mixing erotic fantasies with real memories. But another trait to his personality emerged on our travels, that of a rampant Priapus. Or to put the matter in modern terms, my philosopher magician revealed himself as an old lecher.

This new persona first reared his head in Berlin. On this occasion Conundrum was interviewing a frosty female bureaucrat in the old STASI HQ in a gloomy office compound. Her replies were vague and evasive.

"Let me say just this. We've had some very difficult issues to deal with. So what I am saying is …"

She droned on like this for several minutes. She showed every sign of wanting to be shot of us at the earliest opportunity. Conundrum tried every tactic to get a response. He even cocked his head at her in a knowing way that said he found the interview just as tiresome as she did. But the lady took no notice and continued to utter her ritual formulae evidently learned on a 'how to stall the media' training course.

Finally, Conundrum stood up. Leaving the tape recorder running, he walked over to the window and stared out. Not even this obvious gesture of boredom brought about any change in her recital of defensive phrases.

"At the end of the day, on a level playing field, we would welcome a transparent dialogue and an informed debate. I've dealt with every conceivable aspect of the matter in a series of published articles you might care to consult."

At this Conundrum sat down again.

"Very good, *Frau Doktor*. Now, with regard to freedom of information and transparency in public affairs, may I ask you a specific question?"

"I also dealt with all that in one of my recent articles. May I give you a reference?"

At this, Conundrum switched off the tape recorder.

"*Frau Doktor* I feel I should be reading you in a library instead of attempting to talk to you in the flesh."

Perhaps it was simply the way Conundrum slowly mouthed the word 'flesh' that had such a startling effect on the lady. First she blushed and then she removed her wire-framed spectacles. This simple act could not have been more erotic if she had taken off her clothes. Meanwhile Conundrum continued to look her firmly in the eye seemingly at a loss what to say next. At last she broke the silence.

"Very well, let's get on with it. Ask me your questions and I will answer them. I can be very direct when I chose to be."

"I don't have any more questions, *Frau Doktor*."

The lady replaced her spectacles and fixed Conundrum in a vice-like stare, as if seeing him properly for the first time.

"You are a very clever man. I see the little drawers in your mind opening and shutting. Filing away index cards covered with strange writing."

"Well, I hope you can't read what is written on them."

"Why not?"

"That would put me at a grave disadvantage."

He said this with a sly smile and a monstrously suggestive wink. At this the lady removed her spectacles again and gave an embarrassed laugh like a teenage girl.

"I don't know what I should make of you."

"You, *Frau Doktor*, can make of me what you will."

Flustered, she replaced her spectacles once more just as Conundrum gathered up the tape recorder.

"Have you finished already?"

Conundrum closed his notebook.

"Did you get all you wanted?"

"For the time being, *Frau Doktor*. Except for the snaps."

"The snaps?"

"Yes, indeed. Young Henri here will do your portrait."

I don't think she had been aware of me until then. Now it was my turn to be flustered. But I did my bit and took a few snaps of the lady bureaucrat at her desk, bespectacled once more, looking the model of prim bureaucratic efficiency.

As we left, Conundrum spoke a few words in German that made the lady blush even more deeply than before. Once outside, he absented himself for the rest of the afternoon and so we went our separate ways.

When I next saw Conundrum that evening back at the hotel he was sauntering across the landing, head in the clouds, his mind clearly on other matters. I waved to him but he didn't notice me. Nor did he notice a silver tray of half-consumed food carelessly left on the floor outside a guest room. He stepped right on it, lost his balance and suddenly came sliding down the grand staircase one foot planted on the remains of a club sandwich, the other on a piece of Black Forest gateau. Like a skateboarder, he raced at breakneck speed on this large silver tray down the elegantly curved stairs and through the open door of a salon where the cream of Berlin society was gathered for a reception.

I looked on in amazement as Conundrum cut a broad swathe through the noble throng of dinner jackets and evening gowns. Finally he came to rest in the arms of an ambassador's wife, pinning her against a column, his head buried deep in her ample bosom. He took an uncommonly long time to extricate himself. Far from being offended, the lady seemed flattered by his close attentions. She graciously proffered her hand for Conundrum to kiss, which he did most gallantly as he procured a serviette from a waiter and mopped the champagne from her heaving breasts.

Now he spotted me hovering in the doorway and waved me in as casually if he were the genial host of this distinguished gathering. Another waiter appeared bearing champagne and we helped ourselves. He told me about his afternoon.

"*Frau Doktor* turned out more forthcoming at the second time of asking. Showed me my STASI file. Must take off my hat to Teutonic thoroughness. They even had a note of my cavortings with one of their top female agents during a walk in the woods in the Harz Mountains on 17 July 1964. And to think *Frau Doktor* had all that on me while giving me the run around with her bureaucratic nonsense. No wonder she didn't bother to answer my silly questions. I don't blame her. Anyway, to cut a long story short I gave her a damn good going over while she clung on to a filing cabinet for dear life. Hope she updated my file afterwards. Want them to know I'm still up to scratch. Matter of personal honour, don't you know?"

Up against a filing cabinet? Had *Frau Doktor* really given in to Conundrum's charms? I could hardly believe it. Surely this was the fantasy of an old man. But the very next day I had proof that his sexual powers, far from declining, were as keen as ever.

"I've fixed us up with a couple of prostitutes, Henri."

"Oh, really?"

"Don't look so shocked. It's all above board. More's the pity. A whore's tour of the red-light district. Sex tourism without the sex. Should be right up your street, Henri."

Conundrum was for some reason in a foul mood. He even seemed intent on antagonising the two prostitutes whom we met in a dingy room. He pointedly ignored them while he spoke into his recording machine.

"About to record interview with a couple of tarts."

The two ladies exploded in a double salvo.

"A couple of tarts?"

Conundrum beamed his rotten lop-sided smile at them.

"Who do you think you're calling a couple of tarts?"

"We'll have you know we're a pair of sluts."

"And dirty little sluts at that."

Conundrum seemed delighted with this.

"So be it, my dirty little sluts. What a joy to meet you."

The girls introduced themselves by their working names *Klit* and *Ekstase*. The interview that followed was a riotous affair, partly in German but mostly in English, their preferred language for talking shop. Conversation sparkled like wildfire between the three of them huddled in a close triangle liked a merry *ménage à trois*. I sat on the fringes, playing with my camera waiting for them to finish.

When it was time to do the snaps, *Klit* and *Ekstase* threw off their coats to reveal full working gear of thigh-length boots, fishnet tights, lace corsets and black suspenders. We went out into the street for the shoot. For my benefit, the ladies struck up a variety of lewd poses, hanging on street lamps or draped over car bonnets. I recorded their lascivious glances directed not at me, but invariably at some vague point over my shoulder, or wherever Conundrum positioned himself.

We ended up in a gloomy courtyard and I fitted a flash on the camera. For some reason, it refused to fire.

"Do let us know when you are functioning properly, Henri. We do look forward to seeing you in action."

The ladies laughed themselves silly. This only encouraged Conundrum to goad me further. So pleased was he with himself that he even launched a firecracker at the ladies.

"But how can I be sure, my dear ladies you really are dirty little sluts and not boring housewives from the suburbs?"

Klit and *Ekstase* eyed Conundrum appraisingly, then exchanged complicit glances. Suddenly, they grabbed him by the elbows and frog-marched him through a doorway and up a dark staircase. I was left alone in the courtyard. Half an hour passed before the three of them reappeared. A rather flushed and ruffled Conundrum was still adjusting his clothing.

"Do forgive me, dear ladies, for casting aspersions. I think you have just authenticated your sluttish credentials quite conclusively and comprehensively."

After an exchange of friendly compliments, *Klit* and *Ekstase* parted with a formal handshake. When they were gone, we retired to a pub for a glass of beer.

"You know, Henri, getting a freebie off a couple of hard-nosed whores must rank as an ultimate achievement."

How did he get away with it? He proceeded to tell me.

"It's a fair exchange. I bathe in their valley. They scale my mountain. Together we make a complete landscape. Or to put it in musical terms. I am the bow to their cello. Together we make music. You do know what I'm talking about, don't you?"

I nodded rather unconvincingly.

"But they weren't exactly beautiful, were they?"

"Beauty doesn't come into it. A beautiful woman with no appetite for sex, stirs the blood no more than a marble statue. We admire her bodily perfection and remain unaffected by her charms. The sort of disembodied aesthetic experience you seem so obsessed with. I see I shall have to take you in hand, Henri."

Take me in hand? What on earth did he mean by that? I didn't dare to enquire. Thankfully he left it at that.

Next morning we were due to fly home. But I found a note from Conundrum pushed under my door wishing me *bon voyage* and telling me he was staying on in Berlin for a few days. I wasn't surprised. He had several options. *Klit* and/or *Ekstase*. *Frau Doktor* with or without her spectacles. Perhaps all three plus others I wasn't even aware of. Why not? By now I was ready to believe the old lecher capable of anything.

Our next trip was to Russia. We met up at Heathrow for the flight to St Petersburg. When, after a long wait, it was our turn to check-in, Conundrum slumped onto his suitcase.

"Are you feeling alright, sir?"

At last, Conundrum spoke.

"This is the traditional Russian way of preparing for a long journey. We must sit quietly on our suitcases in order to allow our souls adequate time to take leave of home."

Conundrum continued to wait patiently perched on his suitcase. At last, he produced a thin smile.

"I am now ready to depart."

We checked in. Nothing further happened until we were on the plane and just about to take off, when he cheerily waved several small colourful packets in my face.

"Help yourself, Henri. Banana, raspberry or coconut. Take your pick. Got them from a machine in the gents of all places. Should stop your ears popping."

Conundrum put one in his mouth. I don't like sweets, but he insisted and so to humour him I slipped one in my pocket for later. After take-off he leaned across and mumbled.

"Nice and fruity, but a bit chewy."

Conundrum blew a small bubble. By the time the hostess arrived with the champagne, it had grown into a tennis ball. He blew harder until it grew into the size of a football. The hostess looked aghast. I checked the small sachet in my pocket. He was chewing a fruit-flavoured condom. Conundrum punctured the enormous balloon with a toothpick. There was a loud explosion. Fearing the worst, several passengers screamed and went into the bracing position. Calm as a cucumber, Conundrum pulled out of his mouth what remained of the rubbery membrane and stuffed it between the pages of the in-flight magazine.

"Bubble gum wasn't that tough when I was a lad. But fear not, I have disposed of the offending item."

He continued in the same breath.

"I have been asked by our Russian minders to wear something distinctive so they can recognise me on arrival."

"Oh yes?"

"Well, I thought it would be fun to wear one of the Queen's corgis on my head."

"One of the Queen's corgis?"

"Yes. It seemed distinctive and suitably patriotic too. Or, failing that, then a dead cat."

"A dead cat?"

"Yes, of course. Must be dead to get it through customs."

He rummaged in his bag.

"So how does it suit me?"

His hat did indeed resemble a dead cat. Tufts of ginger fur detached themselves and landed on his shoulders. Others floated down onto the half-eaten meal on the tray before him.

"First time in Russia, Henri?"

I nodded.

"Well, take this bit of advice. Throw away the cork. I may have mentioned it before. You'll soon see what I mean."

On our first day in St Petersburg I took some pictures of people playing volleyball on a small beach by the river near the fortress of St Peter & St Paul. Conundrum had wandered off. I was going to look for him when I stopped in my tracks at the sight of a sexy young woman in a blue bikini leaning against a stone bulwark. Eyes closed, she soaked up the sun through every pore. I recalled a piece of sculpture I had photographed in Rome, an antique beauty so lifelike she seemed actually to be stepping out of her marble frieze into the real world. And here I stood in

St Petersburg confronting a twin sister of that Classical statue, no longer a cold piece of marble but a woman of flesh and blood.

My heart was in my boots. I raised my camera. My finger trembled on the shutter release. Her eyes fluttered open. I froze. Conundrum now stepped between us. He held her gaze as he stroked her cheek with the back of an index finger. Her eyes narrowed. Soon she was purring like a cat. Then he passed a hand across her face like a hypnotist putting a patient into a trance. Her breast heaved with the rhythm of sleep.

Like a craftsman admiring his handiwork, Conundrum surveyed her body from head to toe. Then he reached out to touch her. But he checked himself, shook his head with a faint sigh and turned away, leaving the lady leaning against the wall, immobile as a piece of sculpture for which I had earlier mistaken her. I took my picture and slipped away, full of rueful thoughts. Perhaps statues of cold stone really were my level? And for Conundrum the hot living flesh?

But that was nothing compared to what lay ahead for us in Moscow. The overnight train from St Petersburg, far from exhausting Conundrum, put a fresh spring in his step.

"St Petersburg may be cosmopolitan, but Moscow is metropolitan. It's Mother Metropolis. A regular colossus of a conurbation. Paradigm of the universe. Vast, exciting, dangerous. Just how big cities are meant to be."

Moscow was uneventful until our penultimate evening in town. Strolling back to the Metropole after a marathon operatic performance of *Boris Godunov* at the Bolshoi, Conundrum teased an organ grinder's monkey. It promptly jumped in his face and bit his nose. Perhaps there were some limits to his magic? And some justice in the world? He dabbed the blood with a dirty handkerchief and pretended it was of no account.

We reached the hotel without further incident. On our way to the lift we passed through a secluded seating area. Three girls lolled about in huge armchairs. Conundrum slowed to give them the once-over. There was no mistaking which one had caught his attention. A classy maiden sat on the arm of an ornate *belle époque* sofa. A sable coat hung loosely over her shoulders, revealing a minimalist black cocktail dress from which a pair of long legs extended alluringly. High cheek bones, ice-blue eyes, blond hair and a proud bearing gave her the air of a Russian countess from a 19th century novel who might have travelled here in her personal troika. A real stunner.

Conundrum whispered into my ear.

"Now there's a birchy one, Henri, and no mistake."

"A birchy one?"

"Russians revere the birch tree and compare a beautiful woman to its slender form. Consider her willowy if you like, Henri. But that always makes me think of cricket. So for me she is birchy, decidedly birchy. I think we should get acquainted."

Conundrum mumbled a couple of words to the other two girls, both of whom were distinctly unbirchy. Then he came to the countess in the cocktail dress. She introduced herself as Nikita from Siberia. For a man normally so skilled with words, his opening gambit was woefully inadequate.

"I expect Moscow is a bit hot for you, Nikita."

She responded with a look of derision.

"Nothing is too hot for me. Besides, I never discuss the weather with someone who wants to fuck me."

Delicious. I fell for Nikita on the spot. She had swatted Conundrum like a fly. Or so I thought. But he was completely unfazed. Boldly, he met her eye and uttered a brief remark in Russian. The effect was dramatic. With a languid movement that conveyed no particular emotion, she rose majestically to her feet. Her legs were even longer than when she was seated.

Until that moment I had never thought of Conundrum as being either short or tall. He always seemed of adequate stature. Perhaps he had mastered the art of adjusting his height to every situation? If so, this ability now deserted him. Nikita towered a head above him as she accepted the arm he offered her. I looked on in disbelief as this ill-matched couple wandered off down the plush red carpet and turned a corner.

I now received speculative glances from the other two girls. But after Nikita they were a decidedly unattractive duo. I mumbled an awkward goodnight and beat a hasty retreat.

Next morning over breakfast, Conundrum looked tired but happy as the saying goes. I knew he was going to tell me all about it. But first he couldn't resist having some fun.

"How did you get on with Miss Ukrainian Forklift Truck 1992? Or did you go for the champion weightlifter from Tblisi? Don't look so aggrieved, Henri. We don't always get what we want. You must learn to take the rough with the smooth."

Conundrum passed from teasing to gloating.

"The lovely Nikita has a brain as well as a body. Studying law at Moscow State University. No shame attached to earning a few dollars on the game to finance her studies. All her friends are at it. Just imagine. In a few years time she might be a top Russian politician making headlines around the world. And I'll be able to say she screwed me senseless in the Metropole."

Conundrum looked exceedingly pleased with himself.

"Amusing she was too. Even made a little joke about you, would you believe? Now what was it she said?"

I didn't want to know.

"Oh yes. You looked like a man who packs his galoshes and forgets his condoms. Spot on, don't you reckon?"

I winced.

"A real mine of information she was. The knowledgeable Nikita gave me all I need for my article on New Russia."

"Did she, indeed?"

"And you know what that means?"

"No."

"I can charge every cent of my $100 as research."

"$100?"

"Yes, that's what I paid her for the interview. Trouble was, she actually wanted $200. Going rate for a whole night, she

175

said. And wasn't she worth going the distance? I told her she was very welcome to stay but I wasn't going to pay cash for sex."

I must have raised an eyebrow.

"Indeed not. Where's the fun in paying for sex? Takes all the spice out of it. I only did so once, and the lucky lady derived far more pleasure than I. So I gave that up as a bad job. Mind you, with Nikita, I must admit I was sorely tempted."

Conundrum sipped his coffee with contentment.

"I told her I wouldn't pay the extra $100 as a matter of principle. But Nikita was persuasive. And turning down a lady goes against the grain. So I felt had to oblige in some way."

Conundrum now looked indecently pleased with himself.

"In lieu of the extra $100, I promised to give her a shag to remember, the full crime and punishment. And I didn't let her down. Didn't get much sleep. God, she was a goer. Gave as good as she got. Insisted on conjugating my rusty old irregular Russian verbs. Said she wanted to see them all well oiled and in good working order. Sadly, not enough time to start declining nouns."

Trust Conundrum to mix sex and linguistics.

"Want to hear how the Cyrillic alphabet was invented?"

I didn't have much choice.

"Well, according to Nikita, some Russian monks got riotously drunk one evening, tanked up to the eyeballs on vodka. A right old symposium they had, talking all sorts of nonsense. Each outdoing the others with silly suggestions for brightening up life in the scriptorium. Just about everyone had their say when one of the brethren, a scholarly soul by the name of Cyril, came up with an ingenious suggestion for alphabet reform."

"Alphabet reform?"

"Brother Cyril's brilliant wheeze was to create phonetic havoc by writing a capital R back to front as Я and pronounce it as Ya. Must have been the way he told it, for this brought the house down and won him first prize for utter foolishness. The Cyrillic alphabet bears the name of Brother Cyril to this day."

I said nothing.

"Anyway, back to Nikita. Thought we had settled the matter. Dam good shag, no extra $100. But come morning she demanded another $100. I reminded her I'd made myself clear. Never knowingly pay for sex etc. Something must have got lost in translation. We had a regular lovers' tiff. Our first and last. I reminded her I'd already given her $100 for her 'interview' which involved no sexual services. In any case I didn't have any more money. She didn't believe me until I showed her my empty wallet. So off she goes in a huge Siberian sulk, claiming I 'owed' her. Said she would be back later with a 'friend', someone I'd rather not meet, to 'collect'. And I'd better have the $100."

Conundrum lit a cigarette.

"She was deadly serious, Henri."

I knew what was coming.

"Don't suppose you could tie me over?"

I shook my head defiantly.

"Thought you said it was a matter of principle."

Conundrum looked genuinely disappointed with me.

"So I did, Henri. Quite right. So I did."

He went over to the breakfast buffet and fetched himself a bottle of Russian champagne.

"Oh well. Let's see what she's capable of. A woman with a good arse can be forgiven anything. At least, the condemned man will have eaten a hearty breakfast."

Midway through his third glass Conundrum yawned, displaying the full rancid glory of his 'English smile'. Then he stood up and sauntered off unsteadily clutching the half empty champagne bottle. I assumed he wanted to drown his sorrows in private. I didn't give much thought to his remark about the condemned man eating a hearty breakfast. I figured it was just a melodramatic turn of phrase to make me take pity on him. Well, this time he could sort himself out and not at my expense.

On returning to my room after breakfast, I found a note pushed under the door.

177

"Have checked out. Pick up yours truly tomorrow 11am sharp outside British Embassy en route to airport."

Then I heard a sharp knock. I turned the handle just a fraction and the door flew open in my face. Over the shoulder of a big man in dark glasses and double-breasted Versace suit I saw Nikita. So this was the 'friend' coming to 'collect' on her behalf. Pinned up against a wall with a gun to my throat, I knew it was pointless saying Conundrum's debts were none of my business.

Using Nikita as interpreter, the gangster ordered me to hand over the $100 owing. Impossible to resist with a revolver barrel stuck in my mouth. I nodded meekly. As I handed over the $100, the man snatched my only other note, also $100. He handed one to Nikita, the other he pocketed.

"Service charge. For personal collection."

Nikita's helpful translation was clipped, matter of fact. Equally so was the disdainful look she gave me as she left.

"Do you always pay up so easily for your friend's pleasure? You could have spent the money on yourself."

Nikita departed with a scornful toss of the head. My heart was thumping. Was it the shock of the ambush? Or the lingering presence of her perfume, taunting me with what I might have had for the $200 that had just been taken from me?

I cursed Conundrum a hundred times. To dull my anger I went for a walk. I headed for Kazan Cathedral in a corner of Red Square where Russian Orthodox priests with bushy beards and jewelled crowns paraded like kings bearing gifts through clouds of incense. Amidst the flicker of a thousand candles the chanting of human voices carried me up and away. But not even this impressive religious theatre could lift my depression for long. Then I trailed glumly through the Kremlin Museum. Its rich treasures looked like fancy baubles. But what did grab me was a set of horseshoes emblazoned with hearts. I fantasised about a fur-wrapped Nikita in her troika leaving a trail of passion stamped across the frozen Siberian tundra.

The memory of Nikita's parting words when she said I could have spent the money on myself left me burning with desire and a jealous resentment that Conundrum had coolly stepped in and conquered where I had feared to tread. Lost in morbid introspection, I wandered at random and found myself stranded the wrong end of Red Square. The army had thrown up a cordon of steel barriers. I had to return to the hotel by a circuitous route through a rabbit warren of courtyards and passages barred by iron gates like a high-security prison.

That evening, on the way up to my room I encountered Nikita and her pals draped across the same sofa by the lift. Cool as a cucumber, my tormentress looked me up and down with a wry smile. Was she giving me the come on? But I had already spent my last $200 paying for Conundrum's shag. The bastard!

Next day, I checked out and ordered a cab. According to Conundrum's instructions I told the driver to go to the airport via the British Embassy. There was no sign of him anywhere. Long minutes ticked away. At last, a battered old Lada spluttered to a halt behind me. Conundrum emerged from the vehicle and exchanged enormous bear hugs and kisses with a dubious individual wearing a string vest under a leather jacket. Both were unshaven and bleary-eyed.

"What a ball! What a perfect ball! Spent all night drinking with some shady characters right out of Gogol."

I was in no mood to listen to Conundrum's exploits.

"Spare me the details. I had a heavy visit from Nikita's 'friend'. On account of your unpaid debt. As a result of which, you owe me $200."

"$200?"

I explained about the $100 outstanding on account of the shag and the further $100 service charge for personal collection.

"I am so very sorry to hear that, Henri."

Conundrum fell silent while he reflected.

"And did you get a receipt?"

"A receipt?"

"Yes, Henri, a receipt."

"What for?"

"So you can claim it."

"Claim it? You mean you aren't going to pay me?"

"Don't see how I can. I never pay for sex, Henri. Matter of principle. Thought I'd made that perfectly clear."

"But you were going to pay, weren't you? You actually asked me for the money at breakfast yesterday, remember?"

"Well, perhaps. But since you didn't help me out, I couldn't do it. So you have only yourself to blame, Henri. You'll have to put this one down to experience I'm afraid."

"To experience? Do you realise the time I've had being beaten up and threatened on account of your debt to a whore?"

"A whore? Tut tut, Henri. Nikita's no whore. At least, not with me. As you are all too aware, I didn't pay her for sex."

My blood boiled. We didn't exchange a single word on the flight back. We were just coming in to land and I was checking my pockets when I found the unused fruit-flavoured condom. I stuffed it into the sick bag. I wanted nothing to remind me of my mishap in Moscow.

Barely three days passed after our return before I received another call from Conundrum. I had decided I would say no this time. Definitely no. No, as in never again. But, as it happened, he gave me no chance to speak.

"Grab a pen, Henri. And write this down."

No sooner had I scribbled down the flight details on the back of an envelope than the line went dead.

Next morning found me seated next to Conundrum on a plane to Zurich. From the airport we took a train to Grindelwald. Our hotel, the *Alpenrösli*, was a folksy Alpine chalet. Conundrum approached the place circumspectly.

"This place has everything, even a one-eyed woodcutter lurking in the cellar, I shouldn't wonder."

I had no idea what he was talking about. We were in the hotel and I stood mesmerised by the sexiest creature I'd ever seen 'manning' a reception desk. With her shimmering make-up and body-hugging dress, she might have been the hostess of a luxury brothel. My hand trembled as I shook hers offered in welcome. She spoke and behaved as if she owned the place.

"We have great pleasure inviting you to enjoy the stupendous views of our glaciated mountain peaks."

Conundrum chuckled as he scribbled the phrase in his notebook. When the receptionist had handed us our keys and disappeared into the office, he drew breath.

"Just looking at young Heidi has given me an erection it's painful to walk. You wouldn't mind carrying my bag?"

I lugged Conundrum's luggage up the wooden staircase with erotic fancies of my own racing through my mind. But when we came down from our rooms there was no sign of the sexiest woman in Switzerland. She must have clocked off for the day. Nor was she there next morning. Breakfast was served by a sullen Croatian waiter. I tried to make conversation commenting on the wonderful views.

"Damn the wonderful views. What views? These ugly, cursed mountains are always in the way."

I tried to reason with him.

"But the mountains are the view. They have their own beauty. Surely that is what people come here for?"

At this point Conundrum chipped in.

"The gentleman's meaning is perfectly clear, Henri. Just look at all that scenery crowding in on all sides. Bucketfuls of bloody scenery. What on earth is one to do with it all? Go up the mountain and look down? Go down into the valley and look up? That's about it. Your view is indeed getting in the way of the view he would prefer to see."

The waiter warmed to Conundrum and poured him a cup of coffee from my pot while leaving me to serve myself.

We spent the day walking in the mountains. Conundrum had me shoot picture postcard views of the scenic type he had just been deploring. Late afternoon back in the wood-panelled cosiness of the *Alpenrösli*, the sexy receptionist popped out of the office and greeted us like old friends. If we were agreeable, she announced, then she would invite us for dinner. It turned out she was the daughter of the hotel owner and would be happy to talk about the beauties of her wonderful mountain valley.

Conundrum's next comment surprised me.

"Dark forces stir. *The Old Man of Hoy* rears his ugly head. But my fragile frame can't stand the strain. I'm counting on you to take care of Heidi. If you think you can handle her."

A novel proposition. Perhaps Conundrum was trying to make up for my humiliation in Moscow. I couldn't imagine he didn't have it in him to take care of Heidi himself. How naïve could I be to even think him capable of such a gesture?

That evening, the three of us sat at a small round table in a cosy alcove. The restaurant window framed stupendous views tinged with fire by the setting sun. But I only had eyes for the red-hot girl who sat between us, like a cone of hot lava into which I would gladly plunge my being in a final all-consuming moment of ecstasy and self-destruction.

I had the greatest trouble eating the fondue. Dipping my fork alongside hers in the bubbling cheese sent shocks of excitement through my limbs. I found it impossible to make any sort of conversation. I have no recollection what she said, but every word she uttered breathed sex, sex, sex. Not that she was trying to turn on the charm. It was simply there, oozing out of every pore of her amazing body. From her lips the Shipping Forecast would have been an act of gross indecency.

By contrast, Conundrum babbled away easily. In fact, he was on song. Occasionally, he lapsed into what I took to be Swiss German. It was an effective little party trick that made her giggle in the most alluring way. All right for Conundrum, I thought. Having ruled himself out, he could be laid back. But I had a serious strategy to plan. To ease my nerves I knocked back the sour country wine while dipping chunks of bread in neat schnapps before I plunged them into the fondue.

As Heidi spoke, her pupils dilated. I plunged into their dark vortex like a bucket down a well. A smile played across her red lips. My pulse was racing. If only Conundrum weren't there I would ravish her on the spot. I felt faint with desire. Finally I could bear it no more. Why wait any longer? I slipped my hand beneath the tablecloth and tentatively fondled her leg. She let it happen without a murmur of dissent. Thus encouraged I slipped my hand beneath her silk dress just above the knee. The touch of her tender flesh drove me wild. Now there could be no holding back. My fingers moved slowly up her thigh while Conundrum babbled on about obscure Alpine dialects. I was no longer in control of myself. This was action before thought at last, and in the presence of the master to boot.

Then my trembling fingers met an unexpected obstacle. Something hard, dry and bony sat on Heidi's silky soft thigh. Squatting like a lizard was a hand. A man's hand. Conundrum's hand. The old bastard had beaten me to it!

Suddenly I felt sick. Head spinning, stomach heaving. Everything went hazy. Last thing I remembered was Heidi's face bent over mine with a look of concern. I melted at the touch of her fingers on my fevered brow. Then I passed out.

When I awoke the next morning, I was lying on my bed, still dressed except for my shoes. I had the most excruciating headache. My shirt smelled as if it had been wrapped around a cow's udder. I staggered over to the wash basin and drank a glass of water. Seconds later, I threw up. Mercifully, I couldn't yet recall anything of the previous night's *débâcle*. A monumental hangover physically crushed all memory from my addled brain.

At last I pulled myself together and went downstairs. I took my seat opposite Conundrum merrily dipping croissant into a cup of coffee. He seemed pretty pleased with himself.

"I say, you are looking well this morning, Henri."

"You must be joking."

"I'm only trying to apply some complimentary medicine. But, to be frank, you do look decidedly out of sorts."

At that moment, Heidi appeared. I recalled looking into her face shortly before I passed out. Other memories stirred. She seemed embarrassed and giggled after a strange fashion.

Did I want tea or coffee? Moments later, she set a pot of tea in front of me. As she did so her hand brushed Conundrum's shoulder picking a piece of fluff from his jacket. A casual but intimate gesture. He was wearing a large silk handkerchief tied in a most unusual manner around his scrawny neck. It didn't quite conceal a series of red blotches, so vivid he might have been sucked dry by a jarful of leeches.

"Affectionate girl, young Heidi."

In a flash I recalled every last detail of the nightmare I'd been through the evening before. How he had cynically used me as a stalking horse for his own move. I almost passed out all over again at the extent of his duplicity and of my own gullibility.

"Excuse me for reviving painful memories, Henri. But when I saw what a hash you were making I thought I'd better give you a hand. Yes, quite literally. And then after you had withdrawn from the fray, what else was I to do? How could I ignore a woman in need? Every bit of love withheld is a piece of one's own soul flushed down the drain. Sins of omission are invariably the worst. It's not what you do, but what you don't do that returns to haunt you in the end."

The bastard! Now he treats me to a moral lecture. Why can I not rid myself of this cruel tormentor?

"And so after we had laid you to rest, one thing led to another..."

My gut turned. I'd had enough. I was just about ready to tear into Conundrum with my bare hands when he pulled open his shirt to reveal a chest scored with cuts and scratches so recent some were still bleeding. I had to look away.

"Never a pretty sight love's battlefield the morning after. Well, at least the dear girl has given me a hearty appetite for breakfast. Fancy a croissant, Henri? They're awfully good."

I made for the exit. Outside on the terrace I came across the Croatian waiter gazing with fury at the mountains just as he had been the previous morning.

"God, I hate these bloody peaks. Every morning I hope someone will have blown them up during the night. But it never happens. They are always there. How I hate them."

As a gesture of solidarity I raised two-fingers to the north face of the Eiger, confident I would not be climbing it now or ever. Back in my room, I threw cold water on my face. I looked out across the valley. Every single chalet sported window boxes of geraniums so violently blood-red I winced at the sight of so much bleeding flesh. Suddenly, I had an intense desire to soar up and fly over the great wall of rock hemming me in.

I felt an overwhelming need to be far away from this place, and above all far away from Conundrum. Wherever I went, this man was destined to cause me the cruellest pain. I stormed out of the hotel and strode up the path out of the village. I followed close behind two French tourists discussing the aesthetic merits of the *Schreckhorn* and the *Finsterhorn*. Which of the two mountains, the *Peak of Dread* or the *Peak of Darkness*, was *le plus joli*? I didn't give a damn about their verdict and I cursed Grindelwald from the bottom of my heart.

I reached an open alpine meadow and lay down in the long grass just wanting to vanish from the face of the earth. At that moment I would have gladly traded my life for that of a bee buzzing contentedly from flower to flower. And then, in spite of myself, the photographer in me awoke and I fell to admiring how delicate were the soft blobs of rich colour in the foreground that merged into a vibrant carpet of petals framed by a distant vista of snow-capped mountains. I felt inspired to take some pictures.

But I hadn't shot a single frame when a farmer came chugging up the track on a tractor with two strapping young daughters walking along behind. Then he hooked up a mower and I could only look on in horror as he proceeded to make short work of the meadow. In a couple of minutes he hacked my perfect picture to pieces. My beautiful tableau of Alpine flowers was ripped to shreds in front of my eyes. In my paranoid state it felt as if the man had responded to an SOS call to prevent a devious act of arty photography.

His job done, the farmer unhitched the mower, wished me a good day and pointed the tractor back down the hill. The two girls waved cheerily to me as they set off back down the path. Now my whole world was in ruins. Game, set and match to Grindelwald. My spirit was broken.

When I said just now that my spirit was broken, I meant precisely that. The next day, when we took the train to Zurich, I had no more punch left. I didn't care what was to become of me. I was Conundrum's creature to dispose of as he felt fit. And so what? To be honest, there was a certain relief in having been brought so low. I realised I wasn't fighting him any more, and that brought with it a kind of merciful release. In fact, I didn't even have the energy left to hate him as I knew I should.

From the terrace of the *Dolder Grand Hotel* we observed some hang-gliders riding the thermals high over the distant *Uetliberg*. I envied them the miraculous sense of freedom they must be enjoying. Conundrum also seemed captivated by the soaring of the colourful kites from which tiny human figures were suspended. At last, he turned away shaking his head.

"Free as a bird? Perhaps that's what true freedom looks like. But if I were to aspire to such a thing as freedom, I would elect to be the lowliest slave worker on the pyramids. No decisions to make, just the implacable will of the Pharaoh to shape my days and set a limit to my action. Real freedom can only come from accepting a bondage that delivers the spirit from the horrid perplexities of choice. The only true liberation comes from within. So embrace your servitude, clutch it to your breast, devour it, swallow it whole. Make it your very own."

What was he trying to tell me? That serving him was my highest purpose and my liberation too? Conundrum's eyes were wild, dangerous. They brooked no argument.

"All very well floating up there with a fancy apparatus to hang on to. Child's play. But flying without wings, Henri. Just imagine that. Flying without wings."

Leaving that unreal vision hanging in the air Conundrum now came down to earth.

"Time for a spot of work."

We proceeded downtown to an appointment in a quaint cobbled street just off the *Bahnhofstrasse*. I wasn't required to do anything more than take a snap of a brass plaque with the name of a private bank. Conundrum was to interview one of those secretive Swiss financiers who didn't want his face to appear in the magazine. Afterwards, we strolled along by the lake. What happened next took me completely unawares.

"Henri, I want you to do me a favour."

Do him a favour? Strange. He usually gave orders.

"What's that?"

We were standing outside a bathing station at a place called *Utoquai*.

"I want you to take a dip in the lake."

"A dip in the lake?"

Even by Conundrum's eccentric standards, this was a singular request. But I had no strength to argue, no will to resist.

"I want you to swim across the lake until the church towers of the Lady Minster and St Peter's are exactly aligned. It's not that far. Half a mile, there and back. It brings good fortune. Just do as I say Henri. Believe. Have faith."

"But I don't have my swimming trunks with me."

Conundrum beamed his louche grin and presented me with a cloth bag containing a towel and a bathing costume.

"I took the liberty of borrowing this from the concierge."

I accepted my fate.

"Swim out across the lake until the two steeples come precisely into alignment. Not a stroke further, mind you. Then stop and swim straight back. The guardian spirits of the lake will not help you beyond that point."

"But what is the purpose?"

"Don't be such a bore. Just get on with it."

Before I knew it Conundrum was waving me off from the sundeck of the bathing station. I gritted my teeth and took the plunge. The water was colder than expected. The initial shock had me gasping for breath. I spat out a mouthful of Lake Zurich as I struck out boldly with an energetic crawl.

Soon the water felt less cold. As I pulled out further and further from the shore I felt a miracle happening. I was breaking free from a place of confinement. I was escaping the internal prison of my ordinary self. I was at one with nature. On and on I swam, full of purpose, measuring my progress now and then against the narrowing gap between the two church towers. I reckoned the middle of the lake was well within my range.

It was a moment of triumph when the slender steeple of the Lady Minster fell in line with the squat, square tower of St Peter's. I stopped and was about to swim back, anxious to follow Conundrum's instructions to the letter. But then an irrational urge took hold. I felt so good in the water, re-energised and renewed. Why not continue to the other side? My spirit was not that broken after all. I had played along with Conundrum's little game. Now I would play my own. I would go all the way. I would define my own limits. And to hell with Conundrum!

I struck on regardless of a small voice telling me I could no longer count on the guardian spirits of the lake. Whatever that meant, I had no idea. I fixed my sights on a bathing station directly opposite the one from which I had launched myself. As it came more clearly into view I could see the floating platforms of sunbathers. I pressed on, anxious to rest my cold and weary body for the return swim. My legs felt weak and shaky as at last I grasped the iron rail of the steps leading up to a wooden raft covered with human bodies basking in the sunshine.

Without my glasses, I could not see clearly, but just well enough to note that all the bodies on the deck were female, most of them topless. At that moment, I shivered from the cold and sent a few drops of water onto the back of the nearest lady. She sat up and grabbed a towel to cover herself. Then she spoke.

"This place is for women only. You must go."

I couldn't make out her features except for two dark eyes and a tress of black hair falling onto slender shoulders. Her voice captivated me, gentle, feminine, the accent charmingly oriental. I felt flooded with warmth and well being, an incredible sensation. In that moment I knew that she was the purpose of my epic swim. Conundrum had told me to swim no further than halfway across the lake. But I had disobeyed, gone the full distance and reached the other side. And now here I was in the presence of this mysterious being. I tried to take in every detail of her face, but my vision was clouded by the water in my eyes and the bright sunshine that made me squint. So her face remained tantalisingly undefined. At last I managed to speak.

"You might not believe this, but I swam over the lake to meet you. Tell me who you are. Then I will swim back again."

A couple of other women now looked up, shocked to find a man in their midst.

"Just give me your name and phone number."

She hesitated.

"Please. I beg you. I have come so far to meet you."

She took my hand and started to write on it with a ballpoint pen. The touch of her flesh melted mine.

"Tell me what it says."

"You must go now. Someone is coming."

"I'll call you."

"Goodbye."

That was all. So with the precious information printed on the palm of my hand, I set off on the return trip. I swam on my back, right arm held aloft to keep the writing dry. I fixed the girl in my sight as long as possible. But gradually she became smaller and smaller until indistinct from all the figures around her. Just another dot of female flesh. I was once more a solitary swimmer charting a lonely course back across Lake Zurich.

Swimming on my back and using only my legs for propulsion was no easy matter. I took a quick bearing on the two spires but they were still a long way apart. The coldness of the water numbed my limbs. But I struggled on, happy in the knowledge I had for once made a brave existential choice. Not only had I picked up the gauntlet thrown down by Conundrum, I had also committed action before thought at last. Exhausted and jubilant in equal measure, I checked my progress against the two church steeples. They had come together. I was halfway across. The rest would be a simple matter of endurance.

Then I was almost blasted out of the water by the boom of a ship's horn. I looked up to see a steamer bearing down on me. Basic survival instinct kicked in. I broke into a frantic crawl to avoid the paddles. I was that close to being sliced up like salami. Only when my strength was drained from my body, did I dare look around to see the ship steaming blithely on towards the eastern end of the lake.

I resumed my swim in a less exhausting sidestroke. I needed to ration what energy remained. It took an eternity before the bathing station at Utoquai came into view. At my painfully slow rate of progress I thought I would drown. I'm not sure what happened next. Did I get picked up by a boat? I recall someone pulling me out of the water, telling me off for my rank stupidity. Someone else threw a towel over my shoulders. After that I sat in the sun to get some warmth back in my body.

Now that I was safe I had only one thing on my mind. I wiped my eyes and put on my glasses. But my vision was still smeary. I couldn't read what the girl had written. So I held out my right hand, palm uppermost towards Conundrum.

"What does it say?"

"What does what say, Henri?"

"My hand. Tell me what's written on my hand."

Conundrum looked at me over his half-moon spectacles.

"I'm not a fortune teller, Henri."

"Just read it for God's sake and tell me what it says."

At last, Conundrum spoke.

"It's a bit faded."

I feared the worst. It had been washed off in the lake.

"But I can make out a faint inscription."

"Well, what is it?"

"It's not in English."

"I thought you knew every language under the sun. So which is it?"

Conundrum looked again.

"Chinese."

"Chinese?"

"Or Japanese."

"Japanese?"

"Or Thai."

"Thai?"

"Actually, it's hard to tell. But it's definitely something oriental. Perhaps I'm reading it upside down."

Conundrum twisted my hand with a sharp wrench that almost snapped my wrist.

"No, right second time. Japanese. Definitely Japanese."

Japanese. Yes, that figured. I waited to hear more.

"But I can't tell you what it says."

"You can't? Why not?"

My heart was in my mouth.

"Most of the ink has been washed away."

"That can't be true."

"Afraid so. I do hope it wasn't anything important."

Conundrum seemed remarkably unconcerned.

"But I can tell you in general terms what it was."

"In general terms?"

"The outline of the characters is faint. But I can see they were written in three lines consisting of a total of... 17 syllables. That can only mean one thing, Henri."

"And what's that?"

"A *haiku*, of course."

"A *haiku*?"

"A common Japanese verse form."

"Are you sure?"

"Oh yes, Henri. Quite sure."

So she had written me a poem instead of her name and phone number. What could that mean? I looked at my hand and studied the faint blue lines dancing across my palm. All I had to go on was a *haiku* that could no longer be read by a nameless Japanese girl I had only perceived as a blurred vision. Perhaps I wouldn't even recognise her if I passed her in the street? But beyond that layer of doubt a deep inner certainty told me I would recognise her immediately. Of course, I would.

"And you really can't read it?"

"No, Henri. No one could possibly read it."

My first thought was to take a cab straight round to the other side of the lake and wait for my Japanese poetess to emerge from the bathing station. But I must have been utterly drained and exhausted from the swim because at that moment I passed out. When I regained consciousness I was with Conundrum in a taxi heading back to the *Dolder Grand Hotel*.

As soon as my head cleared doubts began to surface. Surely, if she had meant me to contact her she would have given me something more than a *haiku*? Yet none of this depressing logic could destroy my absolute conviction that our paths would cross again. No, it was stronger than that. Our destinies were inextricably entwined. I was so absolutely convinced of this, it was as if I had been given a sneak preview of my life's script. Or to get to the point, I had fallen in love.

"So tell me what happened, Henri?"

I decided there and then to keep Conundrum in the dark. I could just imagine the fun he would have with the comical notion of Henri in love.

"I can't recall. My mind's a blank."

I was able to enjoy the rare spectacle of Conundrum puzzling over a real conundrum. If only in this respect, I felt I had achieved something. I had notched one up against him.

On the flight home, he gloated over Grindelwald.

"You mustn't take it to heart, Henri. If I were a sexy lady I would want a greater test of my erotic charms than some over eager youngster who falls in his fondue at the first fluttering of an eyelash. How much more rewarding to coax an erection out of some thoroughly worn out *membrum virile*, like a snake charmer enticing a geriatric cobra out of its basket."

I didn't argue. I couldn't care less. Let Conundrum milk it. What did I care about Heidi from Grindelwald, or indeed Nikita from Siberia for that matter? I only had thoughts for an anonymous Japanese girl who had penned a *haiku* on my hand. I was in love. And what did Conundrum know of love? Unable to feel love himself, the old lecher was unable to recognise it in others. Love was his blind spot. He had no idea what it felt like. We lived in two separate worlds of love and lechery. My mind took flight on the wings of a delicious idea. By virtue of being in love, I had found a refuge safely beyond Conundrum's reach, somewhere immune to his devious magic. I had discovered a secret place where he couldn't reach me.

Even while I was thinking these thoughts, the old fool continued to rub my nose in my Grindelwald shame.

"You should have seen your face the following morning, Henri. But there is always a useful lesson to be learned. Always the bigger picture to consider."

The bigger picture? I reckoned I was the one who had seen the bigger picture. Quite simply it was love versus lechery. We would see which one would prevail. So I let Conundrum continue unchallenged. He really was barking up the wrong tree.

"What do you do when life spits in your face, Henri?"

I shrugged nonchalantly.

"Same thing you do with spit on your boots. Rub it in to deepen the shine. Absorb all injuries to your person. For they add to the lustre of your innermost being."

By that reckoning, my innermost being must be shining like a mirror, so many hurts had I received at Conundrum's hands. But now it was shining with something else. I savoured my private moment of triumph.

Conundrum's eyes were closed. Inscrutable. What was he thinking? Might he be wondering how I had managed to return from my swim in Lake Zurich with a *haiku* on my hand? He must surely realise I had gone way beyond his strict instructions. Perhaps his silence meant he didn't want to acknowledge the fact that I had disobeyed his orders, that finally I had been my own man. Or what if he was merely pretending not to see what had happened to me for some dark reason of his own?

On arrival back at Heathrow, I popped into the gents in the baggage hall. Some sad soul seemed to have torn out most of his pubic hair and left it lying in the urinal. Recalling my despair in Grindelwald, I could guess just how he felt.

When I returned to collect my suitcase, Conundrum had vanished, gone on without me. Well, good riddance! I resolved this was my last trip. Next time he called I'd tell him politely to stuff it. And I had my opportunity the very next day when the phone rang. But he caught me completely unprepared.

"Ever heard of La Réunion, Henri? Peak of volcanic rock in the Indian Ocean. Tropical paradise crawling with dusky maidens drinking lemongrass tea under the palm trees. Air heady with essence of vanilla? Need I go on?"

This was my moment to say I wasn't coming. But I thought I'd play along for a bit.

"Well, we've been invited down on a freebie to end all freebies. First class flights. Five star hotel."

I was wavering already.

"But don't get excited. I have declined the invitation."

"Declined the invitation?"

"Yes, declined. I must leave one place on earth untainted by an actual visit. So La Réunion shall be the repository of everything I should ideally like a place to be. I'll write the article of course. In fact, I have been inspired to new heights of creative expression. By virtue of not going to La Réunion I have this very morning produced some of my best travel writing, a feat that would be quite impossible to match if I were actually to go."

"And is it professionally ok, I mean ethical, to write about a place without having been?"

God, I sounded pompous. I didn't give a toss about the ethics. I was just peeved at missing out on La Réunion.

"Ethical, Henri? When you have seen as many places as I have, you are fully entitled and amply qualified to make up one or two. Besides, it's a proud tradition: Ibn Battuta, Herodotus, Marco Polo, Jonathan Swift. I'm in illustrious company."

The smugness of his tone annoyed me intensely.

"It's all very well for you to write about a place you haven't visited. But I can't take imaginary photos of La Réunion sitting here in London."

"Poor Henri. I do see your difficulty. Just goes to show the limits of photography."

There was a cold anger in my voice as I retorted.

"So is that why you called? Just to tell me we aren't going to La Réunion?"

"Hole in one, Henri. Precisely. Only right and proper to keep you fully informed."

"Fully informed, is that it?"

"That is indeed it. *Au revoir.*"

The line went dead. He had hung up.

Only now did I realise the full cunning of Conundrum's latest trickery. Not only had he scuppered my brave moment of revolt by proposing a place I would undoubtedly have accepted. He had actually got me interested in La Réunion just before snatching it away from me. And to add insult to injury, he taken yet another swipe at my photography. Damn him!

By way of compensation, that night I experienced my first flying dream. I rose a couple of feet in the air and hung mysteriously suspended above the ground. It was more like hovering than flying, but I could sense the thrill of imminent flight tingle through my body. It didn't last for long but what a wonderful sensation. I was hooked. On waking, I recalled Conundrum's words spoken quietly to himself while watching the hang-gliders over the Uetliberg.

"Without wings, Henri. Now that would be something."

Perhaps one day I might fly without wings. Why not? I might even get there before Conundrum. After all I now had the power of love to inspire me. And what did he have? So why shouldn't I beat the old fraud at his own game?

FRENCH LESSONS ONE

Hate is not really the right word to describe my feelings for Conundrum even after that ghastly business with Heidi in Grindelwald. Hate is personal, and I didn't hate Conundrum for what he had done to me. After all, my connivance in whatever he threw at me formed an essential part of my unwritten pact with this devil. No, it was more like resentment than hate. I resented the way his whole way of being and how he lived his life threw my various inadequacies into sharp relief. Under the harsh spotlight of his merciless scrutiny every crack in my façade was exposed and prised open. But hatred of the most personal kind was there nonetheless lurking in the wings and eventually it stepped out of the shadows.

Meanwhile, I persisted in my futile attempts to make 'sense' of Conundrum, to get to grips with the inner man at the heart of this slippery individual. But try as I might, I could detect no fixed centre to his being. I reasoned to myself that most of us are concentric in nature, our essential core being wrapped in various outer layers of pretence. But Conundrum was somehow polycentric, having not one but various centres of being, and these were constantly in motion like a human kaleidoscope. One small twist and a different pattern emerged.

By allowing myself to be hypnotised by his various protean identities I took my eye off the ball. I lost sight of my original goal of acquiring the knowledge that lay in *Conundrum's Book*. And now that I had hatched the crazy notion of beating Conundrum at his own game, I became even more involved with my own agenda and overlooked the possibility that he may have one of his own, a single-minded purpose, a master plan working itself out with a stubborn relentlessness.

Grindelwald was the significant moment when I might have extricated myself, pleading one personal humiliation too far. But my discovery of 'love' by the shores of Lake Zurich had rekindled my innate romantic idealism and blinded me to the harsh realities. As in some cheap fiction I believed there could only be one victor in the love versus lechery showdown. Little did I know that subsequent events in Paris and Tokyo were to shoot down in flames that ridiculous scenario.

I was lost in introspection when the phone rang.

"We're off to *Gay Paree*, Henri."

Conundrum of course. It felt like he was speaking from inside my head. I shouted at him to go away and leave me in peace. But I could only mouth the words. I was no better than that silly little dog glued to the sound of his master's voice coming through the gramophone.

"Paris?"

"Yes, Henri. Paris. As in Paris, France."

Early next morning we flew out of City Airport. The take off afforded a grandstand view of the *Millennium Dome*.

"Sod the bloody millennium! Why did they bay for the year 2000 like demented dogs? Folk had more sense the last time round. They approached the year 1000 with fear and trepidation. Scared it would be the end of the world and they would all fall off the edge. There squats the *Dome* on the slimy mudflats, a huge cockroach waiting for a cosmic boot to stamp on it. And the supreme arrogance of claiming Greenwich as the *home of time*. As if time gives a toss about having somewhere to live. As if time needed to be invented by anyone."

It was a breakfast flight, but Conundrum had got hold of some champagne.

"You might expect them to conduct themselves with more intellectual *rigueur* in France. But they don't, Henri. They don't. For all their free-thinking, the French think about as freely as a ... as a monkey in a Cartesian strait jacket."

He downed another glass of champagne.

"Oh, the endless folly of humanity. Our silly dreams of perfect order, golden measures, divine harmonies, holy numbers, beautiful mathematics, celestial geometry and all that our elegant minds can come up with. We yearn like children for a higher truth and a divine architect, or some such fairy tale. But what if chaos rules the universe?"

I'd become used to Conundrum calling me Henri with a French pronunciation. But suddenly I was alarmed. There was an awkward feeling about going to Paris, in a sense my mythical home, under this assumed name. Surely this was the one place where my false Henri would stand out as a rank impostor.

Conundrum was on a parallel track of his own.

"An essential part of me is quintessentially French, Henri. And Paris is where it all began for me. Here I learned there was an alternative to the asphyxiating Englishness with which I had been saddled at birth."

I didn't interrupt as Conundrum warmed to his theme.

"Paris is an exotic realm way beyond the stifling embrace of Pudding Island. The pungent pong of garlic, *Gauloises* and *pastis*, laced with sensual *parfum* and *eau de toilette*. Ethereal babble of existentialist banter over marble tables in the *Dôme* and *Deux Magots*. Visceral cries of Piaf in Pigalle, husky tones of Juliette Greco in Montparnasse. And those amazing whores in *Rue St Denis* with fannies like Venus flytraps where men might vanish from sight never to be seen again. But there was poetry too. Tiptoeing at daybreak through the *Tuileries*, the magic of an early summer morning when the whole city held its breath, anticipating the heady whiff of *café au lait* and *pain au chocolat* even while the taste of last night's *amour* lingered on the lips. Love, sweet love swirled and eddied in the very air I breathed."

Conundrum sprinkled the French words like a celebrity chef seasoning a dish with herbs and spices. This was the first time he'd mentioned love in the context of his own life. I listened with bated breath to hear what confidences he might let drop under the influence of champagne flowing fast and free.

"I'll let you in on a little secret, Henri."

I feigned disinterest.

"Paris is paradise for the pursuit of married women. *Ah, les femmes mariées!* Nothing can surpass the pleasures they offer. In Paris you can take your pick. They have a special attraction I didn't properly understand until Gaston, an old friend and a real *habitué* of this kind of *liaison*, put me in the picture."

Conundrum lowered his voice.

"During one of our frequent drinking sessions, Gaston spoke to me of a certain *femme mariée* who excited him beyond measure. He couldn't figure out why. She was not more attractive or adept in the erotic arts than countless others. It took him some time to understand that it was all due to the telephone."

"The telephone?"

"The telephone, precisely so. Her husband would often phone her from the office when she was at home *in flagrante* with Gaston. *Le mari* seemed to have an uncanny sense of timing. Always at the crucial moment. As if somehow he knew. At first, these little interruptions annoyed Gaston and put him off his stroke. But when he noticed that the lady was more than happy to make love to him even while telling her husband what she planned to cook for his dinner that evening then Gaston learned to accept the minor inconvenience of the phone calls. Now listen well, Henri. For the best is yet to come."

Conundrum paused briefly to grab a refill of champagne from a passing trolley.

"Very soon Gaston found himself enjoying far more those moments when the lady was on the phone to her husband than when she gave him her undivided attention. Indeed, he began to reserve his best sexual efforts for when the husband rang and he revelled to hear those simpering *petits cris* that she couldn't entirely suppress when describing the *bifteck saignant* and *sauce béarnaise* she was about to prepare for her *très gentil mari*. Gaston took intense pleasure in her *petits cris* which he reckoned must be clearly audible over the phone. Indeed, he derived a regular *frisson* from the thought that he was screwing the husband as much or even more than he was screwing the wife."

200

Conundrum's eyes narrowed as he continued.

"But Gaston didn't yet understand the nature of the beast he had become. Unbeknown to himself, he now responded like a Pavlovian dog whose lustful saliva trickled every time the phone rang. And before long, he found himself unable to make love without it. He would sit impatiently on the bed chain smoking until the husband made his call. Only then could he spring into action. Then one day disaster struck. The husband didn't ring at all. Gaston sat with the wife all afternoon, drank a bottle of *Veuve Clicquot*, smoked a packet of *Gitanes* and eventually made an ignominious exit without having caused her to emit *les petits cris* to which he had become so dangerously addicted."

Conundrum gulped down the last of his champagne.

"After that, Gaston's *liaison* with this particular *femme mariée* was doomed. His sex life lay in tatters. He could only summon an erection when the phone rang, but could not maintain it without a cuckolded husband listening in. And that proved to be a rare commodity. Gaston went rapidly downhill. Soon a shadow of his former self. One day he decided to phone the lady who had been the cause of all his troubles to find a remedy. He chose the wrong moment. Clearly audible between her words were *les petits cris* the delicious gasps of pleasure that had been his pride and joy. Another suitor had taken his place. Even as Gaston listened she was riding an extended orgasm far deeper and more resonant than anything he had managed to stimulate. But worse was to come."

"Worse?"

"Why yes, Henri. Even in the direst situation there is always the possibility of worse to come. For now the husband grabbed the phone and, between grunts of ecstasy, thanked Gaston profusely for having rekindled his appetite for his wife. Hearing her *petits cris* over the phone while making love to Gaston had stirred his blood, reminded him of carnal pleasures long ago. Now he felt again a desire for his wife deep in his loins. The honour of the marital bed had been saved. *Mon pauvre ami*

Gaston listened impotently to all this until at last the *très gentil mari* gave out a long, low moan and hung up."

A short silence ensued.

"And what do you think happened next, Henri?"

That put me on the spot. But fortunately, Conundrum quickly answered his own question, albeit in a curious fashion.

"Mustn't give away the entire plot. Suffice it to say it's a thumping good tale and I like to think I tell it rather well. You'll get the full *dénouement* when you buy the novel. *FOR WHOM THE PHONE RINGS* is a damn fine title, don't you think?"

Conundrum now spotted the Eiffel Tower down below in the distance.

"Get an eyeful of that, Henri."

Conundrum chortled but since I failed to respond with even a smile, he explained the witticism in his best 'explaining' voice while pointing to his bloodshot eyes.

"*Eyeful Tower*, get it Henri? I don't usually 'do' puns, but that one was too awful to pass up on, don't you reckon?

Thoughts turned to our assignment. August seemed a strange time to be visiting Paris. But, as Conundrum now explained, our story was to evoke the special mood of the city during the summer doldrums when most of its inhabitants had taken themselves off to the *Côte d'Azur* for the month.

"Paris in August has a special charm, Henri. A song has been written about it. Far less frantic, much more relaxed. Time in suspense. The blessed emptiness a balm to the soul. You can hail a taxi, get a table in a restaurant, cross the road without getting run over. Little things like that."

As chance had it, on this particular August day emptiness was in short supply. A global army of young Catholics had converged on Paris where the Pope was to celebrate a monster Mass of epic proportions. As soon we set foot in the *Métro* we walked into a solid wall of rucksacks carried by every one of the 300,000 young Catholics clogging up the city. I got squashed up against a tall Bavarian youth in *Lederhosen* and cutaway singlet that afforded an alarming close-up view of his armpits from which tufts of golden hair sprouted like gorse bushes. These he sniffed alternately like a connoisseur tasting two different vintages, undecided which was of superior quality. I almost passed out.

After some of the young Catholics piled out at *Franklin D. Roosevelt* Conundrum slumped onto a *strapontin*. This brought Conundrum's nose down to the level of a large American bottom in nylon shorts. We alighted at *Charles de Gaulle-Étoile*. I now detected a new aroma lurking in the foetid atmosphere of the *Métro* passages: the stench of stale urine. Since the good old Parisian *pissoir* has made way for those automatic pay-as-you-pee cubicles various nooks and crannies of the *Métro* have been adopted as public conveniences. The hot breath of August now drew up layer upon layer of historic smells from the depths.

We staggered groggily into another train heading south. I watched the stations slide past: *Kléber, Boissière, etc...* It was at *Trocadéro* that the most amazing thing happened. Conundrum must have decided on the spur of the moment to do a runner. I didn't actually see him leave the train. But I distinctly saw him standing on the platform as the train pulled out of the station. He stared me straight in the eye with a look that defied me to comprehend let alone question his action. I noted he hadn't bothered to take his battered old suitcase with him. It was still with me in the train. What was the old fool up to?

I quickly reviewed the possibilities. Perhaps Conundrum was unwell, needed some air? But I didn't believe it could be that simple. Only then did I realise I had no idea where we were going. So what was I supposed to do? My next thought was this must be some kind of test. I would have to make some quick decisions in his absence that would somehow define the future course of events. I had scarcely begun to grapple with this when the train pulled in at the next station: *Passy*.

I couldn't believe my eyes. There was Conundrum standing on the platform in precisely the same attitude I had left him at *Trocadéro*. Incredible! And as the doors opened, he stepped back into the carriage and took up the same place next me he had previously occupied without a single word or even a gesture to acknowledge the impossibility of what he had just done.

"But how? What in the name of …. I mean how on earth did you do that?"

"Do what, Henri?"

"You know very well. I mean getting out at the last station and getting back on again at the next?"

"Are you sure I did that?"

"Of course, I'm sure. I saw you with my own two eyes."

"With your own eyes? You trust them, do you?"

"Of course. I believe what I see. What else can I trust?"

"Well, that's fair enough then I suppose, Henri."

Dammit, here was I trying to tell Conundrum he had just performed an astounding piece of magic. And here was the great conjuror, if not exactly denying it, then questioning my own ability to have perceived things correctly.

"Think it over, Henri. Anyone can appear to disappear. Re-appearing is the tricky bit."

Had I been tricked into seeing Conundrum disappear? If so, then how? Was he able to make me see things that hadn't happened? But if his disappearance was faked there was still the matter of his re-appearance. Here I was really floundering. All I knew was that the master magician had performed another trick. Perhaps by reminding me of his powers Conundrum was laying down a marker to ensure he had my full and undivided attention as we embarked on our Parisian adventure.

The train rattled on through its dark tunnel. After *Passy*, it broke surface like a missile from a bunker. We were launched into space over the *Seine* under a cloudless sky with a spectacular view of the Eiffel Tower. It really was an eyeful and no mistake. Conundrum's eyes lit up like those of a child at the circus. He didn't speak until we reached the next station: *Bir Hakeim*.

"This stretch of the *Métro* never ceases to astound me. One moment buried alive, the next flying free. Who would have thought such wonders are possible between *Passy* and *Bir Hakeim*? I trust you agree it was well worth the agony?"

I nodded. My soul had taken wing. In the excitement I forgot all about the disappearance/re-appearance riddle.

Our journey continued above ground to *Sèvres-Babylone*, where we alighted. We dragged our suitcases in the stifling heat up *Boulevard Raspail*. We passed a couple of swanky hotels along the way. The classy sort of establishment where Conundrum generally managed to have us lodged, fed and watered free of charge. But he ignored them one by one. I wondered what he had up his sleeve for us this time. We paused for breath at the corner of *Rue de Varenne* where Conundrum mopped his sweat-pearled brow as he tried to get his bearings.

"It's been a while since I was last here."

Then he turned into *Rue de la Planche*.

"Used to call this short cut walking the plank. *Rue de la Planche?* Get it, Henri? How is your French by the way?"

I contented myself with a non-committal Gallic shrug.

We turned into *Rue de Commail*, past a tiny square covered in sand, ideal for playing *boules* and exercising your dog. Nothing much around here except for a small bar just before *Rue du Bac*. Conundrum made towards it with carefully measured step. There was nothing else down here so I could only assume he wanted to have a drink at one of his old haunts before going on to our hotel. The shabby exterior of the bar had once been painted a deep shade of purple, a noble Burgundy, but now it was all blistered and flaking. Just before entering the dark, musty interior I looked up at the crumbling façade of rusting balconies and broken shutters. Faintly discernible were faded letters spelling out *HÔTEL PENSION SPLEEN*.

As my eyes adjusted to the gloom I could make out a zinc counter and behind it an assortment of colourful bottles lined up like pretty poisons on glass shelves under a huge mirror. A handful of rickety stools were scattered along the bar. No sign of any customers. The place seemed deserted. Then a slow, rasping voice addressed us.

"*Vous désirez, Messieurs?*"

Conundrum stepped forward. His formal bearing showed respect for the stout old lady seated impassively next to an antiquated cash register. Behind her was a sliding door marked *ACCÈS RÉSERVÉ AUX CLIENTS DE L'HÔTEL*. So was this dubious establishment to be our hotel? I feared the worst.

"*Madame.*"

"*Monsieur.*"

The greetings were spoken in a monotone: succinct, impersonal. But unspoken volumes weighed down on these two simple words. The atmosphere was charged with things unsaid. Without being asked, *Madame* (I never knew her by any other name) slopped measures of *pastis* into smeary tumblers. With a terse movement of a puffy hand she invited us to help ourselves from a carafe of tepid water on the bar.

Conundrum raised his glass.

"*À votre santé, Madame.*"

Madame remained silent. Unusually for him, Conundrum seemed ill at ease, as if walking on eggshells.

"*Et Monsieur Albert?*"

Her dull eyes flickered briefly upwards to the ceiling, then sank solemnly to the floor. I imagined *Monsieur Albert* lying sick in an upstairs room or even gone to a higher place. Conundrum emitted a sigh that could cover either possibility.

The conversation was at an end. *Madame* now placed two large iron keys with grimy wooden tags on the zinc counter, one in front of each of us. My worst fears had been realised. We were actually going to stay at *Hôtel Pension Spleen*. Leaving *Madame* at her post, we struggled up five floors of rickety staircase. Our adjoining rooms were on the top storey under the mansard roof. I was about to enter mine when Conundrum snatched the key from my hand and gave me his own.

"You'll be more comfortable in there, Henri."

I didn't argue. In this dump one room would surely be as bad as the other. To my relief, Conundrum proposed that we go out straight away. We walked for an hour or so in the stifling heat and at last sat down for a drink *chez Fouquet* on the corner of *Champs Élysées* and *Avenue Montaigne*. A few feet away from our table on the most expensive pavement in Paris there squatted a *clochard* who swigged in time-honoured fashion at a litre of *vin rouge* while scratching a flea-ridden mongrel.

Do dogs know what sort of people their owners are? Can they tell if we are winners or losers, social dropouts or A-list celebs? Are dogs blind to our social distinctions? Or is their devotion unconditional? And what about myself, this dog called Henri? Is he unquestioningly devoted to his lord and master Conundrum? I looked again at the tramp's dog. He was perfectly at peace with himself. His owner might just as well be President of France and he couldn't have looked prouder or happier. As for the *clochard*, he wore an expression of pure bliss, as if in his mind the *Champs Élysées* really were the Elysian Fields.

From the café terrace I took some action pics of passing *Parisiennes*. They looked sexy, cool, elegant, chic and all that, but eyes glinting hard as nails. Their menfolk – for all their own well groomed allure and elegance – walked tentatively in their scented slipstream like creatures of a lesser order, anxious not to be crushed like snails under the ladies' sharp stilettos. There were a few children about. I noted one with an eerily adult face was a juvenile dead ringer for Charles Baudelaire, his troubled poetic brow hatching a sequel to *Les Fleurs du Mal*.

Our brief, Conundrum now informed me, was to check out the scene at major tourist spots. So I grabbed a few snaps as we went, casually and without great interest, not knowing exactly what was expected. Another long trek brought us to *Montmartre*. Conundrum was visibly shocked at the sight of a *petit train touristique* taking sightseers up to the *Sacré Coeur*.

"A noddy train to Montmartre! Paris, the theme park. If France cannot defend herself, what hope for the rest of us?"

I would have gladly taken the noddy train. Instead I had to trail along behind Conundrum. We climbed up the hill to *Place du Tertre* where some of the world's worst artists hawked their wares. I reckoned my snaps might be in the same league. But I didn't give a damn. My mind disengaged from what I was doing. Like a dog I followed Conundrum's lengthening shadow through the streets of Paris. On and on we went in the stifling heat. I didn't care where we went, as long as it wasn't back to *Le Spleen*.

At last, Conundrum's thoughts turned to food.

"I've a little treat in mind, Henri. Dinner at *Café de Commerce*. As I remember it, one step away from a soup kitchen, air thick with smoke. Wine like vinegar. Waiters earned more than most of their customers. But we were all fellow travellers in those days. Barely keeping body and soul together."

On the way into the *Café de Commerce* we crossed paths with a group of Japanese tourists on the way out. I scanned the faces for one resembling the young girl who had penned a *haiku* on my hand after my epic swim across Lake Zurich. I drew a blank. No wonder, I had only a blurred memory to go on.

A smartly dressed hostess greeted us.

"Fumeur ou non-fumeur?"

By way of a reply Conundrum re-lit a yellowing home roll clinging to lower lip. En route to our table I took in an interior so spanking new it might have been installed yesterday. Clearly, this was no longer the earthy Parisian dive Conundrum had in mind. He was on the point of giving it up as a bad job when someone caught his attention. Among the bustling team of young waiters and waitresses was an old lady, working twice as hard as the rest. Conundrum flagged her down and asked if she remembered the good old days of the *Café de Commerce*.

"Moi, si!"

Her derisory lift of the eyebrows dismissed everyone else in *Café de Commerce* out of hand. But she treated Conundrum with respect and affection like a personal friend. On her way to serving a large, silver-haired American seated with his back to us at the next table, the old waitress paused to show the wine he had ordered. It was a classy number, *Château Lafite-Rothschild.*

In a theatrical fashion, Conundrum twiddled the stem of his glass and gave the waitress a wink. She winked back like a fellow conspirator. I soon discovered why. For, after uncorking the bottle and pouring our neighbour a few drops to taste, she deftly filled Conundrum's glass. All this happened behind the back of the American who finally pronounced himself happy with the wine and watched the waitress fill his own glass.

That turned out to be the first of several visitations. The bottle was soon empty. The American expressed his amazement.

"Am I getting through the wine that quick? At fifty bucks I'd expect the stuff to hang around a bit longer."

"*Mais oui, Monsieur.* The *Lafite-Rothschild* is indeed a quick one. May I suggest you order a *St Émilion.* It is much slower."

"Quick wines and slow wines? That's a new one on me. What will you sophisticated Frenchies come up with next? Well, what the hell, I'll give the slow one a try."

But the *St Émilion* disappeared as quickly as the *Lafite-Rothschild.* For every time the waitress served the American, she secretly poured Conundrum a generous measure as well. Soon my companion was well away and having so much fun he didn't notice anything amiss until a vast shadow fell across our table.

The American was a massive bear of a man with a thick neck and huge tattooed forearms.

"Perhaps you would introduce yourself. I think I've a right to know who's been siphoning off my *vino* all evening."

Conundrum sat there ashen-faced, for once in his life completely unable to speak.

"Well, who the hell are you?"

Conundrum mumbled his name in a feeble voice.

"It's a conundrum."

The American was not impressed.

"A conundrum? What sort of a name is that?"

At last, Conundrum regained some composure.

"One to tickle the fancy without taxing the intellect."

The American now grabbed a chair. I thought he was going to smash it over Conundrum's head. I wouldn't have minded. Instead, he sat himself down ever so calmly between us.

"I've got to hand it to you, you old son of a gun. That's one helluva scam you've got going there. I salute you, Sir."

Conundrum bowed his head but remained silent.

"Tell you what, why don't you order the most expensive wine on the list and we'll knock it back together."

"Well, that is most civil of you, er ..?"

"Elmer Z. Wiltshire II. Just call me Elmer Z."

A hand huge as a baseball glove squeezed Conundrum's. I heard a faint squeal above the cracking of bones.

"Think nothing of it, old fellow. I must say, you are one helluva guy, Conundrum."

"And so are you, Elmer Z. It takes enormous subtlety to view matters as you do."

"Subtlety, Conundrum? I've never been accused of that before. Just wait till I tell the wife about this."

To my immense relief, I was ignored. Except that when a magnum of *Gevrey-Chambertin* arrived, I also received a helping. There was a great clinking of glasses.

"So here's to subtlety! Up yours Conundrum!"

"And up yours, Elmer Z!"

Soon the wine was doing its work. Even sober, I guessed Elmer Z. was not one to mince his words.

"You're a cool customer Conundrum. Don't know how you get along with them Frenchies. If you ask me they've never forgiven us Yanks for liberating them from the Krauts. So tell me how you charmed that sour biddy. What's your secret? How much horsepower do you pack between your legs, old buddy?"

Conundrum was quick off the mark.

"More than you've got between your ears, I dare say."

It was a tense moment. Anything might have happened. But I need not have worried. Elmer Z. fell apart laughing.

"Ain't you the sassiest, Conundrum? Why, it's a real pleasure to be insulted by you. A refreshing change from the usual charming English hypocrisies."

Conundrum now chanced his arm.

"You're quite welcome Elmer Z. Though there's nothing wrong with a bit of honest, down-to-earth hypocrisy?"

Elmer Z. now walloped Conundrum across the shoulder blades with the flat of his hand. Conundrum's head slumped at the shock. He grimaced as if he had swallowed his teeth.

"Ain't you the funniest, Conundrum? My, how I love your smart limey arse, goddammit!"

When Conundrum raised his head from the tablecloth, he looked a trifle uncertain, as if wary of another blow. I think perhaps he was a bit rattled that Elmer Z. was more than a match for him in the verbals department. The playful banter continued over a few more glasses, the two of them hitting it off like a house on fire with wisecracks exploding like fireworks.

But Elmer Z. had the last laugh. When he called for the bill he searched his pockets for ages before finally announcing he had lost his credit card.

"Don't suppose you could loan me a couple of thousand francs, Conundrum? Just until I get to a *bureau de change*."

Conundrum's jaw fell and stayed down.

Elmer Z. fell about himself.

"You should go see yourself in a mirror, Conundrum, old sport. Like you've pinched your soft old pecker in your hard steel zipper. Just the sight of you makes it worth every franc. Best evening's entertainment I've had in ages."

Elmer Z. pulled out a small piece of green plastic and did the honours. With true American generosity, he even insisted on paying for our meal as well as all the wine we'd consumed together. Conundrum was visibly relieved. Elmer Z. concluded by saying that Paris sucked, France sucked, Europe sucked and this evening had been the highlight of his stay. He was glad to be going back home to good old Texas tomorrow. Conundrum promised he would look him up when next in the States.

We poured Elmer Z. Wiltshire II into a taxi, declining his offer of a lift. Better to quit while ahead. Drunk as lords we meandered back to *Hôtel Pension Spleen*. The bar was dark and deserted but *Madame* still sat at her post, as if she had been waiting up just for us. Without a word, she pushed our keys across the cold zinc counter as if placing a bet. Unblinking, she watched us pick them up and made no response to our softly muttered *bonne nuit* as we withdrew from her presence. On the way upstairs, Conundrum noted we had been given the wrong keys and again swapped his for mine.

That night I had a bad dream. In it *Madame* was standing before me in her night-dress, arms outstretched to enfold me in her clammy embrace. I awoke in a cold sweat. Then I realised the dream wasn't a dream. The real *Madame* advanced towards me. Having dragged her weight up five or six flights, she was out of breath and could only utter a single word.

"*Enfin.*"

Panic stricken, I reached for the light. As it flickered into life I took in the repulsive sight. *Madame* loomed over me, a thinly clad mountain of flesh. Under the cruel neon her skin had the pallor of a ghost. I was terrified. But *Madame* seemed equally shocked at the sight of me.

"*Ah, non. Vous? C'est pas possible ça!*"

Madame turned and retreated. I fell back on my pillow, heart beating in unison with her heavy footfall as she painfully made her way back down the steep, narrow stairs. I listened to the ever fainter thud of her footfall, each step like a muffled drumbeat marking the burial of her amorous hopes.

As the shock receded, so my brain started to work. If I wasn't the intended target of *Madame*'s nocturnal wanderings, there could be no doubt who was. The exchange of keys had been intended to deceive her. Conundrum had set me up good and proper. A sacrificial lamb tethered to a tree for an ogress to devour. Was there no limit to his readiness to use and abuse me? Why not just walk away and be rid of him for good?

Unable to sleep, I speculated on what might have once passed between the them. A romantic liaison behind the back of *Monsieur Albert*? It must have meant a lot to *Madame*. She had made a heroic effort to climb the stairs. Her disappointment had been equally monumental. Had *Madame* been attractive in her day? And had Conundrum come to the *Spleen* to stir the ashes of an old flame? I remember he once said that true love can only begin when human beings start to decay. As external beauty fades so internal beauty shines through.

But with *Madame* there was a thick carapace of ugliness impossible to ignore. And as for Conundrum, an emotional entanglement seemed wildly out of character for a man who scorned human feelings. But who was I to judge? I really knew nothing of his inner workings. And yet curiously, I felt closer now to discovering something of the real Conundrum than ever before. At last I fell into a dreamless sleep.

Next morning I was woken by a sharp tap on the door.

"Shake a leg, Henri. Be ready in five minutes."

Madame looked the other way as I dropped the key on the cold zinc counter. It fell with a leaden ring. Meanwhile outside, Conundrum hopped about excitedly on the pavement.

"Trust you had a comfortable night, Henri?"

I resolved to say nothing of last night's events, at least for now. As for himself, Conundrum gave nothing away.

"Slept like a log, myself. As I always did at the *Spleen*."

Somehow he made it sound like the Ritz or the Carlton.

"We'll have a leisurely morning, Henri. Main event today is lunch. And it will be one to remember."

The prospect of a lunch to remember didn't prevent us breakfasting pretty well off *croissants* and *café crème*. Afterwards, we strolled through shady streets. Conundrum offered no clue where we were heading. By the time we reached *École Militaire* the heat of the August day was heavy with intent. We struggled on to

Boulevard de Grenelle. I recognised the spot where we had poured Elmer Z. Wiltshire II into a cab. For a moment I feared we were returning to *Café de Commerce.* But then we took the *Métro.* The young Catholics were still much in evidence, albeit in smaller groups and mostly without their rucksacks.

We alighted at *Étoile-Charles de Gaulle* and headed north up *Avenue de Wagram.* Finally we reached the premises of *Guy Savoy,* the legendary restaurant in *Rue Troyon,* where we were greeted by a delegation of staff. Each had a particular speciality. First out of the blocks was a charming girl who asked us whether we wanted our water still or fizzy, chilled or tepid. A lovely creature. Sadly, she took no further part in the proceedings.

That was the only choice we were called on to make during the next three hours. What followed was a *menu à dégustation* composed by the *maître de cuisine.* We kicked off with an artichoke soup laced with truffles and parmesan and served with an *amuse-gueule* on the side in the form of a tiny *brioche,* no bigger than a cheese football. Having finished the soup, Conundrum eyed the *brioche* suspiciously.

"When I look back and wonder what did the damage, then I will perhaps conclude that this minuscule *gourmandise* was the culprit. Well, what the hell."

Conundrum speared the tiny *brioche* with the miniature silver fork supplied for the purpose and popped it in his mouth.

"So let the juices flow."

The meal passed largely in silence. Conundrum made great show of scribbling copious notes on every dish, posing outrageously as a serious food critic. What he was really writing in his notebook was anyone's guess. For the first five courses we drank a *Saint-Péray 1995,* a dry white *Côtes du Rhône.* Meanwhile, a more serious looking bottle, *Château Bellegrave 1992* had been decanted before us with full rites. The *sommelier* left it sitting on a small table by my right shoulder. I fancied I could hear the venerable claret drawing gentle breath beside me.

We had just been presented with an elegant *assemblage* of *girolles* mushrooms served with a golden *galette* of crisp potato dotted with specklets of a tangy Spanish ham, when the *sommelier* sidled up and whispered in Conundrum's ear.

"C'est le plat de transition, Monsieur."

We steeled ourselves for the switch from white to red. Time to face the big guns. Conundrum gave the claret three swift passes of flaring nostrils followed by an arched eyebrow subjecting it to soul-searching examination. Then he paused for a moment's reflection. Finally, and still without wetting his lips, he grudgingly gave it the OK with a barely audible grunt.

There was a sharp intake of breath from the *sommelier*. I could see he was quite taken in by the charade. Conundrum had acquitted himself well. The waiter bowed as if to salute the moment. Our glasses were ceremonially filled and we savoured the richer nuances of the *Château Bellegrave 1992*.

Conundrum's appetite was endless, his stomach bottomless. The five starters had me done. How I managed the two main courses that followed I have no idea. But I could only pick at the various cheeses and desserts.

Scarcely able to move, I staggered to the gents. While splashing the porcelain I noted the urinary elegance of the *Delafon* installation. It knocked your average *Armitage Shanks* into a cocked hat. What would dear old Buffy or Muffy or Fluffy make of that? I realised I was very drunk. When I got back to the table, Conundrum was wiping from his lips the crumbs of a tiny *friandise* that accompanied the coffee. Lunch was finally over.

After the air-conditioned restaurant, the hot breath of the torrid August day laced with the excremental hamburger smell of *Rue Troyon* almost brought me to my knees. Conundrum seemed unaffected as we wandered slowly through the sweaty haze back to the *Arc de Triomphe* and made our way down *Avenue Kléber*. Although it was late afternoon, the searing sun obliged us to stick to the shade of tall buildings on an epic trek that finally brought us to the *Palais de Chaillot* and the *Jardins du Trocadéro*.

We paused for a breather. I took in the scene. Young African men had set out their wares on the ground: fake designer handbags, ethnic trinkets, dubious wrist watches, plastic models of the Eiffel Tower, concertina postcards, luminous necklaces. Music played. Arab rhythms from Algeria and Morocco mingled with drums from Gabon and Senegal.

People started to dance. I relaxed to enjoy the show. Soon a small crowd of people was moving and grooving to the beat. Conundrum wandered off. No idea what he was up to I was glad to be left alone. Then I spotted him right in the thick of the action. He was standing still, immobile as a telegraph pole in a forest of trees swaying in the wind. All around him young people gyrated to the rhythmic command of the drums. What was he doing there, if he wasn't going to dance?

Then something amazing. First one foot, I think his left, began a tentative tap on the ground. By degrees, the movement spread up to the knee. Then his entire leg twitched and sprang into action quite independently of the rest of the body, which remained still as before. Next Conundrum's right arm came to life. Like a marionette whose strings were being tugged by an invisible hand, his left arm and right leg now joined in the action. But still his body did not appear to move. By now, Conundrum was at the centre of a growing circle of onlookers.

Then the miracle happened. Conundrum's torso awoke from its statuesque immobility. Suddenly, his back arched like a bow. He launched himself into a frenzied, syncopated movement that responded to every beat of the drums. One by one, the dancers abandoned their own efforts to admire the spectacle of this elderly gent dancing like a man possessed.

The performance lasted for several minutes. Finally, stepping off the dance floor to a burst of applause and even hugs from some of his female admirers, Conundrum grabbed a skateboard from a surprised youth and set off down a slalom course marked out by a colourful array of drinks cans. But he had no idea how to steer the board. Instead of swerving between the cans he ploughed straight ahead and sent them all flying. As the skateboard gathered pace with Conundrum planted on it stiff as a statue, I foresaw a messy end with bits of flesh and broken limbs plastered across the tarmac.

But Conundrum was riding his luck today. Several cans became wedged beneath the skateboard and put a brake on his progress. Gradually, his momentum slowed until he ground to a halt by the very last can, which obligingly toppled over to complete a clean sweep. Those who had witnessed Conundrum's dancing prowess assumed this was yet another party trick. A thundering round of applause detonated on all sides.

It only remained for a suitable *coup de grace* which Conundrum duly delivered. He made a beeline for the fountains. With a cry of joy Conundrum hurled himself fully clothed headlong into the basin. Right on cue a battery of water cannons erupted in an explosion of foam. Half of Paris followed hard on his heels. Within seconds a mass of bodies, mostly half naked, splashed and cavorted. I never saw Conundrum happier than at that moment in his delirious *bain de foule*, contented as a crouton floating in a great soup of human happiness.

Afterwards, he sat quietly on a stone wall waiting for his clothes to dry off in the hot sun. His pupils were dilated, as if he were on some hallucinogenic drug. Then I noted the colour of his waistcoat. After his dip in the fountain it had turned bright silver like the belly of a herring. So beautiful. Sheer magic.

"Humanity in the abstract, Henri. Can't get enough of it. My heart melts in a warm feeling of oneness with the masses. Feeling the same for them as individuals is another matter."

He rolled a celebratory cigarette.

"Never danced quite like that before. And here speaks one who has tangoed by the Bay of Naples, head buried in the breasts of the Duchess of Amalfi and waltzed the ball gown off the Empress of Austria at the Opera Ball in Vienna."

He now gazed across the river to the Eiffel Tower.

"Androgynous architecture. Top half clearly phallic. A monumental erection. Lower half most definitely feminine. Broad hips, legs spread wide open like a pagan fertility symbol, beneath which the *Supreme Pontiff* will tomorrow celebrate Mass in front of 300,000 young Catholics."

Conundrum looked at his watch.

"Time we were pressing on, Henri. We have a dinner to attend this evening."

"A dinner? After that lunch? You must be joking."

"No joke, Henri. It's a formal do. Would have mentioned it earlier, but I didn't want to cramp your style at lunch. As for myself, all that exercise has made me quite peckish. I think I have discovered my second stomach."

We made our way back to the *Spleen* to get ready. But shortly before we were due to go out, a crumpled scrap of paper was pushed under my door. I feared it might be from *Madame*, but it was actually a scribbled note from Conundrum.

"Regret dinner off due to wet socks. C"

Wet socks? I tapped on his door to enquire.

"It's like this, Henri."

He lifted his trousers to reveal a pair of thin sockless ankles protruding from his leather shoes.

"Seems I only brought one pair of socks and they are still wet from my dip in the fountains. So I'm a bit stuck."

Over his shoulder I could see a pair of threadbare socks hanging limply over the rim of the sink.

"No problem. I can lend you a spare pair of mine. Clean, of course. I'll go and fetch them."

Conundrum recoiled in horror.

"Oh, no. Far too personal, Henri. Really I couldn't."

I might have been offering him a used condom, for all the fuss he made. But it was senseless to press the matter. So I went back to my room and stretched out on the bed. I couldn't have cared less about dinner. I was about to nod off when there was a sharp tap on my door which swung open on impact.

218

"Come on, Henri. Problem sorted. Let's be off."

By way of explanation, Conundrum lifted his trouser legs to reveal his ankles stained black with ink to resemble socks.

"Time we were going. Look lively or we'll be late."

We managed to exit the *Spleen* without encountering *Madame*. As we walked down the *Rue du Bac* I asked how come we were invited to the formal dinner that evening.

"Not the sort of thing one is able to talk about openly. Suffice it to say I've done my fair share of *incognito* assignations with persons anonymous fetching and carrying brown envelopes full of greenbacks and all that caper."

Conundrum a secret agent? I now recalled the way he referred to our little jaunts as missions notched up. After each trip, did he not toast another small piece in the great European jigsaw? And had he not likened our Berlin escapade to a drop behind enemy lines? I looked at Conundrum with fresh interest as we crossed the *Pont des Arts*, the footbridge leading over the Seine to the *Palais du Louvre*. Even the trick with his socks added to the sense of intrigue. For who but a master of deception would think of counterfeiting a pair of socks with India ink?

Conundrum paused in the middle of the bridge and stared at *Île de la Cité* its tip shaped like the slender prow of a vast ocean liner anchored in the river. Old ladies stood patiently by their small dogs defecating in the *Square du Vert Gallant*. Then his gaze turned west into the setting sun, which transformed the waters of the Seine into a sea of liquid gold.

"This is where Clamence, the hero of *La Chute* by Albert Camus, was standing when he heard the laugh of the Absurd explode behind him and realised the sham of existence."

At that moment, a *bateau-mouche* packed with tourists passed beneath the *Pont des Arts*. The vessel had rows of seats on its upper deck like a floating cinema auditorium. Although it was not yet dark, the boat projected a battery of probing searchlights along the façade of the *Louvre*.

"But the people down there are being told a different tale. Ridiculous stuff, like how many tons of limestone went into *Notre Dame*, how many kilometres of steel in the *Métro* and so on. As for knowledge of the Camus sort, forget it. The next lot will have to figure it out for themselves all over again."

His literary lecture done, Conundrum continued over the *Pont des Arts*, a wraith-like figure, weightless as an autumn leaf. I caught a fleeting glimpse of those spindly, ink-stained ankles and could not suppress an absurd laugh of my own. Thus distracted I failed to note through which doorway of the *Palais du Louvre* he took me. I recall passing through a labyrinth of passages and then we entered a stately function room. A hundred or so guests were already gathered. Champagne flowed. We grabbed a couple of sparkling goblets as they shot past on a silver tray borne by a flunky in full *Louis XVI* kit. Conundrum cut an elegant swathe through the crowd, exchanging greetings with all and sundry *en passant* as if dancing a courtly *quadrille* of his own devising.

"Lots of lovely smiles, but don't be fooled. These people only show their teeth when they are about to devour something."

I now noticed that Conundrum had sprouted a breast full of medal ribbons to match those worn by everyone else.

"Where did you get those from?"

Conundrum gave me a withering look.

"Sorry, I mean, what did you get those for?"

"Oh, the usual acts of valour. Masturbating under enemy fire. That sort of thing. Like the rest of the crowd in here."

Conundrum bestowed on me one of his lop-sided grins.

"Once got home from a bash just like this, found a half chewed cocktail sausage in my jacket pocket. Tucked away behind my *Chevalier de la Légion d'Honneur* ribbon. Prime suspect, the French cultural attaché. So be on your guard, Henri."

A gong summoned us to table. I could only play with the food as a result of that enormous lunch. Besides, my attention was distracted by the lady opposite. She was, as they say in France, of a certain age. But the years had not dimmed the sparkle in her eye. No, that awful cliché simply will not do. Her look was like a flame seen in the dark silver of an antique mirror. And it was precisely her age that endowed her with such compelling lustre. All skin and bones, not a spare ounce of flesh on her. But what fine bones! And the skin though leathery was smooth and soft like a top quality handbag. In all she was real class. Pure cashmere washed in *Dom Pérignon.*

She introduced herself as Monique and the man next to her as *'mon très gentil mari'.* The very nice husband took no part in the proceedings while Monique gave an effortlessly natural display of *coquetterie* delightful to witness.

The dinner got off to an odd start when Conundrum dropped his napkin. Bending down to retrieve it, he then tucked it firmly under his chin and straightened his neck. As he did so, the *décolletage* of Monique's dress slipped a couple of inches to reveal a fleeting view of her breasts. Calm as you please, she bent down and with both hands pulled hard on something. Conundrum's napkin now popped out of his collar and vanished beneath the table while Monique reeled in a white silk trailer and adjusted her dress. Conundrum, seemingly unaware of what he had done, bent down again to retrieve his napkin and this time he came up with the correct item.

After that Monique could not keep her eyes off him while Conundrum did full justice to the dinner. Monique hardly bothered to lift a knife or fork as one gastronomic *tour de force* followed another. When the final dish, a dark *mousse au chocolat* in a pale sea of *crème blanche* was set before her, she laid down her napkin and looked Conundrum in the eye.

"You eat with such enthusiasm, *Monsieur.* But do you know what is the most important ingredient of a good meal? In fact, the only essential ingredient."

Conundrum remained obstinately silent.

"You really don't know, *hein?*"

Still he held his peace.

"*Eh bien*, then I shall tell you. It is the appetite. Without appetite the most sophisticated of dishes fails to please. But if your appetite is great enough, then you can devour anything with pleasure. Even your execrable English cooking."

Conundrum now initiated a conversation so heavy with sexual foreplay it was embarrassing to listen to.

"Eating is like making love, don't you think? Without appetite it is nothing, meaningless. But with sufficient desire you can devour anything, anyone, anywhere."

I thought Conundrum was coming on a bit strong. Surely she wouldn't fall for corny stuff like that? But she did.

"Ah, *Monsieur*, you speak with such truth. When I am in the mood, I could indeed give myself to anyone."

And so it continued with one egging on the other, raising the stakes higher and higher. Seemingly oblivious to this brazen verbal flirtation Monique's *très gentil mari* remained busy with his nose buried in a bundle of notes. He now stood up and walked over to a podium. There was a ripple of polite applause as the lights dimmed and he began to read out his speech.

I looked across to Monique to study her further. But the lady was nowhere to be seen. She had vanished into thin air. I cast a quick sideways look at Conundrum. His face was a study of rapt concentration as if he wanted to catch every word of the speech being delivered. And a very long speech it turned out to be. Conundrum quickly fell into a deep trance, eyes half closed like a cat. At one point, while others contented themselves with restrained clapping, he nodded enthusiastically and drummed the palm of his hand on the table. Finally, he gave out a loud gasp as Monique's husband reached his concluding remarks and folded his notes before returning to his seat.

At this moment Monique popped up from beneath the table, napkin in hand to wipe away what appeared to be a thin smear of *crème blanche* from her lips before tucking in to her *mousse au chocolat*. She raised an eyebrow at Conundrum.

"*L'appétit vient en mangeant, Monsieur. N'est-ce pas?*"

Conundrum took a moment to catch his breath. A flush of excitement coloured his cheeks.

"Indeed so. And that reminds me of what my dear friend Jean-Paul Sartre used to say about dinner parties."

Monique waited patiently for Conundrum to deliver his *bon mot* which he did with an enormous smirk.

"On ne mange pas. On est mangé."

Monique emitted an unladylike chuckle. Then in a stage whisper Conundrum added.

"But I never dared hope old JPS meant that literally."

Monique could not suppress a burst of lewd laughter. The *très gentil mari* shot a pained look at his wayward wife and then with a stabbing finger tapped insistently on her diamond-encrusted watch. It was time to break up the happy gathering. Pausing merely to pour a last drop of *cognac fine de champagne* down her bejewelled throat, Monique took her leave of us without a word, just a vaguely valedictory gesture of the hand. Her husband trailed behind dejectedly in her perfumed wake.

I could hardly believe what had just happened. Or had I imagined that an elegant sophisticated *Parisienne* had actually pleasured Conundrum under the dinner table.

"Remember what I said about married women in Paris, Henri. Always full of surprises. Monique has given a whole new meaning to the word intercourse."

Dinner over, Conundrum elected to take a different route back to the hotel. His reason for this, so he explained, being that life itself is a circular journey that inevitably deposits us right back where we started out. The very idea of simply returning the same way as taken on the outward leg went against nature. As we exited via the glass pyramids in the *Louvre* courtyard, Conundrum reflected further on the evening's diversions.

"Long live *les femmes mariés*. I think I may have gone one better than dear old Gaston. Nature achieves her ends with such infinite ingenuity and glorious unpredictability. The mysteries of women. Some with breasts like watermelon, others small and hard like crab apples. One of the sexiest I knew had nothing more than a handful of dried dates for tits. And what a beauty she was. Oh, the endless carousel of love. Even as the thrill of one embrace subsides so the tremors of fresh desire for the next shake the loins. But do not think of me as a dirty old man, Henri. Merely harvesting the ripe corn that falls beneath my scythe."

Conundrum may have had his scythe well and truly gilded, but his waistcoat exhibited a dull leaden colour under the sodium glare of the street lamps.

"I'm feeling rather crepuscular tonight, Henri. Tottering off into the twilight. I see the span of my mortal coil shrinking before me like the short end of a vanishing pyjama cord, and I know I will die no further advanced in enlightenment. The Grim Reaper stands at the foot of the bed, and still there is plenty of unfinished business. So many things left undone. I never rode the Catford Loop or the Metropolitan semi-fast to Watford. Now only the last train to Morden awaits and still so much remains to be understood. How did the *carabinieri* get their stripes? Why do dogs walk sideways? And what, for heavens sake, is a dry riser? I have yet to find out. I doubt I ever will."

Stupidly, I responded to the last point.

"Well, actually, a dry riser is essentially…"

"No, Henri. Have mercy. You don't understand. Some of life's little mysteries are best left unexplained. Indeed, that is their very point and purpose."

Now he gazed up at the stars.

"I looked at my razor last night and did some calculations. If one blade lasts a month and twelve last a year, how many will I need to see me through? And what if I buy them all now? Then I can steadily shave my way towards oblivion counting them off one by one. On the other hand, I could grow a beard, keep the blades and live for ever."

He chuckled. But Conundrum sounded sad, as if he had a clear premonition of his own imminent demise.

"They say the universe is expanding. But my own little world is shrinking. I swim in ever-tighter circles. The sands are running low. The whiff of senility hangs about my person. A sweet animal smell of decaying fatty substances. The body is decomposing while still alive. Why is it that the newly born and the almost dead have a distinctive smell? Between babies and oldies yawns the odourless chasm of adulthood that we smother with scents to give off an enticing aroma. Why is that, Henri?"

We crossed the *Pont Royal*. The river flowed fast and swollen through its arches, full of ominous purpose, a huge body of water flooding through Paris during the night, unnoticed by anyone except the tramps sleeping rough on the quays.

"Soon no more letters from Tom Champagne."

"Tom Champagne?"

"You know that chap from *Readers Digest* who used to tell everyone they have been selected to win a million."

I smiled, wondering where this was leading.

"And what happens when I die?"

At last he had spoken the fateful word. I held my breath, hoping this was another rhetorical question.

"Come on, Henri. It's not that difficult."

"Well, er... I'm not sure what you mean."

"We will pay 101% of the full value of your bond."

I didn't know what to say.

"Really, Henri. That was an easy one. I saw that recently in a leaflet from the *Norwich Union*."

I didn't like the sound of this.

"So what can I do but sit in front of the mirror and watch myself rot away as I garden my nostrils? Meanwhile, my old brain cells are popping off by the zillion even as I think these paltry thoughts. But I'm still no nearer to whatever it was I once so desperately wanted to know. Whatever that was. But I guess it doesn't matter anymore."

I found this immensely depressing. Surely my master sorcerer could do better than that? But perhaps I should finally accept there would be no great revelation in the pages of *Conundrum's Book*. I figured if he hadn't written it already, it was unlikely he would do so now.

Conundrum heaved a sigh.

"Young and old, what does it matter? We are simply at different stages of decomposition. What we perceive as youth and age is yet another illusion. After all, what differentiates a young, firm, smooth tomato from an old, soft, wrinkly one?"

Sensing this was a monologue, I kept quiet.

"One for the salad, the other for the sauce. That's about the long and the short of it."

Conundrum's next remark surprised me.

"So what is the point of a tomato, Henri?"

"Sorry, what's what?"

"The point of a tomato, Henri?"

I shrugged.

"The pips, Henri."

"The pips?"

"Yes, indeed. The pips are the sole point of a tomato. The sole purpose of a tomato is to produce more tomatoes. And to achieve that, it must die in order to release the pips. So the death of the tomato is its true aim and apotheosis."

"I see."

"But with humans it's different."

Conundrum tapped the side of his head with some force, as if knocking on a door.

"There are pips in the human cranium too. But, unlike those in a tomato, you must sow your mental pips while you are still alive. Cast them to the winds like dandelion seeds. Watch them take wing and fly away. Open up the brain of the dead Einstein and you won't find a single clue as to the theory of relativity. Absolutely no trace of $e=mc^2$. No point either looking for a note of music in Mozart's skull. And when you die they won't find anything inside your muddled head except for spent brain tissue. So don't bottle up your dreams, Henri. Set them free. That's the only way they will live on. Unless you give birth to your ideas while you are alive they will expire with you."

Conundrum gave me a searching look that cut me to the quick. I felt horribly exposed to his penetrating eyes.

"Worse still, they might even expire before you."

Conundrum had plucked one of my deepest fears from the dark recesses of my mind. I was cruelly aware of all the ideas and dreams even now drying up and dying inside me on account of my incapacity to turn thought into action, let alone put action before thought. Meanwhile, Conundrum continued.

"All we can say with any certainty is that life's purpose is to create more life. Yet people still insist on pointing to the great works of 'civilisation' and ask how can the whole epic endeavour have been in vain when there is all that to show for it? But it has been in vain, Henri. Utterly in vain. For we came from nothing and we will end in nothing. All this is nothing."

We were halfway across the *Pont Royal* when Conundrum suddenly stopped and leaned on the parapet. He looked down into the dark river surging through Paris on its endless journey towards the sea. Conundrum looked unsteady on his feet.

"Everything OK?"

"Nothing serious. Probably overdid things today."

He spoke with difficulty.

"We are all in freefall, Henri. Each and every one of us has been dropped from a different building. No one knows how tall or how short is their particular one. The only certainty is that we will all hit the ground sooner or later. And as we plummet down and destiny rises up to meet us, we can do nothing more than cry out that we are still alive, still alive. Then suddenly, it's time to hit the pavement. And that's the end of it. Splat!"

Conundrum now doubled up, as if he had been struck by a thunderbolt. He clutched his chest. Face white as a sheet. I thought he had died on his feet. Then his knees gave way. I only just managed to catch him as he fell.

"I must get you to a hospital."

Barely able to speak he managed to utter a few words as if his life depended on it.

"No hospital. Just get me to the *Spleen*. The *Spleen*."

No taxis about, so I supported Conundrum for the long walk up the *Rue du Bac*. Our progress was painfully slow. I felt the grip of his bony hand tight on my shoulder. At last, we turned the corner of *Rue de Commail* and for the first time I was deeply thankful to see the faded sign of *Hôtel Pension Spleen*.

The bar was shrouded in darkness. I dreaded having to arouse *Madame* from heaven knows what distant cranny of the building. Fortunately, the glass door responded to my tentative touch. Nor had *Madame* yet retired for the night. I could see her face, pale and impassive as a death mask, feebly lit by the moonlight reflected in the mirror behind the bottles. A cold shudder ran down my spine.

"I'll ask *Madame* to call you a doctor. You look awful."

"No doctor, Henri. I need sleep. Just sleep."

I don't know how much *Madame* caught of this brief exchange. Impassively and without a word, she pushed our keys across the cold, grey zinc of the bar top.

Helping Conundrum up the five flights of stairs was not as hard as I thought. He really was a mere wisp of a man. I wondered what would happen to him once I had laid him to rest. Laid him to rest? What was I thinking? The words felt chillingly apt. There was something fateful about the *Spleen* and its macabre *Madame*. As if she held some occult power over Conundrum. Although no obvious communication had passed between them in my presence, there had been a conflict of purpose, like two unyielding blocks of stone, heavy with mutual history, intent on grinding one another into submission. It now occurred to me that whatever twist of destiny linked Conundrum to this woman, there could be no doubt he had been drawn to this awful place with only one thing in mind, namely to die.

But why had I been dragged into this godforsaken hole? Was my role just a meaningless walk-on part in Conundrum's sordid melodrama? But what more could I expect? I had lost the power to assert myself, even to defend myself. In any case, I had reached a point where my own fate no longer mattered to me. I actually felt a curious sense of relief that I was an irrelevance. It was after all not such a bad thing to be of no significance.

I steered Conundrum to his bed by the garret window under the mansard roof. He stepped out of his shoes, abandoning them in mid-stride exactly as he once anticipated doing. But there was no upward soaring like a rocket. No flying without wings. Instead, he crawled submissively into his burrow like a sick creature. His ink-stained ankles looked perfectly ludicrous. What would the mortician make of that? He already resembled a corpse as he lay back fully clothed like one of those Sicilian skeletons in their Sunday best that hang in the Capuchin catacombs in Palermo.

"And now you must leave me, Henri."

"But you must cover yourself and keep warm."

I pulled the thin blanket and dirty bedspread over him. His waistcoat had assumed a ghostly shade of grey. Again, I insisted on calling a doctor. Still Conundrum would have none of it. The very thought seemed to appal him.

"No, Henri. Just me and mortality. We shall see which of us prevails. I do not want to be helped."

A sepulchral pause, then a thin smile curled his pale lips.

"How impotent is death. I may be about to peg out, but there are more Conundrums in the pipeline. Or should that be Conundra? Possibly even more Henris too, I dare say."

I thought he left things a bit dubious on my account.

"If only one could live to tell the tale."

He shivered.

"And now be gone, Henri. I need to be alone."

There was such finality to his words. No choice but to obey. I withdrew to my room. I pressed my ear against the wall but couldn't hear a sound. Like Conundrum I lay on my bed fully clothed except for my shoes that I placed nearby so I could slip into them at a moment's notice. I stared at the solitary light bulb in the ceiling. I was instantly transported back to our first encounter at that deadly dump in Wales. Then I thought of all the many places we had stayed since. I recalled Conundrum saying that all journeys ended up exactly where you started out. Now I could see what he meant.

A whole lifetime flashed through my mind as I lay there, willing myself to stay awake. It seemed so out of character for Conundrum to depart in so ignoble a manner. I had expected him to sign off differently, to exit on a winning note. Surely the great conjuror would pull a rabbit out of the hat?

There was another consideration. I had assumed all along that one day Conundrum's superior knowledge would become mine. Now I was cruelly aware that however much I had heard and observed, how little I had really made my own. Conundrum's death would leave my ambitions tragically unfulfilled.

The cold calculation behind this unworthy thought when my companion lay dying only a couple of feet away left me gasping at the extent of my selfishness. Then I nodded off. For how long I couldn't tell. All of a sudden I was aware of Conundrum's voice jabbering. I quickly pulled on my shoes and rushed next door. As I pushed open the door without knocking, he sat up wild-eyed, trembling.

"Who's that? Come to watch me croak in this hovel, have you? Damned if I'm going to die with you standing there like a vulture. No, I shall see off the Grim Reaper and live as long as I please. So you might as well bugger off. The party's over."

I don't know who he mistook me for.

"It's me, Henri. I heard you shouting. Thought I'd better check. How are things? You look bad. You need help."

I seemed to get through to Conundrum.

"Help? There's no help for me."

He looked ready to die.

"The *Grey Cairns of Camster* are calling me, Henri. I'm not much longer for this world. No need to give me that pitying look of a young person scared by death. If anyone thinks they will live for ever then they'll have a short think coming."

What started as a dry chuckle at his own witticism ended up a hollow rattle in his throat. I tried desperately to commit to memory what I feared were Conundrum's last words. But now his lips moved again. There was more to come.

"I was so looking forward to spending a bit of time with *Madame*. Watching her moustache grow. Stuff like that."

I think that's what he said. But his voice was frail. I could hardly hear what he was saying. What came next was spoken between sharp intakes of breath.

"My feet. Frozen. Blocks of ice. Must warm my feet."

Conundrum's bony feet with their bands of ink around the ankles protruded from the bedclothes. I wondered if I should attempt a massage or fetch a pair of socks.

"Go to *Madame*, Henri. Ask her for *Monsieur Albert*. Say it's urgent. Only *Monsieur Albert* can save me now."

I was hugely relieved. So Conundrum wasn't ready to die after all. But how could *Monsieur Albert* save him? I didn't dare question his wishes even though the thought of arousing *Madame* in the dead of night filled me with dread.

"Just ask her for *Monsieur Albert*. Tell her my feet are freezing. Matter of life and death. She'll understand."

With that, he fell silent. What choice did I have but to do his bidding? As I made my way downstairs, I reached yet another low in my complex relations with Conundrum. Suddenly, I wanted to go back and strangle the old bastard for getting me into this mess. Here I was creeping about like a thief in the night to awaken the disgusting *Madame* in the sordid flea pit that was *Hôtel Pension Spleen* to ask her for the help of this mysterious *Monsieur Albert* to warm the frozen feet of my sick companion.

At this point I was struck by the irony of me wanting to murder someone virtually on death's door. I almost laughed out loud. But how was I to carry out Conundrum's singular errand? Where did *Madame* sleep? I had only ever seen her perched on the stool behind the bar. Except, of course, for her appearance in my room a couple of nights previously, a memory which now returned in all its lurid awfulness. Then, in this very moment of fear and indecision, the light came on.

"*Vous désirez, Monsieur?*"

Madame presented a scarcely less frightening sight than on our previous nocturnal encounter. She wore a stained housecoat over her scanty *négligé*. Summoning my courage, I came straight to the point. I found I could say my piece in French.

"*Conundrum est malade. Il a besoin de Monsieur Albert. C'est pour chauffer ses pieds qui sont très froids.*"

I had delivered my message. I now braced myself for her reply. To my great surprise, *Madame* received this unusual request with equanimity. She reflected in silence and when she spoke, it was with eyes downcast, as if communing with a spirit.

"*Écoutez, Monsieur Albert. On a besoin de vos services.*"

Then she looked me in the eye.

"*Prenez-le, Monsieur.*"

Still I did not understand. My eyes then followed her stubby finger down to the floor where I could just make out a plump tabby cat lurking in the shadows.

"*Alors, prenez-le.*"

So *Monsieur Albert* was the hotel cat? I couldn't believe it.

"*Monsieur Albert? C'est lui?*"

"*Prenez-le, Monsieur.*"

Fearing I was the victim of a practical joke, I hesitated. At this point *Madame* lost patience. With a deft movement hard to credit in someone of her size, she bent down, scooped up the cat and pressed him into my arms. *Monsieur Albert* meowed, but put up no resistance as I clasped him to my chest.

With that *Madame* disappeared. A second later the light went out to the dry snap of a spring-action timer. I couldn't find the switch. So in total darkness I began the long climb upstairs, wondering what on earth *Monsieur Albert* was making of all this and how he would react to the daunting prospect of doing the night shift as Conundrum's foot warmer.

Surprisingly, *Monsieur Albert* remained completely calm and accepted his fate with perfect good grace as I laid him as carefully as I could across Conundrum's freezing feet. I noted they had turned a dangerous shade of blue to match the ink stain around his ankles. I retired with bated breath praying that the cat would know exactly what was expected of him and not move an inch from his post. I think it was the totally unfeline compliance of *Monsieur Albert* that finally convinced me Conundrum was well and truly endowed with special powers.

Next day I awoke soon after dawn and savoured the delicious cool air laced with the soft splash and gurgle of fresh water flushing out the gutters down below. I shut my eyes to absorb the ritual early morning sounds of Paris. Gradually I recalled the events of the night before. Was Conundrum still alive?

I hurriedly pulled on some clothes. No response to my tap on his door. I hesitated then turned the handle slowly, full of foreboding. I needn't have worried. I should never have doubted that Conundrum would see off the Grim Reaper. There he was sleeping like a baby, still fully clothed except for shoes and socks. The ever faithful *Monsieur Albert* lay draped obediently across his naked feet just as I had left him. The snoring of the one merged with the purring of the other in a sweet melody. It was an image of perfect contentment. Feeling utterly surplus to requirements, I withdrew and crept downstairs. How might I slip out of the *Spleen* without encountering *Madame*?

"Psst!"

Madame had spotted me. Before her on the zinc counter stood a glass of some steaming infusion and a plate of small pastries. With a minimal jerk of her head, she indicated I should take them up to Conundrum. So I climbed the five flights of creaking stairs feeling like room service.

Still no response to my knock on the door. So I placed the tray on the rickety bedside table. Conundrum didn't seem to notice it. I was on the point of leaving when he spoke.

"If that was the dress rehearsal, Henri, then I simply can't wait for the opening night."

So had Conundrum been trying on his own death mask before putting it aside for a future occasion?

"This could so easily have been it. The end of the line. And what a setting. Paris, the sordid hotel room: just the scene for an ignoble death following in the footsteps of poor old Oscar. Not very original. How corny can you get?"

He continued in more sombre tone.

"He who has looked death in the eye will not look back."

I continued to look blank.

"Carl Gustav Jung, Swiss psychologist, 1875-1961. I can give you the quote in the original German if you prefer."

"That's OK. Shall I sit with you for a while?"

"No need, Henri. *Je ne suis jamais seul avec mes platitudes.* But if you have nothing better to do."

Conundrum had entered a different phase: calmer, more reflective. The excesses of yesterday might have been the final glorious eruption of a dying volcano. His eyes glared wide open, like they were seeing far into the distance beyond the walls of this humble room. But now he noticed things closer at hand, like the hotel cat lying on his feet. He gave it a tender glance.

"Thanks to *Monsieur Albert* I live to tell the tale of my skirmish with death. Most instructive. Get your head round death, then make something of life. That's the trick. Let's face it, Henri. You have frittered away the fizz and bubble of youth. So why not reach out for what follows? Be finished with life before life is finished with you. Get acquainted with old age while still young enough to appreciate you aren't yet old. Understand illness while still healthy. And ultimately, know death while still alive. In short, be ahead of the game. Simply being alive is not enough. Happy is the man who has made his farewells. I don't think I'll miss being alive. There's a lot to be said for being dead."

Conundrum now assumed a wistful expression.

"I used to think the longest survivors were the winners by virtue of outliving whoever had died before them. But those who have shuffled off this mortal coil have only caught an earlier train or plane and are well off out of it. So let no one claim victory by outliving everyone else."

He prefaced his next remarks with a sigh.

"I'm tired of life, thoroughly tired. It's like one of those museums or galleries where the guidebook says you can happily spend a whole day. But after less than an hour you are looking for the exit. I can endure the relentless daily routine of shit, shave and shower – hopefully to be followed by a shag – but the same old mind games, aye there's the rub. I'm so tired of having to think my own thoughts and generally being me."

This was not what I expected. The great summing up was turning into a pathetic lament. Perhaps I shouldn't have fetched *Monsieur Albert* and just let nature take its course?

"Maybe I wasn't yet ready for death? Or death wasn't ready for me? Anyway, I'll have to soldier on for a while longer until death, my own death, finally gets its act together."

It was pointless trying to say anything. Even more than usual Conundrum was talking at me rather than to me.

"Trying to become pure spirit in this life is a doomed enterprise. Best accept defeat and embrace all the garbage it is our sad lot to wade through. But it's not all doom and gloom. As one gets older and has release in sight so one's heart gladdens at the imminent prospect of letting go. That's why some old people have a twinkle in their eye. They're demob happy, end of term is coming. Soon it will be over and they can meet their maker, be eternally snuffed out or whatever metaphor they care to name. Of the entire world's religions only Buddhism has grasped the essential truth that the one possible and desirable escape from existence is in nothingness. No afterlife as such, just a series of rebirths until you find the ultimate way out."

Nothingness. Was that Conundrum's game? But for now he was for better or worse back in the land of the living. His eyes had fallen on the tray with the hot infusion and pastries.

"What's this, Henri? You shouldn't have."

"I didn't. I mean it's from *Madame*, actually."

I heard a sharp intake of breath.

"From *Madame*?"

I nodded.

236

"From *Madame*, this *tisane?*"

I nodded again.

"And the nun's farts[2] too?"

"Yes."

He contemplated his little feast solemnly as if about to take Holy Communion. I wanted to ask him about *Madame* and what had brought him – and me – to the *Spleen*. But Conundrum was still too weak for interrogation. He sipped the *tisane* and then nibbled daintily at a nun's fart. His face, tormented and sick yesterday, was now strangely at peace, almost infused with fresh life. And suddenly, he was off on a crazy new tack.

"Surprised I lasted this long. Could easily have died in childhood, you know."

"Really?"

"Oh yes. My father would thrash me to within an inch of my life."

"Surely not?"

"Oh, yes. Things weren't metric in those days."

Conundrum laughed in my face.

"God bless you, Henri. You always take the bait."

Conundrum was back with a vengeance. I now felt no scruples about asking him the question that had plagued me since our arrival at the *Spleen*.

"Why did you come to this place?"

He shrugged. I decided to be more direct.

"What's going on between you and *Madame*?"

"How much experience do you have of women, Henri?"

He eyed me cryptically.

"No, better not answer that one."

Conundrum rounded up the remaining crumbs of the nun's farts with a grubby index finger and then washed them down with the last drops of the *tisane*.

"And what's that supposed to mean?"

---

2 *Pets de nonne* are a very light French pastry.

Conundrum came over weak and weary, a convalescent who has exhausted his stock of energy for the day.

"Later, Henri. I cannot speak of this thing under her roof. When we are out of here, I will be fully frank with you."

"Fully frank?"

"You have my word."

His word? That was a rare promise. I let the matter drop. Conundrum had said enough to confirm my suspicions. *Madame* did hold some mysterious sort of power over him.

Conundrum now handed me a small battered book with a broken spine disgorging well thumbed, dog-eared pages. I felt like a novice priest being presented with a breviary. I looked at the title. *Plan de Paris par Arrondissement et Communes de Banlieu avec la station du métro la plus proche. Nomenclature des rues. Autobus avec Répertoirs. A. Leconte, Editeur, 1964.*

"See how you get along with Leconte, Henri. I'll rest up and take it easy for a while."

I took the hint and left Conundrum resting in bed at the *Spleen*. With the borrowed copy of Leconte's *Plan de Paris* in my pocket, I set off on what turned out to be an amazing journey across Paris. The name of our local *Métro* station *Sèvres-Babylone* triggered magical associations, opened a door to a subterranean realm of weird and wonderful resonances stretching from *Pyramides* and *Le Kremlin* to *Porte des Lilas* and *Jasmin*. Much more exciting, I soon realised, than London Underground's boring old Hounslow West and Aldgate East.

Once in this groove, I scaled a mountain range at *Pyrénées*, slipped over the border at *Place d'Italie*, encountered poetry at *Montparnasse-Bienvenue*. The thunder of battle resounded at *Oberkampf, Crimée, Solférino, Stalingrad*. Havens of happiness beckoned at *Place des Fêtes, Porte Dorée, Gaité, Plaisance* and *Bonne Nouvelle*. On and on it went. I drifted through this parallel universe beneath the streets of Paris. Suddenly, I was intoxicated by the power of words. Exhilarating. I felt the urge to write. Henri the writer. That would give Conundrum a shock.

Then something really startling happened to bring me sharply back to my role as photographer. I was sitting in *Place des Vosges*. Parisian mid-August lethargy hung heavy in the air. The scattering of people in the square resembled ghosts from a century ago reclaiming their lost city. I took a few pictures, thinking how perfect they would look in soft focus, printed in sepia and mounted in an old leather bound album. A lady in a straw hat lay on the grass, motionless and timeless as a fallen statue. I snapped her and then a couple of metal chairs someone had dumped in the fountain, all very moody and artistic, thinking again how wonderful that would look in sepia.

Suddenly, I realised I was no longer just imagining my pictures in sepia, I was actually seeing them in sepia. I blinked in disbelief. No, I wasn't dreaming. Everything I saw was through a sepia-tinted filter. I shut my eyes and counted to ten. But when I opened them again still the grass wasn't green, and the sky wasn't blue. They were, just like everything else, shades of soft brown. Again I shut my eyes and counted to sixty. A minute should be enough to restore my vision to normal. But it wasn't. My whole world was still in shades of sepia and nothing else.

What was going on? For the first few moments I was bemused. Such a novelty to see the world in this nostalgic mood, the present posing as the past, auditioning for a place in the archive. The mood was soon shattered when I realised I had no way to switch back to normal vision. Was this a form of colour blindness? Keep calm, I told myself. It doesn't hurt and it's not life threatening. All to no avail. Panic set in. Wherever I looked, whatever I looked at, it was all in sepia.

I now recalled how Conundrum's colourful waistcoats had shown up in my Spanish pics in exactly the same shade of muddy brown. I was immediately convinced of his part in this. I could find no other possible explanation. Was there no end to his magic? Not content with hijacking my thoughts, now he was inside my head, tinkering with my vision.

I returned to the *Spleen* for a showdown. On entering the bar, *Madame* indicated to me with a vague gesture of the hand that Conundrum needed rest and should not be disturbed. Suddenly, the prospect of sleep was deeply appealing. Perhaps, with my conscious mind disengaged, the subconscious would sort out the visual disorder.

But next morning, things were just the same. The world remained immersed in a tank of sepia. I was about to knock on Conundrum's door, then thought better of it and walked away. I had no further obligation. He was now in the tender care of *Madame* who could nurse her convalescent back to health with her regime of *tisane* and nuns' farts. Well, good luck to the pair of them. I would resolve the sepia vision thing without him.

I left Conundrum at the *Spleen* and resumed my urban wanderings through Paris in August. Without him constantly peering over my shoulder, pouring scorn on my efforts, I could follow my own instincts, do my own thing, be my own person. A weight had been lifted from my shoulders. Yes, today would be a kind of Liberation Day, just for me.

I wandered up *rue Mouffetard* as the street market was winding down. Melon rinds lay in the gutter like discarded smiles. A fish eye stared at me reproachfully from the greasy cobbles. I had a huge desire to take a picture. So much expression in this sad disembodied head of mackerel. I shot a few frames, and then some more. Then I stopped. What was the point? Was this fish's head not sufficient in itself? Did I really need to photograph it? Did anything need to be photographed? There was far too much asking to be photographed. Where to start? Where to stop? Suddenly it all seemed pointless. Feeling low and deflated I trudged aimlessly on through my sepia-infused Paris.

"Get any good snaps, Henri? Very nice sepia tones at this time of year, don't you reckon?"

I spun round. No-one there, only Conundrum's voice inside my head. And soon drowned out by a street accordionist who struck up the opening chords of *Sous le Ciel de Paris*. Song sheets were distributed. An old woman sang *Je suis l'esclave des souvenirs.* Was this reality for real or merely the mirage of some phantom music hall from the distant past? I couldn't be sure.

I continued my wanderings until late afternoon, eventually drifting into *Les Deux Magots* where I ordered a glass of red wine. Sorry, make that sepia wine. For that's how it looked and even how it tasted. I was by now thoroughly fed up with my sepia-tinted universe. I thirsted for colour. In this angry, resentful mood I sat in the café with Conundrum's disintegrating street guide opened in front of me, wondering where to go next and what good it would do me. And then a man forever etched in my memory as *Monsieur Tristesse* sat down at my table and engaged me in a bizarre conversation.

"Comme vous avez l'air bien triste, Monsieur."

I had no problem understanding the literal sense of his remark: 'How very sad you look, *Monsieur.*' Nor was I surprised to hear that I looked sad. Sadness permeated my bones. But he said it in such an encouraging, positively approving fashion as if he were actually paying me a compliment something along the lines of: 'How well you wear your sadness, *Monsieur.*'

I don't know why I chose to lie, but I insisted that I was *au contraire* quite happy, in fact a good deal happier than I had been for a long time.

"Indeed? But I can see through all that."

"Oh?"

Not wanting to breathe a word of my sepia affliction and to show I really was happy, I began to tell this gentle stranger of the sweet pleasures of my long walks through Paris. But every time I told him of something or other that had made me particularly happy, *Monsieur Tristesse* released a wistful sigh.

"Ah, how sad to imagine one is happy."

I looked hard at him to see if he was serious.

"We are all dying, *Monsieur.* From the moment we are born we start to fade away. Our very essence is transience. Only one outcome is possible. All we can do is pluck flowers along the way as our tumbrel rumbles along. *Comme c'est triste tout ça*. Life, the whole human experience – from nothing, back to nothing – is sad, essentially sad. Happiness is unnatural. Against nature."

The very idea of happiness seemed to upset him deeply.

"*Le bonheur? La joie? L'euphorie?* Many words for nothing at all. What is the point of being superficially happy when you can be profoundly sad? How beautiful it is to be sad! I once nursed a wonderful sadness for months. Then, one day, it flew away. *Un beau jour ma belle tristesse s'est envolée.* And I..."

I was about to say 'how sad' but then realised how odd that might sound in this particular context. I looked at *Monsieur Tristesse* with mounting interest.

"And I was left with ..."

His voice broke off again.

"I didn't recognise it at first. It took me a while to realise what it was. *Le bonheur.* Happiness. For what else is happiness but the absence of sadness? Me, happy? *Quel désastre!* Take away my sadness and you take away my soul. There seemed no point in going on. I prayed my so-called happiness would not last. And that when it passed my sweet sadness would be there waiting, a blissful melancholy staying with me like a faithful companion right until the very end when, and only then, the last soft sigh of regret would seep from my body. Fortunately, I didn't have to wait long. The very awareness of my happiness depressed me so enormously that sadness soon reclaimed me."

"But surely that all sounds a little bit..."

"Sad?"

"Yes, I suppose that is the word I'm looking for."

"But there is a bright side."

"A bright side to sadness?"

"Of course. *Certainement.* The sadder you are, the easier it is to say goodbye to this vale of tears and suffering."

"Yes, I can see that. Having no regrets when the time comes. It must be a weight off your shoulders."

"It's much more than that. It's actually a source of a very special kind of – dare I say – happiness."

"But surely that's precisely what you are trying to avoid by embracing sadness?"

"No, not at all. Sadness is its own reward."

Monsieur Tristesse now looked at his watch. Clearly we had already exhausted the subject.

"So many things to do, so little time to do them. Too many possible lives to choose from. Every option equally futile. I recoil before the crushing complexity of choice. Shall I stay? Shall I go? Does it matter? Nevertheless, I must go now. *Comme c'est triste la vie.* Parting is such sweet sorrow."

With a helpless shrug, *Monsieur Tristesse* took his leave and vanished into the crowds on the *Boulevard St Germain*. I wondered what Conundrum would make of him. How I would love to bring the two philosophers together and listen as they debated the big issue of happiness versus sadness.

As I pondered what *Monsieur Tristesse* had said, I stared at the place where he had sat, the imprint of his backside still quite visible on the plastic upholstery. But as I watched, this last relic of his physical presence dissolved before my eyes like a shadow that had become momentarily detached from its owner and now ran off to be reunited with him. Finally, when all trace of *Monsieur Tristesse* had vanished, I wondered whether this curious person had been anything more than a figment of my imagination.

That's when the second miracle happened. As if a switch had been flicked, my sepia vision suddenly turned blue. I don't know the exact term for this particular shade. But how fresh and exciting everything looked in its novel blueness. I was on my feet in a flash, anxious to see more of Paris while this blue mood lasted. Didn't Picasso have a blue period? Well, it wasn't a patch on mine. Blue permeated every shade of every colour. I rushed about in a frenzy, laughing out loud. The world had been reborn! But the novelty of seeing everything in blue didn't last. Blue was cold. Blue was lonely. Blue was depressing. All too soon I missed the warm earth tones of sepia.

Not wanting to return to the *Spleen*, I walked at random, my steps bringing me to the famous second-hand bookshop *Shakespeare & Co* just across the river from *Notre Dame*. On an impulse I stepped inside. The shelves that once held out the promise of infinite riches with their precious volumes now resembled so much merchandise in a supermarket. What did all these words add up to? The way I felt, it was enough to read the titles on the spines to gauge the pretensions and empty promises lurking on the pages between the covers.

But without the human urge to explore and express the mysteries of life, what meaning could there be in the world? Meaning? Meaning what? I recalled Conundrum's caustic words in Cadaques in the shadow of that old impostor Salvador Dalí propped on the crutch of his much-vaunted impotence. Suddenly I felt stupid. I was still barking up the same old tree of adolescent illusions. When would I ever be able to free myself of such childish props as the need to believe in something?

I was a hopeless case. Quite hopeless. I left the bookshop under a brooding sky of dark rain clouds which chose that very moment to burst. No sooner had I pulled out an umbrella to shelter from the downpour than I felt a light tug on each elbow. At first, I thought I was about to be mugged. Then the sound of female laughter burst in both ears simultaneously and I saw my assailants were two young girls who accompanied me across the rain-spattered cobbles of the boulevard by the river.

We huddled close together under my umbrella. Their *joie de vivre* carried me along. I felt weightless. I revelled in a sense of pure ecstasy. I wanted the street we were crossing to be endlessly wide and for the rain to fall forever. Blue was the perfect colour for this watery scene. But all too soon we reached the other side and the downpour stopped as suddenly as it had begun. The girls detached themselves from my arms.

I wanted to detain them somehow but could only raise a laconic smile to their cheery *"merci et au revoir"* as they tripped off nonchalantly. Surely, there would have been a different outcome if Conundrum had been the man with the umbrella? Right now a cosy threesome would be heading for a café and then most probably on to a shuttered hotel room. Damn Conundrum! Why was he always tormenting me? It didn't matter where I went, what I did. Next to him I would always be that poor, pathetic, inadequate creature, Henri.

Now, as the storm clouds dispersed, a shaft of sunshine pierced the sky, lighting up the soaring Gothic towers of *Notre Dame*. For a second I detected something warm, the merest suggestion of red or yellow shimmer briefly in the blue before dissolving. That must be a sign of something.

I headed down *Quai de Montebello* and across *Pont au Double*. The west front of *Notre Dame* reared up in all its Gothic glory. I had no notion what I was about to do. Just a sense I was about to bring off a great existential trick. One that would bring me face to face with my destiny or whatever was waiting. In short, I felt my hour had come. I'll spare you the details because I can't remember them. Did I purchase a ticket to climb the stone steps to the parapet? Were there other people about? What was going through my mind at the time? All I can recall with certainty was the drama of the moment when I reached the top of the stairs and surveyed the scene before me.

At the end of the parapet, the grotesque statue of *Le Penseur* gazed out over Paris. I smiled to myself, imagining the surprise on those scornful stone features when I flew up and away like a bird. And that's when I realised what I was about to do. I was going to live out Conundrum's metaphor and fly without wings. Yes, that was it! I would upstage the old bastard! I would steal his dream! Already I imagined myself flying in triumph past his window at the *Spleen* just to rub it in.

I was deliriously happy. I didn't care if I should fail. So what? It was everything or nothing. Besides, what better launch pad into eternity than *Notre Dame?* Given the enormity of what I was intending, I felt strangely calm and collected. I drew breath, an athlete about to jump. With nothing to hold me back, I waited for an inner signal to act. Several seconds passed. Then I noticed I wasn't alone. Someone stood there almost hidden behind the ugly stone figure. Curious to see who it might be who would witness my moment of truth, I approached quietly.

I shuddered as I recognised Conundrum standing next to *Le Penseur* motionless like another statue of stone. Somehow he must have risen from his sickbed and made his way up here. On seeing him I hesitated, vaguely suspended between earth and heaven. My great project of flying without wings seemed to fly off without me. I was sure Conundrum was fully aware of my intention. But he made no mention of it when finally he cast his eyes in my direction without surprise as if he had been expecting to see me. His face shone with an inner light.

"Back there in the *Spleen*, on what I hoped to be my deathbed, I felt I would soon be a handful of dust scattered to the wind. To be recycled over many millennia through successive states of existence – mineral, vegetable and animal – until my atoms regrouped ready to be launched back into the world as another specimen of *homo sapiens*, a fancy firework that shines and splutters in the sky for a brief moment before being extinguished and once again rejoining the great chain of being."

Conundrum was staring at some invisible object.

"I saw patterns, Henri. Swirling lights and colours. Like cosmic radiation at the birth of time. The Big Bang of creation is inside us. The handwriting of the Creator is right here."

He tapped his cranium.

"Then the scene cleared. Only for a moment. But enough to reveal the nature of things as they really are. I had my worst fears confirmed. We humans are alone in the empty cosmos and surrounded by infinite emptiness. Yet we blithely assert that nature abhors a vacuum. We are scared to acknowledge the grim Truth with a big T that Nature with a big N positively delights in a Vacuum with a big V. Meanwhile, our obstinate Planet Earth upsets the immaculate emptiness, destroys the awesome sterility of the grand design."

Conundrum fixed me in a steely gaze.

"Earth is the odd man out, Henri. In this inanimate universe of dead dust and noxious gases ours is the only place still infected by this curious thing called Life. Our obstinate biosphere is the thin blue line protecting and sustaining us against the combined forces of universal annihilation that long to snuff us out utterly and totally."

Conundrum's world-weary expression was drained of all energy or purpose. He spoke like an automaton. This was nihilism in the literal sense of the word.

"Yes, infection. Planet earth is 'infected' by life. Above all by arrogant humans, the self-appointed lords of creation, with their foolish notions and dangerous ambitions. We pit ourselves senselessly against the underlying desire of the universe to attain nothingness. Like small children we raise enormous architectural follies such as *Notre Dame* to the heavens. We are afraid to acknowledge the vacuum. And so we invent fine and fancy fairy stories for everyone to believe in. And then have the audacity to grace them with the name of Truth."

Conundrum groaned, labouring under a great weight.

"Don't you see what this means not just for religion but also for philosophy, art, civilisation and all those things humanity holds dear? They have less eternal value than cosmic dust? For if our natural world is but an aberration in the grand design then all we have created with our human ingenuity must perforce be an aberration too. We have come from nothing and perforce we will return to nothing. The irony is that humanity should be so complicitous in the destruction of its own habitat. Therein lies the subtlety of the hidden scheme. Humans are programmed, doomed to self-destruct. Nothingness is our end game, our final destination. Perhaps it is even our higher destiny?"

I gulped at the depth of this bleak vision.

247

"Is this the great blasphemy you mentioned in Rome?"

Conundrum sighed and hung his head.

"I have lived long enough with this dark thing. But it will not let me go. Even while thirsting for my personal extinction, I must soldier on with the boring and pointless business of being me. Adieu sweet dreams of whatever else I might have imagined possible. Let me take up once more my tired old role of being the clapped out creature you see before you."

Conundrum leaned on the parapet next to *Le Penseur*, the spitting image of the gargoyle sticking out its tongue at all things in heaven and earth. They were perfect partners in crime.

"Yes, back once more to my poor old fragmented self, a pathetic ragbag of tics, gestures and *bons mots*. Yet I once had an unshakable certainty all I had to do was discard the false baggage and I'd be left only with that which was 'true'."

Conundrum now looked me in the eye.

"Yes, Henri. I too suffered from the same ailment that afflicts you. The enchanting mystery of life once captivated me as a wondrous plaything, an exciting enigma. But it soon grew heavy during the painful paradox years before at last turning into the fully grown conundrum you see before you today."

Conundrum was in full confessional mode. This was the closest he had come to giving a full explanation of himself. At this crucial point he appeared to lose track of his thoughts.

"Where was I? Discarding things? I was convinced that the things we cling to most are invariably those we should let go of first. Trouble was, I discarded so many things so quickly I saw I would soon have nothing left to cover my naked transparency. I got scared. So, to be like everyone else, I cobbled together this shabby shell of borrowed behaviour and misappropriated mannerisms you see before you now."

Conundrum now performed some curious charades.

"Take a good look at me, Henri. This inscrutable leer of lofty disdain I won from a French poker player in the casino at Deauville. This serious intellectual expression I purloined from a

German professor of philosophy in Heidelberg. This air of meaningful concern I acquired from a social worker in Sweden."

I wondered where Conundrum had obtained the louche lop-sided grin that he now directed at me.

"And this rather effective way of breaking wind I stole from a Spanish peasant in the Sierra Nevada of Andalucia."

Conundrum performed a full demonstration, as if I needed reminding of his amazing capacity for flatulence.

"But my question, Henri, is this. Strip away all that stuff, and what remains? What actually lies at the heart of the great edifice of my character? It's no more than an empty room."

Conundrum surprised me now. Just when I expected him to sink even lower into introspection he flared up like the embers of a dying fire. His eyes blazed with excitement.

"And do you realise how dear to me that is, Henri? This vast emptiness at my core is my most precious possession. An empty room, a vacant space waiting to be filled not with anything I might choose for myself, but with something sublime that chooses to make its home in me. Meanwhile, no one can steal my inner void from me, because there is nothing there to steal. All I have to do is to make sure nothing else fills it. It has taken me the best part of a lifetime to create this treasure chamber of my personal emptiness. And now at long last I'm almost ready to display my glorious transparency to the world."

Something miraculous happened at this point. Although everything else I saw was blue, Conundrum's waistcoat slowly turned sepia. Then it drained of all colour and gradually assumed the limpid sheen of an old mirror whose silver backing has blackened with age, just like that one in Rome in which I had observed his detached image.

"I know something, Henri. And even if I don't yet know it fully, I know it is there for the knowing. It will come to me when the time is ready, in the ripeness of the season. I am in no hurry. But when it comes, I shall be ready to grasp it and swallow it whole. And one day it shall be yours too."

Now the waistcoat started to disintegrate, to break up before my eyes. In places I could see right through Conundrum's body to the stonework behind. I could hardly believe it. Was he going to dissolve before me?

"So don't fill your life with meaningful things. Rather rid it of all meaningless things. Make your soul an empty vessel and polish it until you can see through it. Keep at it until finally you will be clear as glass, a fortune-teller's crystal ball showing the way forward. The see-through soul. That's the trick."

A fortune-teller's crystal ball? I recalled *Madame Renée Clairvoyante* at the end of Southend Pier. The crystal ball on her table! My heart thumped. Were the pieces of the puzzle finally falling into place? Suddenly it all made some kind of sense. Then with equal suddenness, it made no sense at all.

I saw Conundrum revealed, not as a man ready to fly without wings but labouring under the dead weight of all the emptiness stored up inside his person. His entire act was a hollow pretence. And he had made me believe in him, he who believed in nothing! I wanted to hurl him over the parapet of *Notre Dame* and watch him plummet to the ground.

He pre-empted me with a doleful expression.

"Well, go on, Henri. Why not push me over the edge? I see your purpose. What is stopping you?"

Even as he spoke, his waistcoat began to lose its limpid transparency. I forgot my murderous designs. The moment had passed. We returned to earth not flying or falling but in pedestrian fashion via the stairs and made our way to the café where just an hour earlier I had spoken with *Monsieur Tristesse*.

Conundrum immediately resumed his train of thought.

"So take my advice, Henri. Empty your soul of all falsehoods, the desire for meaning, faith, hope, love."

I was on to him like a shot.

"Love? Where does that fit in your scheme of things?"

He winced. I had hit him where it hurts.

"Love, Henri?"

So the L word really was Conundrum's Achilles heel. I pressed home my advantage.

"Yes, love. How do you deal with love?"

Again he winced. Just saying the L word was like waving a cross in the face of a vampire. I reckoned I had him on the ropes. All I had to do was jab away until I got a result. But then he wriggled out of my reach.

"One doesn't deal with love. Love deals with itself."

"And what's that supposed to mean?"

"Well, Henri. It's like this…"

Conundrum was struggling. Time to go for the knockout.

"It's *Madame* we're talking about, isn't it?"

I do believe I detected a faint blush.

"*Madame*, Henri?"

Now I had him playing my game of repeating questions he couldn't or wouldn't answer.

"So how does *Madame* fit in this theory of love? You promised to be fully frank when no longer under her roof."

Conundrum shot me a silent warning to back off or else. But I plunged on.

"Your *Madame* paid me a visit on our first night at the *Spleen*. I guess she planned to find you. That's why you swapped rooms, wasn't it? To get her off your back? So what's been going on? What are we doing in the *Spleen*? I've a right to know now you've dragged me into your mess."

"A right to know indeed? Oh, very well, Henri. I'll give you chapter and verse."

"I'm listening."

"Well, love, as you understand it, as in loving another person is far too easy. We usually love people who are easy to love. Where's the merit in that? But try to imagine loving someone unlovable or even attaining the state of love without a love object. That's not so easy."

Already he had me tied up in knots.

"That's all a bit abstract. Tell me about *Madame*."

"Patience, Henri. I'll get to that. *Madame* or *Mademoiselle*, as she then was, caught my roving eye as a callow youth. She excited me as a distant prospect. I loved her from afar. But when she was there before me it wasn't the same feeling. I seemed to love her more in her absence than in her presence. I loved the idea of her rather than the reality. So what to do with my great passion? One day I was inspired to indulge my love by creeping into her still warm bed just after she had left home for the day. I inhaled the perfume of her skin on the sheets, savoured the scent of her hair on the pillow, felt the contours of her body with my own naked flesh. But then she came back unexpectedly and caught me in the act. Far from being outraged, she was delighted at my adoration and took her pleasure of me. So that's really how it started. There, I think I've said enough."

"So what went wrong?"

"Beware of love, Henri. Loving people is fine, but better not let them know it. Or they might start reciprocating. And reciprocated love – in spite of what the poets have us believe – is a dangerous chink in one's existential armour. Well, *Madame* – or *Mademoiselle* as she was then – made a big mistake when she acknowledged my love and chose to love me in return. So I had no choice but to cut and run."

"I don't follow."

"I feared you wouldn't."

Conundrum relit his cigarette.

"Problem was she loved me in my entirety. That left me with nowhere to go. I told her I didn't add up to much. What disarming honesty from a young man! She said she could see that much for herself. But she could also see my potential to mature into a magnificent senility. So even my future self had been assessed and possessed in advance. I was subsumed into her. I had to save myself even though what I was saving was perhaps worthless without her. It was a stark existential choice. To be or not to be. To be happy and dead. Or to be alive and in pain. And in my book being alive to all possibilities is nothing less than a sacred duty. So how could I attach myself to one woman and say no to all others? How could I abandon the entire female species for the sake of one woman?"

So Conundrum had sacrificed his one true love so he could play the field. And what had it brought him?

"I devoted my manly energies to women in general. Over the years I have 'fallen in love' without let or hindrance. My many loves have spanned the globe. Not even the shackles of time have held me back. My most enduring affair was with a pair of ancient Greek lips on display in the British Museum. All that remained of a beautiful lady carved in the third century BC out of Pentellic marble."

I thought I was the one who could only relate to statues.

"Don't look at me like that, Henri"

"Like what?"

"That look of pity. You would do well not to feel sorry for me. Just because you imagine one perfect love to be the cure for all your inadequacies you cannot understand someone strong enough to turn it down. How else does tempered steel acquire its inner strength but by plunging a red hot blade into icy water?"

"Sounds painful."

"Pain is good. Keeps the emotions sharp and clear."

"But that's a sick idea."

"Sick? What is sickness but the flip side of health? And without sickness we wouldn't know we were healthy. So how can you know if you're feeling anything if you're not suffering? A man with no raw and exposed nerves is no man at all."

Conundrum shrugged.

"So there you have it, Henri. You looking for someone who may not even exist. Me turning my back on someone who indubitably did. What a pair."

I was about to tell Conundrum that my 'someone' really did exist in the shape of that Japanese girl who was never out of my thoughts. But I decided to keep that to myself. Meanwhile, he delved further into his bitter-sweet memories.

"*Madame* said my refusal would ruin her life. I tried to explain it wasn't exactly a refusal. More like stopping short of a total acceptance. But she couldn't see the difference. Ever wondered why women don't make great philosophers, Henri?"

Conundrum pulled on his cigarette. It had gone out.

"So I gave the relationship just what it needed. 35 years of absence. But she didn't see it like that. There were tears and recriminations, ugly scenes. Finally she took flight to Algeria. Married *Monsieur Albert*, not the cat, an older man with a tobacco farm near Oran. Not a bad chap. When things went down the pan out there, they scraped together what they could, came to Paris, took a lease on the *Spleen*. Then *Monsieur Albert* died. *Madame* transferred her affections to the cat. Things didn't go well for her. She took to drink. Results are there for all to see."

"So why did you want to go back to the *Spleen?*"

"I didn't *want* to. I *had* to. For the usual lame reasons. To lay ghosts. To get closure. To confirm I had done the right thing. I always intended to go back, you know."

"And have you done the right thing?"

Silence.

"But you must have been pleased to find her in such a state. Not much risk rekindling the embers of an old flame?"

I had overstepped the mark. Conundrum gave me a sad, infinitely world-weary look.

"That remark is unworthy, Henri."

I hung my head in shame.

"I must admit it was a relief I could no longer desire her. But seeing her in that state was cruel. A personal reproach. For it was I who had brought her to that. She deserved better."

I could hardly believe my ears. At that moment, the Conundrum I knew ceased to be. Was he human after all? The great magician had bared his soul to reveal a heart.

"After all, she has served me so well. By pledging my love to her I made myself immune to all the rest. I could love them and leave them as calmly as changing trains. Even while I held a woman in my arms my eyes were already on the horizon anticipating the next. My commitment to *Madame* saved me on many occasions from getting attached. But it was an unspoken commitment. For although she held the keys to my soul, she never knew the burden she was carrying for me all those years."

"And does she now?"

"She knew it the moment I checked in at the *Spleen*."

"And has she forgiven you?"

Conundrum nodded.

"When she let me have *Monsieur Albert*, I knew I was forgiven. The *tisane* and the nuns' farts told me I was absolved."

I looked enquiringly at him.

"There was a note under the nuns' farts, Henri."

He relit his cigarette.

"Brief and to the point."

He inhaled the smoke and let it curl upwards.

"Tout est pardonné. Rien n'est oublié."

Suddenly, he appeared uncertain.

"Unless it was: *Tout est oublié. Rien n'est pardonné.*"

Conundrum blew a smoke ring.

"Amounts to much the same thing, don't you reckon?"

The usual cynical ambivalence had returned. Was he really telling the truth? Or was Conundrum's 'moment of truth' at best 'a moment of half-truth' or even 'a moment of untruth'. Quite possibly the latter. I saw before me the same old rogue, unrepentant as ever. He looked at his watch.

"Well, I've indulged your curiosity long enough. So let me just leave you with one final thought, Henri."

He paused, clearly for dramatic effect.

"How do you know I haven't made the whole thing up?"

"What? You can't have!"

"Why not? Suppose I were to tell you it was all a pack of lies. That I'd never clapped eyes on *Madame* before this trip. Ugly old bag. That's the whole truth and nothing but the truth."

"So it was all a pack of lies? How could you?"

"Quite the outraged innocent, aren't you, Henri?"

"I don't believe you."

"Don't believe what, Henri? What I've only just told you, or what I previously told you?"

He had me in a cleft stick.

"But you can't have made it all up?"

"Can't I?"

"No. Otherwise, what were we doing in a dump like the *Spleen*? Hardly your style. There has to be a reason."

I thought I had him there.

"That's simple. I'm writing a piece on hotels to die in. Sort of macabre take on hotels to die for."

"I'm not buying that. There was something between you and *Madame*. And you won't trick me into thinking otherwise."

"Suit yourself, Henri. Believe what you will. Makes no difference to me. But you've had my last word on the subject."

Dammit! How had he managed to tell me everything and yet leave me with nothing?

"Haven't you worked out when I'm joking, Henri?"

He didn't bother to wait for my answer.

"You must assume I'm always joking. All the time. Even when I'm not joking. Can't stand folk who just turn it on and off. You never know where you stand, do you?"

He looked at his watch again.

"And now we must be going. We leave for the coast."

"The coast?"

"Our train departs in an hour from *Gare Montparnasse*."

"But I haven't even packed. So we'll have to go via the *Spleen* and then I can ask *Madame* if your story is true."

"No time for that, I'm sorry."

"But what about my luggage?"

"I've had it conveyed to the station."

He had covered all the angles. Now he surprised me even more. Conundrum actually paid for our drinks at the café. Hand went into pocket and out came some cash. As we departed, he tossed a final firecracker at me.

"People make such a fuss of *savoir-vivre* but *savoir-mourir* is ultimately what counts. To be a worthy recipient of the melting sweetness of the final moment. The greatest orgasm you'll ever experience. I was really primed and ready to go. I had nothing left to say. I had thought my last thought. I had no further words for posterity. The whole tiresome business was done. Nothing left but crossing over to the other side of the mirror. The thrill of being reabsorbed back into the cosmic void. Really 'up for it' as they say in today's parlance. Ready for my dose of *rigor mortis*."

He now threw me an accusing look.

"Such a shame that *Monsieur Albert* – with the connivance of parties who shall remain nameless – saw fit to haul me back into the land of the living."

Conundrum had asked me to save his life and all the thanks I got was this ungrateful reproach.

"Yes, I really feel I've had my death snatched from me."

The bastard, the total and utter bastard! To my further chagrin I was still seeing everything through a blue veil. I shut my eyes to block out the inky fog that hung over me. Darkness fell as our train pulled out of Paris. I felt as gloomy as the night.

FRENCH LESSONS THREE

The train ride to the coast passed without incident. I lay awake all night trying to pick my way through Conundrum's tangle of truth and lies. Also trying to understand what was going on with my vision. How long would my blue period last?

I passed the long witching hours as the train rattled south racked with doubt and anxiety. Unable to shift the dreadful beast of despair sitting like a dead weight on my chest. My angst-ridden thoughts revolved like a rusty wheel around one central issue. Conundrum. How much longer could I endure him? And why was I so lacking in fight, spirit, resistance and unable to defend my personal dignity, my very identity as a human being?

As I explained right at the outset, Conundrum caught me at a low ebb in my fortunes. Not the lowest point in my life, for he had yet to bring me to that. But I was trapped in a mood of despondency like a jellied eel in a jar, a lobster in a pot, a prawn in aspic. Why all these seafood similes? Heaven knows. The point is, I was congealed in my innermost being, frozen like a fish supper whose sole purpose is to be cooked and devoured at a moment of someone else's choosing.

My lack of fight was also motivated by a sly survival instinct that told me to absorb the punishment and grow strong through it. In fact, Conundrum gave me pretty much the same advice. But I still persisted in the dumb notion that in so doing I could somehow outwit him. Lull him into a false sense of his total mastery over me before delivering the sucker punch.

This was my biggest mistake. As if I could come up with anything that hadn't already been factored into his own subtle scheme or master plan. And to compound my folly, by engaging in a personal struggle I lost sight of the ultimate reason, the long term objective of my association with him: my quest for the Holy Grail of Conundrum's knowledge. To be there peering over his shoulder as he wrote what I have called *Conundrum's Book.*

And this ridiculous business of falling in love with a total stranger, the nameless, faceless Japanese girl in Zurich. How corny was that? A desperate move surely on my part to rewrite the rules of his game or even create one of my own? Love versus lechery, an epic struggle where I would emerge triumphant like an Arthurian knight. Arise, Sir Henri! It seems utterly laughable now. Yet I must have believed in it then. Otherwise, what follows wouldn't have happened. I mean that ghastly business in Tokyo. I still can't imagine what possessed me to make such a monstrous miscalculation, to stoop so low as to do what I did. I tremble at the thought of writing an account of my base and ignoble actions. I pray I will be up to the task. We'll see.

But there is a far simpler explanation as to why I put up with everything Conundrum threw at me. Masochism. I was a pain junkie. I enjoyed the punishment. The more suffering the greater the investment in my habit. And the more I suffered, the harder it was to walk away from Conundrum with nothing to show for my pains, if you will excuse the pun. I had too much at stake. I had placed all my chips on the table. There had to be an outcome somewhere along the line for me. I needed a result.

Such were my thoughts on the night train to Nice. They all revolved around my personal devices and desires. Self-centred delusions, no less. When I really should have been thinking about something of far greater import. I'm talking about Conundrum's great blasphemy. Had he not entrusted me with his revolutionary theory of life as a cosmic infection just a few hours previously? And my response was to think of my own petty self.

My thoughts were still for myself as the new day began. My first concern as I peered out of the smeary train window into the inky blackness only just beginning to brighten in the east was about my vision. For how much longer would I see everything through a blue filter? And where was this leading? Would I sample all the primary colours one by one, until I fell off the end of the rainbow into Conundrum's parallel spectrum?

At this point I finally nodded off. An hour later when I opened my eyes in the bright Provencal sunshine, the blue was miraculously banished. The scene was now bathed in a rich chrome yellow of ripe lemons. Unbelievable. Like I was seeing true yellow for the first time. Warm, radiant, joyous, uplifting. My spirits rose. But not for long. Pretty soon the sharp citrus edge to my vision had my eyes watering. I was anxious to reach the end of this unusual chromatic experience.

On arrival in Nice we took a taxi to the *Negresco* a grand old *belle époque* hotel in the middle of the *Promenade des Anglais*. It was a real vision of paradise after *Hôtel Pension Spleen*. First thing we did was grab some *petit déjeuner*. A quiet elderly couple sat at the next table. Their whispered confidences fell onto the linen tablecloth soft as the golden flakes of their *croissants au beurre*. After breakfast, we strolled along the *Promenade des Anglais*.

"Watch where you step, Henri. It's a veritable minefield. The French should invent a dog with no arse."

With that Conundrum turned tail and – without a single word of explanation – left me to my own devices for the rest of the day. He didn't re-appear until dinner at the *Negresco* when his bizarre conversation now turned to art.

"Cézanne does paint a damn fine apple. Must have got paid by the French Apple Marketing Board. They really should have named one after him."

Conundrum slipped into inverted commas mode.

"I'll have a kilo of your best Cézannes and I'll thank you to serve me from the front of the barrow. I'm not having any of those mouldy old Chagalls you keep at the back."

Conundrum ordered more wine.

"Not so good on humans. All that timeless repose. His portraits are still lives. Madame Cézanne does have nice rosy cheeks though. But that's the apples all over again. She really was the apple of her husband's eye, wasn't she. Oh dear! A pun. How awful. Hope I'm not going to make a habit of cracking jokes."

Perhaps all was not well with Conundrum.

That night I listened to the rhythmic thump-and-sigh of the Mediterranean hitting the beach, feeling something strange about to happen. Indeed, next morning the weather had changed. And my sunny yellow world had been replaced by an overcast, almost English dull green with perhaps a hint of grey on account of the weather. But I found the green tone amazingly calm and soothing after the heady excitement of yellow.

"Fancy a trip to Monte?"

During the drive to Monte Carlo Conundrum waxed lyrical about Scott Fitzgerald, Picasso, various tycoons, film stars and aristocrats as if he had known them all personally.

"Lunch at the *Hôtel de Paris*, Henri."

I raised an eyebrow.

"Yes, the legendary *Hôtel de Paris*, where the *ennui* of affluence finds its highest expression. But money can only buy so many superlatives. The real purpose of astronomic pricing is to shut out those who can't afford it. *Hôtel de Paris* proves there is a point to being seriously rich. But curiously at the same time, it demonstrates that the opposite is equally true."

Conundrum pressed a 20 franc note into the hand of the uniformed doorman who helped us from the car and then drove it off to *le parking*. I was astonished. Although the note was no longer legal tender since the introduction of the euro, still it represented a small fortune by Conundrum's standards.

"Never tip loose change at the *Hôtel de Paris*, Henri. Bad form. Unlucky too. Few years ago a former bell captain received so many tips in heavy metal he had to have extra long trouser pockets to stash all the cash. Each evening he struggled home stiff-legged, heavy with gratuities, a walking piggy-bank."

Conundrum grinned. There was more to come.

"Then one hot August day he collapsed on the pavement. Heart attack. Struck down by a surfeit of small coins."

Before lunch we were invited to sample the seawater spa of *Les Thermes Marins de Monte-Carlo*. We entered a gleaming white marble tunnel that felt just like a passage to paradise. We were greeted, the renowned travel writer and 'his' photographer, by uniformed nurses, wearing smiles set in permanent suntans.

Swathed in snow-white dressing gowns of thick fluffy towelling, we were handed separate programmes. Before I knew it, I was standing stark naked but for a pair of plastic sandals at one end of a long tiled room. The wall behind me bristled with metal bars. Several seconds passed before I heard a female voice.

"C'est la douche à pomme."

I gazed uncomprehendingly at her. Without my glasses, I could only make out a vague white blob at the opposite end of the room holding some sort of apparatus. The green filter of my vision was perfectly suited to the sea watery ambiance.

"Non, pas comme ça. Tournez-vous. Face au mur. Voilà."

Obediently, I turned to the wall. A powerful jet of water hit me between the shoulder blades. The blast struck with such force I was squashed against the tiles. I gripped the bars and braced myself. The treatment continued with an assault on my spine, playing up and down my stiff vertebrae, flicking them to and fro like so many counters on an abacus.

"Tournez-vous."

I obeyed. Dripping with seawater, naked as a newborn babe, I awaited my fate. What next? The jet-shower hit my belly like a boxer's fist. I tightened every muscle in my stomach to prevent the contents being squeezed back up my throat. I wondered how many people, caught unawares, find the remains of their last meal lying at their feet before seeing it washed away down the drain. I was glad lunch was yet to come.

Then it was all over. The lady of the *douche à pomme* withdrew with a cheery *au revoir*. After that, I found my way into a bath of warm seawater where various jets fizzed and bubbled benignly at sundry parts of my anatomy. The treatment ended with a masseur kneading my flesh like dough while chatting amiably about European economic and monetary union.

After that, I wandered about in search of the exit. Through a half-open door I espied a skinny body lying on a slab.

Motionless and covered with green slime from head to foot, it might have been a drowned man wrapped in seaweed. I was about to steal away when the cadaver opened an eye. Just like a toad sticking its head out of a slime-covered pond. I recognised Conundrum. I would never see him in the same light again. I'd always think of that uncanny reptilian resemblance. Then the eye closed shut and the body resumed its previous aspect of death by drowning. I withdrew.

I came across Conundrum again a while later relaxing on a deckchair by the swimming pool. The only swimmer was an elderly gentleman splashing up and down on his back. His body was entirely submerged but for an enormous nose that protruded like the conning tower of a submarine. Conundrum observed closely as this noble work of nasal architecture scythed through the water, menacing as a shark's fin.

"Imagine this great Gallic honk in its infancy sniffing the sweet aromas of *madeleines* and *pain au chocolat,* moving on to *omelettes aux fines herbes* and the headier stuff of ripe *brie* and crushed garlic. Then the olfactory apparatus tuned in to erotic odours. Savouring the perfume behind a woman's ear during an amorous *tête à tête,* or picking up a stronger whiff as she lifts her skirts. Now, in old age, the nose slides back down the scale to end up with lavender soap, camomile tea and *café au lait.* A whole life experienced through a pair of nostrils, Henri."

The owner of the great honk now swam across and peered at us over the edge of the pool.

"Someone showed General de Gaulle a picture of my nose. He was jealous. He ordained it had to be deployed overseas in the service of *la patrie.* So I was forced to serve as a diplomat. There was no dictator's arsehole too dirty this poor schnozzle hasn't been obliged find sweet its most pungent aromas. After that, normal smells could hold no pleasure. The whiff of my own corruption disgusts me. So I swim with my body submerged. It is the only way to escape the stench. *Adieu.*"

With that he sank beneath the water and resumed his lonely progress up and down the pool. I turned to Conundrum, expecting some comment. But he was now in the jacuzzi where a middle-aged lady appeared to be in some difficulty. It took me a moment to figure out what was going on.

She was thrusting her pelvic region forward, trying to get a jet of water to hit just the right spot, a rather intimate spot. But the force of the water kept pushing her away. To my amazement Conundrum came to her assistance. Without a word, he placed a helping hand in the small of her back to hold her steady. I was astounded as much by his audacity as by the lady's acceptance of his help. For several minutes they worked at it together. When the business was finally done, she thanked him with a low moan. Conundrum took his leave of the lady with a formal bow and returned to his deckchair.

He had surprised me yet again with his shockingly direct approach. Was there nothing that fazed him? With women he rose to every challenge. He made a mockery of conventional morals and the normal decencies of social etiquette. How did he do it? And how did he get away with it?

"Never ignore a damsel in distress, Henri. I know where women hurt. They know I can heal the tender spot. So it would be unethical to withhold treatment. And now for a spot of lunch. I have worked up quite an appetite."

The crystal-dripping chandeliers in the grand restaurant of the *Hôtel de Paris* were of Versailles magnificence. The curtains hung in opulent, sensual folds.

"A word of advice, Henri. Never order frothy soups in places like this. Steer clear of the *Vichysoise*. I've been careful ever since George Orwell brought to my attention that socialist cooks at the Paris Ritz liked to spit in the soup of the rich."

I smiled, bemused as ever.

"But that's quite restrained compared to masturbating in the mashed potatoes, I suppose."

I did not allow Conundrum's remark to put me off my lunch which turned out to be quite exceptional though not as copious as our gastronomic binge in Paris. We had just finished our dessert when I happened to glance at a copy of the *Financial Times* left behind on a neighbouring table. A small story caught my eye. Two waiters in the south of France had stripped a customer who couldn't pay his bill and tossed him naked out into the street. According to the FT, the penniless diner could face charges for the serious crime of *grivèlerie*, which is ordering food without having the money to pay for it. Having read the story to Conundrum I made what I thought was a harmless joke.

"Are you sure lunch is a freebie? Don't suppose either of us could afford to pay for it. Looks awfully expensive."

Our waiter now approached bearing an ominous piece of paper. Conundrum turned deadly pale. He was not used to receiving bills. The waiter placed the paper face down on a small saucer and withdrew. We looked at it with foreboding.

"My eyes are strained, Henri. Perhaps you might…?"

I reached out hesitantly for the folded piece of paper. As I did so, Conundrum pushed back his chair as if to stand up.

"Excuse me a moment, Henri. Nature calls."

Was he was going to do a runner?

"Don't you want to see how much it is?"

I pushed it towards him. He pushed it back. I then reached out to take a peep. Whistling softly through clenched teeth I pushed it back towards him once again. His face was a picture. Reluctantly, his scrawny hand lifted the paper. His pinched features relaxed visibly as he read it.

"Ah, just as I expected. A charming note from *Monsieur Jacques* at *Le Casino de Monte Carlo* to confirm our visit. It's at 3 o'clock this afternoon."

Conundrum glanced nonchalantly at his watch.

"Come along now, Henri. *Monsieur Jacques nous attend.*"

As if still nervous about the bill, Conundrum scuttled to the door like a cockroach to a drain. He didn't slow his pace until we had passed through the portals of the *Casino de Monte Carlo*.

As if by magic *Monsieur Jacques* emerged from behind a marbled column to take us on our guided tour. We traversed a series of magnificent *belle époque* salons devoted to baccarat, blackjack, roulette and *chemin de fer*. In a private gaming room called *Le Superprivé* several cigar butts fat as dog turds lay in the ashtrays. No sign of any gamblers. The place was deserted. Our visit thus quickly concluded, we drove back to Nice while the rain continued to fall. Green, now tinged with grey, was still the colour of my visual world. What next, I wondered.

Next day the sun re-appeared. *Côte d'Azur* was fabulously blue again. At least I assume it must have been blue. I couldn't see it. A full-blooded red now tinged my vision: red sky, red sea, red beach. Colour saturation on absolute maximum. It seared and scorched my retina. Yet somehow it was a thrill to see a fresh colour in all its intensity.

I hadn't mentioned any of these curious optical tricks to Conundrum. If he was behind it, as I very much suspected, then what was the point in my telling him? Sooner or later he would let something slip, and I would know his complicity. And if he wasn't behind it, then this was a personal experience best kept for myself until I understood the full extent of it.

I sensed there was more to come. Having progressed from sepia through blue, yellow and green to red, I was making steady progress through the spectrum. Each individual colour had etched itself in my mind's eye. My colour awareness had been sensitised and sharpened to a remarkable degree.

Today's programme had me driving to Menton and leaving Conundrum there to explore on his own. Then I was to proceed to *Il Giardino Hanbury* which involved a short hop over the border into Italy. It was Conundrum's idea. For his article I assume. I had never shown much interest before in gardens, just taken a few flower pics of the usual kind. But for some unknown reason I felt a real compulsion to visit this particular garden.

Gloriously free, I felt I had slipped the leash. I wandered about contentedly for half an hour or so, still not knowing why I was there. Then I saw 'her' and suddenly it all made sense. She had her back to me, crouched on her haunches in oriental fashion. The ground all around her was spattered with patches of scarlet and crimson but I may be mistaken since red was the only colour I was registering. She was gathering up fallen petals from a tulip tree. She proceeded with ritual slowness. There was a serene, mystical quality to her actions. She didn't seem to notice my presence. I dared not intrude.

Then she turned and looked up. Her sad, beautiful face melted my heart. Without a doubt she was the Japanese girl who had scrawled a *haiku* on my hand on the shore of Lake Zurich. But for some stupid reason I shut my eyes. Only for a moment and probably just to have the surprise of seeing her once more as if for the first time. But when I looked again, she was gone. I ran to the spot but not a trace of her. She had vanished.

The petals from the tulip tree lay scattered on the ground, bright red like drops of spilled blood. I crouched down to gather them up as she had been doing. Then on an inexplicable impulse I pressed a petal to each eye. And when I removed the petals, the garden was transformed into a psychedelic wonderland. The spectrum had been distorted or bent in a weird and wonderful way. The flowers all around me exploded in an orgy of colours dramatically different from anything I had known. I'd never perceived such colours before. It was like I had passed through a secret door into another dimension.

What was going on? Had I gained access to a previously unused area of the retina? I revelled in the miraculous birthing of this unsuspected inner eye. A whole new world burst through with amazing clarity. Had I realised Conundrum's vision of bending the spectrum, going beyond the rainbow? Or was it all down to the Japanese girl? For she had touched those very petals just before I pressed to my eyes. But I had known what to do with them. Basking in the glory of this new vision, I took a lap of honour through the garden. I perceived images of such awesome power it hurt to look. I absorbed immense abstract colour paintings, strange and exotic as remote galaxies way beyond the scope of conventional photography. Yet a camera was all I had to record this wondrous phenomenon.

But even as I looked through the lens the dream faded. My newly acquired colour perception gradually dissolved. Soon I was back in the realm of the familiar old spectrum. So strong was my sense of loss it took me several moments to be thankful that at least I now had the full spectrum back again after being restricted to seeing just one colour at a time over the past few days. But what should have been a sweet moment of normal colour vision restored was tinged by the dazzling memory burned on my consciousness. I thirsted to regain that magical rainbow of extreme unknown colours.

Thoughts now turned to the Japanese girl. Whatever my part, she had been instrumental in bestowing this gift on me. But where was she? Sensing it was futile, I rapidly scoured the garden. She was nowhere to be seen. So I gave up and strolled about in a daze, inspired and uplifted one moment, feeling lost and bereft the next. But I was buoyed up by an undercurrent of hope. I considered the future with fresh purpose.

The way forward was clear. I could feel the proximity of another dimension that made a mockery of our pale material world that passes for reality. I had had a glimpse of a realm of endless new possibilities. I would find my way back into seeing those magical colours and devise a way to express them and show them to others. And if photography couldn't capture what I'd just witnessed then some other medium would. I had seen the light. Literally. I would see it again. As for the Japanese girl, I would see her again too. Of that I had absolutely no doubt.

Driving back to Menton, I reckoned I was ready to spring some surprises. Henri poised to turn from caterpillar to butterfly. Henri? I laughed. The same name Conundrum had mockingly given me, knowing full well I would never measure up to Cartier-Bresson, might well apply to another Henri altogether, that magician of colour, Henri Matisse.

So Conundrum had hit on the right name, but got the wrong person. Matisse was the Henri I would emulate. So my wizard was fallible after all. Well, I wouldn't put him right. Let him stew in his juice. The wrapping of my own ruse within Conundrum's ruse gave me the keenest pleasure. I had an impregnable shelter where the master of ridicule could not reach me. This true Henri concealed within the false Henri would be my refuge. And to cap it all, I had realised Conundrum's dream of a parallel spectrum ahead of him. I had beaten him to it. And the Japanese girl was my secret too. I punched the air. Yes! Yes! I would outwit the master of existential trickery.

I was a bit late getting back to Menton. Conundrum gave me a searching sideways look. I remained inscrutable. Quite inscrutable. No way would I let him penetrate my little secret. Little? It was enormous. I wanted to shout it to the world. I would soon leave behind camera and tripod and take up the nobler instruments of Art with a capital A. I had seen amazing pictures. Soon I would be able to create them.

Back in Nice, I feigned disinterest in joining Conundrum to visit the *Musée Matisse* - of all places - and announced my intention to do some beach photography instead. He arched an eyebrow. I had him guessing already.

"Beach photography, Henri? Are you serious?"

"Yes, I want to work on my technique."

So, we went our separate ways. At the beach, I paused to observe the scene. Bodies lay all over the place offered up to the sun like so many lizards on a rock, steaks on a grill. I shot a few frames then walked along to where the crowds were thinner. Now individuals started to emerge from the mass. My gaze fell on a woman and child. She was standing in the sea with the water breaking gently around her ankles like a pair of silver bangles.

Her one-piece bathing suit was rolled down to reveal a smooth brown olive skin and soft feminine curves. Her infant son sat astride her right hip, held securely in place by a protective arm. Their faces were trained on the far horizon.

There was something about this isolated tableau of 'mother and child' staring silently out to sea that compelled me to observe them. They were oblivious to me. Yet I was somehow part of their scene, though not intruding on it. Then things morphed in a mysterious way. As if stepping through a looking glass, mother and son were transformed into living statues before my eyes. The cloak of the eternal fell on them.

The clock had stopped. Time stood still. Immobile, they contemplated the great void stretched out before them. I held my breath. Under a spell I took several pictures that seemed to compose themselves. Frame, focus, shoot. Frame, focus, shoot. Simple as that.

Then a man ran from the sea, sprinted across the beach and enfolded them in a dripping husband-and-father hug. Statues no more, they snapped out of their sculptured state of suspended being. The clock started again. They were back in the real world of hours and minutes ticking away, swept along once more on the breaking wave of real life. I walked off cradling my camera as if it contained something precious. I felt it was not just a simple photograph but perhaps a sketch for a painting.

Further along the shore I spotted a topless lady, lean and sinewy as a branch of driftwood sculpted by the sea. She came padding barefoot along the water's edge. I tracked her approach and then, quite spontaneously, fired off several shots in quick succession as she filled the frame. She took no notice. I watched her move on, becoming smaller with every step. The waves swallowed up her footprints in the wet sand behind her. My eyes followed her intently along the shoreline until she was no more than a small dot merged with countless other figures that were no more than mere blobs of colour on a *pointilliste* painting.

I was on song. Shooting great pictures. Action before thought at last. Photography wasn't such a lost cause after all. Then, on an impulse, I stashed my gear, stripped off, ran through the knee-high breakers and threw myself headlong into the sea. For several minutes I floated contentedly on the surface like a babe in a cradle. The occasional soft slap of a wave hit me behind the ear rather like the tap of a powerful lioness playing with her cub. I dried myself on my T-shirt and was just pulling it on when a voice came out of nowhere.

"Suivez-moi."

I jumped out of my skin. It was her. The topless lady. Where had she sprung from? Had she actually told me to follow her? Or did I imagine it? She hadn't slowed her pace, nor did she glance back. What to do? For once, there was no need to think. My body had already responded. Action before thought again. Clutching shoes in one hand, camera bag in the other, I hobbled after her and fell in step a few paces behind. After all, she had said to 'follow' her, not to 'accompany' her. There was a French precision of meaning that I felt compelled to respect.

Walking behind her I took exquisite pleasure placing my bare feet one after the other over her footprints in the wet sand. Following every movement of her body rhythm, I was carried forward effortlessly by her graceful progress. Now she bent to scoop up a towel and beach bag lying on the beach. In one smooth movement she slipped on a cotton shirt. We crossed the road and entered a stylish art deco apartment block. We climbed two flights of stairs. A door opened. The room was flooded with sunlight and sea air. White walls empty like a cinema screen.

Without a word she faced me, eyes engaging mine in a challenge to take full stock of her. I watched benumbed as she peeled off shirt and swimsuit. Now she was without a shred of clothing. Against the stark backdrop of the wall, she stood there larger, more intense than life. My eyes drank in every last detail of her nakedness from head to foot and back again.

Still she didn't speak. But her eyes posed a question as if asking me to declare my intentions. The sunlight revealed every nuance of her flesh. She was better than any fashion model. I bent down and took my camera from the bag. Again I looked her in the eye. But something had changed. I had gone through lust and come out the other side. She had become a piece of raw material I could transform into a work of art. So I framed and snapped with total concentration. No sooner had I taken one shot than I saw another, and another. My lens explored and caressed every angle and aspect of her body. I changed films and still I could not get enough of her. I reached the end of the third roll. Over a hundred pictures. Surely that was enough.

I put the camera aside and drew breath. I looked at her again. Still she stood there staring at me. Now the artist's model dissolved before my eyes. A real woman of flesh and blood took her place. I wanted to take her right there, on the spot, against the wall. I moved towards her, targeting my first kiss at the base of her neck. But I was stopped by an outstretched hand.

"Mais non, monsieur. It's love or art. You can't have both. You've got your pictures, so now you can go. *Adieu."*

She slipped under my outstretched arm and vanished through a door behind me. I was left clutching thin air. I could only look in pain at the shocking emptiness of the white wall, which a moment ago had displayed her body in all its carnal glory. The lady had been there for the taking and I had elected to photograph her instead. But really I'd had no choice. The photography had chosen me. Stunned, I put my cursed camera in its bag and turned to leave the apartment. The front door stood ajar as if it had known I would not be staying long.

I walked numbly along the *Promenade des Anglais.* My fingers touched the rolls of film. I had some brilliant shots, but my artistic triumphs felt like so much dust in my hands. I was tempted to hurl them into the sea. But I didn't, for that would make me a double loser.

Had I really chosen making art over making love? Snaps over a shag, as Conundrum would surely put it. But why couldn't I have both? What about all those artists' models who famously performed both services? I turned things over and over in my mind until nothing remained but a dull ache. In the process even the memory of that amazing experience in the *Giardino Hanbury* turned sour. I had had the artistic colour vision but the Japanese girl had slipped away. So perhaps there too the real business of life and love had passed me by. Or rather, I had passed it by.

I drifted sadly along the *Promenade des Anglais* in the lowest of spirits. There were plenty more topless ladies about, every bit as desirable as the one that got away. Why not see if the beach photography routine would produce a result? I got as far as framing a shot. A general view in which the individuals were no more than blobs of humanity. But suddenly, one of the blobs was right in my face, wagging a finger.

"Non! Non! Non, monsieur!"

Perhaps the lady wished to invoke her copyright against infringements of her reproduction rights? Useless to explain I only saw her as a figure in a landscape, a small blob of paint on a larger canvas. Oh, foolish blob! You think I am really interested in your personal identity? Would you like to sign a model release? I bet Cartier Bresson never had to put up with this modern contractual nonsense.

I was getting angry, working myself up into a lather. Having only just rediscovered the joy of photography, I was falling out of love with it all over again. What point in any more images of an increasingly meaningless world? Soon we would have more pictures of stuff than actual stuff itself. Perhaps, with every click of the shutter a piece of real life must die. And today everyone is a photographer. Collectively we are exhausting the world by representing it too many times over. That is surely what Conundrum would say.

"Gotcha! Caught in the act, Henri."

There he was once again, right on cue. It seemed I only had to think of him and he would appear out of nowhere. Conundrum cast a mocking eye over the topless beach scene I had been about to shoot and laughed in my face.

"So that's what you call beach photography, Henri?"

He allowed himself another chuckle or two.

"I'm glad to see you appreciate the eternal wonder of the female breast. What a vista of mammalian magnificence. What infinite guises lactic tissue can assume. All the many forms of the humble nipple, from small pale button to big dark saucers. What we would have given as young boys to be treated to such a feast for the eyes. But now it's all spread out before us like so much fruit in the market, perhaps it's not so interesting after all."

God, the verbosity of the man! I didn't have the wit or the will to respond. And why did Conundrum have to drag everything down to his sordid level? To add insult to injury yet again, he now had me filed away as a *voyeur*. It would be pointless to protest. So I kept silent and let him enjoy his joke.

Mercifully, that was the last day of our Riviera trip. That evening we flew back to London and went our separate ways.

UNHOLY WEDLOCK

There are some things you do in life that are so huge you can only think in terms of a before and an after. There was the Henri prior to that disgraceful episode in Tokyo, a man who still had a spark of romantic idealism and hope in his heart. Then there was the base creature following that 'moment of madness' who could do no more than crawl away into the shadows to conceal his shame. The irony is that I thought this thing I did was a defining, selfless act that would raise me to a higher level. My spectacular fall from grace had been intended as the glorious rebirth of a sparkling new Henri.

I could always blame my great iniquity on Conundrum. This whole business was his doing. But what had happened to my moral judgement? Why didn't I stand up for what was right? I'm sure you will groan yet again at my passivity. Why did I freeze, unable to take evasive action, like a deer dazzled by the headlights of the truck speeding toward it?

Well, in order to retain a modicum of self-respect a man who has been badly deceived has a perverse need to maintain belief in his deceiver. Or, to put it another way, the deluded party needs to delude himself that he hasn't been deluded. Which I guess is what being deluded is all about in the first place.

At least, that's how I can now, if only in retrospect, interpret the reasons why I convinced myself that in spite of everything there resided deep within Conundrum an essential something that was would eventually take me in the right direction albeit by a roundabout route.

One fact helping me in this optimistic assumption was the miraculous transparency that had fleetingly appeared on Conundrum's waistcoat on the parapet of *Notre Dame*. There could be no mistake about that. I had surely not been deluded in witnessing a close up vision of his see-through soul, that sacred emptiness he had spoken of with such passion. I felt privileged to have been present. I thought again and again over the words he had spoken on that occasion.

"I know something, Henri. And even if I don't yet know it fully, I know it is there for the knowing. It will come to me when the time is ready, in the ripeness of the season. I am in no hurry. But when it comes, I shall be ready to grasp it and swallow it whole. And one day it shall be yours too."

So I clung on to a belief in Conundrum's pot of gold at the end of the rainbow. I had my moments of doubt but I didn't seriously allow for the possibility his precious treasure might turn out to be counterfeit. Come what may, he had in me a gullible accomplice desperate to believe in his sorcery.

The situation was further complicated by the unreal colour vision I had all too briefly glimpsed in that enchanted Italian garden. If that had nothing to do with Conundrum, then the logic was I could be my own man and fulfil my personal destiny not just through him, but also independently of him and even in defiance of him. Perhaps the apprentice upstaging the master was actually part of the plot? So even while playing along with Conundrum's game, I was always on the lookout for ways of pursuing my own agenda. So with all these complexities, no wonder I came so spectacularly unstuck in Japan.

Add the magic ingredient of Love, with a capital L of course, to the equation, and you can see why my judgement may have let me down. In short, anything was possible. I had no way of tracking down the Japanese girl I had met only twice and briefly at that. But I was utterly certain there would be a third meeting. And it would be decisive. My life would be resolved one way or the other. With her everything that had gone wrong would be redeemed. She was the key to it all, the one person who could never be an instrument of Conundrum. She had been my discovery after I had gone against his strict orders.

While biding my time, I held on to that dream. My final destination on the road ahead would be that mysterious Japanese girl. Had she not put her mark on me when she penned a *haiku* on my hand in Zurich? And was it not our meeting in the *Giardino Hanbury* that had triggered off that explosion of abstract colour? I felt so sure that with her Art and Love would come together in holy triumph to sweep away all doubt and confusion in one great healing torrent. Together we would inhabit a pure world in which Conundrum could not meddle. I was more certain of this than I had been of anything. Deep in my bones, I knew it would come to pass of its own accord at the appointed time and place. I would be ready and waiting at the third crossing of our paths. Destiny would not be denied.

Meanwhile, back in the real world, I was getting on with my life. After our return from France, things had fallen into a lengthy silence on the Conundrum front. I used my 'freedom' to good effect. While waiting for the right moment to embark on Art with a big A, my photography blossomed again, quite literally, as I explored the natural colours of flowers. I penetrated each shade in all its nuances. I probed and plumbed the redness of red, the blueness of blue, the yellowness of yellow until I had captured the quintessence of the conventional spectrum. But still I was thirsty for a second dose of that other parallel spectrum I had glimpsed in *Giardino Hanbury*.

It was late summer and I squeezed the last drop of colour out of the season. It was a compulsion. My portfolio was bulging with new work. What I would do with all these images I hadn't yet thought through. The important thing for now was just to follow my instinct. I had tapped a new source of energy. Like a surfer riding his dream wave, I was flying down the tube and wanted it to go on forever.

Then one day the phone rang.

"Gird up your loins, Henri."

"My loins?"

"We're going to the land of the one hand clap."

"The one hand what?"

"Don't be obtuse. I mean Japan."

"Japan? Oh, really? When?"

My hand trembled as I took note of the flight details. Japan! Surely this was it? My third and definitive encounter with the Japanese girl was imminent. What else could this mean? Then something else occurred to me. If the Japanese girl in the *Giardino Hanbury* had opened my eyes to the world of extreme colour, then maybe Japan would take to my new portfolio of flower pictures she had inspired. So I hastily put together a book proposal, looked up some addresses of publishers in Tokyo, composed a short letter, which I intended to mail from the hotel the moment we checked in.

Such was my eagerness for Japan, I didn't pause to think things through. Japan was to be my tryst with fate, destiny knocking on my door. I was going 'out East' at long last. Any doubts about Conundrum's role in all this were conveniently overlooked. In fact I fancied it might be my own doing. Perhaps my desires had forced Conundrum's hand. Why not? But there was no time for deep analysis. We were to fly out the day after tomorrow. He gave me no chance to get my head straight, thus wrong-footing me right from the start.

We met at Heathrow. As I lifted his battered old suitcase next to mine onto the scales at check-in, I noted how light it was. As usual I was heavily laden with camera gear. I wished I could just blink and take the pictures with my eyes.

"First time in Japan, Henri?"

I nodded nonchalantly.

"Everyone should go. Just to make sure it exists. We have seen the ants everywhere and admired their culture and industry. Now it's time to inspect the anthill."

I said nothing, anxious to keep my Japan agenda private.

"The train of human progress may be going nowhere. But it will be exciting – albeit briefly – to sit up front next to the driver of the locomotive."

"Driver of the locomotive?"

"I'm talking me-ta-pho-ric-al-ly, Henri."

He stressed each syllable deliberately in his best explaining voice, as was his wont when I was being particularly dense.

"Japan, where the future is devised, concocted, manufactured. What the Japanese do today, the rest of the world will embrace tomorrow, or the day after. And yet the Japanese are reputed to be at heart merely imitators. It's a bit of a ..."

I attempted a quip.

"...conundrum?"

"My, you are on form, Henri. The riddle of innovation versus tradition is indeed our story. The old versus the new."

Conundrum now permitted himself a deeper observation.

"If Japan did not exist, it would have to be invented."

I had nothing to say about that, so I held my peace while Conundrum scribbled furtively in his notebook.

Flight BA005 to Tokyo, was called. Conundrum grabbed the window seat and sat staring into space as we flew due north over the Arctic. A tiny screen right in front of my nose showed beguiling pictures of the country we were leaving behind. A collage of ancient stones, thatched cottages, ruined castles dissolved to images of swans gliding beneath a medieval bridge, sheep grazing on green hills. Then it switched to CNN. Snippets of world news burst like popcorn. Sausage price in the Ukraine had become the measure of economic performance. A new sect in L.A. worshipped the Source God. Temperature-wise it was getting hot in Chad. Now the screen went blank and turned into a dark mirror from which my own face stared back at me as if from the depths of a murky pool.

The champagne arrived. We clinked glasses. Conundrum presented me with a slim paperback volume: an outline of Japanese etiquette to assist the foreigner. I read at random. Some public toilets are unisex. One should try to maintain a poker face at the urinal if a lady walks past. Visiting cards are to be studied carefully. A sharp intake of breath through clenched teeth accords a hiss of respect to the person whose card is being scrutinised. Would a photographer merit much of a hiss?

The eleven hours twenty-five minutes of BA005 passed slowly. That was fine by me. I savoured every delicious moment of anticipation. As we flew via the polar route over the Arctic wastes I sensed a *froideur* in Conundrum's manner equal to the terrain we were crossing. He peered icily through the clouds at the frozen waste below. I felt he was clawing back personal territory he had unwillingly conceded in Paris. Well, that was his affair. For my part, I had no wish to be drawn any further into the shabby secrets – true or false – of his past.

I dozed fitfully until we came down to land at Narita Airport. As the clouds parted I had my first sight of the awesome megalopolis. Tokyo's street plan extended endlessly in all directions like the electronic circuit board of a monster machine. We passed through the deserted terminal and caught a train into town. Under a grey sky we rode past a drab cityscape that occasionally gave off iridescent glints, like oil on water. Long suffering commuters sat asleep in their seats. A look of permanent exhaustion etched on their faces. As yet no evidence of the Japan of my dreams. The oriental faces that had stood out with such clarity in London were here submerged in a vast mass of uniformity, anonymous as fish laid out on a slab.

Yaesu Terminal Hotel was located near Tokyo Central Station. I was allocated room 920. *NO SMOKING IN BED* said a sign by the phone, but the place stank like an old ashtray. The bathroom was a minuscule module of shower, sink and toilet all in one. It was so tiny there was no room to turn round. I had to exit backwards. I switched on the TV. A chap in a shell suit with a large, fluffy pair of white angel's wings stuck to his back was doing a soft-shoe shuffle. A choir of children belted out 'The rain in Spain falls mainly on the plain' with full orchestral backing. Another notice pinned to the back of the door advised: *PLEASE CONTACT THE FRONT DESK IF THERE IS ANYTHING STRANGE.* How could I begin to tell them?

I awoke the following morning at precisely 6am to the sound of a demolition gang starting work over the road. An earth mover sat on a mound of rubble delicately picking up pieces of twisted metal like a swan repairing its nest. Then back to sleep. An hour later I met up as arranged with Conundrum for breakfast at a local coffee shop.

"The Japanese sell to the world their electronic gizmos which aim to eradicate entire layers of middle managers and secretaries while they hang on to obsolete armies of salarymen and superfluous office ladies."

It was strange to see Conundrum grappling with the 'real' world of business and economics. We were seated on a bench at Kamiyacho station where the Tokyo Subway disgorged load after load of workers every minute or so. All were kitted out in standard salaryman uniform of grey suit, white shirt, black shoes. Briefcases sprouted on the end of their arms like a natural extension. Many wore white masks over mouth and nose, a thin strap behind the ears. The clinical whiteness of a hospital bandage suggested God knows what horrific mutilation beneath. I might be watching a sinister sci-fi movie.

Morning rush hour at Shinjuku. Green-jacketed, white-gloved attendants went at it like sheepdogs driving their charges into the carriages until the last human body was crammed inside. The train moved off, sad faces drained of life pressed against the windows. I couldn't imagine my beautiful Japanese girl among these washed out creatures.

Commuters waiting for the next train stood marshalled in orderly groups. Some had eyes closed. Sleeping? Meditating? Others read folded newspapers or books held two inches in front of faces pinched with concentration. Short-sighted on account of lack of space? The next train arrived and disgorged its load. At the given signal those waiting moved in unison like a drill squad and drove forward as a single coagulated mass joined at the hip. Those reading or sleeping didn't even look up, carried along by the others through the carriage doors shuffling in lockstep like extras auditioning for Fritz Lang's 'Metropolis'. Their collective self-discipline was awesome.

Conundrum was also clearly moved.

"Grey-suited though thou art, thou playeth a noble part."

I raised an eyebrow.

"Opening line of my ode to the Japanese salaryman, Henri. For these humble folk are the lifeblood of modern Tokyo. If I were mayor, I'd commission a monumental bronze of the Anonymous Salaryman. Like one of those superhuman statues of Lenin in Russia. I would order identical copies to be erected outside each of Tokyo's main stations. Should give a moral uplift to millions of salarymen as they go forth to work."

We headed for the Tokyo Stock Exchange. From a balcony enclosed in thick plate glass we stared down onto the dealing floor in the sub aqueous atmosphere of a neon-lit aquarium. Clerks in blue jackets darted about like tropical fish. Occasionally, when a seriously big transaction was completed, everything stopped for a round of mutual applause. As if they were trying to gee up the others to splash out a few billion yen. I had a vision of my own meagre pension fund slushing around with everyone helping themselves to a bit.

Conundrum watched the screen of Reuters Financial.

09.50 *JAPAN ECONOMY SLUGGISH WITH SOME BRIGHT SPOTS*

Two minutes later there came an update:

09.52 *SOME BRIGHT SPOTS EMERGING IN SLUGGISH JAPANESE ECONOMY*

Conundrum smiled and made a careful note.

"Now that's what I call fast-breaking news, Henri."

Outside the Tokyo Stock Exchange we were almost run over by a salaryman riding his bicycle on the pavement with a briefcase under one arm. We retreated into a bookstore. The customers were browsing not in the casual way they do at home but with huge intensity of effort as if memorising the entire contents of the books, desperately cramming for an exam.

"Just look at that mental concentration, Henri. They are not just reading the text but deciphering the watermark as well."

Their eyes seemed to lift the text off the page, hoovering up every comma and full stop. As if the aim were to end up with an empty book, the bare bones of a carcass picked clean. I took some pictures in the bookshop and afterwards of other people reading in public places with the same manic concentration.

Next we went to a big department store, where Conundrum spent several minutes silently contemplating a white Yamaha piano that played itself, the keys depressed by invisible hands. Out came his notebook and he scribbled something. Then he studied a plastic meal in a restaurant window, spaghetti cascading from a fork suspended in mid air. Again, he scribbled in his notebook and then he spoke.

"More appetising than the real thing, don't you reckon, Henri? And with this little plastic dinner on my table, I'd never go hungry again. Just need to dust it off from time to time to keep it looking fresh and tasty."

Conundrum now announced he had private business to see to and sloped off for the afternoon. I headed for the Tokyo National Museum to see Hokusai's *Breaking Wave Framing A Distant View Of Mount Fuji*. The ultimate art cliché, I know, but I felt compelled to see it nonetheless.

My way there was hindered by well-meaning people who insisted on giving me directions the moment I stopped to get my bearings. One old man grabbed my street map, held it upside down and pointed me the wrong way. I thanked him and followed his instructions until safely out of sight. Then I retraced my steps in the correct direction. When at last I got to the Tokyo National Museum, I discovered the Hokusai was not on view. It had gone to a department store in Yokohama.

The next couple of days passed in an exciting confusion of delightful discoveries. But I will spare you the details. After all, this isn't a travel book. It was the evening of our fourth day that the real business finally got started.

I returned to the Yaesu Terminal after a long afternoon out snapping to find Conundrum deep in conversation with a

Japanese girl. She had her back to me. But I knew immediately who she was. My heart thumped loudly in my chest. I was surprised she didn't hear it. I realised my foolish presumption in assuming I could keep this secret from Conundrum. Perhaps he already knew her? They looked like old acquaintances. How so? With mounting disquiet, I watched them from a distance. Conundrum seemed to be conversing in Japanese with an intensity of purpose. There was a mischievous expression on his face as he caught my eye.

"Ah, there you are at last. Henri meet K. K meet Henri."

K? Not much of a name, but that's all I ever knew her by. K turned toward me, smiled and said hello. I almost fainted. Yes, she was the one. The girl of my dreams. There she was standing before me, I couldn't believe it.

My blurred memory of the mysterious young creature who had penned a *haiku* on my hand in Zurich came into focus. She wore her face like a beautiful mask, skin smooth as eggshell yet soft and supple. She gazed out to me as if from inside a room through an open window. Her eyelids like small shutters. She held a hand outstretched. All this was beyond my wildest expectations. I had set out for Japan with a vague notion of tracking her down and here she was, standing before me. I took her hand and held it lightly. My flesh tingled.

How on earth was this possible? Conundrum? The only possible explanation must lie with him. He seemed to know her. Surely, he had summoned her? Why else would she be here? So Conundrum must have known about my mysterious Japanese girl all along, the sly old fox. But I was so happy, I didn't care through whose agency she had materialised. This was my reward at last. With a great leap of faith in Conundrum's good intentions toward me, I accepted K as part of his wondrous grand design unfolding around me. Somehow I had earned this.

Conundrum now took his leave with a well-executed bow. As he departed he whispered in my ear.

"Don't get any amorous ideas, Henri. Be hereby advised that K is one of Sappho's sisters."

"Sappho's sisters?"

"I mean Sappho as in Sappho of Lesbos."

"Lesbos?"

"Yes, Lesbos. Thought you'd better know."

As he sidled off, Conundrum gave me a sly wink heavy with innuendo to underline his Classical allusion. Sappho of Lesbos? K a lesbian? Surely not? She looked 100% feminine. Yet the warning was clear enough. Even I understood the reference to Sappho and her legendary island of Lesbos.

Not even this disappointment could dent my euphoria. I was in seventh heaven. The woman of my dreams stood right there in front of me. Details didn't matter. I'd take things as they came. I did not intend to mention our previous encounters. That was history. What was the point in going back? I would reach out for the baton and run from here. I would live entirely in the blessed here and now, no questions asked. I would not even enquire how K and Conundrum came to be acquainted. I would simply take things as they presented themselves.

As for the Sappho of Lesbos business, I resolved to navigate circumspectly around that issue in the hope that a union of souls would lead ultimately to something even better. Or perhaps, with patience and devotion, I would even reclaim her from the sisterhood. Possibly that was all part of the quest. I saw my role in heroic almost mythical terms.

Not wanting to say anything banal or predictable, I gave K an enigmatic smile as we stepped out of the Yaesu Terminal. Who was leading whom? No idea. I had the sweet sensation we were both guided along by a force beyond our awareness. We rode the Subway to Shinjuku, one of Tokyo's livelier nightlife areas and drifted from bar to bar. I think we stopped first for something to eat, a bowl of noodles, nothing fancy.

Then we hit a couple of bars. Our saké-fuelled talk slipped straight into the big subjects. I found myself saying far more than intended, not about my travels with Conundrum – his name would not pass my lips – but about my artistic ambitions with the parallel spectrum of extreme colour I had discovered in *Giardino Hanbury*. I didn't quiz K about her part in that. Let her reveal all when the time was right. For now I had so much to tell her. She seemed to understand everything I said. Uncanny how K appeared to know exactly what I was talking about and with what intensity she listened. Like she was totally familiar with me, my dreams, my whole being.

While all this was intoxicating and a balm to my soul, I couldn't help noticing how sexy K was. That Sappho of Lesbos stuff was hard to believe and even tougher to accept. Then the unexpected happened. Physical desire dissolved into something deeper, richer. I passed, as if through a secret door, into another world where I not only fully accepted the fact of K's sexuality but actually welcomed it as a gateway to an excitingly different, more enduring kind of relationship.

Knowing upfront K wasn't available in the carnal sense had some advantages. I didn't have to jump through the usual hoops. No need to plan my moves, risk making a clumsy pitch. I was free of all that. Totally free. K must have sensed what was going through my head. For now we were even more at ease with one another. And after a few more drinks I even found myself wishing more women could be sisters of Sappho. Life would be so much simpler. Pretty soon I was totally intoxicated. With K. With life. With myself. With everything. And with drink too, for I had been consuming saké and beer with reckless abandon.

We now made for the seamy side of the red light district. Streets wall to wall with Friday night people out on the town. We were carried along on a tide of pleasure seekers. Right in the thick of it K took my arm to avoid our being parted. Delicious. Everything went into meltdown. I had no idea where we were heading. I didn't really care. I was in a complete daze. All that existed was the soft touch of K's hand on my arm. We moved in a bubble of our own, a pair of atoms drifting in the cosmos.

K wasn't guiding me in any way I could detect. And I was in no state even to guide myself. So how we landed up in the doorway of this particular erotic establishment is beyond me. We hadn't chosen it. Rather, it had chosen us. That was how it felt. Just like everything else we had done that evening, our presence here seemed to come about of itself, without intent.

I reached for the door handle. I wasn't in command of my actions, just responding to what the situation demanded. Man opens door, ushers woman inside. We entered a dark space crammed with people. Standing room only. We threaded our way through the throng. The crowd parted mysteriously before us. In dreamlike fashion people melted away as we approached. We fitted ourselves into the last cosy space by the bar, as if it had been held in readiness just for us.

Lights dimmed. People behind surged forward just like the salarymen in the Subway. In the crush K's body pressed against mine. My desire for her returned stronger than ever. I faced up to the novel prospect of witnessing some kind of sex show with a sexy lesbian adhering to me. Would the act turn her on? Perhaps we could both get high on the fantasy to be played out right before us. After all, we both liked girls.

Seconds later, a stripper came prowling along the bar top. Strobes bounced off her sequins like fireworks. The stripping part of the routine was quickly done, being but the prelude to some earthier stuff. But my awareness of K and what I imagined her to be feeling turned me on much more than the stripper. Her silky body moulded against mine was a thousand times sexier than the naked woman a few inches in front of our faces.

The show ended with the stripper treating us to a long rear view through legs splayed wide apart, a real close-up. After a brief round of applause she took her bow only to re-appear moments later bearing a tray of what looked like sweets. She offered them round like candy. There weren't any immediate takers. Then one of the customers reached out and helped himself. Only than did I see what was inside the wrappings. A salaryman – obviously familiar with the routine – removed a condom from its sachet and rolled it slowly over his middle finger. The stripper fell to her knees on the bar top, her legs spread apart. The man inserted his finger deep inside her. The stripper writhed and groaned in mock ecstasy while he worked on her for a minute or so before she pulled away.

Gradually she edged her way down the bar, obliging a couple more customers. Then there she was, planted before me. She held the silver dish right in my face daring me. I wondered what K would want me to do. Suddenly it didn't seem such a big deal. It was all so public, just a spot of harmless fun, rather like a stag night and I was in a mood for devilry.

So after a bit of token resistance I reached out and selected a condom. The stripper then took it from me, opened it and slid it on my middle finger. Then she guided my hand and drew my finger deep inside her. Again she went through her mock moaning and groaning routine for a couple of minutes as I probed the soft contours of her flesh.

If only I had stopped there, things might have turned out differently. But when the stripper had done with me she didn't move on. Again she offered me the dish. Surely, I wasn't being asked to have a second go? Only then did I know what was being proposed and what I was meant to do. The diabolical idea took me unawares, unscripted, unpremeditated.

I was a stunned spectator as I watched my hand stretch out and take another condom. I could hardly believe what I was doing as I saw my fingers now take hold of K's dainty hand and slip the sheath over her middle finger. It was done before I'd even thought about it. Action before thought at last.

A collective intake of breath arose from the audience of salarymen behind. I had earned a huge hiss of respect, but at what price? The stripper permitted herself a knowing smile as she now turned to K and offered herself. But K just stood there immobile, frozen. So I helped her hand towards the place I had explored myself a moment previously.

An electric shock seemed to convulse K's body from head to foot as she made contact. Her eyes half closed like a cat. Her chest heaved. She gasped for air. I thought she'd pass out. If I'd wanted proof she was one of Sappho's sisters, this was surely it. As for the stripper she seemed to be getting off on it too, obviously content for K to go on touching her forever. This time her pleasure wasn't feigned. Her hips turned so delicately and precisely as if to draw every ounce of ecstasy.

My actual thoughts during this moment of madness are hard to recall. There was a demon inside me, a rabid monkey in my brain urging me on. A clever little devil he was too, making me believe I was performing a sacred ritual to cement my relationship with K, like a wedding ceremony in which the stripper served as high priest, the bar as altar and the audience of drunken pleasure seekers as the guests. While this perverted vision lasted I was as happy as any bridegroom.

Finally, the stripper groaned in a shuddering orgasm and slowly pulled away. K let out a soft, hurt cry. I removed my hand that had been supporting hers, which dropped onto the counter and lay there like a broken twig, the condom still wrapped around her finger. The stripper gave her a curious searching look, before skipping off down the bar top and vanishing.

The lights went on. The audience burst into thunderous applause. It was all over. I turned to K. I had never felt closer to a woman. We were totally as one, absolutely complicit partners in pleasure. We had drunk at the same source, celebrated the consummation of an invisible bond. We had forged a rare connection between man and woman, deeply sexual and yet way beyond sex. At that point I was incredibly proud of my night's work. I had broken free.

The glorious prospect before me was a lifetime of holy wedlock to K. I fantasised about a golden future in which K and Henri would be hailed as the greatest union of all time. We would hunt together, feasting on the same prey. Since we had no physical claims on one another, we could never grow tired or drift apart. Our love would be continually renewed. Romeo and Juliet, Dante and Beatrice, Tristan and Isolde, all other paradigms of perfect love would fade into insignificance beside that of K and Henri. I was so certain of it. I felt I could take on the world. I was ready for anything and everything.

But what next? I looked into K's eyes to see if she was feeling the same. But she was still in a trance. Then suddenly she snapped out of it. Without a glance in my direction, she made for the exit. The crowd parted as if shying away from her. I made to follow her. But a barman held me up. There was the bill to be settled. I fumbled desperately in my pockets for cash. Vital moments elapsed before I could hurry after her. I had to fight my way through the crowd. Like swimming against the tide. I was getting nowhere and K was getting away.

At last I was outside. Desperately, I looked about. No sign of K. I thought I spotted her further up the street. Yes, it was her. She looked uncertain where to go. I called out but no sound issued from my throat. Then a limousine pulled up next to her. The rear door opened. A female arm reached out. K looked unwilling to be drawn inside. But the stronger woman had her way. As the car sped off the heads of two women were projected on the lace curtain of the rear window like a silhouette drama. I watched numbed as K was engulfed in an amorous embrace, eaten alive by a hungry mouth swallowing her whole.

My sweet vision had turned into a nightmare. My silly world of illusions collapsed around my ears. The sky had fallen on my head. So much for my absurd notions. Infantile dreams. But my pain was real, undeniably real. I had done such wrong that could never be put right. K was gone for ever. Who could blame her? The unattainable image of K was etched in my soul, stamped on every fibre of my being. Now I knew what it was like to ache for somebody utterly out of reach.

Abandoned to my own sorry devices, I drifted at random through Tokyo streets filled with gaudy neon-lit signs offering all earthly pleasure. Now totally empty, without substance. I had committed a great obscenity, performed an unholy wedlock, leaving a stain that could never be removed.

What to do? I had to explain myself to her. See if she'd understand. But how to find her? I had only the initial K to go on. So who was she? Conundrum would know more. Didn't he always? One of Sappho's sisters, he'd said. It would have been better if he hadn't told me that. That dangerous bit of knowledge had led me to the unspeakable act I'd done. Only then did I draw the inevitable conclusion. Conundrum had been pulling the strings behind every false move I'd made. He had set me up right and proper, just as in Grindelwald. But why? Why?

I had a sudden urge to return to the spot where I'd parted company with K. I'd pick up the trail from the scene of the crime. But I was lost, hopelessly lost. No clue where we'd been, no clue where I was now. Couldn't even read the Japanese signs. All gobbledygook. I continued my aimless wanderings through the urban maze of Shinjuku with as much free will as a metal ball inside a pachinko machine.

A few drunken salarymen were still out and about on the town, rolling and stumbling with every step. One slid on his arse down a flight of stairs into a cellar bar. His colleague tumbled after him. They climbed back up and resumed their homeward walk. Like a comic double act in an old film they took it in turns to fall over and help one another up with swaying bows of exaggerated politeness and mutual deference. The sacred rites of the Friday night binge being observed. I felt partly consoled. I was just another sad, boozed figure in an inebriated landscape.

I saw a girl waiting for a night bus. A carrier bag at her feet displayed a stanza of poetry in large pink letters:
WHICH STAR WILL YOU WISH UPON TONIGHT?
LIMITLESS UNIVERSE
UNLIMITED
THE MOON, THE STARS AND PLANETS
DREAM OF FARAWAY ROMANCE

The girl was asleep on her feet. In her dreams she was out there in some distant galaxy. I wished I could trade hers for mine which lay soiled and shattered in the gutter. I passed on down the street, a heavy hollow in the pit of my stomach. No idea where. I wandered about for hours. I didn't want to go to bed. That would mean waking up next morning with the full weight of guilt and remorse coming back to haunt me with even more intensity in the cold light of day. Better to keep walking and walking. Perhaps I could walk it all off if I just kept on going until exhaustion would wipe the slate clean.

By the time I got back to the Yaesu Terminal the new day was already well underway. And as my cursed luck would have it, I bumped smack into Conundrum.

"So how did you get on with the delightful K?"

He certainly knew where to stick the knife.

"I need a coffee."

He followed me in to *Dunkin Donuts.*

"Well, spill the beans, Henri."

I tried to put a brave face on it. Damned if I was going to let him know the extent of my shame and disgrace.

"Oh, we had a great time. Been up all night, actually…"

I attempted to catch Conundrum off guard.

"And thanks very much for that tip about K."

"Tip about K? What tip might that be?"

"You know. About her tendencies."

"Tendencies, Henri? What are you talking about?"

"Lesbian tendencies. Not to get amorous ideas, you said. That stuff you told me about Sappho of Lesbos."

"Lesbian tendencies, Henri? Did I say that?"

I didn't like the sound of what was coming. I tried to remember exactly what it was Conundrum had said.

"Yes, 'one of Sappho's sisters'. That's what you said."

"Ah yes, so I did. That's exactly right."

At least Conundrum had the grace to concede the point.

"But I only meant Sappho in her capacity as poetess. Did K tell you about her poems? She turns out a mean *haiku*."

K, a poetess? A composer of *haikus*? Of course, she was. Hadn't she written one on my hand in Zurich? So Conundrum hadn't meant anything more than that and I'd gone and …. Oh hell and damnation! I couldn't think straight any more.

"But why put it to me as a warning? What's so dangerous about a poetess? And surely Sappho of Lesbos is more generally known as the patron saint of lesbianism. That's what you wanted me to believe, isn't it?"

"I can't comment on popular misconceptions, Henri. Except to say the real claim to fame of Sappho of Lesbos is her poetry. And poetry is dangerous stuff for an impressionable young man such as yourself. That's all I meant. The lesbian stuff is neither here nor there. Misguided tittle-tattle possibly. Or possibly not. Who knows?"

I spluttered incoherently. I had run out of words.

"Perhaps I shouldn't have risked a Classical allusion on you, Henri. I'll watch my step in future. Anyway, I trust that little misunderstanding didn't cramp your style."

"Little misunderstanding? Is that what you call it?"

I swallowed hard, unable to say anything more.

"Well, it didn't, did it?"

My pained expression said everything.

"Oh, dear. What a shame."

K a poetess! Was that all he'd wanted to tell me? K not a lesbian. And I'd pushed her into a lewd act with a female stripper. Even held her hand. And if K now ended up as one of Sappho's sisters, it would all be thanks to me.

"Everything all right, Henri? You don't look very well."

"You must be joking. After the damage you have done."

"Damage? I don't see what this has to do with me. I suggest you give the lovely K a call and sort things out."

Give her a call? I had not even thought to exchange cards with K in the course of our evening of drunken debauchery.

"I don't have her number. We didn't get around to cards. So just tell me how to reach her and I'll do it."

"How should I know?"

"I thought she was a friend of yours."

"A friend of mine? Whatever gave you that idea? I just happened to be here when she called to ask after you."

"She called to ask after me?"

"Yes, of course. Who else?"

"But why? Did she say what she wanted to see me for? "

"This is really most bizarre, Henri. You had a whole evening with her to find out the nature of her business. So surely you are in a better position to know than I."

Things were getting worse with every word.

"Though I do seem to recall she mentioned something to do with your flower pictures."

"My flower pictures?"

How on earth did she know about that?

"Yes, Henri. Now I recall, that's what K came to see you about. She told me her publisher thought your flower pictures and her *haikus* would go rather well together in a book."

"Go rather well together?"

"Yes, exceedingly well, if I remember correctly. It would be a unique artistic collaboration. Or so she said."

Conundrum stared at me with a singular intensity.

"I didn't know you were photographing flowers, Henri?"

There's a lot about me you don't know, Conundrum. That's what I wanted to say but the words just wouldn't come. I'd been knocked sideways by the enormity of my error. Nothing was making sense. Then I remembered those book proposals I'd mailed to publishers on arrival in Tokyo. I'd given the Yaesu Terminal as my contact address. So K's publisher must have received one of these and sent her along to see me in a purely professional capacity. She had come to suggest an artistic collaboration: her poetry and my pictures. And I'd forced her into an act of the greatest obscenity. Oh God! I had to find her.

"So where do I reach her?"

"How should I know?"

But she must have given you her card?"

"No, definitely not. She only told me her name."

"Her name? Well, tell me that at least."

"Surely, you know that already. It's K."

"K? Is that all?"

"There was a bit more to it. But I can't recall. Probably short for Kyoko, common enough girl's name in Japan."

"Dammit! And damn you! I've just messed up the chance of a lifetime in more ways than you could ever comprehend – and all thanks to your devilry."

It was a puny effort, impotent indignation rather than red-blooded rage. Fear of mockery stopped me saying what really hurt me: the loss of a perfect love and spiritual soul mate. I had done no more than fire a distress flare. Even so, I dreaded the reaction to my outburst of temper. A steely look shone from Conundrum's eyes as he stared into mine.

"Yes, Henri? Is there something more you wish to say?"

Now I was floundering. Like an upset child.

"Yes, there is, as it happens..."

"Yes, Henri? Spit it out."

"As it happens, my name isn't Henri. It's ..."

"Yes, Henri?"

"It's ... It's ..."

All I could manage was a weak whimper, a strangulated non-sound that died in my throat. Had I forgotten my real name? Or was I simply unable to pronounce it? How had I been reduced to this? My undoing was total.

I stood up and rushed from Dunkin Donuts. I only just made it back to my room at the Yaesu Terminal before throwing up in the washbasin. To think I had pushed K's pure loveliness into the filthy clutches of that depraved stripper. And all because of Conundrum's whisper in my ear. This was far worse than any nightmare. I threw up again. Then I lay down on the bed. My head throbbed. My stomach churned. I stared at the ceiling. I wished I was dead, knowing in a sense that I already was.

Hours passed in this state of desolation. Then my vacant gaze fell on a little orange book lying next to the telephone on the bedside table. Distractedly, I picked it up. *The Teaching of Buddha* fell open in my hands.

"The world is full of suffering. Birth is suffering, old age is suffering, sickness and death are sufferings."

Not to mention countless other sufferings. I closed my eyes. I couldn't face the world any more. There could be no redemption after this. I had blown my unique chance to emerge from the miasma of being Henri or whoever. The very thought of seeing Conundrum made me sick.

I now realised this was our last day in Tokyo. We were due to leave for the airport in an hour. Well, Conundrum could fly home without me. No need to see or speak to him now or ever again. To hell with him. I dreaded he would call to remind me we were leaving. But he didn't. So I lay low until I reckoned he must have departed. Then I phoned down to reception to see if he had checked out. Yes, he was gone. I was free.

One weight was lifted from my shoulders. But that awful business with K had to be resolved. How to find her short of calling round all the publishing houses I'd contacted to ask after a young *haiku* poetess whose name began with K? And even if I tracked her down, after what I'd done, how could I just show up and look her in the face?

In the end, I spent the afternoon visiting bookshops thinking I might pick up some clues in the poetry section. But the Japanese titles were all indecipherable. I examined the authors' pictures on the jackets. I asked at a couple of bookshops if they had anything by the famous young *haiku* poetess, named K. What name did you say? What has she written? Perhaps she's not yet published? I quickly gave that up as a bad job.

Instead I took to scrutinising every female face in the teeming crowds. But K was nowhere to be seen. Then I started seeing her everywhere. Suddenly, every girl had something or other that reminded me of K. I rushed about in a frenzy, staring hard at complete strangers as if the intensity of my look could force K to come out of hiding. My close attentions were not appreciated. I muttered humble apologies to countless young ladies. Just as well I had learned the Japanese word for sorry from that book Conundrum had made me read on the plane.

Come evening, I had no more energy left for walking. So I rode the Subway. There was a moment of high drama when the train gave a sudden lurch and threw everyone off balance. A girl reading a book came waltzing down the aisle towards me. For one sweet moment I thought this was K and she would fall right into my arms. I was poised and ready to catch her.

But some nimble footwork carried her away at the last moment into the arms of a surprised salaryman who hissed angrily at her. All the while, she barely glanced up from her book. She finally came to rest against the doors just as they opened and then she tumbled out onto the platform, still holding her book to her face. Now she looked up and our eyes met. There was a hint of a smile on her lips. K! K! It was K! I'm sure it was. But the doors had already shut. The train took me away.

The dark tunnel swallowed up any hope. I alighted at the next station, caught the first train back and raced to the spot where I'd last seen her. But she was gone. As I knew she would be. This was like one of those bad dreams where everything goes wrong and the torment only ends when you wake up and realise you've been dreaming. But this was no dream. I roamed about for hours through a maze of tunnels, stairs and escalators until I was no longer sure who I was looking for. With the tiny bit of sanity remaining I realised I was losing my mind. Something snapped inside. I felt a huge need for space and solitude. I had to get out of Tokyo. But I couldn't leave Japan until this business was settled one way or the other.

Next day I caught a train to Kamakura, highly rated by my guidebook. I'd decided to be a good tourist. That would put a framework on my wanderings. The *Great Buddha* in the *Kotukin Temple* just outside Kamakura was the big local attraction. The huge bronze effigy sported a notice: *DON'T CLIMB ON THE STATUE AS IT IS CONSIDERED SACRED.* But for 20 yen I was able to follow the others tourists and climb about inside the sacred image. I looked up into the hollow space inside the head where the *Great Buddha* mind should have been located. But there was absolutely nothing. It was just air and emptiness filling the internal shell of the enormous bronze skull.

Perhaps that's what enlightenment looks like from the inside? Pure emptiness. A vacuum. The presence of something expressed through an absence of everything. Conundrum would have enjoyed that. Conundrum, damn him! Why should I care what he might have thought? Hadn't I already suffered enough on his account? But I was powerless to shake his thoughts out of my thoughts. My life no longer belonged to me. At that moment I would have given anything to swap my tormented head for the vacant brain of the *Great Buddha.*

Out in the open air once more, I studied the expression of the *Great Buddha.* His air of calm omniscience was tinged with a hint of amused detachment clearly visible in a slight upturn of his lips. This elusive wisp of a smile possessed the force of a vast grin of truly cosmic proportions. Like all things in Japan, it only required a minimal gesture to suggest something quite immense. Conundrum was right. He'd said God must be a Minimalist. Or something very much like that.

Conundrum again, dammit! When will I step out from his shadow? I looked again at the statue. The *Great Buddha* seemed to find it all faintly comic. OK airhead, go right on smiling. It's all right for you. You're well off out of it. And then I thought of all those tourists climbing about inside his head and still that enigmatic smile. There was more than one joke going on here, and that small smile encapsulated them all.

I returned to Tokyo late evening and slumped exhausted on the bed. Physical exhaustion was sweet after all the mental torment I'd been through. Just before falling asleep I reached out and picked up *The Teaching of Buddha*.

The little orange book fell open at random: *"Oh my mind! Why do you hover so restlessly over the changing circumstances of life? Why do you make me so confused and restless? You are like a plough that breaks in pieces before beginning to plough; you are like a rudder that is dismantled just as you are venturing out to the sea of life and death. Of what use are many rebirths if we do not make good use of this life?"*

That message was addressed to me personally, as surely as if it began with *Dear Henri* and ended with *Yours truly, Buddha*. So I slipped the little orange book into my bag. It was intended for me. It would be my companion.

Next morning I checked out of the Yaesu Terminal and wheeled my suitcase over to Tokyo Central. The *Hikari Super Express* to Kyoto pulled out of the station right on schedule at 9.07. Although determined to be the good tourist, I managed to fall asleep and missed the fabled view of Mount Fuji as the Bullet Train shot like a projectile through the Japanese landscape.

In Kyoto I checked in at a *ryokan*, a traditional Japanese inn. The *Hiraiwa* was the real thing at last after the faceless modernity of the Yaesu Terminal. A notice warned: *'Be Careful. Some Guests Like To Pinch Your Shoes. Lock Up Your Valuables.'* I carried my shoes to my room. I thought I should try the communal bath. This was a deep stainless steel tub filled with water so green as if they had just finished boiling broccoli. I put one toe in and screamed as my flesh started to cook. In the corridor I met an Indian lady from Bihar drawing cool water from the dispenser. Her *yakata* fell open as she offered me her hand. I went to the bathroom to brush my teeth. An American lady was already in occupation.

"Please do come in. There are two sinks."

My sink had no water. I wetted my brush under her tap. It was that intimate, we might be married. Behind us two cubicles. I checked out the *Western Style* but the toilet had a heated seat. So I tried the *Oriental*. Back in my tiny box of a room, the bedding was laid out. My clothes hung on the walls. The only item of decoration was a Japanese print stuck on a round plastic tray. It showed a stylised female face mouth contorted in a tight triangle of laughter. Amusement at the antics of yet another foreigner, no doubt?

Snores, coughs and heavy breathing of the other guests punctuated the night through the paper-thin partition walls. But the nocturnal noises were soothing: animals grunting and farting in a barn. I savoured the anonymous companionship of solitude among strangers with Conundrum thousands of miles away. The sheer bliss of being far removed from his nefarious influence.

Yet I continued to mull over his cruel deception in that awful business with K. What did it say about me that I accepted any bit of misinformation Conundrum tossed in my direction? I imagined how he would justify his action: *'The fool is there to be deceived, Henri. Just as the hungry man is there to be fed.'* Then it struck me I had conceived a thought worthy of Conundrum. I smiled at the irony of that. Then I fell into a dreamless sleep.

Next morning, I set out to walk to the *Imperial Palace*. On the way I discovered a narrow street bordering a canal crossed by elegant bridges. An old lady was watering her tiny front garden. Oh Kyoto, you old charmer, so there are some lovely corners left, but do you really expect this vignette to cancel out all the urban ugliness? Nonetheless, my hand reached for the camera. Before I knew it, I was recording folkloric images of *old Kyoto* that would suggest the entire city was just like this. I was doing my bit to give people what they wanted to believe in.

The quaint street soon petered out and I was back in the modern jungle. I stopped for breakfast at a café. To piped strains of a Viennese waltz I devoured ham, eggs, toast and coffee while thumbing through a porno mag called *Men's Non-no*.

I joined a guided tour at the *Imperial Palace*. Gravel, gravel everywhere. Deafening sound of thirty pairs of tourist feet tramping through acres of gravel. The noise drowned out the guide's commentary which switched between Japanese and

English without warning. By the time my ear had figured out which language she was speaking, she had switched back again. Life at the *Imperial Palace* must have oozed with ritual tedium. There was nothing to delight the eye apart from one small garden with an artfully contrived bridge. It seemed to say: *'Look, aren't I lovely? The bridge of bridges. One of me is quite enough.'*

After an hour of gravel crunching under a fierce sun, I escaped into the broad acres of the *Imperial Park*. Here it was yet more gravel. A fresh consignment had just been delivered. A pocket-sized bulldozer was spreading another layer. The 'strolling garden paths' overflowed with gravel onto the grass.

Perhaps Japan has a problem with a surplus of gravel pouring out of the ground and everyone does their bit to dispose of the stuff? By the time I reached *Nijo Castle*, stronghold of the fearsome *Tokugawara*, my stomach was in revolt. Something I ate last night? I made a bee-line for the conveniences. I was glad of my practice run in the *Oriental* loo.

"Practice run? Was that perchance a pun, Henri?"

"Oh, sod off, Conundrum!"

Ignoring the mocking voice, I went down into a squat, hoping I would not dump the lot in my trousers knotted around my ankles. I was lucky. But afterwards I couldn't stand up. My knees had locked in the bent position. Don't panic. Keep calm. No hasty movements. I eased myself into upright mode.

Forehead damp with sweat, I took a walk in the fresh air to restore myself. That meant tackling another gravel path where gardeners with tweezers and magnifying glasses were removing tiny blades of grass that had dared sprout. Elsewhere, children playfully poured handfuls of gravel down the necks of their sailors' suits. I felt weak, feet heavy as lead. I sat down on a bench and removed my shoes. Every nook and crevice on the soles was crammed with of bits of gravel. I was carrying a sizeable chunk of Kyoto on my feet. Oh for a Swiss army knife!

I couldn't shake off the gravel that day. Late afternoon, in the famous stone garden at *Ryoanji*, I overheard snatches of a bizarre conversation. The voices were familiar, unmistakably so.

"It's a very nice patch of gravel, isn't it, Arthur?"

"Prefer a nice spot of grass myself, Gladys."

"But it does look lovely at this time of year, Arthur."

"Don't be daft, Gladys. Gravel is gravel. And why did they leave that heaving great boulder right in the middle?"

"That's intentional, Arthur."

"Is it really, Gladys?"

"It's supposed to be an island in the sea of life, Arthur."

"Pull the other one, Gladys. Doesn't add up to two rows of peas. They won't win any prizes with that."

"Gravel watching by moonlight is the real thing, Arthur. It's what the monks do when the tourists have gone home."

"Never heard of anything so daft, Gladys."

"I read it in the guidebook, Arthur."

"Reckon our garden will end up dry as that if *Yorkshire Water* don't lift their perishing hosepipe ban."

I didn't look round. There would be no one there. Those voices existed only in the empty space between my ears, a radio intermittently switched on by someone. I mean by Conundrum, of course. I sensed he was tracking my every move.

Taizo-In Temple was my last gravel session of the day. Twilight sun shining low across neatly raked ridges casting shadows over miniature valleys. All was calm. The evening breeze let out a gentle sigh. Autumn leaves lifted on the bough, settled back under their own weight. The tree drawing breath. No more than that. At that precise moment my eye was caught by a single falling red leaf. It detached itself and came wafting down. I followed it until it touched the ground. As it landed the falling leaf turned from an ordinary red to a brighter, more intense hue. A wondrous sight against the gravel.

It was doubly wondrous when I looked up to see the tree tinged with all manner of twilight colours. My extreme colour vision had been restored. I thought of K in *Giardino Hanbury* gathering up the red tulip petals. I wished I could just reach out and grasp the single red leaf and keep it in her memory. But it was too far away. Then by some piece of magic another red leaf landed in my hand resting open on my knee.

I felt I was forgiven. Now I was at peace with myself. A lone heart floating in a sea of happiness. I could ask for no more. Time dissolved. So did place. Like I was actually nowhere, not somewhere. I had arrived at the ultimate destination.

I reached for *The Teaching of Buddha* and placed the leaf between the pages at the place where the little orange book fell open. *"The world has no substance of its own. It is simply a vast concordance of causes and conditions that have their origin, solely and exclusively, in the activities of the mind that has been stimulated by ignorance, false imagination, desires and infatuation. It's not something external about which the mind has false conceptions; it has no substance whatsoever. It has come into appearance by the processes of the mind itself, manifesting its own delusions."*

When I entered a restaurant for dinner that evening five smiling waitresses burst into a merry chorus of greeting as if I had triggered off a burglar alarm. Ten eyes watched me deploy my chopstick skills on slippery cubes of tofu. Having passed that tricky test, I decided to show off by taking a delicate nibble from a deep fried sage leaf which I then placed respectfully on the edge of the plate while I chewed the tiny morsel slowly like a Zen master. I was healing, on the mend.

Last day in Kyoto. My planned visit to the *Kiyomizudera, Temple of Pure Water* was thwarted by a torrential downpour. A real monsoon. Divine sense of humour? The rain fell at a forty-five degree angle like a shower of arrows in an ancient Japanese woodcut. After the storm, I dragged my suitcase to the station. As I waited to cross the road, a tourist bus drove through a deep puddle, splashing my trousers, filling my boots. Peering through the misty window, schoolgirl faces peered apprehensively at the grey sky wondering why one day it shines and the next it pours.

One looked just like a younger version of K. But the bus moved off before I could examine her closely.

Next stop, Hiroshima. I visited a pachinko parlour, a de luxe two-storey affair, noise deafening, endless explosions in a ball-bearing factory. Chap with a vacuum cleaner did the rounds, sucking out the ashtrays. I went to the gents. As I unzipped my flies, a twittering of birds erupted all around me. The avian equivalent of hysterical canned laughter. I spun about. Realised I was holding my member in my hand. Just as I started laughing too, so the birds stopped twittering. I was laughing on my own. I fell silent, relieved myself, zipped up and exited.

My *ryokan* in Hiroshima was wedged between railway tracks. The trains passed by so close they seemed to come in one ear, go out of the other. Nothing so sad as engine whistles in the wee small hours. In the morning I reached for the thermos flask. The hot water had been standing there by my futon all night long, my future waiting for me to catch up with it. I had travelled through the night to arrive at this moment lying in ambush while I slept. Now it was time for me to stumble into the open jaw of the predatory beast. I poured the hot water on the tea bag and sipped the green tea. It was lukewarm, but tasted good.

I had to move fast for an early start. There was a train then a ferry to catch. Around mid-morning I disembarked at the sacred island of Miyajima materialising like an oriental version of Capri out of a thin mist hanging over the water. I saw a sign: *'Welcome to Miyajima! One of Japan's Scenic Trio.'* A tourist map brought to my attention *'Places of Historic Interest, Cultural Assets and Promenades Full of the Beauties of Nature'*. An old lady approached, presented me with a handful of photos of her in traditional costume striking a variety of poses, one with a samurai sword. My scrutiny completed, off she went with a stiff bow.

I set off for a promenade through the beauties of nature. Far away, I heard the hammer blows of a woodpecker attempting to coax a reluctant lunch out of a tree. Apart from that all was quiet in the forest. I tried to imagine the sound of one hand clapping, but all I could hear was the thumpity-thump of one heart beating. I was walking too fast. *Mount Misen* was only 530m high, but it went straight up from sea level.

I struggled on at a slower pace and crossed a rivulet of clear water bubbling effortlessly down the hill. With a pleasant gargling sound it flowed merrily through a narrow gap between the rocks, then broadened out into a thin, silent sheet of translucent silver draping itself over a smooth grey boulder. Making mockery of my strenuous efforts, it advised me to take the easy course: downhill. I pressed on to a wayside shrine where someone had discarded a blue plastic bottle and a beer can. Hoof prints of a deer that had crossed the path while the concrete was still fresh were preserved for posterity.

My feet ached, heavy as lead. I staggered a few yards further before stopping to take off my shoes. I stepped onto a wet boulder in the middle of the mountain stream. The icy cold water swirled around my feet. Small red leaves of autumn circled slowly around my toes before being picked up by the faster current and carried away. Could there be a *haiku* here waiting to be born? I reached for my notebook. But my effort was no good. It didn't work at all.

K would know what to say. I still couldn't believe how I had managed to wreck things so completely. I tore out the page and threw it in the water. I watched my useless words dissolve and flow away downstream after the red leaves. Farewell my failed *haiku*. As I dried my feet with my cotton pullover I saw a solitary red leaf had attached itself to my toe. I peeled it off, put it back in the stream of life and watched it race away. Perhaps there was a *haiku* here after all.

Not far now to the summit of *Mount Misen*. Although my feet tingled fresh from their immersion in the cold mountain stream, my body felt old and heavy. I managed to get going again, but every step was a huge effort. Would I make it to the top? Then my ears picked up the rhythmic beating of a drum. I felt lighter. The mighty boom-boom lifted me physically like a heartbeat far stronger than my own. Something or someone was carrying me. Now I was walking on air. My own fading energy reinforced by waves of sound. Is such a thing possible?

Something prompted me to slow down. I was about to reach the apex not just of *Mount Misen* but of my Japanese trip. After this it would no longer be onward and upward but backward and downward. A relentless homeward trek, retracing my steps via Hiroshima, Kyoto, Tokyo, and so to London where I would pick up the pieces. Now I understood Conundrum's preference for circular journeys where you keep travelling out until the very last moment when you get back to base.

Still the boom-boom of the beating drum carried me on as if with winged feet. Just as I stepped out of the forest to arrive at a temple in the clearing, it stopped. So did I, tripping over, as if a moving pavement had been switched off. No one about but a lone monk who was putting down the large, smooth piece of wood he had used for beating the drum. He turned at the sound of my boots scraping on the path. For one startling moment, I caught a glimpse of a very un-Japanese face. It was Conundrum. I blinked and looked again, but the monk had gone.

Could I have been mistaken? Was I projecting an image of Conundrum onto someone else? But this rational explanation brought me no comfort either. It meant I had Conundrum on the brain. Either way, it was impossible to escape him. At any moment, his thoughts, his voice and even his physical image could pop up on my mental screen, as if a hacker had placed hidden files on my hard disk.

A sudden twittering of birdsong brought me back to reality. Just like that burst of mocking laughter in the pachinko parlour toilet. What sort of country is Japan, where even the wildlife makes fun of humans?

"What is it?"

I put the question to a man standing behind me, a pair of binoculars stuck to his eyes. He took his time before replying.

"It is a bird. A Japanese bird."

I thanked him for the information. It was time to go. The piped music on the JR ferry back to the mainland went *dum tee dum, dum tee dum, dum tee dum tee dum dum* without let up. The first bars of The Archers theme tune on an endless loop. Rain returned with a vengeance during my train ride from Hiroshima to Tokyo. Clouds so low it was impossible to see Mount Fuji through the thick shroud of vapour. Twice I had missed the sacred mountain. What did that mean? That K remained just as elusive? Yes, that must be it. No doubt. So there was nothing left to hold me in Japan.

Back in Tokyo, for my last night at the Yaesu Terminal, hoping there might be a message from K. There wasn't. Before going to sleep, I opened the little orange book one more time.

"If the accumulation of false beliefs is cleared away, Enlightenment will appear. But, strange enough, when people attain Enlightenment, they will realise that without false beliefs there could be no Enlightenment."

Yes, that made sense, after a fashion. Without my silly false beliefs I would not even be in the starting blocks. But how long would I have to go on suffering like this?

"Be on guard against thinking of Enlightenment as a 'thing' to be grasped at, lest it, too, should become an obstruction. When the mind that was in darkness becomes enlightened, it passes away, and with its passing, the thing which we call Enlightenment passes also."

So what was the point of Enlightenment, if it too passes away? But perhaps that was precisely the point. The ultimate paradox. Why ever not? The glaringly obvious point being that there was no point. Everything pointless. Ignorance pointless. Enlightenment pointless. Me pointless. Life pointless. That was surely the point. Elementary, my dear Henri! Why has it taken you so long to crack such a small nut? Conundrum's cosmic joke revealed at last perhaps? On this occasion I didn't resent his interjection. Thanks to the little orange book, I felt I'd taken my own route through the maze of words and concepts. I'd come through to my personal destination.

By now I'd had my fill of words. But I was about to find yet more reading matter in the hotel bathroom. Among the guest supplies, a disposable toothbrush and razor, each packed in a small box bearing a printed message.

First word from the toothbrush:
"Ah, you look so good to me.
With my eyes open wide I can see.
Ah, it feels so good to me.
And it's so good when you're here.
Cause I'm free."
Then a response from the razor:
"Oh but it's clear skies we're under.
When I am together, when I sing my song."
On an impulse I joined in this insane duet between razor and toothbrush. I felt a surreal surge of delirious joy. Like I was supercharged. There was a glimmer of hope after all. Even if the only direction it could lead to was total insanity.

"Yes! Yes! When I am together! When I sing my song!"

I placed toothbrush and razor in my suitcase. They would always remind me of this amazing moment. I laid them alongside *The Teachings of the Buddha* like precious relics. Before putting out the light, I opened the little orange book one last time.

"To Buddha every definitive thing is an illusion."

It was a great comfort to be told that all my struggles and pain were illusions. But I also knew they wouldn't go away just like that. Life must go on. Even after my great revelation, it wasn't over yet. Not by a long chalk. And sure enough, it wasn't.

On the flight home from Tokyo, I wasted the long hours over the Arctic figuring out how to settle accounts with Conundrum. Somehow I would bring him to book[3] for his cruel, wicked deceit over K. He had known exactly what I would make of that pointed reference to Sappho of Lesbos. Anyone would have drawn the same conclusion. He had stitched me up yet again. But this time he had gone too far.

I agonised over K's role in all this. Conundrum must have arranged things with her in the first place. How could I have been so naïve as to imagine I had something going with her independent of him? And that could only mean he had known I would disobey him and swim right across Lake Zurich for my pre-arranged tryst with K. So he had set things up for me to do his bidding even while making me believe I was acting on my own account and keeping him in the dark. God, what a laugh he must have had at my expense.

What kept me going now in spite of all that was the conviction I was finally entering the end zone. I could sniff the finishing line. The pieces of the puzzle were up in the air. Who knows how they might fall. My life could yet be salvaged. It didn't need to be a non-event, coming from nothing, going back to nothing. So I would hang on in there. I was still up for it. Whatever it was. I had paid in full upfront for what I was about to receive. I would have my pound of flesh and be truly thankful. Even if turned out to be rotten and riddled with maggots.

I drank a lot more champagne and then some. Getting seriously drunk was hardly the thing for someone who just a day earlier had stood trembling on the verge of Enlightenment. But having grasped – all too superficially – the message of the little

---

[3] There is some irony here. Bringing Conundrum to book in the same sense as bringing a cow to calf had been my original purpose.

orange book, I failed to absorb it completely. I didn't make the knowledge my own. And so the false beliefs returned. Of course they hadn't really departed, just gone for a walk round the block while I was playing with this new state of being.

I even came up with a new theory to make allowance for my situation. It went as follows. Enlightenment is not for this world. Surely all this confusion, these illusions and delusions are what actually define the human condition? Show me someone who isn't confused and deluded, and I'll show you someone who isn't truly human. At any rate, the Buddha would have to wait. I quietly hoped he would still be there when I had finally run my course. With spiritual matters thus on hold and my brain running on pure champagne, I dozed fitfully.

Almost immediately I had another of those strange flying dreams in which I hovered a few inches above ground. But on this occasion I progressed from levitation to gliding, arms outstretched like wings, an eagle riding the skies. Then on an impulse I folded my arms and dared to defy gravity. But instead of plummeting to earth, I soared upwards like a rocket. Quite the opposite effect to the normal operation of the laws of nature. It didn't last long, but it took my breath away. The ecstasy was too much to bear. Where had the force come from?

I awoke in a state of bliss. In a flash of blinding clarity I saw that the only reason we need wings to fly is in order to overcome gravity. But if we can achieve weightlessness then we would have no need for wings. So that could be the way forward. To become weightless, both spiritually and physically. Crazy as it sounds, I felt I had it in me to break my earthly shackles. I could realise Conundrum's dream to fly without wings. Then finally I could dispense with Conundrum altogether.

I got home exhausted but in high excitement. No sooner had I entered my flat stepping over a pile of brown envelopes in the hall than the phone sprang into life. I shouldn't have picked it up. It was bound to be Conundrum. And so it was.

"Safely back from the land of the one hand clap, Henri?"

310

How on earth did he know the precise moment of my return? Would I never be free? My pent-up anger exploded.

"You bastard!"

Conundrum took it on the chin. He made no excuses whatsoever for the ignoble part he had played in the K affair.

"An understandable reaction, Henri. But there's always a good reason why things happen. Or don't happen, as in your case. Some unions are simply just not meant to be in the way we imagined. Besides, you should look on the bright side."

"There's a bright side?"

"Why yes. There's always a bright side. In your case the realisation, or so I hope, that there are better things to do with your life than spend it with a perfect soul mate."

"Like what?"

"Like being alone with your own good self. Being truly alone in perfect oneness. Other people are merely diversions, distractions along the way from the one true path."

The one true path? Conundrum talking like this?

"So you mustn't take it to heart, Henri. What was it the poet said? A pleasure deferred is a joy forever."

"I don't give a toss what the poet said. It's what you said to me about K that bothers me. First you gave me to understand this about her. Then you said it's that."

"Don't get all thissy and thatty with me, Henri. You sorely disappoint me, boy."

"Boy?"

Never was a single word calculated to do so much damage. It punctured my balloon.

"Yes Henri, your general air of hesitation and lack of real answers to so many basic questions has a certain boy-like quality. A modicum of self-doubt can be appealing to women. Brings out the maternal instinct. Beyond that it scares them witless."

My fury had been quickly spent and to no effect, and I now had to endure a brutal analysis of my shortcomings.

"Poor Henri. You have devised a sentimental screenplay full of fine feelings. You go about like a casting director to fill the noble parts you have dreamed up. You had pencilled in K as your leading lady. But she isn't an actress. She doesn't belong to you. So come down off your precious little cloud, Henri."

He now passed to more general comments.

"Besides, real men are not intended to fall in... I mean to bond 'ro-man-tic-ally' with women."

Conundrum was in explaining mode again.

"Of course, one hears of men who are 'in love' with their wives. I don't think I would necessarily ban it. But Nature with a big N certainly does not require it. Men are not needed to be 'in love' for longer than it takes to launch sperm to ovaries. The rest has been put in our minds. 'Love' is just another 'thing' we humans have invented. So try the Conundrum method. Accept every invitation on offer and move on before things get serious. Don't get too fond of people, or places for that matter. Attachments tie you down. In that way you can always stay in palaces without waking up one day to find yourself in prison. It's like our little jaunts, Henri. A series of five-star hotels and off we go before we outstay our welcome and the manager gets the daft idea we should be presented with a bill."

So much for my big revolt. I had nothing more to say.

"And so back to business, Henri. Imagine an island far away to the west, an outcrop of volcanic rock, soothed by Atlantic breezes, embalmed by the scent of tropical flowers to which we are drawn hoary with age to while out the autumn of our lives. You may not yet have reached that stage, but I feel ..."

The line went dead. A tropical island? I recalled the La Réunion fiasco. But I was intrigued. Did he have another trip in mind? Or was he about to embark on a journey of his own that would effectively mark the end of our little jaunts? I waited for him to ring back. He didn't.

Suddenly, I felt dog-tired, exhausted from the overnight flight from Tokyo. I slept for the rest of the day. It was late evening when the phone woke me. Conundrum took up the conversation at the exact point where he had been cut off many hours previously.

"You may not yet have reached that stage, but I feel the weight of the years on my shoulders."

"Meaning?"

"Meaning it's time for Madeira."

Madeira. So that was it.

"As I was saying, it's hardly your cup of tea."

So Conundrum was going solo this time.

"But you'll find a few flowers for your Japanese project. So be at the TAP ticket desk, Heathrow Terminal Two, three o'clock tomorrow afternoon. Hand luggage only."

How nice of him to remind me of my lost publishing deal illustrating K's *haikus*.

"Fuck you, Conundrum!"

I could curse and swear as much as I wanted. He had hung up. I was under no obligation to go but I knew I would be there tomorrow, as instructed. Silly to pretend otherwise. In my rage, I hadn't asked why he had said hand luggage only.

Conundrum was inscrutable on the flight to Funchal. We drank the usual rounds of champagne, but he was withdrawn, unusually preoccupied. He stared wistfully out of the window. He hardly spoke until we were approaching Madeira.

"The ocean down below looks peaceful enough, but beneath the waves it's primal anarchy. Everyone is someone else's dinner. Whereas, at this altitude up here in the clouds, there is no threat, no aggression. All benign and benevolent. Fluffy cotton wool shapes no more menacing than a flock of sheep or a bunch of barristers' wigs put out to pasture. No wonder we see heaven as a place in the sky. The serenity is overwhelming. Not even the sound of this silly plane can disturb it."

Madeira announced itself as a huddle of clouds draped over mountains. Why were they gathered here at this tryst in the middle of the Atlantic? Do clouds have a herd instinct, a spirit that moves them to meet at certain places?

"I do like the Portuguese, Henri. They are so at ease with themselves. Been everywhere. Done everything. Conquered and converted this. Plundered and exploited that. Far-flung memories of imperial dreams from Brazil to China. Calm people buffeted by the remorseless Atlantic beating on their beaches, nibbling at their cliffs, bringing the wide salty wind from the west."

There was a valedictory tone to Conundrum's voice, suggesting season's end at a holiday resort, a wrapping of beach umbrellas, stacking of sun beds. As if he had a premonition. But of what? Perhaps of things coming full circle and achieving their secret purpose. It was as vast and intangible as that.

We checked in at *Reid's Palace*. Not bad. The grand hotel promised to purge memories of the *Spleen*. But it didn't lift Conundrum. There was fatigue in his gait as he paced slowly through the stately lounges. He paused to examine a cabinet of curiosities, his attention riveted by a black and white print of George Bernard Shaw at his melodramatic best posing for the camera during a tango lesson on the hotel terrace.

The picture was inscribed to his dance instructor: *'To the only man who has taught me anything.'* Conundrum poked out his tongue at the picture of the bearded writer.

"GBS was really a Frenchman. No true Irishman could sustain that level of pomposity."

We visited the tropical gardens belonging to *Reid's Palace*. We were shown around by a young lady, eyes black as olives, dark pools in which one could plunge forever. There were indeed plenty of flowers, just as Conundrum had said. Bright red *hibiscus*. Pink and yellow-pink *frangipani*, *bougainvillea* in shades of purple, red, pink, orange, yellow and white. But my heart was no longer in flower photography. That cursed business with K in Tokyo had spoiled it all for me. I wondered what K's *haikus* were about and what the Japanese publisher had seen in my pictures.

Nonetheless, I snapped away mechanically. I even took some pleasure photographing a prickly *Dragon Tree* standing like a strict Victorian chaperone at *Lover's Corner*. The lone bench at this scenic spot was empty. No sign of any lovers. We were shown a rare, snake-like climbing plant that only blossoms in the dark. Come morning the blooms fade. This shy flower, the *Queen of the Night*, took Conundrum's fancy.

"If I were a flower, I too should bloom only at night and have done with it by dawn. I wouldn't want people staring at me, picking me, putting me in a vase."

Why was Conundrum suddenly so keen on flowers? Next day it was more of the same. He seemed anxious to rub my nose in them. The *Palheiro Gardens* vibrant with violet *tiboushina* from Brazil, fleshy pink *arum* lilies, silvery blue carpets of *agapanthus*. Sandy yellow paths of the *Jardim Botânico* littered with purple *jacaranda* petals. In spite of Conundrum's irksome presence I found myself still fascinated by the intense world of colour that opened before my eyes.

I managed to get him off my back at the Monte Tropical Garden and strolled about on my own. I came across a Japanese *Buddha* statue and all my recent memories flooded back. The setting itself was so reminiscent of K in the *Giardino Hanbury*. I realised there would be no escape from the past: always something there to remind me of K. I wandered on down the garden paths. Strange faces of the Koi fish in an ornamental pond were almost human. One looked just like Conundrum. Could that be possible? I didn't have time for a closer look when the real Conundrum caught up with me.

"So you've moved on from flowers to fish, Henri? That's evolutionary progress, I guess. I always thought pretty flowers were the last resort of the emotionally inadequate."

He was his usual mocking self.

"Nature is all very well, Henri. You can relate to it. But it won't relate to you. So it's a rather one-sided affair."

I framed a shot of some blood red *hibiscus*.

"Always snapping the obvious, Henri."

I didn't respond.

"I wonder if you know what colour really is?"

What was he playing at?

"What you see as red is simply that bit of the spectrum reflected back after all the other colours have been absorbed by the object you perceive as being red. So the red *hibiscus* you are snapping is not really red at all. What you see is merely the absence of blue, yellow, green etc, i.e. the colours the flower has kept for itself. In short, what you see is the rejected bit of colour that has been thrown back in your face."

Where was this leading? Did he know about my ability to perceive colours beyond the rainbow?

"With me so far, Henri?"

I nodded hesitantly.

"So what you see at any given time is simply a chromatic reject, the result of everything else being held back. Now apply the same principle right across the board to existence in general. And what do you have? Every certainty falls apart. Nothing is what it seems. Everything on earth is an illusion."

Now he was talking like the little orange book.

"And the self is the greatest illusion of all. You are what you are by virtue of what you are not. All those other selves that might have been you are hidden away inside. What you appear to be on the surface is made up of those bits that have not been held back. So our true natures may be the exact opposite of what they seem. Behold my intelligence. It is nothing more than a lack of the stupidity I have bottled up inside me. You may apply this to everything. Love is the absence of hate. Kindness the absence of cruelty. Happiness the absence of sadness."

Happiness the absence of sadness. Where had I heard that before? Of course. In Paris. From *Monsieur Tristesse*. So that had been Conundrum playing me along in yet another charade? And to think that I had wanted to introduce the two of them. I wondered just how many of the people I had met during my

316

travels with Conundrum had actually been Conundrum in a different guise. Meanwhile, he continued talking.

"The only pure happiness is one which has no reason. Where there is nothing in particular to be happy about. Like a baby smiling at nothing. And why are babies so happy? Because they are born knowing nothing? Or perhaps because they know everything worth knowing?"

Conundrum suggested merely through his tone of voice that the latter was the case.

"Sadly from there it goes downhill all the way. Acquired human knowledge corrupts the divine. Slowly but surely that wonderful all-embracing smile is wiped off our faces. But the outlook is not hopeless. The totality of knowledge we had as a child may return to us as we close in on death. If only in a brief, blinding moment of transfiguration as we slip over to the other side. That's the moment I am waiting for."

There it was. Conundrum yearning for his own demise.

"We are born knowing all the answers. Without seeing the need for questions. But as our insane hunger for questions grows the corresponding answers vanish like so many exploding light bulbs. We think we're pretty smart with all our questions. But the more questions we put, the less knowledge we have."

He paused to make sure I was keeping up.

"So it is with your great illusion of Truth with a capital T, Henri. You think it is something to capture, frame and hang on the wall. But Truth is simply what remains after you have dumped all the lies. It is not anything in itself. Truth is nothing more than the absence of falsehood. Indeed, it cannot properly exist without falsehood."

Now Conundrum really was speaking just like the *Buddha*. Had he absorbed the *Buddha* nature too?

"In short, nothing exists except by virtue of the absence of its complementary parts. No day without night. No dry without wet. No good without evil. No health without sickness. What you see is always only one half of the story. Nothing stands alone. And so, what I am is simply the flip side of what I am not. That's about as far as any honest philosopher can go with certainty. And by certainty I mean of course nothing more than the absence of uncertainty. Even life is no more than the absence of death. For you can't have one without the other."

Conundrum beamed a tired expression at me.

"But what does all that mean in reality?"

"Haven't you taken in a word of what I've been saying? Let's get back to colour. When you put all the colours of the spectrum together, what do you get?"

Was this the moment to tell Conundrum about the other spectrum? I thought better of it.

"You get nothing. Except for pure light. And since pure light is invisible we can't even see it. So when we say 'we have seen the light' meaning we have understood something, in fact we have seen or understood nothing at all."

I couldn't quite get my head round all this.

"Can't you grasp it, Henri? We humans mistake our own thoughts for reality. Our life is a total illusion from start to finish. And the biggest joke of all is that we think we are the lords of creation, masters of the planet and so on."

Conundrum fell silent as he watched a steady procession of elderly tourists study the little Latin labels tagged to the trees and plants in the garden of *Santa Catarina.*

"How do we know the plants aren't the ones running the show? They came before us in the chain of being. They will still be there when we have destroyed ourselves. Humankind is doomed. Only question is how many species we'll take with us. But once we're gone the first job of the plants will be to restore the conditions that made our life on earth possible. Meanwhile, to pass the time while we're still around, they use us as best they can, beguiling us with sweet scents and pretty flowers to carry their seeds in little packets across the oceans."

Conundrum broke off abruptly.

"Shouldn't you go and do the market snaps, Henri?"

As if a hypnotist had snapped his finger I was back in the 'real' world. So I set off for the covered market in Funchal. I did some close-ups of fruit and veg, then some scabbard fish, their big eyes full of reproach. They had every reason to be resentful. Man's endless hunger had invaded their realm a thousand metres down in the ocean deep. How beautiful the aquatic elegance of silvery tuna, one of the most perfect shapes ever created. Stalwart men hacked with steel choppers at huge pieces of their flesh thick as tree trunks. A fat glob of tuna blood landed on my shirt. Close to my heart. Like a mortal wound. As if I'd been shot. Or hit by one of K's tulip petals. An omen?

I was soon done with the market, not having shot a single human, when a flower girl caught my eye. A pretty, waif-like creature, she looked at me calm, unblinking, somehow willing me to take her image away with me as a personal gift. I obliged. She smiled as she walked off. I was redeemed.

I rested under the shady palms in *Jardim de São Francisco*, a haunt of old men whiling away the hours watching the slow shunt of the taxi rank. I was sinking into the general somnolence of the place when Conundrum appeared out of nowhere.

He dragged me into a nearby courtyard. Moments later we were seated in a medieval cellar beneath a vault lined with dusty bottles. A dozen glasses of finest Madeira stood before us in two rows of six. We indulged in a tasting session from driest Sercial to sweetest Malmsey and all the way back again.

"Want to see a miracle, Henri? Wine into words. Watch closely. Pour alcohol in mouth. Swallow. Wait a couple of minutes. Words start to spout from the same orifice. Can't hold them back. Is that not a miracle?"

He drank some more.

"Well, I've gone one better, Henri. I can even turn words into wine. Want to know how it's done?"

I nodded wearily.

"Simple. Sell some books, spend proceeds on wine. And hey presto! A used copy of *Das Kapital* becomes a bottle of *Dom*

Perignon. And then you piss it down the toilet. And so the words go down the drain where they belong."

Conundrum drank his way up the line of Madeira glasses. I matched him sip for sip. As we reached the end, he sighed.

"We've flown quite a few missions together. I do hope our little jaunts have offered you some entertainment, Henri."

There was an unfamiliar edge to his voice.

"And I trust they have been instructive too?"

I did not reply directly except by nodding to confirm that our little jaunts had indeed been most instructive.

"Excellent, Henri. That is most reassuring."

We were entering new territory. I waited for Conundrum to reveal his purpose. The musty old cellar fell silent, holding its breath. I looked Conundrum in the eye to fathom his thoughts. But when at last he cleared his throat, it was only to call time on whatever he might have been about to say.

"Well, come along, Henri. Let's be moving on."

So that was that. At least, for now. As we emerged from the cellar, my eyes narrowed in the blinding daylight. My legs were unsteady. I tottered after Conundrum through the *Jardim de São Francisco*. He strode purposefully to the head of the taxi rank. Minutes later, we were on the highway heading west. The taxi stopped at *Cabo Girão* one of Madeira's scenic lookouts. Leaden-footed, I hurried after Conundrum who skipped along so nimbly he might be walking on air. We reached a railed viewpoint on the edge of a cliff. He wore a look of utter exhilaration.

"Sheer drop of 580m down to the sea. Ideal spot to…"

Conundrum didn't finish his sentence. He swung one leg onto the balustrade. He was going to jump. The bloody fool! In the nick of time, I grabbed him and pulled him to the ground.

"What the hell do you think you are playing at?"

"And I could ask the same of you."

We dusted ourselves off. Nothing more was said. But I knew what he was up to. His 'flying without wings' was more than a poetic metaphor. But did not the same mad dream lurk at the back of my mind? I recalled my sudden urge to throw myself off the parapet of *Notre Dame*. Yes, all his talk of 'flying without wings' stuff was intended quite literally.

Back at *Reid's Palace*, Conundrum went to his room. I took a dip in the heated seawater pool. I floated in the warm briny and looked up into the cloudless sky. I was sure something was brewing. Yet I had no way of telling what or when. But if something was going to happen on this trip, then it would have to be soon. Tomorrow we were flying back to London.

Next morning Conundrum appeared bright and breezy as if nothing untoward had happened. We caught our scheduled flight to Lisbon where we were due to connect with one to London. But Conundrum headed out through immigration and customs and made for the Hertz desk.

I followed in his wake. What was he up to? So that's why he had insisted on hand luggage only. We were jumping ship. His plan must have been hatched long ago. Why had he kept me in the dark? But it was better this way, me not knowing what was afoot. Having travelled such a long road, I wanted and needed to be in at the kill. The thought made me shudder.

"We'll need a car. Do the necessary, Henri."

Conundrum had me drive inland for a couple of hours almost due east, before directing me onto a smaller country road.

"Follow the signs for Almendres."

Almendres turned out to be a prehistoric site. Rounded stumps of stone protruded from the ground like teeth from the half-buried jaw of a long dead hippopotamus. A dog ran about confused for choice. It didn't know which ancient stone to piss on first. If there was any megalithic magic in the air at this ancient place, I did not feel it.

Now the first spots of rain started to fall. We continued along a pot-holed track to Zambujeiro, according to the sign another prehistoric site. Conundrum sidled off while I wasn't looking. He had vanished into thin air. Now the rain was coming down hard. I stayed in the car and waited. Just like that time at

Avebury, the start of our travels. So would Zambujeiro be the end? Yes, I was sure of it. It would be so typical of Conundrum to link his fate to the alphabet, starting at A ending at Z.

The rain eased up. I wandered about in the soggy grass, trying to find him. There was nowhere else a person might go except the prehistoric monument. I found Conundrum inside the dolmen. Lying on the earth floor curled up like a foetus. I stole away silently. I sheltered in the mouth of the dolmen and waited. Was Conundrum planning to die here in the ancient tomb?

About ten minutes later he reappeared.

"I feel pleasantly revived. But I don't think I shall opt for the crouched pot burial method after all."

That evening, Conundrum retired early.

Next day in Evora, a sullen-faced dog followed us in a quiet pensive manner wherever we went. It had such an attentive air I felt it was listening to what we said. Then we drove east to Monsaraz. A solitary white cloud in a big blue sky sat right over the hilltop village. Eerie sensation it was watching us. I stopped the car and pulled out the camera.

"You don't have to take snaps, Henri. You're off duty. It is not obligatory."

Off duty? What did he mean? If not for snaps, what was I here for? Now I definitely knew something was up. We drove south through wide Alentejo landscapes of red earth, blue sky, green meadows, purple flowers. Colours of elemental power and simplicity. Groves of cork oaks, trunks stripped naked of bark, cropped like poodles. Limbs twisted in grotesque contortions. Alpine music of cowbells struck an incongruous note.

The countryside flitted past as if on a vast cinema screen. Lonely figures walking down empty roads carrying plastic bags of groceries to remote places. Like the opening of a film. Eyes of hidden faces peered out behind closed shutters as we passed through sleepy villages deep in Portuguese dreamtime. Gnarled old men, immobile as olive trees, leaned like bookends on barns and houses. As if without them they would have no attachment to the earth, at risk of being blown away by the wind.

"What would happen if all the old men propping up the walls of Portugal were to stand up and wander off? Would the whole country come tumbling down like a house of cards?"

Conundrum's words coincided with the approach of three horse-drawn carts, heavily loaded with people and all their worldly possessions. Nomadic group on the move. As our paths crossed my eyes met those of a woman breast-feeding her child. Proud, defiant gypsy fire in her fleeting glance that briefly registered my presence then discarded it as she hurtled on into the future. Her future. Was this for real or just a scene in a film? When I looked in the rear-view mirror the road was empty.

Late afternoon we glimpsed the Atlantic, a distant smudge of blue. Stopped at Estoi where goldfish lay immobile in the weed green water of a Baroque fountain. Strands of saffron in mint jelly. German tourists filed past muttering *"klassisch Barock"* nodding wisely. We put up for the night at *S. Brás de Alportel* in the hills with the Algarve coast shimmering below. Other guests at dinner included an English family. The man wore a cricket sweater. It looked odd. Conundrum hardly spoke.

Next day, we walked on the beach at Albufeira. A stream cut a broad swathe through the sand on its way to the sea. Just for a second the outgoing breakers sucked the water out of its bed. Conundrum chose his moment with absolute precision and scampered across. A cry of triumph announced he had reached the other side. He hadn't even got his feet wet. Now it was my turn. But I got it badly wrong. My shoes quickly filled with water. I had to wade across. My trousers were soaked to the knee. Yet Conundrum had virtually walked on the water. What next?

Little conversation over dinner in Lagos. We sat staring at a TV screen reflected in an aquarium. Figures of miniature footballers darted about dementedly among tropical fish that glided serenely in their own element. Then the footballers disappeared. Their place in the aquarium was taken by a meeting of the Portuguese Cabinet. The fish were as unimpressed with the politicians as they'd been with the footballers. Conundrum looked spellbound at the flickering TV images in the aquarium as if they were the most fascinating thing in the world.

"So it's possible for a football match and a meeting of the Portuguese Cabinet to take place in a small aquarium. And neither the politicos nor the footballers have a clue they are cohabiting with the fish. There is the germ of an enormous idea here, Henri. Most probably, something to do with parallel universes, I think. I'll tell you when I've cracked it."

Conundrum the mad professor? His attention now shifted to another aquarium. A solitary jellyfish illuminated in ultraviolet light hung in the water like a drowned ballerina, its diaphanous skirt billowing gracefully. A spectacle more beautiful than the most inspired production of *Swan Lake*.

Conundrum filled our glasses.

"I propose a toast to the jellyfish, Henri."

The jellyfish?"

Don't you get it, Henri?"

Get what?"

"The joke."

"The joke? The jellyfish?"

"Yes, well not really the jellyfish. It's us, Henri. You, me the entire human race. We're the joke."

"How do you figure that?"

"Our childish notion that we are fashioned in the image of the Creator is so wide of the mark it's perfectly ludicrous. For there is more perfection here in the spiritual transparency, the spineless strength, the mindless intelligence of the jellyfish than in the most sophisticated posturing of the human species. So might not the Creator justifiably take more satisfaction in this flawless act of creation than in us?"

I took a sip of wine.

"The conclusion is inescapable, Henri."

"Being?"

"For all we know, God is a jellyfish."

"God, a jellyfish?"

"Yes, why ever not?"

This was at least a step away from the bleak view of life as a cosmic infection Conundrum had expressed in Paris. But to see God as a jellyfish surely made a mockery of everything. Michelangelo's Sistine Chapel ceiling, for example, would have to be repainted with images of jellyfish instead of men.

"Do you have a problem with that, Henri?"

The glazed look in Conundrum's eye told me he was in his cups. But he stuck doggedly to his theme.

"The cells that make up a jellyfish and the ones that gave us Ludwig van Beethoven have a common origin. Once they are decomposed and recycled they go on another journey to make up something else. The same life source exists throughout the whole creation but permanence of form is not in the script. Flux and reflux is the name of the game. Ultimately everything is on loan. Atoms which in one life are part of you Henri can the next time round be something quite different. For example, a..."

"Yes?"

"A digestive biscuit!"

"A digestive biscuit?"

"No need to fuss over the details, Henri. You take the micro and I'll take the macro. And I'll be in Scotland before ye."

I'd never seen Conundrum so drunk.

"What a pain it is to be thinking all the time. Can't even have a drink in peace without thoughts wanting to join the party. Perhaps yours isn't such a bad trade after all, Henri. With photos it's just snap, snap, snap. As for me, clapped out old hack, I'm condemned always to be thinking about all sorts of things, when I would really much rather be thinking of nothing at all."

He knocked back another glass of wine and immediately refilled it. I'd never seen him this drunk.

"But we are both guilty as charged. You and I. Writer and photographer. We turn reality into unreality through the daily practice of our respective trades."

We were after all in the same boat. Conundrum despaired of words as I did of pictures. A fine pair of disillusioned failures we were. Was that why we had become fellow travellers?

"Remember Port Lligat, Henri? North-eastern point of Iberia where Dalí boasted he was the first man in Spain on whom the sun shone every morning. Well, tomorrow we shall be at Cape St Vincent, south-west point of Iberia, where we shall be the last to see the sun go down. In ancient times, people thought the world stopped there. If you went any further you would fall off the edge."

That afternoon we checked in at the *pousada* in Sagres. Before dinner I wandered out along the cliffs. I came across a dead rat, big brute lying in the middle of the path, pool of blood oozing from its muzzle. I know a bad omen when I see one.

Next morning we headed to the fort at Sagres. I took pictures of the crazy cliff anglers perched perilously close to the edge on tiny rock ledges. Around lunchtime we reached Cape St Vincent. The road ended in a vast car park and an array of stalls hawking souvenirs. Not many tourists about. A hotdog stand proclaimed *LETZTE BRATWURST VOR AMERIKA*. This had been translated, presumably with the help of a British tourist as *LAST JUMBO KRAUT BANGER BEFORE AMERICA*.

I became aware of a stray dog shadowing us. It might have been the brother of the one that had followed us in Evora a few days previously. Why is it that dogs walk sideways and turn in a tight circle before sitting down?

Conundrum, in a world of his own, scuttled on ahead. I fell in behind without a murmur, unquestioning as the stray dog behind me. What follows a stray dog, I wondered, in this chain of mindless submission to a higher purpose? We stopped at the outer gate of the lighthouse.

"I give you the lighthouse of St Vincent, Henri. Take a look inside. I think it will repay the effort. It's not often you get a chance for such an insight into the true nature of things."

I hesitated.

"Go on, Henri. The door is open. I'll take a walk."

With an oblique glance over his shoulder, Conundrum sauntered down a path towards a walled enclosure overlooking the sea. The last I saw of him before he turned his back on me was his lopsided grin. Like that of the *Cheshire Cat* it hung in the air long after its owner had gone.

The stray dog hesitated for a moment, uncertain which of us to follow. It opted for Conundrum. I entered the outer gate of the lighthouse. It admitted to an austere arcaded quadrangle, like a monastic cloister. A solitary door at the far end opened at the touch of my finger. Now I entered the lighthouse itself.

There was no one about. A chipped dish containing some small coins lay on a wooden desk. I spotted a man in uniform. Presumably, the lighthouse keeper. Did he say something or did he indicate with a flicker of the eyes I was to follow him upstairs? Several flights of steps culminated in a tight spiral stair which brought me to the very top of the lighthouse. Now I was standing right under the great light, a huge cube of shining crystal pieces held together with gleaming brass fixtures. The glass prisms broke the invisible white light of the sun into all the colours of the spectrum. It was like being inside a rainbow. My brain buzzed with speculation.

I inspected the apparatus while the man polished the optics with a cloth. The task was possibly a pretext for keeping an eye on me. I made a tour of the installation, admiring the intricate patterns of refracted light. Then I spotted a gap where one of the pieces was missing. I peered inside. I was amazed by what I saw. Rather by what I didn't see. There was nothing but a relatively modest light bulb. The mighty luminescence visible for miles out to sea was created by a cunning arrangement of mirrors and prisms that magnified the tiny source of brightness until it dazzled the eye. It was all achieved by deceit and trickery.

So what did Conundrum wish me to learn from this? That the pot of gold at the end of his rainbow was nothing more than an empty crock? So what would that make him? A wizard without spells? A sheep in wolf's clothing? No, there must be more to it than that. Was he trying to tell me yet again that the whole world was the work of a master illusionist? Perhaps even the sun at the centre of our universe was just a feeble candle light magnified by some cosmic backstage trickery.

I made another circuit to check out my observations. The light bulb was no bigger than a glass valve in an old wireless set or the crystal ball I'd glimpsed in the salon of *Madame Renée Clairvoyante* on Southend Pier. *Madame Renée?* Why should I be thinking of her at this moment? There must be a reason. Right now everything had a specific reason. I felt certain she must fit somewhere in Conundrum's elaborate charade.

Something began to bother me about her name. *Madame Renée? Renée?* I repeated it over and over, probing the linguistic contours of the word. Was *Renée* an anagram? Then the pieces fell into place. *Renée* in French meant *reborn*. Her name in English translated as *Madame Born Again!* Why hadn't I seen that before? Rebirth? So that's what Conundrum's obsession with prehistoric burial mounds was all about.

I struggled to recall a forgotten line of scripture that first a man must die before he can be born again. Unless of course it's a spiritual rebirth. Though that didn't seem too likely given Conundrum's views on religion. But what did I know? Anyway, the details could wait. I felt I was close to sussing Conundrum's game. He had dropped enough hints that he was on the verge of some great transformation.

I felt an urgent need to see Conundrum before it was too late. He couldn't be far away. I careered down the spiral stairs at breakneck speed, raced out of the lighthouse through the courtyard and back to where I had last seen him. No sign of him anywhere. But the stray dog was still there hanging around. It watched me approach, stood up lazily and ambled off with a slight backward turn of the head as if to make sure I was following. The dog led me down the cobbled path Conundrum had trodden a few minutes earlier for his walk around the lighthouse. But, after turning a corner the path ended a short distance ahead, blocked by a chest-high parapet wall. There was a stark finality about this barrier. It seemed to mark the end of the line, the place where you really will fall off the edge.

I approached with trepidation. The stray dog stood there with an air of detachment, inviting me to take a look, analyse the evidence, draw my own conclusions. It was then that I noticed the pair of shoes. Conundrum's shoes lay abandoned just in front of the wall, positioned in mid-stride as if their erstwhile owner had taken an enormous leap and launched himself into space. That stirred a distant memory: the man who vanishes like a genie on finally understanding the cosmic joke. And to confirm it, now there was the voice of Conundrum inside my head.

"That is precisely how I shall hope to end, Henri. Vertical lift-off, in mid-stride, leaving my shoes behind me."

I realised I would not find him here, or anywhere else for that matter. I walked up to the wall. It was covered with graffiti. I half expected to read something like *CONUNDRUM WOZ ERE*. He was capable of a cheap trick like that. Then I peered over thinking I might discover him lying on a ledge like Arthur in Tossa de Mar. There was indeed a small grassy platform not far below. But it contained nothing except for a clump of piercingly pink flowers. Beyond that, a sheer drop hundreds of feet down to the rocks and the turquoise ocean, all milky bright at the edges with the foam of air trapped in the breakers.

I took several photographs, quite mechanically, as if I were recording the scene of a crime to be used in evidence, if not at an inquest then at least for myself, that I might later believe what my eyes were only half taking in with disbelief.

I looked up into the immensity of the sky. It exuded a radiant Atlantic azure no photograph could capture. I gazed out into the big blue yonder, as if it held all the answers. Now I was certain of it. Conundrum had finally taken the enormous leap he had always dreamed of. And he had done it in a suitably dramatic way. Had there been any witnesses? A ridiculous question. Even with a crowd of people in attendance, Conundrum would have performed his disappearing act like a practised conjuror in such a way no one would have noticed. But what was the outcome? Had he really managed to fly without wings?

Then it struck me the dog must have seen what had happened. I took the animal's head in my hands and looked into its eyes. I gazed into black pools of canine pupils. As I stared intently into their limpid depths, I saw the reflection of a solitary bird fly past against the backdrop of blue. Then I looked up to examine the real bird in the sky.

It was flying low, very low, and heading in my direction. As it came closer I recognised the form of a gannet from its white plumage, wing-tips tinged black as if dipped in ink. Now it was almost upon me. I could make out a beady eye staring at me. It looked familiar. Did I know any gannets? It may even have winked at me before veering off sharply. I felt a wet dollop land on my right shoulder. Do such details matter? I don't know. I had already concluded that this was the latest and last guise in which I would see Conundrum. I was certain it was him.

I watched the gannet head out to sea. Now it folded its wings and dropped like a stone, piercing the waves with a tidy splash. Several seconds later, it emerged, a silver fish trapped in its bill. With a deft movement, the bird flicked its head, tossed the fish, caught it and swallowed it whole. Why, Conundrum, you old devil, you frightful show-off! What antics! He had done it at last. So this was the realisation of his ambition to fly without wings. I tried to imagine how a wingless Conundrum might have flung himself off the cliff and been transformed in mid-air into a gannet. A final piece of scintillating magic.

I watched him fly west until he was a tiny speck against the horizon. About to be absorbed by the blueness of the sky. My eyes ached following him to the point of extinction. Numb with a sense of bereavement, but also a huge joy Conundrum had pulled it off so brilliantly. He had thrown himself off the edge of the world, launched himself from the sacred promontory into the great beyond. He had taken the ultimate risk. Having made the leap of faith and dared to fly without wings. He had grown a set of his own just when he needed them.

So now the old scoundrel was 'moving on' at last. As if to bring me down to earth with a bump, the dog cocked a hind leg, urinated against the wall, splashing Conundrum's shoes. I smiled. Everyday life would continue in its tragi-comic way with an infinite capacity for banalities such as this. I turned away from the piss-stained shoes, last relic of Conundrum on earth.

Now the full impact of his departure hit me like a kick in the stomach. I gasped at the realisation that my life was entirely in my own hands. Conundrum had shown me all he could show me. But was it all I needed? His words came back to me.

"All the cards have been dealt. No point looking for new ones, Henri."

Henri? Another shock to the system. Only Conundrum knew me by that name. I knew it wasn't me. But I didn't know who else I was supposed to be. I had become Henri in a much fuller sense than whoever I had been before. So would I now have to revert to my former self? I recoiled from that awful prospect. I was terrified to re-become whoever or whatever I'd been previously. I felt dizzy. I was going to faint. I don't know how I made it back to the car. The stray dog watched me drive off. It wasn't worth his while to follow me any further.

I didn't get far. I stopped the car and staggered past the *Fortalezza de Beliche*. A scattering of tourists were soaking up the sun on a sheltered terrace. Where was I going? What was I doing? I saw myself like a sleepwalker go through a small gate in a stone wall. A rough rock path marked by rusty iron stanchions headed down the cliff, dipped and dived into the abyss. Instinctively, I followed it down. Gasping for breath, I paused on a rocky ledge. Hundreds of feet down below the ocean crashed repeatedly on a shelf of rock. Another dizzy spell.

Then my senses cleared. I knew what had to be done. This was the time, this was the place, my own launch pad into eternity. I too would fly without wings and head west into the setting sun. I braced myself for lift-off. But I was unable to do what I desperately wanted to do. I tottered precariously on the brink and wobbled to and fro until vertigo buckled my knees and I crumpled to the ground. I had no more substance than one of those soft self-portraits by Salvador Dalí.

I don't know how long I lay there. When I came to I was helped to my feet by an elderly couple, German tourists out walking along the cliff. Tears started to flow from my eyes in a mighty stream. I just stood there crying. No I wasn't crying. I wasn't doing anything. A river of grief – abstract and anonymous – flowed through me. But tears of pure joy mingled with those of sadness. Hidden things from deep inside gushed up and cascaded forth. My heart and soul were in meltdown.

The sun shone in my eyes. Through my tears I could see a rainbow. My very own rainbow, a private mini spectrum. Now I was smiling. Curiously, all I could say to my two rescuers, anxious to get a word from me, was a line in a foreign tongue.

"Alles Vergängliche ist nur ein Gleichnis."

Without being asked, the man translated, as if for my benefit, my own words back to me in English.

"Everything transient is only a metaphor."

His wife interrupted.

"I'm afraid that's a bit literal, dear. It's much more poetic in the original German."

Meanwhile I continued to spout words I had never heard before in a language I couldn't even begin to understand.

"Das Unzulängliche, hier wird's Ereignis."

The husband persisted in his faltering interpretation.

"The inadequate thing becomes a real event."

Again the wife was unhappy with his efforts.

"I don't think that's elegant, and certainly not correct. I'm not even sure it means anything in English."

I was already speaking the next couplet.

"Das Unbeschreibliche, hier ist's getan."

"The indescribable has happened here."

This time the wife is more pleased with his translation.

"OK, that's not too bad."

By this strange means I got to know roughly the sense of what I was saying in German, this mysterious language flowing from my mouth so sweetly as if I'd been talking it since birth.

"Das Ewig-Weibliche zieht uns hinan."

"The Eternal-Feminine draws us ever on."

"Yes, that's better."

The wife was finally pleased and so was I on her behalf. I wanted to say something else in German. But nothing more came. I looked to the German couple for an explanation.

"That's all. You've reached the end of the play."

"Play?"

"Goethe's Faust, Part Two. The final scene. You've been reciting the closing words of the play. Faust's last will and testament to posterity. Your German accent is pretty good."

Faust? The sorcerer? Last will and testament? My German accent pretty good? So had Conundrum bequeathed me the gift of tongues as some kind of farewell present? A symbolical gesture in the pentecostal tradition? Or was it the quotation itself that was significant? Yes, that must be it, especially the final bit.

"The Eternal-Feminine draws us on."

For me that could only mean K.

The German couple kept a watchful eye on me as they helped me back up the steep, rocky path. They asked if they should call a doctor. They invited me to join them for coffee and cakes. I thanked them for their kindnesses, accepting only a glass of cold water. It tasted delicious. I was now desperate to be away, to get back to the hotel at Sagres. I felt sure Conundrum must have left a message. Or if not, then some small clue. Yes, a tiny clue. That would be his style. But nothing too obvious.

I decided I would not report Conundrum as missing. I recoiled at the prospect of all those officials and their endless questions. I feared I might end up in a mental institution if I gave my account of what had happened, that Conundrum was at this very moment flying west in the shape of a gannet as he digested his fresh fish supper. Besides, since there was no body, there was no need to report anything. I knew Conundrum, with his dislike of bureaucracy and paperwork, would thoroughly approve.

I took his key from reception. Trembling, I opened the door to his room. The bed was unmade. A pair of striped flannel pyjamas reclined on the sheets in a rakish contorted pose as if dancing a jig in a gale. His battered leather bag lay on the floor. Feeling like a thief to be rummaging about among his personal possessions, I emptied the contents onto the bed. Items of soiled underwear, miscellaneous travel brochures, crumpled papers. No magic waistcoat. He had been wearing that right up to the end.

The only thing of any real interest was a bunch of keys. This was a prize beyond words. Access to Conundrum's flat, his private realm. But I would need an address. In typical fashion he had supplied only one half of the puzzle. I scanned his handful of papers. I quickly found what I was looking for. Conundrum's home address was printed on a letter sent to him from the Madeira Tourist Office with details of our recent itinerary. It was 7 Moonbeam Mansions, Hanway Place, London W1

A curious address. Entirely worthy of the man. But I felt a twinge of anti-climax that what Conundrum had taken such pains to conceal from me, should now fall into my hands as easily as a ripe apple. Then I thought this must be all part of his master plan. Now that Conundrum had departed or 'moved on', it suited his purpose that I should be put in the picture. His game was entering a new phase. That was all.

I tried to let nothing surprise me. But something did. Conundrum had a first name. It began with an A. The letter was addressed to Mr A. Conundrum. I scrutinised the initial A. Mr A. Conundrum? In a flash I recalled that was exactly how he had first introduced himself to me. *'It's A. Conundrum.'* Only I had misconstrued what he said as *'It's a conundrum.'* He had played the same trick on Elmer Z Wiltshire II in Paris. I also recalled the name card in capital letters marking his place at the Savoy dinner: *A CONUNDRUM.* I had again ignored the evidence staring me in the face and interpreted the A as an indefinite article, crediting Conundrum thereby with a devious joke in keeping with his character. So all along he had been telling me the truth, yet somehow tricking me into a simple misinterpretation.

I wondered what the A stood for. Anthony? Archibald? Adrian? Algernon? Nothing seemed to fit. Aristotle? That was more like it. But still it sounded wrong. And also superfluous. If ever a man could dispense with a first name, then surely it was Conundrum. The more I thought about it, the sillier I felt that I should have made such a basic mistake. I hadn't even got his name right. My confusion over such a small thing as a wrongly attributed indefinite article must have pleased him.

Still ruminating, I stuffed his paltry belongings into the bag. Then, on an impulse, I checked the mini-bar. The old fraud had drunk the champagne, filled it with water, replaced the foil and tucked it away at the back. Or had a previous occupant left it like that? No, that bore Conundrum's signature. I poured the water away and left the bottle on display for room service to find. I'm not sure Conundrum would have approved of my action in owning up on his behalf. In fact, I'm sure he wouldn't have. He was quite shameless in such matters.

What now? My first instinct told me to check out and fly home immediately. My next told me to stay the night at the *pousada* at Sagres and take the flight home the next day exactly as planned. It was important to follow the script.

After dinner I took a walk along the cliffs. There was a glorious afterglow to the evening sun. I was overcome by more tears. This time these were unalloyed tears of joy. Conundrum had flown without wings. He was free. Free as a bird. Quite literally. I felt happy for him the way a member of the Escape Committee feels when a fellow prisoner makes it over the fence. In spirit, you are right with them. Escape Committee? That was exactly what Conundrum had said to me that fateful night in Wales. Now everything was coming full circle.

The sun dropped into the Atlantic like a big red tomato. As I gazed into the ruddy gloaming, I had the distinct impression Conundrum was still observing me with mild amusement, faintly curious what I would do next. There was only one choice.

The keys to 7 Moonbeam Mansions weighed heavy in my pocket. Symbolic tokens laden with destiny. They would lead me on the next leg of this journey just as surely as if Conundrum himself were there in the flesh guiding me along. Strangely, now I was on my own, I felt even more of a puppet than before when Conundrum had been there in person pulling the strings.

Next morning I checked out of the *pousada* at Sagres, settled the extras – including Conundrum's champagne from the minibar – and headed east along the main highway to Faro airport. I drank much more champagne than usual on the flight back to dear old London. As if I wanted to consume enough for two. I was drunk and drained when I got home.

REAL DREAMS

Back home things seemed, at least on the surface, no different now that Conundrum had 'moved on'. After all, we had no regular contact in London between trips. He only called when there was another assignment. Several weeks could slip by without a word. But this time I knew it was finally all over. Yet while the logical part of me fully accepted the reality of Conundrum's departure another part refused to rule out entirely his possible re-appearance. For although I was not expecting ever again to hear his real voice at the other end of the phone, that other voice inside my head, the one that had last spoken to me on the cliffs at Sagres, had not been of my imagining. So in that sense, he was and would always be with me.

Something huge had changed however. Previously, I had only the haziest notion where he lived. Now I knew the exact location of Conundrum's lair. The address was printed on a slip of paper I kept folded in my wallet lest it should go astray. I even had his door keys in my pocket. My initial instinct was to rush round to Conundrum's flat and … and do what?

What would be my purpose exactly? To rifle through his personal affairs? Like a vulture picking at the carcass of a lion. I didn't like to see myself in that role. But I really didn't know what was my role. So I bided my time. Several days passed. But the longer I ignored the keys, the heavier they became, like a dead weight in my pocket.

Meanwhile, old habits died hard. I kept thinking of new trips we would do. One day I browsed through the travel titles in a bookshop imagining we were about to go off on yet another assignment. Then suddenly the prospect of all those flights to be caught, hotels to check in and out of, cars to be hired, waiters to be tipped, people and places to be snapped, induced in me the exact opposite of *wanderlust*. A man thoroughly tired of travel needs a word of equal power to express the intense urge to stay put. I came away from the bookshop reeling with fatigue and I didn't give travel another thought. That chapter was closed.

Even going out in London became stressful. Fear of eye contact with strangers made me give people a wide berth. I crossed the road to avoid an aggressive beggar. He cursed me roundly, told me to drop dead. I wisecracked one day soon I would indeed oblige him. And the way things felt it wouldn't be long. In any case, I wouldn't have minded particularly if I had dropped dead in front of him at that very moment. It no longer seemed to matter one way or the other.

With nothing better to do, I spent long hours alone in my flat, ruminating on this and that. On the windowsill pigeons puffed up with eggy intent were going about the endless business of creating more pigeons. Before I had taken possession of the flat it had been empty for months and a colony of pigeons had gained entrance through a missing ventilation brick in the bathroom to make the place their own. From the way they now eyed me through the glass I could tell that they regarded me as the intruder on their patch. I suspected they were plotting among themselves how to move back in.

The sexual antics of the pigeons were hardly passionate – penetration and ejaculation as fast as a flu jab – but their general air of togetherness really got to me. Somehow it underlined my own isolation. Why had I chosen the lonely road? Surely I'd had my chances to *bond romantically* as Conundrum, with his habitual cynicism, had described love.

But instead of that I'd chosen this lonesome life of mine, and when it failed to deliver the goods, I'd reached out for whatever elixir of life Conundrum had been peddling. Flying without wings, was that it? God, what a fool I was to let such an insane ambition lodge in my brain. But I was hooked. I caught myself repeatedly eying tall buildings, imagining which would be my launch pad. Eventually I settled on *Senate House* overlooking Russell Square. Its totalitarian style made me think of a *Ministry of Truth*. How very appropriate for someone who was now ready to accept the Conundrum doctrine that Truth with the big T was biggest delusion of all.

How had I got to this point? From everything meaning something suddenly to nothing meaning anything. Where could I go from here? What did my future hold? What would *Madame Renée Clairvoyante* of Southend Pier see when she gazed into her crystal ball? And why did I keep thinking of her? I found the very idea of her scary, very scary.

To escape the heaviness of my thoughts I went out for a spin on my bike. Oh, the joy of slipping the Sturmey-Archer into third and feeling the wind in my face. I followed my favourite route from Bloomsbury through Covent Garden to Trafalgar Square, along the Mall to Buckingham Palace, then up to Hyde Park Corner and the ultimate goal of the trip, a traffic-free spin round the Serpentine. Who needs to live in the country?

I stopped for a breather on the south side of the lake and gazed back across the water to where I'd been cycling just a few moments earlier. I could see the bright blue pedalos all neatly moored. I'd thought of taking a picture. It was the sort of image I shot when I was in the mood.

But I had other things on my mind. A fevered thought had taken hold. Only five minutes ago I had been over there the other side of the water. Now I was here. The decision not to take a photo had been made. I had not stopped. That was history. How quickly present turned into past. And how quickly the future would follow suit. It hardly seemed worth going there.

Then something else occurred to me. It took me a while to tease out the thought. It was this. Supposing I had stopped to take those pictures then conceivably right now I would still be there on the other side of the Serpentine hard at work framing my shots trying to get that ultimate image just right. In which case someone sitting here where I was sitting would be able to observe me in real time over there at this very moment.

My speculations didn't stop there. I fell to thinking that if I had stopped to take those pictures then what followed would be influenced by that act. I would conceivably make other detours, chose other directions. In short, my entire future would turn out differently than it will now with me not having stopped. And then I realised these multiple choices are happening almost every moment. For the one real Henri there could have been countless alternative Henris wandering about like lost souls in parallel dimensions doing those things I had elected not to do.

God, this time and space business is weird. The breaking wave of the present seemed trapped in a freeze frame. Myriad tiny droplets of water suspended. Meanwhile, my mind raced forward like an arrow shot from the bow that was me. I felt I was on the verge, just beginning to understand something new. Something huge. The scales were falling from my eyes. Like a dream becoming reality.

Before I knew it I was back in the present sitting on my bench by the Serpentine. Tingling with a new awareness. Was this the now? The blessed here and now? An acute sense of every nanosecond passing, every brain cell popping into oblivion. Me thinking I'm thinking. Me thinking I'm thinking I'm thinking. And so ad infinitum. An endless coil of mental awareness spanning the great wheel of time in a mighty arc, a serpent catching up with itself and swallowing its own tail. In my confusion I started talking out loud.

"I can't make sense of it."

"I can't make sense of anything."

"I can make no sense of anything."

"I can make no sense of it."

"I can make no sense of nothing."

"I can make sense of nothing."

"I can make sense of no thing."

"Yes, that's it."

"I *can* make sense of *no* thing!"

I punched the air like a madman. I'd nailed it.

"Yes, I *can* make sense of *no* thing!"

I had turned a negative into a positive. I couldn't make sense of anything. But I could make sense of no thing. No thing at all! It was a small triumph but somehow a real one. I recalled a story we learned as kids. How to break out of jail using only a matchstick? Well, you snap the match in half. Two halves make a whole. You climb out through the hole. But you have no escape vehicle and the prison wardens are hard on your heels. So you shout yourself hoarse. Then you jump on the horse and ride away. Magic. Sheer magic. The power of words over reality. What had Conundrum said about writing?

"It's not about being good with words. Being good with words can be a handicap. Writing is about being good at having thoughts and feelings. For what is the point of eloquence if you have nothing much to express?"

Now I felt depressed. My paltry thoughts and feelings would never amount to much. I was probably better off taking inanimate pictures of inanimate objects. Perhaps that was the trouble with my photography. I was pretty good at it. I could see pictures. But all too often my heart wasn't in it. I was questioning the need to take yet another picture of whatever it was. For if everything was worth photographing then where was the border between reality and art? Conundrum had it much easier, letting visual reality pass through his eyes or simply wash over him, and then calmly watch it flush down the drain.

I cycled home like a prisoner on parole. After a brief taste of fresh air I was returning to my cell. I reached Trafalgar Square. An old man clutching his can of Carlsberg Special Brew lay prone in front of the National Gallery exactly as he had been an hour earlier. There was someone who had found timelessness, for whom past, present and future formed one big fuzzy bundle of oblivion. But did one have to fall so far in order to achieve this state of beatitude? Questions, questions.

I was drawn into ever darker shadows. Deviating from my route home along the Strand, I turned into Lumley Court, one of the smelliest back passages in central London. The flood of human misery that must have seeped through this narrow piss-reeking, vomit-stained alley over the centuries hit me like a punch in the gut. Abandon hope all ye who enter here.

It was in these unprepossessing surroundings that I found K. There she was lying on the ground in a dirty puddle. Her beautiful face wore a cheap seductive smile as she looked up out of the mire. Even so she was still full of eastern promise. Which is what it said on the cheap postcard on which her image had been printed. The smooth skin of her naked body was pitted from the rough road surface where she had fallen and passers by had trodden her underfoot.

Bending down, I quickly scanned the postcard. It was one of those amateur, homemade jobs that prostitutes put in phone boxes. So K was now advertising herself as an oriental temptress, up for anything and everything, including girl-on-girl sessions. Had I been the one to push her down the slippery slope? There was no doubt in my mind.

Surely this was the moment when I should intervene, reclaim K, and redeem myself? All I needed to do was ring the number on the card and go to her rescue. But the numerals were obscured by a folded corner. I tried peeling it back carefully from the tarmac. But the water-sodden card came apart and dissolved in my fingers. Soon K's image disintegrated into a few soiled, soggy fragments. Her phone number was now as indecipherable as the *haiku* she had penned on my hand in Zurich.

My brain clicked into action. Whoever had dropped this postcard must have got it somewhere. Surely there would be plenty of others of K stuck up in nearby phone boxes. All I had to do was check them out. Feverishly, I did the rounds of the phone boxes. Not trusting first impressions, I tore down the image of every Asian beauty to examine them later. If a phone box was occupied I stared unashamed through the window to examine the faces on the cards. I got some strange looks, rude gestures and narrowly escaped getting beaten up for my pains. But I was on a mission. There was a job to be done.

I covered every phone box between Covent Garden and Russell Square. I crammed so many postcards into my pockets they were bursting at the seams. Time to go home and examine my findings. There wasn't a table large enough so I spread the cards out on the floor. Scores of lovely oriental girls stared up at me with beguiling eyes. I hadn't spotted K yet though I was sure she would be in there somewhere in this erotic beauty parade. But as my eyes sifted through their ranks, all the girls turned out to resemble someone else. I eliminated them one by one and flipped them over until I had just rows of blank cards face down on the carpet making a mockery of my efforts.

I repeated the process several times over, but with no result. Once or twice I thought I was close, but there was always something to disqualify the girl as K. Then, out of the blue, the cursed artist in me reared his ugly head. I had this powerful vision to create a massive collage of all these girls. I would rent a poster site and cover it end to end. Or I would display them all hanging from a washing line as a symbol of a fresh beginning. Or perhaps stick them on empty bottles like wine labels.

These ideas paled before something better. To make one huge portrait. It would be of a serene, perfect, unsullied and very respectable lady. Her beautiful image composed of all these postcard snapshots of sordidly wasted individual lives. I felt these girls deserved better than their fate, to be remembered, even celebrated. Then a quasi-Victorian notion of redemption took hold. I would take my own pictures of these Japanese girls, give them back their feminine dignity. Perhaps in this way I could begin to atone for what I had done to K in Tokyo.

That's when I remembered the topless lady in Nice. Her stark choice of art or love. So here I was choosing art again, not just over love but art over life. Even in this awful situation I was still getting a kick out of the creative possibilities it contained. My sense of self-disgust was overwhelming. I couldn't imagine falling any lower. All I could do was shut my eyes and hold my head in my hands. How on earth to stop the flow of these terrible artistic ideas? I needed the mental equivalent of white noise. Something to blank out these absurd creative notions. Ideas, please go away. Leave me in peace, not in pieces.

When I got home I booted up an old computer and sat there gaping vacantly at screen savers. When that failed to numb my brain sufficiently I ran *Disk Defragment*, the old *Windows 95* version. The monitor filled with row after row of gaily coloured squares that were massaged by a healing digital balm working its way relentlessly through them one by one. After an hour or so watching that, I wished there was some software to re-order my brain cells, my person, my life at the click of a mouse.

I saw my existence as the dotted blue line of a download well past its halfway point. And when this programme Henri.exe was safely stored on the hard disk, what would that amount to?

Things were starting to unravel. I was losing it. Good and proper. Going into meltdown. I wasn't unhappy to be alive, not discontent with life and being part of it. But why did I have to be someone in particular? Why not an indeterminate anyone? A no one even? But above all, why did I have to be me? Why Henri?

Next morning, I took a walk through Russell Square and south on Montague Street. I had just reached the corner of Great Russell Street when I stepped right into a huge pile of fresh dog shit smack in the middle of the pavement. My right foot skidded away. As I struggled to regain my balance my left foot slipped too, spreading the mess over several paving slabs. Somehow I remained on my feet. Drawing breath I leaned against the railings of the British Museum to inspect the soles of my shoes.

"Oi, mate!"

A loud Cockney voice was bellowing at someone.

"Oi, mate!"

It was bellowing at me.

"Oi, mate! Yes, you! I'm talking to you."

A pot-bellied, bald-headed thug in a string vest with a rottweiler straining at the leash stood before me.

"Oh dearie me! What a mess we've made, haven't we?"

I had no idea how to respond.

"And why do you think Reggie dumped it right there in the middle of the pavement?"

The man was clearly barking mad, if you'll excuse the pun. And dangerous with it. I backed away.

"Oi, where do you think you're going? I'm fucking talking to you!"

There was nowhere to go.

"So why do you think Reggie plonked it right there where everyone can see it?"

I had little choice but to hear him out.

"So no careless bastard would go and tread it all over the place. Now just look at the bloody mess you've gone and made. It's all over the bleeding show."

Reggie underlined the point with a low growl.

"See, you've gone and upset him."

Indeed, Reggie didn't look best pleased.

"So what are you going to do about it?"

"Me? Do about it?"

I guessed what might be coming. He was going to tell me to put it back how it was. Well, if he did, then I would tell him he could bloody well put it back where it came from and see how darling Reggie liked that. Pot-bellied, bald-headed thug in string vest would probably kill me. I smiled at the thought.

Would that matter? It would be the perfect answer to all my problems. My life terminated, snuffed out by a homicidal maniac near British Museum following futile argument over heap of dog shit. What a way to go! What a mockery that would make of all those lofty notions and aspirations. A fitting conclusion to my pathetic stab at the human experience. And all I had to do to bring down the curtain was to tell this psycho where he could shove his dog's turd. I was about to put this daring plan into operation, and to hell with the consequences.

"Aren't you going to say sorry to Reggie?"

That stumped me. Was that all he wanted? My instinct for survival now took over. I mumbled the necessary apologies.

"So sorry, Reggie old chap. I mean for making a mess of your mess. Now I really must dash."

And dash I did, making good my escape before any further demands were made. As I rushed off down the street, I left behind a series of brown footprints.

I hadn't gone far before I suspected Conundrum to be behind this. It was just his style. I guessed he could still put on his acts and impersonations from beyond the whatever? What was his game? Trying to provoke me, to prod me into action?

"No, Conundrum. I won't be rushed. Yes, I've got your damn flat keys. I'll go and check out Moonbeam Mansions when I'm good and ready. Not before."

I realised I was speaking to myself. In any case, I couldn't go anywhere before I'd cleaned up. So I backtracked to Russell Square and set about wiping Reggie's pride and joy off my shoes on the grass. Then I rinsed them in the fountains.

While engaged on this menial chore, I saw the sublimely ridiculous nature of things. Here I was polluting the fountains of Russell Square which, in a fit of poetic musing, I had seen as a holy well, a sacred spring marking the very centre of the universe. But no matter what I did to sully the waters they would always come bubbling back crystal clear, sweet and pure. It was a moment of cosmic absolution. My puny acts would leave no lasting impression. Everything would be washed away. I was of no more substance than the shadow of a shadow. I couldn't decide whether to laugh or to cry. In the end I smiled. It was funny. Sad but really funny. So my smile was a bit crooked.

I set off for home with this silly smile on my face. Feeling inexplicably and deliriously happy. It was the very best kind of happiness, having no cause, no origin, being not about or on account of anything, just a state of mind. Suddenly I saw the whole world with huge affection. Like Tiny Tim I was in God bless everyone mode. God bless even the overweight pigeons taking a shower in the fountains washing their feathers just as I had washed my shoes.

My legs were melting into socks out of sheer joy about absolutely nothing. Nothing! I had tasted the heady brew of nothingness. I was about to go into vertical lift-off. I recalled Conundrum's shoes abandoned in mid-stride. Was I about to go the same way? Surely it was my turn now? Without looking I stepped off the pavement with no more thought than to see if my feet would actually stay on the ground. I was almost run over by a cyclist coming the wrong way down the bus lane.

"Fucking dickhead!"

Fucking dickhead? Yes, that's me. Spot on. I wanted to thank him for putting it so eloquently. But already the cyclist was speeding off on his pointless errand.

An even stranger encounter happened in Gordon Square of all places where thoughts would normally turn to Virginia Woolf and the Bloomsbury Group. But here was this old woman in period dress, right out of one of those Georgian prints that illustrate the street cries of the London of yesteryear.

"Fanny! Fresh fanny!"

I stared at her in disbelief. She looked me straight in the eye and muttered under her breath.

"Well, not that fresh, actually."

She then resumed her cries.

"Fellatio! First rate fellatio!"

At this point she cracked a broad grin to reveal the sore red gums of a toothless mouth. I turned and fled.

After that I didn't go out unless I had to. For this I had some reason. Exposure to sunlight caused an angry rash across my forehead and a painful red swelling under my right eye. The photographer's skin had become photosensitive. One of those little ironies in which real life so easily surpasses the imagination. If I had to go out, then I hugged the shadows and sought the dark side of the street, as a cockroach charts a direct course to the nearest drain. Might I wake up one morning metamorphosed into a hideous Kafkaesque insect? Surely I was paying the price for something. I fell into deep introspection. I felt like locking myself in, pulling up the drawbridge.

So I stayed in most of the time. This brought with it an unexpected dividend. My photographic eye started seeing things it had never seen before. An empty green bottle by the kitchen window catching the sunlight struck me as the most beautiful thing ever. I photographed a series of bottles: blue, brown, green, clear. I was going one better than Conundrum's party trick of turning words into wine. That was merely a play on words. I was really turning wine into art. My portfolio of empty bottles would put me a jump ahead of Conundrum. The beauty of it was that my modest windowsill was all the studio space I needed in order to explore an entire visual universe. It was that simple.

What was it Conundrum had said? People don't give a damn how many things you are passably good at. All they want is one thing you can do brilliantly. So why not the bottles? Could they be my thing? Georgio Morandi had spent a lifetime at home in Bologna painting over and over again the same handful of nondescript jugs and bottles. Inspired and uplifted by this, I sat for hours contemplating the sublime glint of sunshine captured in an empty wine bottle by the window.

I saw the Holy Grail of beauty in every single drop of refracted light. I felt in full possession of all my senses. My third eye had been opened. I could now perceive the innermost core of nature's secret energy. I was filled with a sweet sensation. I was as close to the ultimate aesthetic experience as if I were to travel to the ends of the earth. Everything I needed was right here. My life's purpose could be achieved within these walls. I could stay put in this small room and yet reach out to the furthest limits of the human imagination.

I had another good reason for staying in. Bloomsbury was full of young Japanese girls who reminded me painfully of K. I even had the strangest dream about her.

K was lying naked on a bed. She was old, exceedingly old. But I wasn't. I was still my present age. And in this dream I ran my hand gently over her shrunken breasts, softly pressed the sagging folds of her once firm flesh. I explored her entire body like an archaeologist uncovering the streets of a lost city, entering deserted houses, turning over abandoned objects. I felt I could reclaim her just as she was in her prime and somehow build an erotic bridge across the chasm of time. Like breathing life back into an Egyptian mummy. At this point the decadent dream dissolved. I awoke with tears falling down my cheek.

I was haunted by other dreams, equally strange and alarming. Little bits of random memory and chance associations stirred up like autumn leaves by who knows what cerebral breezes wafting through the deep brain.

In one such dream a budgerigar had taken up residence in my mouth. It came and went as it pleased, as if I were merely a nesting box. As if my thoughts were not my own? Conundrum drifting in and out of my head as the mood takes him?

In another dream my arm had been seized by a mastiff while I slept. Its jaws closed firmly on my wrist. If I made the slightest movement the teeth would tighten, break the skin and chew me to the bone. My only hope was to lie quite still and wait for the brute to get bored and relax its grip. But it didn't. Was this Conundrum too? Would he never let go?

I dreamed I was sitting on the loo. Having a crap. Only I had just given birth to a fish. I mean I had actually shat out a real live fish. Nothing too large, about the size of an adult anchovy. I watched it turn in tight circles in the toilet bowl. Anything to do with the silver fish caught by Conundrum in his guise as a gannet off Cape St Vincent?

In yet another dream I entered a ruined castle in the depths of winter. A pack of polar bears lay hibernating in the great hall. Their white bodies were covered in snow flakes that fell through a gaping hole in the roof. They lay cocooned under an enormous duvet of cotton wool. I felt no threat, just peace.

I wished I too could sleep for months and wake up as someone else with my life renewed. Or perhaps just sleep and sleep never to wake again. But all too soon I was woken by something. The air tasted strange. It took me a while to register the aroma of onion soup wafting in from a flat below.

"I say could you turn down the volume on your smelly *soupe à l'oignon*. Some of us are trying to get some sleep."

But I didn't say anything. Didn't want the neighbours to think me mad. Well, I wasn't going mad, was I? Unable to go back to sleep, I stared out across the street. The flat opposite had its curtains open. I peered into a room painted blue from floor to ceiling. Like being underwater. And in this blue room a solitary Chinaman was leaping about as if being attacked by demons. I took me a long while before I twigged he was dancing.

How silly his movements looked without the music. Was that why life always appeared such a grotesque charade? Because I couldn't hear the background music, the accompanying score of the human comedy? All I saw were people twitching this way and that, moving to the rhythms of a silent band.

I was woken again by a soft whimpering noise. A low moan came through the wall from the flat next door. Like a baby crying. Then the sobbing suggested a woman making love. Then it was a baby again. Only this time much louder. Now I was certain it was a woman having multiple orgasms. Then it struck me. Baby crying and woman moaning were simply two different phases of one single act of creation. How typical of nature that the cry of childbirth should be prefigured at the moment of conception by a cry of pleasure.

What was it Conundrum said? Everything contains its opposite? No it wasn't that. Dammit! Was I now thinking his thoughts? It was nothing more than a damn fine shagging. Dammit again! That might have been Conundrum too.

I fell asleep once more. My dreamscape stretched out in an endless desert of rolling dunes. Nothing but sand and sky. I walked alone under a burning sun putting my feet mechanically one after the other into a line of footprints that were laid out like a trail before me. My inescapable destiny leading me on?

I watched my feet step forward as if they belonged to someone else. But when I looked back over my shoulder I was surprised to find I was leaving no tracks behind me in the sand. Absolutely none at all. Each footprint seemed to vanish after I had stepped in it. Even asleep, my mind sought to analyse the dream. Was it my role in life to walk in footsteps already trodden, while leaving behind none of my own?

I awoke in a cold sweat. Lying awake was even worse than the dreams, leaving me prey to every doubt and confusion. A big black dog sitting on my chest. I felt undecided, undirected, unresolved. There was no lynchpin for my life to turn on, no fulcrum to my lever, no ballast in my hold, no keel to my yacht. I was all at sea. So much chaff to the wind. Mercifully, I fell asleep once more. I embraced oblivion with total abandon.

Just before waking, my dream screen filled again with shaky images as if an old projector had spluttered back to life. I saw myself in the film. I watched the camera track my every movement as if in a video diary. I saw myself wandering about the flat exploring like a stranger in my own home.

I stumbled across a secret entrance to an extra room concealed right here in my apartment. I entered this new room so wondrous and perfect I could have wept for sheer happiness. The discovery filled me with excitement. Even awake, when I realised it had all been a dream, the thrill was with me still. I looked everywhere for the secret door. But found none. I felt I was locked out of paradise.

I sat for ages on the toilet staring at the floor. My feet on the bathroom mat waited patiently in a state of eternal repose, like bits of sculpture. Soon, I thought, they will be making their way to Moonbeam Mansions. But motionless for now, since their owner had no stomach for the task. And so my feet bade their time. Then I heard the postman at the door and the faintest sigh of a letter falling on the floor. It hardly made a sound. Those are the dangerous ones, Conundrum had once said.

I picked it up. It felt curiously light. I opened it, but there was nothing inside. I was holding an empty envelope though with my name scrawled on it in large flowing capitals. This must be a sign of something. I didn't know his handwriting but I immediately knew Conundrum to be behind this ruse. Was he trying to tell me something? An empty envelope would be about right for a communication from him.

He would let me make of it what I wanted. Suddenly I knew exactly what it meant. I could put off the fateful day no longer. So I took the keys to Moonbeam Mansions in my hand. With that one small act, my life moved out of dream mode. I shook off the torpor of recent days and weeks. I had been living in a dimension of time suspended. Having been on pause I had somehow hit the play button. The programme was running again and could not now be stopped.

MOONBEAM MANSIONS

My life slips into real time. And so I slip into the present tense. I am now in action mode. Every fibre of my being tingles with anticipation as I set about doing what needs to be done. I step cautiously over two drunks on the front step of my block. They tell me their presence is not entirely a nuisance since they will keep away any other undesirables. I recognise there is no choice but to accept them as a kind of *cordon insanitaire.*

"*Cordon insanitaire?* I say, Henri. That's good. You are making progress in the *bons mots* department."

Having Conundrum with me, albeit as a disembodied voice, makes me feel less like a burglar as I prepare to enter his den. Hanway Place turns out to be an insalubrious loop off Hanway Street, an obscure back alley linking Oxford Street and Tottenham Court Road. It reeks of piss and old garbage, the familiar whiff of high summer in central London. It doesn't bother me. My senses are numb with foreboding. For as long as I knew him Conundrum conspired to withhold his address from me. And here I am about to violate his private realm.

Moonbeam Mansions reveals itself as a seedy, run-down Edwardian block at the far end of Hanway Place. I immediately recognise it as being out of the same mould as Conundrum himself. It suits him perfectly. Its dingy but once distinguished red-brick façade has hardly been touched since the day it was built. I pause on the threshold, trying to assume the pose of one who has legitimate business here. I detect a twitch of net curtains as I stand on the front step, weighing the keys in my hand.

Still I hesitate. I sense a malevolent presence behind me. I glance over my shoulder. But there is nothing of any material substance, only the merest suggestion of a shadow produced by a hazy cloud passing over the sun. I push open the front door and step inside the entrance hall. No one about. The building has an abandoned feel, a *Marie Celeste* of mansion blocks. A peeling hand-painted sign informs me flat number 7 is at the top. The ancient cage-lift is out of order. I wouldn't trust it anyway. Slowly I walk up the three storeys counting each step, a man mounting the scaffold for his final appointment with destiny.

My heart is in my mouth as I insert the key in the lock of 7 Moonbeam Mansions. The brass door handle feels cool in my sweaty palm. I want to turn back from the brink. A nameless force more powerful than fear drives me on. The door opens a fraction, then meets resistance from a pile of letters wedged behind it. I have to reach round to remove them to gain entrance. It appears no one has been here for a long while.

As I take a step forward down the hall, Conundrum's voice stops me in my tracks.

"Welcome, and thank you for choosing 7 Moonbeam Mansions. With so many premises available for casual burglary we really do value your custom. Time is of the essence, so please do listen carefully to this announcement which will make your task much easier. We regret you will not find the usual consumer goods in this establishment but we can offer a wide range of excellent reading material located in the living room which is the first room to your left. Where, you may well wonder, is the dying room? I'll leave you to find that on your own."

Conundrum's voice disintegrates and breaks off. I enter the living room. The floor is covered with books, journals, newspapers and pamphlets like an overgrown garden. Scribbled notes are stuck to the walls, even pinned to the curtains. Several well-trodden routes lead through the mounds of paper as trails in a forest. The walls are lined with bookshelves from floor to ceiling as in a second-hand bookshop. The volumes are arranged by subject: archaeology, history, travel, science. Psychology and religion lurk on a top shelf, safely out of reach.

For someone who proclaimed such disdain for the mundane stuff of factual information, Conundrum's books are a revelation. It's a proper library. So he was working on something. The manuscript of *Conundrum's Book* must be here. I am not to be disappointed after all. I now relax a little. I can take my time. No point rushing. Mustn't overlook anything. I see a hand note in block letters written on a card pinned into a bookshelf.

THERE IS ALWAYS A BIGGER PICTURE

Yes, I remember him saying that, more than once. Then a thought of my own kicks in. How can there always be a bigger picture? Surely there must come a point when things get as big as they can? And things can't get much bigger than the desolate vision Conundrum laid before me in Paris after his close brush with death. Namely that the ultimate purpose and inevitable end game of the universe was self-destruction. That humans amount to no more than cosmic compost. What could be more final, and more chilling than that?

I now spot other hand-written notes stuck on the wall.

THE PERFECT THOUGHT
HOMO NOT SO SAPIENS
THE FOURTH REVELATION
THE WELL DUSTED SHELF
DIVERSION ENDS
NASAL GROOMING MASTERCLASS
LAST TRAIN TO MORDEN

It reads like a list of book titles or possibly book projects. My brain is buzzing with questions. Why didn't I quiz my teacher when I had the chance? Curious, now he isn't with me that my mind suddenly seeks answers. *The Fourth Revelation?* Might *Conundrum's Book* have something to do with religion and metaphysics? Did he not say that the nerve cells in the human brain are like a map of the heavens? That the universe is in us just as we are in the universe. What was it exactly? I can't believe what a poor student I have turned out to be.

An antiquated manual typewriter squats on a desktop overflowing with yellowed press clippings. There is a sheet of paper in the machine with a few words typed on it. Must be what Conundrum was working on when he… I still can't say the word even silently to myself. I lean over for a closer look.

"No good depending on older people to light the way. They won't be around long enough to see you through."

It's eerie how these words form a direct response to the thoughts inside my head. Yes, I am missing Conundrum, and rueing all those missed opportunities.

I pull open a drawer. It's filled to the brim with corks from wine bottles. So the man who urged me to 'throw away the cork' was a secret hoarder of them. There are literally hundreds of corks. At random I inspect one. *Château Léoville Barton 1988*. A nice *St Julien* from the *Médoc*. Not bad. Not bad at all.

What possessed Conundrum to collect them? What hidden store of memories did these corks contain? And who were his drinking companions? Probably no one. I reckon he had drunk all this wine on his own. What was it he had once said?

"I'm strictly a social drinker, Henri. When I've had a few I talk to myself."

I smile at the memory. I open another drawer and pull out a handful of papers. I stop smiling. I even stop breathing. These are bank statements in the name of, in the name of... I have to read the name several times over to make sure I'm not imagining things. In the name of Arthur Conundrum. Yes, it's true. Conundrum's first name was Arthur! I can hardly believe it. Arthur! He must be kidding. After all the jokes he had cracked at the expense of 'our Arthur, which art in Yorkshire'.

I study the statements. No harm in that. I'm not stealing anything. They relate to investment portfolios managed by one of those exclusive private banks in Zurich. I recognise the name of the outfit Conundrum had interviewed and then given such a glowing write-up. So he had been doing his Swiss bank manager a favour. I look again at the statements.

The zeros send my head spinning. The sums are simply astronomical. The old miser who never willingly put his hand in his pocket and who preached the virtues of the non-material existence was a millionaire many times over! He who despised the accumulation of worldly goods had amassed a nest egg of monumental proportions. Will there be no end to his duplicity?

Another drawer is full of old photographs. Faded holiday snaps of people who must long since be dead. Small figures in front of ancient ruins, scenic views from around the world. That sort of thing. Some are of young women with hopeful smiles of tender affection. Old flames discarded after Conundrum purged emotion from his breast? I wonder if there is one of *Madame* when she was young. I can't see any. But then I can't imagine what she would have looked like without all that flesh.

I root around further, seized by a morbid curiosity to sift through all the most intimate remains of Conundrum's vanished life. Now I am staring at a face I recognise all too well from our recent travels. That sultry sex kitten from Grindelwald. The back of the photo bears a lipstick imprint of a hot kiss so voluptuous I can taste her breath. Another familiar face: Nikita, the birchy Siberian beauty Conundrum slept with in Moscow. More bad memories for me. She has penned a dedication in Russian. I'm glad I can't understand it.

There are plenty more pictures. Next one up is a shot of *Frau Doktor* from Berlin. Stark naked on a filing cabinet. Great body. Takes me a while to recognise the serious civil servant without her clothes. But I am shocked to discover a picture of that young student in Cambridge to whom Conundrum had made literary love in the meadow by the river. I would have thought, after his cruel fun at her expense, she would be immune to his dubious charms. I gasp in disbelief at what she has written on the back of her picture. *'Come plant your maypole in my tunnel of love.'* How gross. I had her down as a much more refined creature. By what legerdemain had Conundrum hooked these victims? How had he fooled them into finding him attractive? Too many questions. My head is reeling.

There's one face I don't want to find in Conundrum's collection of sexual conquests. I hope and pray that K doesn't figure among the specimens in his trophy cabinet. The rest don't mean anything to me. I go through all the pictures. But I don't find one of K. Thank heavens for that.

My eye now falls on a shoebox tucked under the desk. I bend down to pick it up. Stuffed inside, yet more photographic evidence of Conundrum's past. A pile of vintage black and white prints. The top one immediately grabs my attention. Two men wearing baggy tropical shorts stand in front of a 1950s Citroen parked by a ruined Buddhist temple. Clearly, they are somewhere 'out East'. There is a wartime atmosphere to the scene. Indo-China perhaps? All this is remarkable enough.

Then I take a closer look. One of the men bears a striking resemblance to the youthful Cartier-Bresson. He has a brotherly arm around someone I now recognise as Conundrum. Beneath the traveller's sun tan I can make out the familiar scrawny features of today's Conundrum. Or should that be yesterday's Conundrum? My head can't cope with that on top of everything else. For I have now just read the dedication: *"À mon très cher ami, Arthur, un plus grand photographe que moi, qui m'a montré le chemin."* It is signed: *"Merci, Henri."*

There can be no doubt. Cartier-Bresson and Conundrum were once bosom pals, travel companions. But fellow photographers? And Cartier-Bresson acknowledging Conundrum as the greater of the two, the one who showed him the way? Surely Conundrum was always a writer? I grab a magnifying glass lying on the desk and inspect the picture.

Both men are holding cameras. Conundrum's machine, a stately old *Hasselblad*, not the handiest apparatus for reportage, is slung casually almost dismissively over his shoulder in the manner of a seasoned old pro. Cartier-Bresson cradles his *Leica* in the palm of his hand as if it were a newly acquired possession. So Conundrum looks like the senior partner. And now I can see that he is much older than young Henri, in fact about the same age as I knew him until only recently. My brain fires another urgent question. But if Conundrum was already that old all those years ago why hasn't he grown older? By rights he should be long dead, making it impossible for me to have met him.

There's too much to take in. Must keep a clear head. I quickly flick through the other pictures in the shoebox. Beautiful scenes in exotic locations, consummate images of human life infused with a powerful poetic realism slip between my trembling fingers and fall to the floor. A treasure trove of photojournalism from the 40s and 50s. And all in the trademark square format that must have come from Conundrum's *Hasselblad* rather than the rectangular shots from Cartier-Bresson's *Leica*.

I'm numb with shock. Conundrum an intimate friend of Cartier-Bresson? His photographic mentor as well? I look again at Conundrum's pictures. Grudgingly I have to admit they are good. Damn good. The crafty old bugger! So why was Conundrum's work unknown? Why had he kept quiet about his photography? And why hadn't I guessed that Conundrum was a photographer? How could I have missed that?

There had been plenty of clues. As in the cable car above the port of Barcelona when I'd petulantly refused to follow his orders and grab that double page spread shot. Then his lecture on photography without film to that beautiful young woman in Rome. So if Conundrum was a top photographer no wonder he knew precisely when to toss his acerbic comments at me. He had surely seen all the images I planned to take long before I saw them myself. Plus many more to which I was blind.

So just how many great pictures had Conundrum seen and stored away with his own inner eye while I floundered about in the dark? I must have been so predictable. What a laugh he had been having all along at my poor attempts to be the great photographer. God, how he must have sniggered every time he called me by that infernal name of Henri, knowing I couldn't hold a candle to the old master.

"Conundrum, you bastard! You total bastard!"

I am screaming for real. Angry as hell. This is a killer blow. Still I can't stop myself looking through his pictures. I now discover some colour prints of flowers. Not just one or two but an entire portfolio. Conundrum a closet flower photographer? What was it he had said about that genre? Last resort of the emotionally inadequate? Damn his eyes! Conundrum's flower pictures are a cut above my own. One in particular, an exquisite composition where the shape of the flower dissolves in the intensity of its colour, has me spellbound.

Suddenly, I've had enough. I give the shoebox a violent kick, send it scudding across the floor scattering photographs in all directions as it crashes into the wall. I curse Conundrum's memory. He has poisoned my photography, destroyed my Art with or without a capital A. He has outdone everything I'd ever aspired to achieve. I vow I will never take another picture. I want to trash Conundrum's flat, to destroy every trace of a life that casts a deep shadow over my own, a constant reproach to every ambition I ever held dear.

I breathe deeply to regain some self-control. Then my eye alights on a scrap of paper pinned to a tiny door. *ABANDON DESPAIR ALL YE WHO ENTER HERE*

My heart skips a beat. This must be Conundrum's inner sanctum. Surely this is it, my real reason for coming to number 7 Moonbeam Mansions?

There is no handle. I push open the door. I have to stoop to enter. In stark contrast to the chaos of Conundrum's living room, this smaller space is almost empty. At the same time it's completely full. All four walls, floor and ceiling are plastered with pages of typescript. Everywhere I look – left, right, up, down – I am confronted by fragments of a disjointed narrative. The pages have been roughly edited with bold strokes of red ink splattered like blood on the white paper.

So the old bugger had been writing a novel. So much for his alleged derision of literature. He loved words so much he had built a personal shrine composed entirely of words. He had been a truly passionate practitioner of all that he took such delight in scorning. Even without reading the words, they are exciting to look at. The black and white typescripts with their sexy red scribblings fizzle with energy. I can't take it all in. Am I meant to read it or just look at the general effect?

It's an astounding artwork of huge visual impact. I catch my breath at the audacity of the concept. Conundrum has created a three-dimensional masterpiece. He has published something that can only be described as literary wallpaper. No, it's more than that. A walk-in installation. Behold all my wonderful ideas, he is saying, do they not provide a nice décor for your lounge or living room? What a brilliant notion!

The only item of furniture is a tall desk. On it lies an open leather-bound volume. Golden letters on the title page spell out the words that I tremble to read: *CONUNDRUM'S BOOK*

On the facing page there is an inscription written in a confident, flowing copperplate hand.

"All events described herein are guaranteed true and authentic, including those that didn't happen exactly as described and others that didn't happen at all."

Well, that's typical Conundrum. Nothing surprising there. Yet my heart thumps as I turn to the next page. It's empty. I recall his wish to write a book about nothing. I turn another page. Empty too. I don't know what I'm looking for or expecting to find. Perhaps a brief dedication from Jean-Paul Sartre with a word of praise for Conundrum's literary skills?

But why the empty pages? Can there be some trick? I take a closer look at *Conundrum's Book.*

Invisible ink perhaps? Suddenly, I get a crazy idea. It's to do with the nature of light. If all the colours of the spectrum combine to make pure light that cannot be seen, could not something similar apply to thoughts? Suppose there is a mental spectrum with a finite number of thoughts, and if you could think them all simultaneously, then to all intents and purposes your thoughts would be invisible. Perhaps they would cancel out one another so you'd be thinking nothing? So the written equivalent would be an empty page.

Conundrum's voice supplies an answer.

"Nice try, Henri. But it's a lot simpler than that. Silence speaks louder than words. Electing not to write specific words in a particular context is a creative decision of the first magnitude. Not anyone can create the perfect blank page. It all comes down to the quality of that which you decide not to write."

God, the man is infuriating! How can one put this ridiculous theory to the test? Am I supposed to imagine what he might have written? One empty page looks just like any other.

In spite of myself, wary of being fooled by the apparent emptiness of *Conundrum's Book* I inspect every single page just to make sure they are all empty. I can't afford to take chances with such a slippery customer. So I keep going through page after page of immaculate blankness.

I look about the room, wondering what to do next. Should I try to read the story plastered all over the walls? But that would take days. And there is no clue where to begin. The pages are stuck up in no particular order.

I am about to turn away and retreat. But now I see them, neatly stacked up in a corner, a pile of about twenty A5 volumes, their bindings all the colours of the rainbow. I pick up the top one and open it at random.

An envelope falls out. It is marked: *To Whom It May Not Concern*. I tear it open. The letter is headed: *'Some Pips for Henri'*. It's for me! *Some Pips for Henri?* I recall his discourse in Paris on tomato pips. So the notebooks must be the pips of the decomposed tomato that was Conundrum's mind.

I peruse the letter with mounting interest. *'Well done, Henri. You have tracked me down at last. Sorry to disappoint with the magnum opus. I know you would have expected more from me. But I trust the notebooks will be of interest. I would have handed them over in person, but that would have required explanations. Questions needing answers. Boring, tiresome, don't you think?"*

The conversational tone makes me feel Conundrum is in the room. I turn round. There is no one. I read on.

"As you will have gathered, there were urgent matters for me to attend to. Flight to catch. Fish to swallow. Ocean to cross. That sort of thing. Shame we couldn't make the trip together. I did so enjoy our little jaunts. My notebooks should offer some recompense for your pains. An account of our travels. They do contain various matters of personal interest. All those amusing adventures you had. And a few home truths, naturally. Given the excellence of the material I'm confident you will find a suitable publisher and I'm happy to bequeath you the royalties."

So my humble but necessary part in this charade will be to act as midwife for Conundrum's wayward brainchild. He wants me to be his literary executor. To oversee publication of a work in which I will appear as a total loser.

Had I been set up for precisely this? Had there ever been anything in it for me personally? The idea that I would learn something for myself from Conundrum was an illusion, a delusion. All along I had been a mere cog in his machine. I had simply played the part of the sorcerer's apprentice who would never acquire the dark arts, never inherit the magic wand.

Incidental to his purpose from start to finish. Unwitting accessory before, during and after the fact. A handy nest for his cuckoo's egg. He had encouraged me to think I could one day move on and up to a higher level of understanding. But now my true role is clear, simply to carry the torch he had lit. And doubtless for his own greater glory.

Seething with anger, I crumple the letter in my fist and cast it aside. I look for the last notebook and turn to the last page. I search for an entry on the day of Conundrum's dramatic disappearance at Cape St Vincent. I am not registering the words, just the fact that they had been written in Portugal. That can only mean that somehow Conundrum must have returned to London and deposited the notebook in his flat. How else could it have got here? So he isn't dead or departed in any material sense. The whole thing has been carefully staged. As usual, I have been taken in. It is all a complete hoax.

Something makes me look up. The net curtains are being sucked softly into the windows like the room is breathing. Then a light tap on a pane has me jumping out of my skin. I spin round, fully expecting to see Conundrum standing before me. But still there is no one. Just a pigeon on the sill pecking at the glass. As if it wants to come in. The bird cocks its head and gives me a curious sideways look. Conundrum? Perhaps he has changed his disguise? From gannet to pigeon, why not? At that moment I am ready to believe anything. I approach the window, but the bird flies off, just like a normal pigeon.

I feel faint. Urgent need to breathe fresh air. Above all a desperate desire to be someone else, somewhere else. Anywhere but here in this cursed apartment. I turn to go. There is a long mirror on the back of the door. I am drawn to it like a moth to the flame. Rooted to the spot I stand before it contemplating my own image in the glass. What is it about mirrors? Then I start to pace up and down, my eyes riveted to my own reflection.

I realise I am doing the same parallel walk I had observed Conundrum executing in Rome. How did it go? Without thinking I make a sudden leap beyond the edge of the mirror and then an equally sudden one back. Yes, that's it. My own reflection has followed me faithfully. Then I look at it again. Takes a while to realise what's wrong with it. My image in the mirror is not reversed. It is not my reflection. It is actually the real me looking at myself. But which one of the two is the real me? I fear neither is. I think Conundrum has somehow got under my skin. He's inside me. Oh my God! Tell me this isn't happening.

FLYING WITHOUT WINGS

In mounting panic, I rush out of Conundrum's flat and tumble headlong down the stairs of Moonbeam Mansions. I plunge into the teeming crowds of the outside world. I let myself be jostled along, just another bundle of bruised humanity on the ebb and flow with all the rest of the flotsam and jetsam. I am carried on the tide all the way along Oxford Street to Marble Arch. Then I turn and start drifting back.

I am pushed off the pavement by some drunken football supporters singing loud and off key.

"You'll never walk alone."

The hideous truth behind the mindless dirge strikes me with sinister intent. All I want is to walk alone. To walk without the shadow of Conundrum falling over me.

"You'll never walk alone. A-a lone. Alone..."

I don't want to go back to Moonbeam Mansions. Really I don't. Every step is a huge effort. It's happening against my will. An unseen force pushes me on. I have no choice. Pointless to resist. It takes me three times as long to cover half the distance. By the time I reach Oxford Circus my knees are like rubber. My tongue sticks to the roof of my mouth.

People are pressing postcards and brochures into my hand. Most of them urging me to learn English. What would it be like if I had to learn my own language all over again? A Hare Krishna disciple tries to engage me in conversation. I fend him off with words that seem to speak themselves,

"Thank you for your pains. But I have already found the truth. Or rather it has found me. I can't escape it. Even now it calls me. I must follow. Even if it turns out to be a lie. Which it probably will. All truth is a lie. Conundrum said so."

Hare Krishna disciple gives me an anxious look. I think he's scared. He's all too keen to see me on my way.

"Take care, man."

Take care? What difference to him or me if I take care or not? And how should I take care even if I wanted too? Life will take care of me one way or the other. What do I mean will? It already is. The future is an illusion. It's only the stuff that hasn't yet happened. But it's going to happen, like it or not.

I am now within sight of Hanway Street. I knock back a large whisky in Bradley's Bar. Now I have strength to continue. On entering Hanway Place I hear an almighty bang. I dive for cover. It's just like a war zone. Stuff flying everywhere. When the thick cloud of smoke clears I can see clear daylight at the end of the street where Moonbeam Mansions once stood. The block has been reduced to a gaunt brick shell. The empty windows of flat 7 gape like the eye sockets of a skull.

Incredible. Quite incredible. A gas explosion maybe? But I suspect some other agency at work. How can all this have happened in the twinkling of an eye at the very moment I choose to appear? I feel that somehow I have detonated a booby trap.

A number of separate fires rage amidst the rubble. I spot the colourful bindings of the *Conundrum Notebooks* going up in flames. Isn't it my job to edit them? So perhaps I should try to save them. But the fire is too hot to approach. Charred embers swirl in the air. I am about to turn away when a scrap of paper among the rubble catches my eye. I pick it up. It's Conundrum's letter. Is this his way of making sure I note its contents? Well, to hell with you! I screw it up into a tight ball and toss it into the fire. It flares up briefly as the flames consume it.

I thrill at my first act of rebellion. A delirious sensation of freedom overwhelms me. The destruction of Moonbeam Mansions has liberated me from the tyranny of Conundrum and the quest for *Conundrum's Book*. But what next? I am bereft of purpose. My existence has no definitive meaning.

Now I hear the sirens of the emergency services. Last thing I want is to be detained as an eye-witness. Must get out of here. I sprint to Tottenham Court Road and race down the steps into the Tube. Not wanting to return home, I ride around at random. To get my bearings I glance at the map of the London Underground. Familiar names rearrange themselves in a surreal manner. *Claphands Common, Chancers Lane, Grudge Street, Mornington Croissant.* Oh God, there's a parallel universe out there. The one I know is deconstructing.

I change trains several times. I end up on the District Line heading west. It has begun to rain. I face backward at what Conundrum once called the Maori view[4].

I recall that dream of me crossing the desert stepping in footprints that had been laid out in the sand for me to walk in and which vanished the moment I stepped on them. These were Conundrum's of course. Who else? So it has been my destiny not only to follow faithfully in his footsteps, but also to remove all trace of his passing from the face of the earth. Hadn't he said something about leaving no tracks in the snow? That means my role is somehow to clean up after him.

I sit in the District Line train watching helplessly as the past races away behind me on tracks of steel. As for the future, it feels like a Maori war club raised behind me that could fall and deliver a killing blow at any moment.

"The present is merely a mirror through which the future passes in order to become the past."

The present a mirror? I look at my reflection in the window. My image stares back at me through a veil of tiny water droplets wiggling across the dirty glass, an endless procession engaged in a mad dash, mindless as sperm racing to hit the ovaries. Again I note with horror that my reflection is not reversed. There is another Henri out there. In mounting panic I get off the train at Kew Gardens. The mood is autumnal.

---

[4] Katharine Cox, Nancy G. Tayles and Hallie R. Buckley writing in *Current Anthropology*, explain that the Maori concept of time is fundamentally different from that of the West: *"While Westerners see time as stretching from the past behind to the future in front, Maori see the past in front of them and the future, which cannot be known, as stretching behind them."*

"Autumn, sweet autumn, Henri. A season for grown ups. Smell of winter in the air, kiss of death on the lips. Spring is for adolescents bursting into life with their ridiculous hopes. Not knowing that summer, like all great expectations, can never deliver. But autumn will not cheat you. Dying is guaranteed and yet you are still alive for a while to survey the whole infernal cycle of being. A death-in-life-in-death experience. Oh, the sweet bliss of it all. Cries of I'll be back! See you next year!"

Shut it, Conundrum! Bugger off! Leave me in peace.

The wind is up. Blowing a gale. Trees stripped bare. I reach Kew Gardens. I race through the fallen leaves faster, faster, trying to get Conundrum's voice out of my head. I run and run until I am exhausted and collapse on a bench.

A small plaque catches my eye:

GEORGE'S FIRST LOVE WAS NATURE AND NEXT TO NATURE HE LOVED HIS ART.

A vandal has added a letter F, turning art into fart. Suddenly, I see the light. I have cracked Conundrum's cryptic clue. The four-letter word spelled with three letters!

"Fuck art! Fuck love! Fuck nature! Fuck George!"

I run off in search of a less annoying bench. The next one also bears a plaque:

FRED AND MARY SO LOVED THIS SERENE AND PEACEFUL SPOT.

Peaceful spot? Fred and Mary must have been stone deaf not to hear the constant roar of jets booming in overhead to land at Heathrow. I feel a deep anger at all these stupid dedications. Every damn bench bears a plaque to remind me this was the favourite place of Daphne and Sidney, Henry and Deidre, Tom and Daisy. Their invisible hands tap me on the shoulder.

"Ahem, not here, if you don't mind. This bench is taken. Sacred to the memory of someone dear and departed."

"Damn your benches! A pox on Reginald, Archibald and Percy who so loved these gardens! You should all rot away in silence like the compost you put on your flowerbeds. Garden benches should be for the living, not shrines to the dead."

I am seized by a wild rage. Truly, deeply angry at last. A divine fury has gripped my entrails. I'm out of my skin, off my rocker. Sod it all! Sod everyone! Sod me! Yes, above all, sod me! To hell with me! Wish I could throw myself away. Like a piece of garbage. I take it out on the flowers, kick off their pretty heads and trample them underfoot. Bloody flowers! Don't need me to take pictures of them. Hell, they can take care of themselves. They'll outlive us all. Conundrum said so, didn't he?

I'm really losing my grip. What if I am? No worries. If this is madness, give me excess of it. I'm glad I'm losing my mind. Bloody good job! About time too. Should have lost it long ago. Now I'm fizzing inside. Vintage champagne just after the cork's popped. A well of happiness bubbles up and gushes out. Release is better than sex. Meltdown of the soul as well as the senses. I'm not me any more. Henri is dead. Perhaps I should have a bench dedicated to my departed self. Freedom at last. I scream for joy. Startled *Friends of Kew* rush for cover as I overturn their precious benches with gay abandon. But soon I am exhausted and collapse on a bench which I have no energy left to overturn. I read the inscription. It's a long one.

FOR ARTHUR WHO ALWAYS KNEW BEST

No, Surely not?

WHO PASSED AWAY FAR FROM HIS NATIVE YORKSHIRE

I read on.

BUT EVER A TRUE LOVER OF THE SOUTH AND ITS PEOPLE

I can't believe it.

THIS BENCH IS DEDICATED BY HIS LONG SUFFERING WIFE GLADYS.

Yes, it's 'our Arthur which art in Yorkshire'.

Always knew best! Ever a true lover of the South and its people! Gladys has struck back. And with a vengeance! What panache! What style! What a stroke of genius! What a woman! Hats off to you, darling Gladys! I want to kiss you! Did you do him in first or just take sweet posthumous revenge?

Either way, I am uplifted by her example. If Gladys can get back at her pain-in-the-arse Arthur, surely I can do likewise with mine? Arthur Conundrum, you are history! I feel a surge of energy. Huge. Immense. All things are possible. I sprint on over grass, through flowerbeds, bushes.

Chinese Pagoda catches my eye. I race towards it like a guided missile. Japanese Gravel Garden lies before me. Memories of Kyoto and all that one hand claptrap.

"One hand claptrap? Very good, Henri. You're getting quite good at puns. Keep it up."

I charge on wildly through the carefully raked gravel of the Japanese Garden, destroying meticulously arranged waves in the eternal ocean of life. More *Friends of Kew* scuttle off at my approach. Only one person is not running away. It's a girl. She stands there, more bemused than alarmed. Oriental looking. Maybe Japanese? Reminds me of K. Can't be though. So many girls have been pretending to look like K. But she's waving to me. No, pointing. Pointing at something behind me.

I turn around. A posse of blue uniformed officers and a couple of men in white coats are bearing down on me through the long grass. Like beaters at a pheasant shoot. Well this bird is not about to be shot. I sprint on towards the Chinese Pagoda. The door is open. I rush up the stairs with wings on my heels. So light of foot I am almost flying. Flying? Now I realise what I am about to do. It's that *Notre Dame* thing all over again.

I quickly reach the top of the Chinese Pagoda, peer over the balustrade. My pursuers are fanned out in a broad circle around the base. One man is holding a megaphone. So they are going to try and talk me down. I've seen it in films. My purpose wavers. No longer sure what I am going to do.

Far down below, the girl who looks like K is looking up. I can't see her eyes but I know she is staring right into mine.

Suddenly convinced she is the key to everything. Yes, she must be K. I want to reach out and touch her.

Then I am alerted by something. I am not alone. Yes, there he is. I can see him now. A blue-uniformed official is standing there just a few yards away. How did he manage to get ahead of me? Or was he already up here in anticipation? He is showing no apparent interest in me. His gaze surveys the broad acres of Kew Gardens. Now he turns toward me. Slowly. Ever so slowly. His face is concealed under the shadow of a peaked cap. Now it comes into view. I see that louche, lopsided grin.

"Oh no, not you!"

His lips move. Voice speaks. I hear words.

"So here you are at last, Henri. About time too. Your moment of truth awaits. Think you can do it? There's only one way to find out. You've come this far. Might as well give it a go, eh? Seems like a long way down though, doesn't it? But that shouldn't worry you. You know it's possible. You've seen me do it, haven't you? So what are you waiting for? Which is it to be, Henri? Action or thought?"

I want to scream that I will have neither of these absurd choices. I am tired of mind games and existential riddles. To hell with action! To hell with thought! And to hell with Art, Truth, Beauty and the rest of them! It is only Love I desire. Love. Just Love. Nothing more than Love. Something you can't understand. But I cannot speak. It's too late. My fate is already sealed. He who has looked death in the eye cannot turn back.

"What are you waiting for, Henri?"

I will be tormented no longer by this monster. Sacred anger returns. I am galvanised. Overwhelming desire to be rid of Conundrum. Great urge to seize him by the throat. Let him have action before thought if he can handle it. I rush towards him, hands outstretched, filled to the fingertips with murderous intent. But just as I am about to throttle him, Conundrum vanishes into thin air. I charge on regardless. Now I am truly inspired. Of course I can fly, fly without wings. I'll show him I can do it. I leap into space. I am airborne. Yes, I am flying. The wind roars and rushes against my face. I stretch out my arms then fold them just as I'd done in my dream. I am flying, aren't I?

But the ground rushes up to meet me. Briefly, I see into the eyes of the Japanese girl. It *is* K! Oh, my God! It *is* K! Then the earth hits me. The breath of life is knocked out of my body. It's all over. The lights go out.

Hours later I wake up in hospital. I have survived my fall with cracked ribs and severe bruising. It's a miracle they tell me. I fell onto a pile of autumn leaves. The police will prepare a report on my vandalising the park benches, flowerbeds, Japanese gravel garden etc. Charges are expected to follow, unless my behaviour can be explained as a temporary loss of sanity. There is no mention of my attempted assault on Conundrum.

I contemplate my actions. I feel absolutely no guilt that I had tried to kill Conundrum. Actually I am rather proud of that. Perhaps I can now revise my idea of myself as his creature. Has my abortive act of violence set me free?

They say I will be allowed home after a brief spell under observation. Perhaps by the end of the week. I fall asleep. When I awake I think I must be dreaming. K is sitting on my bed. But this is no dream. The real K takes my hand in hers. I recall our evening in Tokyo and under what sordid circumstances I last held her hand. I blush at the memory of my shame. Now she looks deep into my eyes. No words are spoken.

Why hadn't I asked K what had brought her to see me at the Yaesu Terminal Hotel? Why had I automatically believed what Conundrum had hinted about her in his sly, disgusting way? She seems to read my mind. There is a look in her eye, a tiny hint of a smile on her lips, as subtle as that of the Great Buddha at Kamakura. At the touch of her hand on mine I melt inside.

I am no longer Henri, no longer Conundrum's poodle. No longer even me, whoever that is. I am becoming no one. Yes, that's it. A delicious metamorphosis is underway. I would so like to be no one. Now it starts to get hazy. K's face goes into soft focus. I pass out. When I come to my senses, a man in a white coat stands at the end of my bed. Now he looks up from his reading of my chart.

"You've had a nasty shock, Henri."

It's Conundrum dressed up as a doctor.

"Fortunately, it's nothing that can't be cured."

He addresses K still sitting on my bed.

"You'll have to go now, my dear. Henri is tired."

I look at K, willing her to stay. Her eyes tell me she must go. My eyes beg her to take me with her. But I know she cannot. Then please take with you my love, all of it, and grant me your forgiveness. A bow of the head tells me she has accepted. I can ask for no more than that. I sigh and fall back on the pillow as if giving up the ghost. I feel my love and my entire capacity for loving depart with her. She holds the title deeds to my soul.

My final sight of K is masked by Conundrum placing a scrawny hand on the small of her back as he steers her through the door. Testing the flesh no doubt. I let out a silent scream, as K vanishes from view. Conundrum delivers his parting shot.

"Don't worry about a thing, Henri. You'll be well taken care of here. And I'll take good care of K. Just remember, she's a poetess. She has a dream world of her own. So she has no need of yours. Trust me on this one, Henri. Trust me."

Trust Conundrum? That's a joke. But I say nothing, feel nothing. Mute acceptance of the inevitable spreads numbness. I realise there is room for one person only in my dream world. Me. That is why I am condemned to remain Conundrum's creature, at least until I have cracked my personal riddle. There is nothing left for me to say. Besides, Conundrum wants the last word.

"Before I go, I really must thank you, Henri. You were the key to everything. I have been carried aloft on the wings of your dreams. I couldn't have done it without you."

The door closes. He is gone. I mull over his last words. Conundrum thanking me for what? For everything? For being carried aloft on the wings of my dreams? Couldn't have done it without me? Couldn't have done what without me?

Suddenly, I see the Truth with a capital T. Conundrum achieved his precious emptiness, his transparent soul by dumping his dreams on me. So that weightless he can float away serenely like a balloon. Why couldn't he simply have cast his dreams aside? But already I know the answer to that. Once dreamed, dreams cannot be undreamed. They have a life of their own and will always demand a human host to be dreamed in.

I am trapped. No, it's the reverse. I am the cage not the captive. I am host to this alien being known as Conundrum. And I can never escape him. Because I am the prison inside which he is doing time. How long? Perhaps for ever. I know I can never be free until my uninvited lodger decides to move on.

Meanwhile, I'm still earthbound, tied down by the weight of his cursed existential baggage. He is gloriously free to 'move on' and ride the thermals, while I'm left behind as the guardian of his awful legacy. All thanks to me he can become pure spirit. I haven't liberated myself. I've liberated Conundrum. Even in trying to kill him I was unwittingly following his orders. And in so doing, I've condemned myself to become him. He has finally got what he wanted. Someone to take his place. He passed me the baton. And I reached out to grasp it. End of story.

I now realise, that in spite of all his cynical affectations, Conundrum had not for a moment given up on the big things that were his dreams. What gave him the right to pretend to care nothing about anything was perhaps that he cared passionately about everything. Number 7 Moonbeam Mansions had been a shrine to his great quests and aspirations. But in the end his way of keeping faith with his dreams was by proxy, guiding my unknowing steps down the primrose path so I would take up the running on his behalf. I had been forewarned. Had he not said as much during that stormy night on our long drive down the M4?

But I had chosen to ignore the health warning on the packet. And now he has done with me, I must come to terms with what I am left with. Could he have achieved his purpose without me? He did say I was indispensable, didn't he? But I mustn't flatter myself. Surely he would have found some other person to play my part. For all I knew he could have been grooming a whole string of Henris all over the place.

So I'm left in a kind of double-bind. I can never be rid of Conundrum until I too learn to fly without wings. But I will never achieve that and emerge from his shadow unless I follow the same script. For if Conundrum needed me – or the likes of me – in order to achieve his aim, then I too will need someone before I can reach the end of my term and 'move on'.

I shall have to ensnare another unwitting soul to serve as my acolyte, to take up the baton and finally set me free. Perhaps I will enlist an aspiring young writer? Anyway, someone with his head in the clouds. Plenty of them about even in the cynical age of today. And so the existential game of pass-the-parcel can have no end. I am but yet another link in the great chain, passing on dreams I cannot keep faith with on my own account.

I let this realisation of my small place in the larger scheme of things sink in like a dagger to the hilt. I feel no pain just the tingling of a recently exposed nerve. It tells me I am poised on the cusp of a new dimension. It is my destiny to find my own way through to the other side. Not even the thought of losing K must deter me. The lesson of Conundrum's pact with *Madame* in the *Spleen* shall not been lost on me.

Even though I will never enjoy K's embrace, have I not already appointed her as the guardian of my love? And has she not accepted me in full and without reserve? I shall never again love any woman in that absolute way. I am a man whose heart has been removed. Yet still he lives. Perhaps, when the time is ripe, I shall call on K in Tokyo or wherever, say fifty years hence when she is old and wrinkled as in that dream. Meanwhile, I am immune to feeling anything for anyone.

Better that way. Indeed, the only way. Am I not turning out to be a brilliant pupil? Already the fabric of Conundrum's life adheres to mine, fold for fold. Furthermore, I have some ideas of my own for attaining my ultimate goal that will leave even the master gasping with admiration. I wonder if he will monitor my efforts from wherever he is. Maybe not. Now that Conundrum has 'moved on', I doubt that I shall hear from him ever again.

I spend the next two days in hospital drifting in and out of consciousness, tuning in always to the same dream sequence in an endless loop. I am leaping from the Chinese Pagoda in Kew Gardens over and over again. But it's not a nightmare. I am not afraid. There is no point in fear. This is my big moment. Nothing can happen to me. Except a man be born again. Only someone who has been comprehensively destroyed can start afresh. And so I willingly embrace my death in life.

But what's happening? I am not falling so fast. I am not falling at all. I am floating, floating in mid air. I extend my arms. They feel like wings. Now I am gliding. Hovering in the sky. Like an angel. I fold my arms. With a great whoosh I soar up like a rocket. Every fibre of my being tingles. So it is possible. I can do it. I can fly without wings. I know I am ready to pay any price to turn this dream into reality and fulfil my destiny.

My destiny? Will there be something more to what's left of my existence than merely being Conundrum's creature? Yes, I feel it in my bones. I cannot accept that my fate is just to travel in his slipstream. In fact, the whole point of driving dangerously close to the man in front is to be ready for the magic moment when you pull out of his slipstream to overtake. Where is all this coming from? Suddenly I am having thoughts of a different kind. I am philosophising just like Conundrum. Only this time the thoughts I'm thinking are mine. They belong to me. I'm buzzing with ideas, as if I've tanked up on something mysterious.

Even from my hospital bed I am preparing myself for great things ahead. I detect big flaws in Conundrum's relentless nihilism. What was his cosmic joke at the heart of the universe? That life is an infection, that everything humanity has achieved is a bacterial growth that will one day be eradicated when the God of destruction finally works his purpose out. Not much a joke that. Not funny at all. But say we humans do have a role in the great scheme of things? What if our creation through the chaos of the evolutionary soup is part of the master plan? What if there is a meaning after all? If I could prove Conundrum wrong and demonstrate that life not death is the driving force of everything then there would be purpose to my own being as well.

My mind goes into overdrive. I have a vision of an epic Hollywood production. Humanity, seeking final answers to the eternal riddle of life, storms the celestial citadel, battering down its defences. As we prise open the inner doors of the cosmic command control centre, what do we find? Probably a vacant space, an empty seat still warm, the previous occupant having departed at the very instant of our intrusion and slipped away into a parallel universe. Then we will panic as we realise that we are to be left alone running the show on our own.

So will human ingenuity finally usurp God? Will the very idea at the heart of creation be revealed in the minds of us the created beings? Doubtful. Though science might perversely end up proving the existence of a supreme being. For when we reach the material and physical limits of our quest for ultimate truth we will have to concede there must be something like a Creator beyond the scientific facts. Then a universal God will no longer be just an act of religious faith but the only possible explanation for that which cannot be explained.

So let us press on to the outer rim of knowable things until we tumble head first over the edge into the divine abyss. Then we can at last leave behind us this silly dualistic game of reason and argument, fact and fallacy. Bring on the big mystery. I await it with wide-eyed wonder.

So what was the reason for Conundrum's ironic lopsided grin? Did he know where humanity is heading? Children of the revolution taking possession of a magnificent royal palace which in their ignorance they are doomed to destroy? I see our dear old Planet Earth as a brave bubble of dreams and desires, ugly and beautiful in equal measure, cruising all alone through lifeless space like a solitary galleon on the high seas. No captain of the ship. The crew has mutinied. It's anarchic, overcrowded and leaking badly. We squabble endlessly among ourselves as we run out of food and water, with disease and pestilence rampant. Meanwhile, unspeakable acts are committed below decks.

Yet still we put proud capital letters on Art, Religion and Philosophy. Although possibly irrelevant in the cosmic scheme of things, these human truths are relevant to us humans. In this world of illusions and delusions they are all we have to hold on to in face of the nightmares we must confront. We may not understand the cosmic joke but we can laugh at everything and nothing. As long as our sense of humour prevails there is hope for us all. Only when the spontaneous smile is finally wiped off our faces will that be the end of the show.

And what will be my role in this amazing production with a cast of billions? What difference can one weak human make? We'll see. How did it go, that great quote by St Jack? Google takes only 0.58 seconds to present me with the inspiring words of Jack Kerouac in his novel *The Dharma Bums* written way back in the heady days of the 1950s: *"But let the mind beware, that though the flesh be bugged, the circumstances of existence are pretty glorious."*

So that shall be my purpose, to explore the glorious circumstances of existence. I'll show Conundrum that there is so much more beyond his base, cynical view. Life is sacred. The creation is holy. It's so much more than a chemistry set. I'll make it my mission to celebrate the glories of this confused and confusing world of ours. I'll seek out the divine spark that infuses all things. It's a huge task. Where to begin? Better take it a day at a time. First I must probe the frontiers of my new theatre of independent action in the post-Conundrum era.

On the morning of the third day, I am discharged from hospital with a strong recommendation from the doctors to seek counselling in order to prevent a recurrence of my temporary derangement. On arriving home I notice something is missing.

The blob of red paint on the pavement is no longer there. Not that it has been eroded; rather the entire pavement has been dug up, carted off and re-laid with fresh slabs while I've been away. So my personal hourglass, the yardstick of my former existence has vanished. I am free to make a fresh start.

It certainly feels like a new beginning. I discover absurd pleasure in everything, even delight in the mundane business of daily chores. Making toast. Dusting a shelf. I feel I am living, fully existing for the first time. I breathe every breath like sipping vintage champagne. All things sufficient unto themselves. Each second of equal potential. Being aware of every instant – good, bad, indifferent – as it passes. For when all these tiny moments are strung together, that is the sum of my life.

I am floating, savouring the joy of being part of things, a tiny droplet of water in an enormous breaking wave. I am no longer me, not myself. Or have I found myself? Rather I may have lost myself. That's it. This great feeling has nothing to do with self. Something oppressive has departed. Conundrum? No, not him. In fact, I owe it all to him. Not that he taught me this, but he so utterly destroyed everything else, eradicated every last vestige of self, crushed out every atom of me in me. So I am left with an abstract sense of everything and nothing. I may have found my crock of gold at the end of the rainbow after all.

I set off to do some shopping with a spring in my step. But my steps do not take me to the supermarket. Instead, I push open the door of the *Relief Fund for Romania*. I've never been in there before but I enter the premises like a regular. I advance between rows of second-hand clothing. The woman at the till turns towards me. I know her face. But I can't place her. Without a word, she leads me to the back of the shop. Suspended from a hanger is a garment that makes the hairs on the back of my neck stand on end. She takes it down, holds it up to the light. It's a gentleman's waistcoat. Conundrum's magic waistcoat. She wraps it in brown paper and hands it to me. I reach for my wallet. But she doesn't want anything for it. She leads me to the door.

I rush home, unpack the waistcoat and slip it on. It fits perfectly. Like a second skin. Now I remember the woman in the charity shop. Suddenly I know who she is. *Madame Renée!* I rush straight back to confront her, still wearing Conundrum's, no it's my magic waistcoat. But there is no sign of *Madame Renée*. The only person present is a much younger woman. I enquire after her colleague serving there just a few moments ago.

"You must be mistaken. I've been minding the shop on my own all afternoon."

Pointless to argue the matter. I am about to withdraw.

"Perhaps I can interest you in something?"

She gives me an alluring look, such a direct come-on I've never had before. I respond with a louche lopsided grin that comes quite naturally even though it too feels brand new. I also manage to arch an eyebrow in a way I've never done previously. I see I'm going to have to keep myself in check if I am not to become a mindless clone of Conundrum. Still, my new powers do have certain advantages.

"Yes, I'm sure you can."

She invites me with a sultry, seductive gesture to take a leisurely look at her wares. Seems like a promising encounter. I'll see what's on offer. Meanwhile, my thoughts are plotting every step of the long walk I know I'll soon be making far out over the mud flats to my appointment with *Madame Renée Clairvoyante* in that mysterious wooden shack at the end of Southend Pier. I'm curious to discover what she'll reveal in my personal crystal ball. But one thing I can say with absolute certainty. It won't be Conundrum's destiny but my own that begins there.

AND FINALLY

The events and people in this book are imaginary, or if at all real then treated in a way that is entirely fictional. I must stress that the jacket photograph is not of Conundrum but of an anonymous gentleman who bears no resemblance even to the mental image I may have of the character. I took the picture years ago, long before Conundrum introduced himself to me.

I would like to offer some kind of rational explanation why I wrote this book. But I cannot. Suffice it to say that Conundrum has been like a mad, bad voice muttering his diabolical dictation in my ear for at least a decade. At first I ignored him. Then I found the only way to shut him up was to write it all down in bits and pieces just as he delivered it. For years I consigned these disjointed jottings on scraps of paper to a black box hoping they would never see the light of day.

But Conundrum would not leave me in peace until I had worked 'his' material into some sort of literary shape. I sensed that a book, nothing less, was what he wanted. *Conundrum's Book*. It was a daunting challenge. I needed help. To poor Henri fell the unenviable task of placating this monster. He has my full sympathy, sincere apologies and eternal gratitude. I couldn't have managed without him. So Henri, in his thankless role, was quite indispensable. I would like to think that he has for all his pains found some measure of fulfilment at the end.

As for myself, I should make no claims for authorship of this work, at least in the conventional sense. For it was not a premeditated act of creation. So I cannot really call it my own. As the title says it is *Conundrum's Book*. My only feeling is one of profound relief that the deed is done. The monkey is finally off my back. I have closure. That's all I ask for. I pray Conundrum will now leave me in peace.

www.ingramcontent.com/pod-product-compliance
Lightning Source LLC
Chambersburg PA
CBHW020637030726
47498CB00002B/252